THE BATH DETECTIVE

CHRISTOPHER LEE

The Bath Detective

A Bath Detective Mystery

faber and faber

This edition first published in 2011
by Faber and Faber Ltd
Bloomsbury House, 74–77 Great Russell Street
London WC1B 3DA

Printed by CPI Antony Rowe, Eastbourne

A CIP record for this book is available from the British Library

ISBN 978–0–571–27640–0

One

The royal visit had gone well. The Queen had been charming, the Duke still handsome, the clergy fawning, the city's gentry obsequious, the gawpers, onlookers and kindergarten flag-wavers bewitched. In the morning, the weather had threatened to spoil it all. By the afternoon, it had changed its mind.

The Bath stone, as mellow as the tourist board described, had warmed to the sun's rays. Down and along smart Milsom Street the hanging baskets had rarely been so colourful, the brass plates on consultants' offices had shone expensively and the carriage horses waiting for tourists at the curve of New Bond Street had been groomed until they were slippery to the guttersnipe's palm. Her Majesty had seen little of this.

Her motorcade had rolled by the Avon at eleven o'clock precisely.

The Bishop, slightly stooped yet not bowed, had welcomed the head of his Church. Richly escorted by dean and chapter well versed in greeting and obbligato, and with the smile of a contented herdsman, he paced the flagstones with his gold crook and escorted his visitors to the abbey doors and beyond the civic chains and beavers' fur. A new shrine was to be blessed and royally signalled. On cue, shafts of June sunlight through the great windows roused even the toneless to anthem that glorious things were indeed spoken, although of whom few felt inclined to ponder.

Then, having been praised by scarlet-cassocked clerks, having been bowed and curtsied to by the city's most worthy, the monarch had been led to the unworthy, the waiting crowds outside. Pausing every five paces to speak but hardly hear the answers and to accept eagerly and sweetly the prepared posies, she had moved along the lines of galvanized barriers until she was beneath the colonnades by the Pump Room. The faces beamed on and a young man with a clown's powdered and rouged cheeks cuddled a great overstuffed charity teddy bear. The Queen laughed and pointed; her consort peered as a scion of the World Wide Fund for Nature should.

Then, when it appeared that the painted fool and his rattling collection box might approach too close, the royal party was safely ushered beneath the arches where, on more typical afternoons, travellers, vagrants and sometimes buskers lolled with their mongrels. But, on this day, the pavements were bare of all but the curious and loyal. Within moments royalty was secure and wrapped in the waiting maroon limousine. The journey to the station and the safety of a royal train, which would not call at Chippenham, Swindon and be late at Paddington, was mercifully short.

At the reception the Chief Constable was congratulated on the arrangements he had made and everyone congratulated each other on the way the Georgian city had looked. Royalty long gone, those who were left relaxed as parents might once bride and groom were safely away. Montague James, elegant in morning coat – his own, not hired, as everyone would know – felt the warmth of success.

'She was splendid. Don't you think so, William?'

The Bishop did not particularly mind being called William. After all, it was his name, but it suggested a familiarity that could not possibly be, as his friends never called him anything but Bill. But he knew why. Montague James had ideas which were not above his station and certainly not beyond those of the city. Therefore, Montague was never Monty, not even to his wife. In that case it followed that the bishop of one of the most important dioceses in England (had not the previous incumbent been preferred at Canterbury?) could not be a Bill. Bishop William sipped at his dry sherry, then at his wet lip, and nodded.

'Splendid. Yes, of course. And she was so interested.'

At his side there came a grunt, almost a growl of agreement. 'Always are, you know. Always are. And did you notice? The Duke semed to know more than she did.'

The speaker was a tall, bluff man with a bushy yet well-trimmed moustache. His dark uniform with its silver buttons and scrolls was clearly that of a senior man, yet it lacked the tailoring of a general's or the confidence of an admiral's. Montague James nodded at him and smiled the smile of a patronizing insider.

'Ah but, my dear Chief Constable, Prince Philip does rather tend to brief himself as much as any man might. He is a stickler for detail. His staff tell me.'

Montague James paused for full attention. Sure of it, he continued.

'His staff tell me that he has his own computer and produces veritable rain forests of notes on even the most minor visit.'

The tall woman who approached did so at speed. She was blonde, quietly tanned and elegant in fawn silk. Montague James would have called it a costume. She held no drink and carried her short cotton gloves as a badge of office, although what staff would have been suitable for the city's director of public affairs was not clear. The three men smiled. The Bishop thought her lovely. The Chief Constable, in his own Sedge-moor way, lusted after her. James thought her exquisite but was far too vain to be in love with her, or with anyone else for that matter.

When she spoke, her soft accent suggested an Australian origin. She was a woman who never publicly asked a question unless she knew the answer or the one she wanted to hear. Yes, the voice was Melbourne, not simply Australian.

'Pretty good? Not a hitch. Not a single hitch. Even the weather knew its place.'

Patsy Bush dazzled the trio with her smile and shook her head as a hovering waitress offered wine.

'My dear Patricia. A triumph. The monarch graced us with

3

her presence and you, my dear, with your expertise. A bewildering combination.'

They all laughed and the waitress moved on to seek the gaggle of serious drinkers who had gathered across the room about the editor of the *Evening Chronicle*.

'You must be used to this stuff, huh, Bishop?'

The Bishop sipped and smiled. He was not certain what 'this stuff' might be, but he supposed he did.

'There is a certain calmness in liturgical drama which allows for the presence of everyone "whoever and whatever", as the late Canon Worplesdon reminded us. But, yes, one has the advantage of having the ball at one's feet and therefore knowing when to kick it.'

'Mm?' The policeman was confused.

The Bishop smiled and dropped his head to the other side.

'In any form of service and celebration, one has only to move slowly and with as much dignity as possible and then the setting and the occasion allows one to make it up if one wishes to, especially if one has forgotten what to do or lost one's place. The ball, you see, is not only at one's feet, it is after all also one's ball.'

Montague James raised his eyebrows over his glass. He was tall and, once, in his twenties, thin; now, thirty years on he was slim. His tailor adored him almost as much as James adored himself. Patsy Bush smiled back in confidence. She detested him. But he was one of the most influential men in Bath. She needed him, or his influence. He turned his attention away from the Bishop to the Chief Constable, who was busy trying to fish a slice of lemon from his gin-drained glass.

'But, my dears, you should know that if, to continue your sporting metaphor William, we should needs select a man of the match, then there is no doubt: I give you our own dear Robert.'

He raised his glass in the direction of a surprised Chief Constable. Surprised not because he'd been caught chewing the lemon slice, but surprised because he had not a clue what Montague James was talking about.

'Me? What on earth are you on about?'

Montague James's pause was dramatic enough for a Theatre Royal matinée.

'But, Robert, you must know.'

Robert did not and shrugged his silver-crowned shoulders to say so.

'Simple policing job. The lads did well. They always do. But, frankly, it's not the old days when the Queen was such a crowd-puller. As I say, frankly, we have more trouble when Bristol City's playing at home.'

Montague James shook his head, dismissing the policeman's modesty. If Montague James decided a hero stood before them, then that gallant fellow should accept his plaudits like a man.

'It's what didn't cause any problems. Oh yes. Oh quite yes. Her Majesty came here to see the finest city in her land. And she did. The city, as my dear naval cousin would say, was dressed overall and splendidly so.'

The Bishop sipped some more and agreed.

'Pretty as a picture.'

'My dear William, of course. Why John Wood himself would have been proud of his city. And let me tell you all, the view was not spoiled one iota, thanks to dear Robert and the way in which his merry men handled the unwanted.'

The Chief Constable looked down and dropped the chewed peel in the slowly melting ice.

'Oh, them. Yes, well, least said the better.'

Patsy Bush looked across to the noises from the newspaper-man's corner and thought she might make her excuses. The Bishop sucked his teeth. Montague James carried on.

'Oh, them. Yes, *them,* dear Robert. The dreadful creatures were nowhere to be seen. You are to be congratulated. I shall make sure that –'

The Chief Constable interrupted him.

'If you do not mind, as I say, the least said the better, to anyone at any time.'

He put his empty glass on a nearby table and did his best with a smile. It was not something the Chief Constable did naturally.

'If you'll excuse me, I've got to change for tonight. Black tie, you know.'

And with that he was off. A big man in all ways and, for the moment, not entirely happy nor proud.

By nightfall, the travellers had returned to the city. Before morning, one lay dead.

Two

James Boswell Hodge Leonard was in his garden eating a very soft boiled egg when he heard that a vagrant had been found dead in a Roman bath.

The local radio station was brief although the reporter would have liked to say more, but knew even less than he had said. Leonard eyed his cat sunning itself on the wall overlooking the river. The cat was as ginger as Leonard was freckled.

'Mm. What d'you make of that?'

Johnson had never been in a Roman bath so made nothing of it. Not a whisker twitched.

'Not even curious?'

Johnson was aware that, for cats, curiosity was rumoured to be dangerous. No, not curious. She may have moved, but few would have noticed.

'Odd.'

Leonard looked up as if remembering. The bulletin had moved on. Leonard had not. Johnson's fur was warm. Leonard peered at the still animal.

'You notice they didn't say male or female. Odd? No?'

Johnson knew the difference between male and female even if others were confused. She yawned.

The news had moved on. Another voice, this time eager and punchy as a tabloid's splash, crowed that the Somerset side was smitten with injuries, bad luck and few spectators. The captain, a new man this season, claimed his team's misfortune could be put down to 'one of those things'. Leonard wondered what those things were. The captain conceded that the other side, Sussex, had bowled well. He had more to say in defence but Leonard was no longer listening. His eyes closed, he could see the downs. The trees. Below, the silent harbour. The screams that would not go away. He had spent a year forgetting. He took off his rimless spectacles and polished them on his napkin, all the while staring at Johnson. A blurred cat. But he knew what she looked like.

Leonard picked up his plate from the warm wooden bench and went inside. The kitchen was neat. No units. A polished pine table with brass-handled drawers. A glass-fronted dresser. A butler's sink. A scrubbed wooden draining board. He switched off the radio and watched hot water splash in the sink. No point in forgetting. It was there. Sometimes it was blurred. But he knew what it looked like. The telephone shrilled at him. He took his time. Turned off the tap, dried his hands carefully.

'Yes?'

The voice at the other end was sharp. Leonard did not bother to look at the clock. Of course he knew what time it was. Yes, he had heard the news. He listened some more, said goodbye and slowly buttoned his brown tweed waistcoat. The matching jacket was over the chair back. Leonard slipped it on, bolted the French doors which led to the small garden and waved a slim finger in goodbye to Johnson. On the way out he picked up his green cycle clips from the hall table. Thought about the hill. Put them down again. Went to the door. Went back and picked up the clips.

The editor was standing in the middle of the newsroom. Without looking, everyone knew he was there. Peter Dover was a big man. He neither stooped nor sagged. Not dumpy. Big. His blue-striped shirt made him taller and everyone else crouched. The black braces were three fingers wide and functional. The tie tightly knotted and tasteful. He was a quiet man. He called himself a hack. Maybe. He had been around. He had seen most of it. What he had not, he knew about. When he twitched, it was inside. His staff never saw it. That morning, he had by chance heard the local radio report. He had twitched. Now he wanted to know when, who, how and who again. When had the body been found? Who had found it? How did it die? Who was it?

It was gone nine. There had been no mention of it at his morning news conference. That was at twenty to eight. There had been no mention because none of his staff knew about it. But that could wait. The first edition was due off in forty-five minutes. That could not wait. Dover did not like being scooped, especially by local radio. In his book, local radio's idea of a scoop was to get the date right. This was Bath. His city. Not theirs. The news editor had every spare reporter working on it. She had just tried the police again. Dover's eyebrows niggled behind his spectacles.

'Well? What are they saying?'

Jessie Wright shook her head.

'Nothing. Said there's nothing to tell. They'll have a statement later.'

'How later?'

'Soon as they have something to say.'

The man at the head of the desk nodded. Typical police.

'Shit.'

Most agreed. Only he said it. The deputy editor sometimes said things like that. Not often. He was a slight, earnest figure; Decision Maker, it said on his confidential file. He scrubbed at his dark, close-cropped hair and said it again.

'Shit. Who told the Beeb, then?'

The news editor shrugged.

'Don't know. Hughie's gone down there. But the last we heard the whole place is taped off.'

The editor gazed in the air. Instinct was as annoying as a whining midge in a darkened bedroom. His instinct said this was wrong.

'Which one was it?'

The news editor didn't look up. She was scribbling a Must Do list.

'Cross Bath.'

'But that's just round the corner.'

The deputy shook his head. He did most things by head movements.

'Not for him, it isn't.'

Dover would not interfere. He was not that sort of editor. He would nudge and glide. He was much older than all but a couple of his staff. He had seen it. Most of it. His job was to make sure they did. The deputy was tapping away at a terminal. Dover's voice was quiet.

'You pulling it together?'

The other man nodded. Hardly anything to pull together. But there'd be enough. Basic fact. Scene-of-crime colour. Probably a picture of the area. Couple of quotes from locals. A couple of lines from the nick. Maybe something else from headquarters. It would be enough for the county edition. It was good there was no colour run in the paper that morning. They could hang on until the last moment.

A reporter had been calling the police-line. She had nothing to tell the desk. The police were playing out a recorded message like some well-Organized kidnapper. The girl had not expected much more. Dover scratched at his belly. Once there would have been a senior officer prepared to brief them. On background, of course. No one gets dropped in the clag that way. Now it was all centralized. A press desk the other side of Bristol. Fat lot they knew. Get to the office. Put the coffee on. What's in the papers? How did City do last night? Parrot's sick again. Wasn't the traffic bloody atrocious. Civilians, all of them, civilians. Civilians still with the taste of marmalade at that time of the morning. So no one knew anything until hours after the event. So much for streamlining. He made a mental note to mention it to the Chief Constable that evening. Again. The girl was waiting. Loitering. Brushing at the dusty fronds of a forlorn fern. A sense of urgency would not hurt. He nodded his thanks and she went back to her desk.

The newsroom carried on. Why not? It was just a death. Not even the Mayor. Nowadays they liked good news first. The agenda had changed. But. The editor sighed and looked about. There wasn't much that could be done. People, mostly youngsters, at their desks. Busy. The place was filthy. No point in being houseproud in a newsroom. From the ceiling, the dangle of power lines hanging from the cobweb of electricity supplies kept the green screens lit. Writers and sub-editors made them dance with paragraphs and headings. But the electricity kept itself to the desk-top displays. The room was tense because there was not much time. Lose ten minutes and they would lose a hundred readers. In London, they'd laugh at that. In Bath, they cursed.

Dover stopped scratching and rubbed instead. His scratching had been too aggressive. He turned towards his room. Then stopped. His deputy looked up.

'Well?'

The older man squinted through his glasses. Calm. Perfectly calm. Outside.

'Ask the police if they suspect foul play.'

'They won't tell us.'

'Ask them anyway.'

Hilary James had not heard the morning news. Her husband had. Hilary James never listened to the news. Never watched it. Never read it. The news had nothing to do with her. Why should it? She was neither a politician nor poor. So now she lay back in her morning bath as she did at this time every morning. She bathed three times each day. There was a lot to wash away. The bathroom was ivory but mostly mirrors. Hilary James cared to see herself. She watched for the slightest wrinkle, the slightest sign that her body might be catching up with her age. There were few signs. She knew each one and made sure no one else did. She lifted one long leg in the air and sighted along its slender lines as a stalker might measure a stag. She knew they were good legs. Hilary James liked her body. Slowly she rose from the water. The light froth clung here and there. An exotic dancer slinking from a stage pool. It was a game she played. Cleopatra, she imagined. She stretched and was pleased the way her body lifted in response. She turned. Admired herself in four mirrors and dropped her head back and smiled at the ceiling mirrors exaggerating her full breasts. She stepped out and onto the pile of soft towels and switched on the drier. She had found it in Rome. A tall mirror with channels all round its ivory frame. She watched and turned as the hot air gently blew away beads of water and the dampness as, legs apart, she swayed before her illuminated reflection. Montague James heard the gentle roar of the drier as he passed her closed door. He smiled at the Filipino girl who waited to empty his wife's bath and collect towels and cloths while her mistress, once gently oiled, dressed next door. In the drawing-room, James's smile, no longer needed, was put away and he picked up the ivory handset and dialled an unlisted number.

'Explanation?'

He gazed through the window at a peaceful city. His face barely wrinkled at his annoyance.

'Not satisfactory.'

The answer was short. Unsatisfactory.

'I want to know. It is essential.'

He listened for perhaps six or seven seconds. He had heard what he had expected. The anger was deep. He put down the receiver as if it were not and without bidding goodbye. He thought it quite unnecessary.

Three

James Leonard had pushed his bicycle the last few yards up the hill to lean it against the wall of the small bakery he fancied in narrow Broad Street. On impulse he had bought a gingerbread man. He'd dropped it in his canvas satchel, said goodbye to the girl who appeared more buxom than ever, and now, with his haul slung across his back, was pedalling slowly past the old Empire Hotel.

At the lights he stopped. He did not mind. He was in no hurry. He rarely hurried, not nowadays. There had been nights long before in the loneliness of the orphanage when he had hurried from one dream to another. In the mornings he would try to remember, but never did. Never could. They were not those sort of dreams.

An elderly man who had been standing with his wife at the kerb started to cross, then changed his mind. Started again. Lost his grip on his wife's arm and stepped back onto the pavement. He stumbled, angry at his age. He stared at Leonard, then glanced up at the red light. The light was about to change when the man asked Leonard if he knew where the Royal Crescent was. The man's arms were scrawny. So was his voice. Mid-Western. Maybe Arkansas. They were both wearing powder blue and the man a white cotton cap. Leonard was surprised they did not know Royal Crescent. He assumed that was the sort of thing Americans would know, instinctively. It took some explaining. They produced a tourist map. She pointed to the grand curve of Ionic memorial to John Wood the Younger. Leonard nodded, smiled and explained that, although on the map it looked miles away, it was not. When he said so, the man smiled. She did not. She looked doubtful. Probably thought her husband a fool. And Leonard.

All men. The couple were in their late seventies, maybe older, grotesquely preserved. He with black blotches on his withered face. She with a tuck and lifted glare and determined to see everything. She wore new boating shoes with leather laces bunched in stiff bows. She did not believe his directions. Leonard did not care. Eventually, and when the couple started to argue in front of him, Leonard said that if they went to the abbey, turned right and kept walking until they came to the T-junction, they would then see signs to the left. The man thanked him. Called him sir. The woman did not. They went off and along the bridge, she looking back a couple of times and determined to ask someone with more authority than a cyclist wearing a three-piece tweed suit and brown leather boots on a warm June morning.

Leonard smiled to himself. It didn't matter. Not now. He had time. They did not.

The lights changed for the third or fourth time and Leonard hitched his satchel into the small of his back and cycled across into Pierpoint and coasted along Manvers Street until he came to an ugly three-storey building opposite an electrical goods discount store. Instead of stopping outside he swung to the left and down the slope to the basement courtyard. The security gates were supposed to be shut across the ramp. They weren't. Never were. In the yard, dusty cars dumped for weeks on end blocked everything but the walker and Leonard chained his green cycle to a crooked and rusted wing mirror, put his pump in his satchel and crossed to a small blue scratched and gashed door in the corner of the yard. A man coming out nodded, held it for him, saving him the bother of remembering that month's door code. Leonard climbed the tatty biscuit stone backstairs to the first floor. There were a few people about. No one said good morning. He went into his office, a tiny outer room with a radiator and an aluminium-framed dirty window overlooking the discount store, and sat behind the only desk. He thought about some coffee, then decided to save the gingerbread man for later. From a bottom drawer he took three green cardboard files. Each was marked New Management Strategy. He flopped them in front of him and again thought about coffee. He was close to making up his mind and was sitting back, hands clasped behind his neck, when a short, dark-haired woman in a black skirt and white blouse appeared in the open doorway.

'Ah, there you are, sir. I was trying to get you on your bleeper.'

Leonard looked at the gingerbread bag. He looked up and returned her smile.

'It doesn't work.'

'No, sir.'

He smiled. It never had. He hummed tunelessly and lifted the edge of the paper bag. The gingerbread smelled good.

'And?'

The woman didn't like him. He unnerved her. She felt safe with red-blooded and suggestive comments from the man who usually sat behind Leonard's desk.

'Well, sir. The boss was looking for you. Could you pop along?'

'Now?'

'I think so, sir.'

Then she was gone. Leonard sighed and put the gingerbread man back in his satchel and headed back along the corridor to the large corner office. One sign said SUPERINTENDENT; the other, COMMANDER Superintendent Stainger was one and the same. Senior officer in the Central Police Station, or CPS as it was known in the constabulary, and also Commander of the police district. CPS was the only station in Bath. If it happened, then it happened here.

Stainger was not a huge policeman. He was a stocky, solid man with a twice-broken nose and thick black short back and sides. He had played rugby union in Scotland, first at his high school and then at Edinburgh. He had a much younger brother, a famous three-quarter. The Superintendent looked battered enough for outsiders to think it was he who had thrilled the crowds. No one ever asked the brother if he were the policeman. When he spoke, the accent was there, but an untuned ear might not have placed it north of the border. It was that sort of family. Now he nodded to the chair and tapped the blotter with a polished steel paperknife. Leonard sat with one ankle resting on his left knee, polishing his spectacles on a green silk handkerchief. Stainger eyed the other man's brown dull boots and mentally shook his head in disbelief. He sighed.

'What d'you know about the crusty?'

Leonard blinked as furiously as a naval telegraphist's Aldis. Alarums. Why should he know anything?

'The . . .?'

'The crusty. Come on, our body of the month.'

'You mean the vagrant.'

Stainger was easily annoyed.

'Listen, don't tell me what I mean. I mean the C-R-U-S-T-Y, the crusty. What d'you know?'

'Only what I heard on the wireless. He or she was found in one of the baths.'

Stainger looked up sharply. Was Leonard trying to be clever? He had known him for four months. He could never tell.

'He or she?'

'The news report did not say whether it was a man or a woman.'

Stainger had heard the report. Had not noticed. Yet instinctively, as with most things Leonard said, Stainger believed him.

'Male. About twenty. That's about it for the moment.'

Leonard was blinking again. The most obvious point was missing. He had loosened his waistcoat and now he hurried on and rubbed at his spotlessly clean spectacles with his tie. He looked up, still rubbing.

'Excepting one thing.'

Stainger nodded.

'Right. Murdered.'

'Sure?'

'He was done over. Not very nice, I'm told. He could have died after that, in which case it isn't necessarily a big one, manslaughter, but it's still pretty rough. Same to us. We're not in the business of deciding. Just finding.'

Stainger was in his shirtsleeves. His superintendent's crowns firm on his broad shoulders. He swung in his executive high-backed chair and glared at the wall of shields, trophies and honours and then back at Leonard.

'I want you to handle this.'

He waited for Leonard's reaction. Silence. Just a furious blink. Stainger pointed the paperknife at the wall behind Leonard. The wall-chart made good reading in what Stainger called daylight. Ram-raiding and thieving he could handle. If this turned out to be a full-blown murder hunt, then 138 officers including the halt and the lame looked thin. It took at least forty men and women to make up a murder team.

'You've seen where we are. I'm down two inspectors out of six and this one has senior officer written on it. It's got to be you. Thank God it wasn't a kiddie.'

'Why?'

'I'd have had to take it on myself. The wee folk rate a superintendent. Crusties get a senior inspector. You. That's the way we work here. You'll find out.'

Leonard had found out quite a lot since the day six months ago when he had arrived in Bath.

Officially he was on secondment. Avon and Somerset Constabulary was going through a major restructuring exercise thanks to the destructive notions of a commission of inquiry and a Secretary of State with a record of causing havoc at whichever ministry he entered. The problem for the constabulary was that it had been ahead of the political game. The Chief Constable had made his own changes. Chief inspectors had gone. The rank of detective had gone. CID was simply a plain-clothed version of everyone else.

Stainger had been one of the brains behind the scheme.

He wanted to make sure that CID lost its elitist identity before it thought it was above the law. It had happened elsewhere. The result had been detectives using their own methods to get convictions at almost any cost. When it had all surfaced, the police were discredited, the job harder than ever. Stainger and the Chief Constable had seen the signs and altered direction. So, although Leonard had been a detective chief inspector in his own constabulary, here in Bath he was officially an inspector.

None of this should have been Leonard's problem. There had been another place. A place in which the most terrible violence and the most questionable methods had left a trail almost impossible to disguise. The irony was that Leonard's background was exactly what Stainger was trying to avoid. Stainger did not know what had gone on. No one in the force did. It had been hushed up at the highest Whitehall level. But blood stains. There had been much blood in what became known as The Madrigal Case. But Leonard had not been the leading actor in the drama. He had been swept along the bloody stream. A combination of this, a single friend at court and the fact that he knew so much had saved him. But he was still a problem with no safe pigeon loft. So, when, at a conference of chief constables, Avon and Somerset had mentioned they wanted an outsider to redraw the wiring diagram of the Bath police, Leonard's senior officer had eagerly offered Leonard's services. Leonard, with his academic background and legal training, looked, on paper at least, the ideal man to process buff folder after buff folder until the new structure fell into place.

The Superintendent had never wanned to Leonard. It was not a matter of liking or disliking. It was something that Stainger could not place. Leonard was not objectionable. He did not cause trouble. He was clearly good at the job he had been brought in to do. His analytical mind had swept through the dross of administration in half the time Stainger had anticipated. His questions had always been discreet and pertinent. But to Stainger it was simply that Leonard was not a person to warm to. Stainger liked to know where he stood with his officers. Leonard did not let anyone in.

Most of all, to Stainger, Leonard did not look like a copper. Slim, almost thin. Gingery curly hair. Round spectacles. Scratchy tweed and the brown scuffed boots of an Edwardian baker's boy. Most of all, Leonard was a loner. The canteen, for example, was a small, cramped room. Yet the couple of times Leonard had gone in he had managed to be by himself in the crowd. The story was that when he joined the force they had called him the professor. He looked the part. But it had not lasted. Leonard had never been popular enough for a nickname to stick.

Stainger did not like loners. They were unpredictable because you couldn't catch the signs. In Stainger's book, a loner spelled trouble. Stainger did not want trouble. The fact that no one talked about Leonard's past meant it had to be full of trouble. A dead crusty could not, must not, mean trouble. He said so.

'Should be straight up and down. Probably one of the brothers. Argument over drugs. Something like that.'

'We know he was doing something.'

'They're all doing something. Crack. Smoking. You know.'

'What about this one?'

Stainger looked at his paperknife.

'Well, nothing yet.'

'Then why should I know if you don't?'

Stainger shifted. A bell was ringing somewhere in his mind. He did not like it.

'Look. This is straightforward, as far as we know. OK?'

Leonard said nothing. He started to hum to himself. Hardly a sound. But still a hum. Stainger got up and stretched and walked to the window. The public car park was half-empty but his officers could not find a space in their own. In ten minutes he was due to hold a meeting about personnel problems. He wanted Leonard to go. Get on with it. Bath did not have murders. Had not had one in a decade. He should be handling this himself. Thanks to reorganization he could not. He did not want trouble.

'Look, James. This is not Crime City Inc. Get on with this one, tidy it up, get a nick, then we can all get on with life. You know, boring old files.'

The hum was softer. But it was there. Leonard would have sooner stuck to his files.

'Who've I got?'

Stainger told him. He wondered how Leonard would get on with his sergeant.

Four

Leonard was glad to be out. He thought about his bicycle but left it chained to the beaten-up Ford. Instead he walked towards the abbey. The late-morning sun was already scorching the pavements. Bath was airless. Leonard thought of his quiet stroll along the towpath the previous evening. The chilled wine when he returned. The pages of Sassoon and the sounds in his mind all night of the poet's wretched war as sister steel stabbed at his sleeplessness. He did not want this.

He had come to Bath to restructure an impersonal system. Maybe even his own. His files were orderly. Safe. Lines and columns. Redesigning forms. That was why he was here. Safety in numbers. Safety with Manual General Numbers. Form MG 2. File Front Sheet. Tick If Attached. Custody Remand. Plea File ABB. Plea File Full. File For Summary Trial. File For Committal. If Available. Requires Typing. File Boring. File Escape. File Forget.

The spiteful snarl of a septuagenarian brought him back. The sour-faced American woman was side-on to him, peering at the menu in the window of Sally Lunn's. Five hundred years of bun- and teacake-making did not impress the Arkansas matron. She was taking it out on her husband. They'd crossed the goddam Atlantic. Paid goddam too much to the goddam railroad company running out of London. And hell, look at the goddam prices. What the goddam hell did these people think she was? Something out of the Lease Lend Program? Her husband did not like her when she spiked like this. He needed the John. He glanced away from the menu he did not understand, peered at Leonard and seemed to recognize him. Seemed was enough and he smiled. He looked tired. Leonard wondered if they had found the Royal Crescent. He hoped for the husband's sake that they had.

He crossed the shopping precinct and dodged a ragbag of travellers. One of the dogs snapped at another and its owner yanked on the rough string lead and, for good measure, kicked it in the ribs. The mongrel, perhaps numb, perhaps used to being kicked, did not yelp but cowered at their laughter. One of them, a fire-eater from Glastonbury, was laying out a mat and charred stick ends, all set to earn from the small crowd and onlookers that milled up from Bath Street.

About halfway down, yellow tape criss-crossed the road. Leonard started to take out his identification card, but the constable, whom Leonard did not recognize, let him through with a solemn nod.

The body was gone. Someone had drawn a thick chalk outline. A blob. Policemen, and one woman, were searching the narrow flagstone pavement and nooks of the high walls about the steaming water. There was no conversation.

A short, grey-haired, muscly man looked up from a notebook and waved as Leonard went through the wooden doorway into the open bath. Inspector Ray Lane was one of the few people Leonard had got to know and the only person who had got to know Leonard. Not long promoted, Lane had returned to Bath after two years in Bristol. There had been two commendations. He kept them in his drawer. He did not smile much but when he did it was the real thing and usually showed up enough scar tissue to make a prize fighter's mother wince. Stainger had once said that Lane slept in his face, but it was said with affection.

'You just missed the star of the show. Doc's looked him over. Well dead.'

'Where is he now?'

'Royal United. That's where they all go.'

Lane paused, looking closely at Leonard's twitching lower lip.

'That all right? Seemed no point in hanging about.'

Leonard shrugged. Looked about him.

'What's the time?'

Lane was wearing a thick, black diver's watch. He was not a diver but it stood up to rough treatment. He called it his Bristol watch.

'Eleven-forty-five. Why?'

'Thought it would have gone long ago. No?'

'Home Office pathologist had to come over from Cardiff. Nearest one's got his leg in plaster. You'll meet him. Nice man. Don't mention rugby. Not even at this time of the year. "We wuz robbed, boyo." Know what I mean?'

Leonard did not. In Bath, rugby union was bigger than soccer. Leonard liked watching cricket, preferably from a deck chair through half-closed eyes. He looked at the chalk line, then at the scene of crime team.

'Anything?'

Lane shook his head.

'Nothing you couldn't get on a postcard. Male. Twentyish. That's about it. No weapon. No bangs. No knife. No nothing. Face down. Just there. But nasty.'

Lane pointed to the chalk lines. By the side of the pool.

In the middle, hot mineral spring gushed out just as the Celts had known it would. The dead had been here before. Leonard stared at the outline. Tried to imagine a man. Instead, a long oblong blob. Face down? One leg bent. A blob climbing a sheer mountain side. A blob without a name.

'Who was he?'

Lane didn't know. Someone did. Leonard was cleaning his spectacles. He nodded over his shoulder in the direction of the open grille in the wall.

'What about his friends? They know him?'

'Maybe. They say no.'

Leonard hissed and hummed and walked to the side of the Roman bath. The steam was too theatrical.

'This genuine?'

Lane laughed.

'D'you mean does it come straight off the mains? A con?'

Leonard nodded. Most things were. Lane joined him.

'Real all right. This used to be marshland. Steam every-where. Real horror-movie stuff.'

'I thought it was Roman.'

'No. Donkey's years before the wops. It's the real thing.'

Leonard glanced down at the chalk outline.

'And this?'

'Real? I think so.'

'Who found him?'

'Some woman. Customs and Excise. They've got an office down by the bus station.'

'What was a civil servant doing out at that time of the morning?'

Lane shook his head. He had wondered. He would ask her.

A tall, elegant man approached through the arch. He was in his late twenties. Dark-blue three-button suit. Summerweight. Pricey. It all came together. The tie, the shirt, the shoes, the pocket handkerchief, the styled, not cut, hair. The tan exaggerated his smile. Very pricey. Lane sucked his teeth. Wiped a summer cold with the back of his hand. The other man stopped, turned up the smile. Put out a strong hand in Leonard's direction.

'Hello, sir. We've not met. Somers-Barclay. I'm your sergeant on this one.'

Leonard looked at the hand. The dangling gold bracelet. He hummed and turned back to the chalk.

'Who says murder?'

Lane grinned at Somers-Barclay. The younger man was put out, but would not show it. The Inspector liked Leonard.

'Until we get to the coroner, I suppose no one. But the doc said he wasn't sure how. Fully clothed, see? But there were enough signs to say it was violent.'

Somers-Barclay had recovered.

'Perhaps we could go over to the Royal United, sir.'

Leonard nodded as if considering the idea. He was rubbing at his glasses again. Same green silk handkerchief. He slipped the wire arms over his ears. He had to look up to the Sergeant.

'How did he get in here?'

Somers-Barclay waved at the white wood doors.

'Pretty simple, sir. Through there, I imagine.'

'Why simple?'

'Only way in. More or less.'

Leonard looked to the wall. Ten, twelve feet?

'Ladder?'

'I suppose . . .'

'Were the outside doors open then?'

'Well . . .'

'Were they locked when he was found?'

Lane tapped his book.

'Nope. It's locked most of the time. There's a custodian. The lock's simple, galvanized padlock. Clasp. Take it off with a lolly stick.'

Somers-Barclay was eyeing the door which opened through to the outer double doors.

'So we need to know if anyone heard anything. Right.'

It was not a question.

Leonard was looking at the high wall and the uniform blob. He searched Somers-Barclay's face. It was an honest face. Open. Bright even. Leonard wondered. He started to hum. Somers-Barclay would have liked to place the music. He was wasting his time. Stainger was right. Leonard really was a loner. He even had his own music.

'Why?'

'Well, the breaking in, sir.'

'What if they had keys?'

'Then why break the lock, sir?'

Leonard turned away. Lane answered for him.

'To make it look as if they didn't have the keys. Gottit, dimbo?'

Somers-Barclay looked suitably enlightened.

'Oh. Right.'

Not that bright. Leonard nodded a friendly farewell to Lane and started back towards Bath Street, but turned left. Somers-Barclay fell in step.

'Where to, sir?'

Leonard carried on walking. He was heading through a back lane. Didn't want to play with the crowd and fire-eaters.

'Find out who had keys to that place.'

'Inspector Lane said it was the custodian.'

'He said there is a custodian. Not the same thing, is it?'

'No, sir.'

'Find every key to that place and who has touched them, or even seen them in the past month.'

Leonard stopped. Somers-Barclay was smiling again. Leonard wished that he would not.

'And then I'll see you at the Royal United at two-thirty. I'll want to see the body.'

'The crusty.'

'The body.'

'Yes, sir.'

'And look out for a dumped rucksack, duffle bag, something like that. OK?'

'Any particular reason, sir?'

'There wasn't one there.'

Somers-Barclay was a good policeman, but this quiet, strange man had speeded up. He'd got away from him.

'Where, sir?'

'In the bath. Inspector Lane would have said if there had been one. We'd have been through it. There wasn't one.'

'I see.'

Leonard doubted it.

'If he's what everyone says he is, then he doesn't have much. He travels light. Mm. They keep themselves in a bag. There wasn't one. Mm? Who he is, what he is, is in a bag somewhere. Find it.'

'But he could be in a squat. Somewhere like Hampton Row. Beckford Gardens. Anywhere.'

Leonard had started off again. He was speaking over his shoulder.

'There's no such place as anywhere. Everything and everyone is somewhere. The keys and his bag.'

'Where will you be, sir? If I need you, that is.'

'Lunch.'

And he was gone. Into the next lane, leaving the tiny street empty except for the elegant Somers-Barclay.

Five

Leonard stumped on through the back streets. His head was down. He was thinking. Stainger had said to be quick before some other crusty went the same way. No fuss, Stainger had said. Probably straightforward. Leonard did not think so. Unless there was blood in a doorway, this was not straightforward. He hummed nothing in particular and thought in particular. The blob had been too neat. Could blobs be neat? The body had been arranged. Placed. From the chalk marks, the wall, the door, whoever he was had not come to die. Who did? Depended on what you took for a living? Leonard had stooped at the outer door. No wrenched paintwork. He did not need a large magnifying glass and a gasp of admiration from Ray Lane to see that. Could have been killed in the bath and then arranged. But how? Why so neat?

Leonard did not like murder investigations. Mostly they were quick. Domestic arguments. Someone in the family. Husband, wife, boyfriend, lover, mistress. He did not like them because of the undercurrents. He did not like the cruel gash across the face of a family which had once loved. To Leonard, violence in something so precious as a family was unbearable. Procedures were supposed to protect people like Leonard. They never did. Better to be alone with his instincts than crowded by procedures. A very correct inspector had told the young Detective Constable Leonard that policework was about choices. So, he had said, there had to be procedures; otherwise the policeman became judge or, worse still, mourner. One day he, Leonard, would have to choose. On the outside it was just as miserable. Just as lonely. For now, he would stay. He would always be alone. But he would stay. He understood aloneness. Liked it. Hated loneliness.

In Florence, he had been alone. Then, one day, he had met a barrister and his family. Dined in their house high in the Tuscan hills. In London, the barrister had welcomed him once more. He became a pupil. But then disillusioned. He thought the law corrupt. The law worked by the fee not the cause. Leonard had been young enough to believe there was no such thing as cheap justice. Only cheap law. They had smiled and had said there was always legal aid. They knew you got what you paid for. He had not smiled and had returned to Florence.

One quiet morning there had been love. When that love perished he left. Had returned. But not to the cream-painted chambers and the Temple's smug safety. He had joined the police. Not in London. Another escape. In Sussex, they had given him uniform and shoes and a hat. All had been his size, perfectly so. None had fitted him. The CID took him in, fed him on irregular hours and not a little freedom. He was not a policeman naturally inclined to the feel of a villain's collar, but he had the wit and logic which allowed others to do so.

While his superiors thought of his future, he thought of his past. He remained a loner. They said it would come to no good. It had come to no good.

In his thoughts, he tripped on the uneven cobbles and kerb. Somewhere above him a clock chimed. And in his subconscious a clapper agitated a nagging instinct. Why was everyone so relaxed? Bath had not had a murder in a decade. Then why so relaxed? Because it was a traveller? Did not matter? Or because it did? Stainger had told him to clear up. No fuss. No need for that.

At the top of Queen Square he turned right and, in George Street, stopped for hayfever tablets, swallowed one and slipped the packet into his waistcoat pocket. He would be fine until the morning. He tapped a finger on a basement railing and wondered about a glass of wine below. At the antique market he wondered about an Afghan rug. Too much. One day. Not this one. A short walk full of incident, of everyday people, everyday lives getting on with every day while a stranger lay ready for the pathologist's knife and saw.

At the top of the lane he turned left and into Woods.

Selsey was standing by the bar. It was early, but the inner rooms were already busy. He was thinking about evening menus. Or should have been.

Selsey had a problem. He had broken the habit of a lifetime and got involved with flat racing. Mistake. Selsey, as everyone in racing knew, was a National Hunt man. Had been since the days he had run a book in the school dormitory. That had been his second term, which was about right because in the Selsey family the second of everything was into racing. His grandfather had been a bookmaker, long before the days of licensed betting shops. His mother said that the second son in the family was always a gambler. It was true. But Selsey would never have bet on it. Because Selsey was not that sort of gambler. He only backed horses. He did not flutter on the Boat Race, the Cup Final or even Miss World. Selsey, like his grandfather, was a proper racing man. In his family that meant over the sticks. Cheltenham on that big week. Wincanton on a bitter cold day surrounded by farmers. A proper place for a hip flask. Proper racing, he would tell anyone who listened. Most would when he talked.

He saw Leonard come in and sit, not in the restaurant but where he sat most lunchtimes. In the front, in the corner by the window. A table for two if neither made much mess. For Leonard, who never made any mess, a table for one. Selsey took across an already-open bottle of white wine and two glasses and sat down.

'You look glum.'

Leonard glanced at him. Selsey was nearly smiling. He was always nearly smiling. At his own funeral he would be wearing a grin just coming up. Now with his thick dark hair over his eyes he had a look that said he had a story to tell. Selsey usually had a story to tell. Leonard sensed a story.

'Glum? No, that's you. Have a look in the mirror.'

Selsey let the grin through. He poured the wine.

'But I am, I am. The most terrible glum. The most terrible glum. Food?'

Leonard fancied an omelette. He liked eggs and ate too many. They'd cook him one though it wasn't on the menu. On the blackboard it said duck and something in cherries. It said wonderful things about fillet of pork. It said sea bass in a special way. They'd cook him his eggs with herbs and then he would drink too much coffee. Small cups. Brown sugar. He sipped at the chilled wine.

'So what's the problem?'

Selsey shook his head in his own disbelief. When he spoke, it was softly. Maybe if he kept his voice down it wouldn't be true. His problem would disappear.

'I think I may have bought a horse.'

Leonard sniffed.

'You told me you would never buy a horse.'

'That's right. That is exactly right.'

'You've got a problem, then.'

'Don't tell me.'

Leonard polished his spectacles. Blinking all the while.

'What sort of horse?'

Selsey looked heavenwards.

'Not that simple.'

'I thought horses were. Simple. So what happened?'

Selsey hunched his shoulders. The pain of it all was taking a superhuman effort. His ruddy face was in agony as reality and devilment vied for his affection.

'You see, I'd had a couple yesterday. There's a trainer in here and he says he's got one going that'll not bother to get up until three minutes before the start and then he'll walk it by half the course.'

'You mean he told you he's got a winner on his hands?'

Selsey nodded. He was warming to the tale.

'Winner? This one, according to him, that is, could sit on the rails as a backmarker and trot to the front any time he wants to.'

'So?'

'Well, we have a few more. And apparently, apparently, I promise you, I say that if he's that good I'll put a few on him and, if he wins me something, then I'll buy a horse from him.'

'Rash.'

'Rash? Rubbish! I was pissed.'

'And he'll hold you to it?'

The restaurateur looked offended. He was.

'No, I will. I said I would. That means, well, it means I'll have to.'

Leonard laughed. The first time that day.

'If it wins.'

'Right.'

'Well, if it does, then you'll be able to afford it.'

It was Selsey's turn to laugh. The humour, though, was hard to pin down.

'You know how much one of these beasts costs? Go on. You

know how much? Maybe one, two, hundred thousand. Then you have to do something with it. They eat their heads off and it costs half the national debt to keep it training. No, James lad, not my league. Anyway, it wouldn't be a jumper.'

One of the girls brought his omelette. She was very pretty. The black skirt was very short. He watched her go. Stainger would have been surprised. He picked up a fork.

'When's the great day?'

'Week today.'

'And no way out of it?'

'I could put on some big money. Which I haven't got. Mind you, I could always get myself bumped off. It's very fashionable. Especially in the Roman bidet.'

Leonard stopped chewing.

'You know about it?'

'Only heard this morning.'

'It only happened this morning.'

'That would explain it.'

Leonard put down his fork. Wiped his mouth with a white napkin.

'Come on. What do you hear?'

Selsey spent his life listening, telling and racing and, when he had time, running the best restaurant in the city.

'Nothing. Well, hardly nothing. I heard there'd be one or two of Bath's finest wetting themselves. But you know how it is.'

Leonard shook his head.

'No. I don't. Who's saying this?'

'Oh, there's nothing sinister, your honour. Nothing at all. The freemen and aldermen scare easily, you know. This town runs on tourism. Find some poor bastard face down in your main attraction and the coaches carry on to Cornwall. Especially if it's a crusty.'

'Why "especially"?'

'The poor always ye have. All right for the gospel to know that, but it doesn't go down too well in this place. Law-abiding Bath. Built by the rich for the rich, lived in by the rich, toured by the rich. The fat cats around here don't like beggars at the gates of their monuments and shop fronts. If anyone's going to rip off tourists then let it be done through the members of the Chamber of Commerce, not some sponging refugee from Glastonbury.'

Selsey grinned. He was an honest man. Kind when others were cruel because it might be easier. He wasn't a cynic. Leonard knew this. They liked each other. Leonard was eating again.

'You still haven't told me who said this.'

'No one exactly said anything. Look, James lad, is this official?'

'No. I'm running the inquiry. But no. Just you and I.'

'Not me?'

Leonard smiled.

'If you wish. So, tell me a little.'

'Nothing much. You know the publicity woman? Patsy Bush?'

Leonard did not. Selsey was surprised. She was the sort of high-powered woman he detested and who knew everyone. He figured she probably knew Leonard's boss. She did. Selsey shrugged and waved at a pretty woman crossing from Saville Row. Selsey knew a lot of pretty women. Most of them knew him.

'Patsy Bush? She's the city's mouthpiece. You know, give it a good name? As if it hadn't got one. Waste of money, if you ask me.'

'Go on.'

'Well, she was in this morning. About something else. And she mentioned it, that's all. Said it was bad for the image. Me, I said it was bad for the poor bastard. She just said it was a pity they let them back in.'

'What did that mean?'

The door opened and the woman entered. Selsey waved again and called for another glass and a bottle, and she came over. Selsey had escaped. His instincts did not easily take to a friend being a policeman. This was beginning to be one of those moments. Selsey opened both arms with all the warmth of a baptist preacher.

'You know each other?'

They did not. They each said so at the same time. They each laughed. Selsey laughed loudest.

'Harriet Bowles, James Leonard. James Leonard, Harriet Bowles.'

Selsey poured wine. The other two said hello.

'Harriet is a paper-maker. Melincourt. You know, special paper? Outrageous prices?'

Leonard knew the shop. There were two or three in Bath. Melincourt was tucked away. A side-street off a side-street. He wondered how it survived. She smiled easily at Selsey and handed him a package.

'Then you shouldn't be so vain. Here you are. Two days early.'

Selsey was a good customer. He liked the best. It was a good recommendation. She turned to Leonard but Selsey started to tell her the tale of his impending financial ruin at the hands of a trainer with a good memory. While Selsey talked and she listened, Leonard watched her.

Harriet Bowles could only be English. The soft brown hair, the slightly rounded, lightly tanned face. Not glamorous. But something. Yes, very English. Knew what sensible shoes were, even if she never wore them. She was perhaps early thirties, tallish and for a few years more would turn husbands' heads and make less than confident wives snarl. When she moved, so did the brilliant white cotton shirt. A man's shirt. She moved. Caught him looking. Leonard wondered if he had blushed. He might have done.

'You're visiting Bath?'

Selsey grinned. This was fun. He poured more wine. He was about to say something, but Leonard got in first.

'I work here. For the moment.'

'I'm sorry. Yet another of Selsey's friends from his cupboard.'

Selsey's surname came easily. Leonard could not remember anyone calling him by his first name.

'James lad is a lunchtime acquaintance. Isn't that right?'

Leonard nodded. He had taken off his clean glasses once more. The silk handkerchief was out. She wondered why this man seemed so comfortable dressed for winter.

'And, when you're not listening to nonsense from Selsey, what brings you to Bath?'

Her voice said too many cigarettes and too many late nights smoking them. It wasn't what her complexion and eyes said.

'I'm a policeman.'

There was, in the old manual of police interrogation, a chapter on Dislocation of Expectancies. In that chapter are ploys and schemes to dislocate a villain's confidence and so score points that when added will bring about his breakdown and his confession. There is nothing in the book about a quietly lovely woman in a fashionable Bath restaurant in June being told by a tweed-suited man in his late thirties or even early forties, rubbing a pair of rimless spectacles with a green silk handkerchief while humming under his breath, that he is a policeman.

Harriet Bowles sipped her wine.

'A policeman. I see.'

Leonard hurred on one lens, rubbed and then hooked the wire arms over his ears.

'Yes.'

'And what do you police?'

Selsey chuckled and clinked the bottle against the rim of her glass.

'He is, Harriet my love, as you can see by the heavy disguise, a detective. And so be careful. Anything you may say may be taken down and forgotten instantly.'

The three laughed. Leonard not loudly. Selsey continued.

'And, I have to say, I have never seen him, nor do I know

anyone who has seen him, doing his detecting thing. Is that right?'

Leonard sighed. Took a sip. Murder seemed far away. He had to leave.

'Where do I find Miss Bush?'

Harriet Bowles looked amused. Selsey answered.

'Just across from your body, my son. Opposite the Colonnades, God rest their bankrupt souls. She's got an office there. It's all very smart.'

Leonard got up. He went to the bar and gave the girl money. There weren't that many left, she thought. Leonard had never had a credit card. He went back to the table to say goodbye. They were talking. Harriet Bowles put out a hand. The grip was strong.

'So you're finding out that Bath does things by numbers.'

'I am?'

'Account numbers, isn't that so, Selsey?'

The other man nodded. He grinned up at Leonard.

'She's right, James lad. Damned right. You see, Bath has Austin Reed, Moss Bros, Liberty, Laura Ashley and Droopy and Brown, all within yards of each other. Now, Holmes, what does that tell us about this place?'

Leonard nodded. He understood. Harriet Bowles sipped and looked up.

'And don't forget, Mr Leonard, most of it's old money. Old money means more than bank accounts. It means it owns everything, including the bank. Or thinks it does. I wish you luck.'

Leonard must have looked puzzled. She laughed.

'You can't have been here very long. We don't have murders in Bath. It's bad for the image.'

'You've got one now.'

'A vagrant, wasn't he?'

Leonard nodded.

'There you are, then. The worst kind of publicity. Right, Selsey?'

'Right. Oh, just one word of warning, James lad. It's very much Ms Bush, not Miss. But you'll find out when you meet her.'

Six

The door was locked. It had a buzzer. He could see the outer office. Lots of blue carpet and a reception desk like in a small hotel foyer. The youth who let him in was pleasant but unhelpful. Patsy Bush was out. No, he did not know what time she would be back. Would he like to make an appointment? Leonard said no but he would call later. The youth said it was always better to make an appointment, especially with everything going on. Everything going on meant the yellow tape across from the office. The youth who was not good at conversations tried his best.

'Bad for the image, you know.'

'What is?'

The youth looked smug. He would not have expected this fogey to know.

'The murder, of course.'

'Why "of course"?'

'Hardly good for trade, is it? I mean, is it? People come here to enjoy themselves. We get a better class of tourist in Bath, you know. I mean, Patsy was only saying that times are bad enough without fuzz asking questions everywhere. After all, I mean, he was only a crusty. You know?'

Leonard blinked. Took off his glasses.

'You mean it doesn't matter?'

'Course it matters. People, especially Americans, get frightened. And the police don't help, do they? I mean, well you can see for yourself, can't you? I mean, well, all this tape everywhere and great big plods going into the shops. Mind you, they're about the only people who do go in nowadays, especially down here. You know? But fuzz all over the place is bad news. You know?'

Leonard asked again.

'You've no idea when she'll be back?'

'Three. Maybe four. It's like that. The job, I mean. Never can tell.'

He reached for his multicoloured felt-tip. He eyed Leonard. Made a decision to go through the motions.

'Tell you what. I'll tell Patsy you called. Does she know you?'

Leonard shook his head. Time to agitate muddy water. He headed for the locked door. There was a buzzer click and it opened. Leonard turned.

'Tell her I'll be back later.'

'Who shall I say called?'

'Inspector Leonard. Bath CID.'

He was gone. The youth supposed he had heard correctly. He did not look up from his notepad, fearful that Leonard might have waited.

'Shit. Holy shit.'

But it was OK. Leonard really had gone.

He arrived at the hospital at two-twenty-five. The cab driver had said ten minutes. It had taken six. The main entrance was festooned with blue-and-white direction boards. A smiling and T-shirted man with a sash which said he was a Visitors' Guide wanted to help. Leonard was about to ask the way when he spotted Somers-Barclay chatting to a young doctor. She was very pretty and smiling. She did not look like a Welsh pathologist. She wasn't. By the time Leonard reached them she was leaving. Somers-Barclay was looking very pleased with himself, especially when the woman turned at the corner and gave a half-wave. She had very long legs.

'Oh hello, sir. Knew her brother. He was on my staircase at Cambridge.'

'She's a pathologist?'

Somers-Barclay laughed. The head going back, the mane exaggerating the roar.

'Good lord, no. Cardiac.'

Leonard wondered if such pretty women should be treating delicate men.

'And?'

'Oh, purely social, sir. Purely the old social. Mind you, she said they get quite a few crusties through here. Mostly in the winter.'

'The halt, the sick, the lame and the freezing?'

'And the scroungers.'

Leonard supposed Somers-Barclay right.

'Any in now?'

The Sergeant shrugged.

'Not that she knows. But then she wouldn't unless they had ticker trouble. Not her line, you see.'

Leonard did. He was about to ask Somers-Barclay to keep in touch with the young doctor, but did not. He would anyway.

They were following the arrows. Somers-Barclay was leading him in the direction of the pathologist's den. There was no name on the door. Just the trade plate. Leonard had been told what to expect. Lane had been short and precise.

'He'll treat you like a fool if you let him.'

'Why?'

'He thinks coppers are.'

'This isn't Cardiff.'

'God. Don't tell him that. He knows that all right. That's the problem. Even speaks Welsh to his dog. And you can forget the Celtic Fringe bit. This one's right in the centre and your starter for ten is that he's known in the business as the Screaming Skull.'

Facing the Home Office man, Leonard could see why. The Screaming Skull ignored Somers-Barclay and his outstretched signet ring, sized up Leonard as a funeral director does out of habit, and nodded a greeting.

The head was completely bald. The cheekbones high and

the marbled skin taut. The upper lip, clean-shaven and long pulled back from irregular teeth. When he spoke, it was not a Cardiff accent. No echoes of Liverpool to the untrained ear. This was a man whose father had spat his last long before the final cage had clanged shut and the humourless waters had flooded the deepest coal seam for all time. This was a man who understood straight glasses and tasteless beer and who had escaped the Rhonddas but who had taken with him the prejudices and anger of his father and four brothers. The upper lip twisted. An educated sneer. Leonard did not even look like a policeman.

'What you want, then?'

Leonard saw the signs. Was prepared to play.

'Only what you can give, Dr Griffiths.'

'Not much.'

The body was on the table. The skin was not yet dough and the hairs not yet best seen on a butcher's slab. But it had started. The skin was not his own. The muscles had lost interest. The sinews lost. Death had not stayed long. Long enough, but not long. Whoever he had been was no longer there. Griffiths tapped the bare, empty belly. Somers-Barclay was not good with bodies. He said something about a telephone call and left. Leonard wondered if he would head for the Cardiac Unit, but thought not. Somers-Barclay had lost a little of his tan. He was not at his best. He would only visit the pretty doctor with the large breasts when he was at his best. Griffiths sneered at the closing door.

'So, I'm not sure what you expect. I haven't had a chat with him yet. But it could be interesting.'

'Why so?'

'Well, we'll know for sure how he died, won't we? And, as these weirdos go, he's a bit different.'

'There's a standard?'

'Somewhere between distasteful and despicable.'

'That's a limited view.'

The Screaming Skull tapped the belly again.

'They don't leave here with too many secrets.'

'That doesn't mean they're despicable.'

'They have charity in the police now, do they? Very nice, I'm sure. Let me tell you, when I get my little drill and saw going and when I've run their vital organs through my bacon slicer, then, Mr Leonard, I usually know what sort of life they've been living. Mostly despicable. Believe me.'

Leonard looked away. The pathologist was fingering the belly as a child would a soft pillow. The policeman looked up at the glass-fronted gallery. A couple of people were watching. Waiting. He wondered who they were. He did not ask. The glasses were off. The handkerchief was out again. Leonard held them to the light. Perfectly clean. He polished them.

'OK, Dr Griffiths. Tell me something. What's interesting about this one?'

'Why should there be?'

'He's been murdered.'

'Lots of people get murdered. Lots of people die. Eight hundred came through here last year.'

'None of them ended up with a chalk outline.'

The Screaming Skull backed off. A little.

'Good class of cadaver. Nice to see a bit of class in the drawer. And beautifully clean.'

Leonard looked at the body. It looked dirty. He said so.

'But, Mr Leonard, this is what you people call a crusty. Yes? Well, Mr Leonard, well, he may look dirty, but this is not crusty dirt. It's not deep dirt. It's not there from months of grime and soiling himself. This one's a washer. Very particular, I'd say.'

Griffiths picked up an unfeeling hand. He peered at the nails.

'And look at these. He's not a biter, you see. They're ripped all right. But in anger, not bitten.'

Leonard was interested. He was getting somewhere with this odd Welshman.

'What was that about class?'

Griffiths smiled. At least on anyone else it would have been a smile.

'Ah yes. Somewhere along the line, there's breeding here.'

The face was unrevealing. The body thin. Or was it slim?

'How so?'

'Well, it's the hair. Bit shitty maybe. But look at it. Look at the way it lies. It's a give-away. You see, it doesn't matter how much you pay your crimper, if you've got background there's something in the genes that gives you a certain lie, a certain feel, of the hair.'

Griffiths was running his fingers through the dead man's hair. He was nodding. Leonard felt uncomfortable.

'Nonsense.'

'Maybe. Most things in death are.'

Leonard noticed, for the first time, light and dark patches at the shoulders.

'What about that?'

The Screaming Skull raised his black eyebrows.

'Tell you when I know more.'

'Tell me what you know now.'

Griffiths drew deeply through his nostrils.

'If I turned him over, which I'm not about to do, mind you, but if I did, you'd see for yourself.'

'See what?'

'Bruising on backs of both shoulders. Upper arms. Upper backs of thighs, and look there.'

Griffiths tapped the ankles. There was a small amount of discolouring.

'Which tells you what, Inspector?'

'It tells me nothing, Doctor. I'm a policeman.'

Griffiths went to the head of the table. Moved the head to one side. There was another bruise on the neck.

'At a guess, someone, maybe more than one person, held him down. A despicable act, you see.'

'When he was stripped?'

'Maybe. He's not saying.'

'To kill him?'

Griffiths pushed the body's legs apart. Leonard had not really noticed. Now he could see. The testicles were torn. Beneath the useless sac, deep angry colours and blackened flesh. Leonard did not want to see this. He stared. Fascinated. He tried to sound gruff. His throat gurgled. The Screaming Skull smiled. Satisfied.

'Not very nice, is it?'

'What is it?'

Griffiths rolled his eyes. Dealing with live fools was a job for psychiatrists, not pathologists.

'How do I know? I haven't been in there yet. But, at a guess, it's how he died.'

'Guess once more, Dr Griffiths. This is a murder inquiry, not Trivial Pursuit.'

There was a tone in Leonard's voice which made the Welshman wonder. At the sound of footsteps, he turned to the door. It was not Somers-Barclay. It was an attendant. He was wearing overalls and a shiny apron from chest to ankles. His rubber boots were white. He did not say anything. Instead he turned on a tap and tested a small hose. The next couple of hours could be messy. Leonard was waiting.

'Well?'

'Well, Mr Leonard, for the moment, just for the moment you understand, I'd say that our boyo here has had a dramatic departure.'

The snorting breath rushed through the wide nostrils and the head came up like an ugly stallion's in the paddock of the Apocalypse.

'I'd say, Inspector, that he had some curious friends. At a guess, mind you, and between you and me, mind you, I'd say his manner of departure was unusual, except in classical times, you know.'

'Don't beat about the bush, Doctor Griffiths. *How*?'

The nostrils spread.

'Well now, I'd say that this boyo died because, well, simply put...'

'If you would.'

'Well, Mr Leonard, I'd say that someone took something like a red-hot piece of steel, maybe a poker, and, as you would probably say, stuffed it right up his arse.'

Seven

The reception for the American Tourist Commission had been well organized. The Bath Spa Hotel was used to handling important occasions. For the city fathers, this was an important occasion. For Montague James, occasions were almost always important, especially his part in them. He appeared at everything of any importance because his fingers were in so many pies that it was inconceivable, to him at least, that a feast of civic dignitaries and business interests would be complete without his approval and, more importantly, his presence.

James had given the American delegation an audience, correctly identified the two most influential members and invited them to dine with him that night. At first they had talked about the need to get back to London. The uncertainties of the train, they had said. He first reminded them that the spirit of Isambard Kingdom Brunel lived on in what he, James, still called the Great Western Railway, and then completely won them over by promising to have his chauffeur 'run them up to town' in the Rolls. Montague James smiled. He would take them to Woods. A telephone call before would guarantee extra attention. Personally, James could not stand Selsey, probably because everyone else liked the man. But he was a good restaurateur and this evening would be important.

That done, Montague James was in the main hall, wondering where Mrs James might be, when he caught sight of his wife coming down the main staircase. The man she was with was from Utah – wherever that was. Hilary James had a habit of walking very close to men. The burly travel agent from Salt Lake City appeared a friendly sort. James did not mind. His wife was looking very summery in soft white lawn that folded and moved gently over her breasts. Which was why she had chosen it. James would have liked his wife to have been a little neater. He imagined that he might prefer large breasts on other women. Not on his wife. And he thought her jewellery might have been a little less obvious. Something simple for summer. Perhaps the sapphires were best left for Christmas. Certainly too ostentatious for lunch. But Hilary thought not. She liked men looking at her and women envying her. Sapphires helped.

Montague James smiled. If the American thought he might be making an impression, he would be disappointed. Hilary James did not have the courage to be indiscreet. Once, she had. But Montague James regarded his wife, as he did all his possessions, as expendable once they no longer pleased him. She knew that. On the one occasion when he knew she had nearly been unfaithful, he had been quite explicit in his warning. He had simply told his wife that her beauty was his to destroy. Hilary James believed her husband in everything he said. Now she said goodbye to the surprised American and fell into step with her husband.

'We're not being silly are we, my dear?'

'Don't be ridiculous, Montague.'

'I am never that.'

The conversation got no further. In the entrance, the Chief Constable was talking to the editor of the *Evening Chronicle*. Montague James raised his voice as they approached.

'Ah, Chief Constable! And Mr Dover. My, this is a high-level occasion. A gathering of the informed.'

Dover nodded. Tried a smile. It did not quite work. He was not a man who smiled to order. He was also fascinated by Hilary James's overt sexuality. Dover was wary that any friendliness would betray his feelings. Dover regarded lust with some pleasure. He knew others might need a deeper explanation of his intentions. The Chief Constable was too preoccupied with the day to have such sensitive internal conflicts.

The policeman had not enjoyed the reception and pre-sentation. He did not like being put on the spot by the civic fathers. Nor the visiting firemen. The Americans had wanted to know how he could guarantee the safety of tourists. The Chief Constable's gruff response that Bath was hardly down-town New York had not been well received. The American tourist associations now had a list of what they called safe cities in Europe. A presentation by the Bath city manager had contained one paragraph about beggars and vagrants and that had been enough to stir the doubts of the visitors. It had been an unnecessary paragraph but was three lines in six hundred. The manager's peers were displeased.

But it was the policeman who took the brunt of the ques-tioning. His assurances that Bath was probably the safest tourist city in Europe made little impression on the group of Americans whose stock in trade was the opportunistic use of superlatives. The recent news report had not helped. No, the Chief Constable's morning lot was not a happy one. He said as much.

'I have to tell you, Montague, that you can't expect my men to run a murder inquiry with the flaming tourist board laying the ground rules.'

The editor looked at him.

'So it is a murder inquiry.'

'For the moment. It depends on what we find and what the coroner says, but yes, for the moment it's best to go for the worst-case scenario.'

Hilary James was looking at her profile in a mirror. She breathed in and her breasts lifted. She caught the newspaper-man's reflected gaze as she turned to the Chief Constable. Her tone was almost, almost arrogant. After all, the Chief Con-stable was a servant.

'But surely, Mr Wake, this, this person was only a vagrant.

These folk, well, they do kill each other, don't they? Isn't it all about drugs?'

The policeman shook his square head.

'We don't know that, Mrs James. There's nothing so far. To my people, it doesn't matter what he was. He's dead.'

Montague James nodded.

'Quite right too, Robert. Quite right. But Hilary's also right. Aren't you, my dear? Surely there's nothing in this. After all we wouldn't want a fuss, would we?'

Dover looked puzzled.

'What do you mean fuss, Mr James? Why should there be fuss?'

'I mean that, although we quite understand the need for a proper investigation, it would be wrong to build it up into some tabloid sensation. Would you not agree?'

The editor did not like his newspaper being referred to in such a pejorative manner. To him tabloid sensation smacked of corrupt reporting. He was not in that business.

'You're suggesting that the *Chronicle* is making something of this that's not there? Have you seen today's paper?'

'Of course not. Of course not. Far too busy. I was simply making the same point that Robert did to our American cousins. Bath is not darkest New York City. We do not have murders in Bath.'

Dover was getting tetchy.

'You mean it is bad for business?'

'I'm sure you do not intend to tell me what I mean. But realistically, Mr Dover, you are correct. Murder is bad for business. Bath, do not forget, is a business and that business advertises in your newspaper. Come along, my dear. We must about our own business.'

Montague James smiled. Hilary James smiled. He swept, she swayed, out of the hotel to their waiting car. The Chief Constable sighed. Perhaps seethed. Dover looked at his watch. He needed to get back. But he had a question.

'What the hell was all that about?'

45

'What it's always about. The Bath mafia is speaking. It doesn't like dead bodies littering a prime tourist site, especially on the day it's wining and dining a couple of million dollars' worth of business.'

Dover's warning bells had been tuned by thirty years of almost every type of journalism. He had been guided by the thought of a famous American newspaper editor who started most of his interviews with one question in his mind: 'Why is this bastard lying to me?' The Chief Constable was making his own leaving signs. Dover had another question.

'Come on, Bob. What's going on?'

'Nothing more than you know. Some crusty is dead. We don't know who he is. We're trying to find out. Good God, man, we're not yet sure how he died. Could have been natural causes.'

'Really?'

'OK. Not really. But I tell you, damn it, we don't know.'

'That means he wasn't stabbed, strangled, coshed nor shot.'

'No. It means we do not know what actually caused death.'

'But it was murder.'

'It looks that way.'

Dover moved to the door where the policeman's car was waiting nearby. The afternoon was hot. The driver was in shirtsleeves. Across the way, ground staff tidied the lawn edges and in a herbaceous border a small brown bird was fluttering in a dustbath. All very neat. All very English.

'It would be useful, Bob, if your people could tell a bit more. If this goes for another twelve hours we'll have the nationals down. The Press Association has already asked for a line on it.'

'When there's something to say, we will, OK?'

The back door of the car was open and the policeman was climbing in.

Dover had not finished.

'Who's driving this one?'

'An inspector. A good man.'

'Who? Stainger's number two?'

Robert Wake was clipping his seatbelt. His voice was muffled.

'No. Man called Leonard.'

'Leonard who?'

'No, Leonard's his surname. Look, I've told you all I know. I really don't keep tight tabs on this sort of thing. I've got a whole district of officers who do. Have a word with them, will you?'

He slammed the door and, with a snapped word to the driver, the car moved off leaving the newspaperman standing. He started down the slope to the main road. He was thinking. Leonard? Never heard of him. And one other point niggled. The Chief Constable was a good man. A good policeman. Above all, he was courteous. He had just been very rude. Dover was doubly puzzled. Who was rattling the Chief Constable's cage? More importantly, why?

Deep in the cushions of the rear seat, the Chief Constable rubbed at his lower lip. He should not have been on edge. He had been rude to Dover, which was unforgivable and unprofessional. Dover was a good man. Sound. The Chief Constable kept the press at a distance and had a healthy suspicion of its practitioners. Equally he knew that people like Dover were not out to make names for themselves. Dover was not a cowboy. The editor of the *Chronicle* was just as much a professional as he was. Had to be. He stared from the window. They were leaving the city. It looked normal. Bath always did. Most cities did. But that could change. Dover had warned him. The news agency was sniffing. The next thing would be the sharpshooters arriving. The *Sun*. The *Mirror*. The *Mail*. The *Express*. The tabloids. He shuddered. Each one trying to get a different angle. Each one with a mobile telephone in one hand and a chequebook in the other. It could be that he would need Dover. He picked up the car phone. Tapped out a private number.

Stainger had half expected the call. Chief Constables did not normally go direct to superintendents. But they'd known each other for years. Played rugby together for the police. There's not much rank in a steaming bath of fifteen bruised men. Stainger was not surprised. He told Robert Wake what he did not want to hear. The Chief Constable cut the phone and grumphed to his driver. At the next roundabout, the black Ford, instead of turning right for Bristol, went right round and headed back into the city, in the direction of Manvers Street and the grubby building opposite the electrics discount store.

A few minutes earlier, at the same roundabout, the dark-green Rolls-Royce had gone, not to Bristol, but straight on, through the small villages of grey-blue stone cottages and walls and out into the Mendips.

Montague James did not care to be in these hills. He did not care for the countryside, especially the Somerset countryside, which he regarded as treeless and boring. He felt vulnerable. Montague James understood towns and cities. He understood the structure of smart and unsmart which cities clearly sign-posted. He detested the protocol of Barbour and labrador. He found country landowners ignorant. He thought their wives devoid of any conversation beyond beasts, children, people who were down for the weekend, and innuendo about those absent from the dinner table.

On the other hand, Montague James regarded cities as self-contained units in which self-contained people managed their own interests, not boredom. People who were interesting for themselves and to themselves and did not come to dine in Land-Rovers. Montague James's shoemaker had never been asked to make a pair of brogues. Nor would he be.

His wife had similar disdain for the countryside and even more for its people. Hilary James did not see the point of the countryside. Everything she could ever wish for could be found or ordered in cities. She did, however, like looking at hills, trees and lambs. Equally, she was soon bored with views and would never have contemplated getting out of the car if it meant stepping onto anything less firm than a pavement.

As the limousine whispered along the stone-walled road, neither spoke. Hilary James was wondering what she might wear that evening. She thought something in silk. She liked silk next to her skin. Montague James was preoccupied. The death had been somewhat annoying. He understood the need for what he described to himself as 'the event'. He was furious at the outcome and silently feared the possible consequences. He hoped the police would be diligent. He hoped that Robert Wake's men would rightly select a culprit from among the dreadful people who lived in the netherworld of Bath's slums. It would be better still never to find a murderer. A murderer would mean a trial. It would go on. Evidence might be inconclusive. Better that it should be left at 'a person or persons unknown'.

As the driver turned off by the village store, Montague James took a little comfort in the fact that even the admirable Chief Constable had accepted that the person had been of little consequence. James rested a soft hand high on his wife's slim thigh. The chauffeur never took his eyes from the lane until the car slowed to a stop in the sweeping gravel drive of the gentrified farmhouse. For a moment, neither James nor his wife moved. A person of little consequence. Oh dear. If only that could have been so.

Eight

Leonard's socks were bright green. Plain green. But very bright. Superintendent Stainger kept coming back to them. The Chief Constable looked at them once or twice and wondered about Leonard. The tweed suit when everyone was sweltering. The waistcoat, even odder. The Chief Constable was sweating. Leonard was not. The Chief Constable's brother was a bishop. Maybe that was why he saw through the illogical garb.

Leonard was comfortable dressed that way. But the socks were something else. He glanced up at Stainger. Stainger had his head back in his large executive chair.

'I thought, sir, you would want to hear Inspector Leonard's comments.'

He nodded in Leonard's direction. Leonard was polishing his rimless spectacles. Using his tie. The Chief Constable thought that odd. It was common for officers to wear glasses. Had not been at one time. But times changed. Senior officers adopted half-frames, or half-eyes, as the Manual General sheet described them. That was usually eye strain and advancing years. But Leonard gave the impression of always having worn spectacles. Odd. Again. When Leonard spoke, it was quietly. The spectacle-polishing continued with the occasional peering at the perfectly clean lenses.

'The cause of death, sir, appears to have been rupturing of internal organs, internal haemorrhaging as a result of the manner in which they were ruptured, shock and subsequent heart failure. It seems that he was held down while a heated rod was inserted through the rectum and beyond.'

Silence.

The Chief Constable closed his eyes. For a few seconds he held his breath and then ran a dry tongue across his upper lip. When he did speak, it was a whisper.

'I do not believe this.'

Stainger did not look down. Leonard did not look up. Both knew the Chief Constable did believe it. Leonard continued.

'Dr Griffiths will have more to tell me later today.'

Stainger swivelled.

'You will understand why I felt you should know.'

The Chief Constable nodded.

'Of course.'

He looked at both men, then asked the obvious question.

'Any ideas who? Why?'

Leonard slipped both wire arms over his ears and peered at the no-longer-blurred vision of his Chief Constable.

'No to the first question, sir. No to the second. But classically yes to the second. In history, especially in literature, there have been examples of execution in such a manner. The writer liked Edward the Second to suffer. The death of a homosexual.'

Stainger's arms were outstretched, asking 'why?'

'Was he?'

Leonard did not know. The medical examiner did not know. As the Screaming Skull had observed, drily, the evidence for that had been obscured by the circumstances, or certainly the instrument, of death. The Chief Constable's question was to Stainger.

'His travelling friends?'

Stainger did not think so and said as much, although he admitted it was nothing but a guess.

'When there has been violence among them, it has usually been over a petty grievance. Possessions. Sometimes women. It hasn't been so, er, ritualistic.'

The Chief Constable raised his eyebrows.

'I thought these people were full of ritual. Wasn't there some business about sacrifices?'

'Not human.'

'Even so.'

Stainger shook his head.

'Chickens. A couple of nutters. Then it turned out they'd nicked them.'

Leonard shifted. His legs stretched out in front resting on his heels. The socks very green. He screwed his eyes at the Chief Constable. The sun was bright.

'Once you get over the problems of excise duties, trespass, social security fiddles and exotic substances, they're often more law-abiding than the average family. Lead a simple life and you've only your own codes to break. Mm?'

Having spoken, Leonard looked out of the window. He hummed tunelessly under his breath. Wake could hear a sound but could not identify where it was coming from. The afternoon sun was enjoying itself. It was the middle of the year. Leonard looked back into the room.

'The other thing is that there aren't too many fireplaces on the go at this time of the year. To get a poker, say, to this temperature you'd need a pretty hot fire. Maybe even a furnace. A forge.'

The Chief Constable's imagination had switched off. He did not want to hear any more. He was wondering about Dover and his newspaper. He was wondering about Montague James and his mafia. He remembered the roadworks in Manvers Street. Leonard had missed a point.

'Not necessarily, Leonard. Plumbers use butane gas bottles. Your Edward would have had no hiding place in our modern age.'

The Chief Constable got up. Stumped about. Nodded to both his junior officers. The interview was done.

Somers-Barclay was waiting for Leonard when he returned to the Murder Room. The dark woodblock floor was already scuffed, the blackboard lined and ruled and filling up with information. A corner filing cabinet was open, and two officers followed him in, struggling with a white briefing board. The windows were closed and the place reeked of a too-long-shut-off classroom, its walls lined with notices and lists and regulations. Coffee was bubbling in the corner but it already smelled stale. Someone had pinned the team notice over Leonard's seat.

> I keep six honest
> serving men –
> they taught me
> all I know.

Leonard smiled. Somers-Barclay felt relieved. He needed to. He had nothing to report.

'No sign of the bag, sir.'

Leonard was looking out of the window.

'What bag?'

'His bag. The, er, the crusty's.'

The window overlooked the yard and then the church. Even the constabulary atheists blessed the ecumenical generosity that allowed them to park. A place to leave a car was worth a constable's ransom. He wondered if his bicycle was still chained to the half-wrecked car. He supposed so. Like a good disciple, Leonard looked beyond the spire unto the hills and Rainbow Wood on the far horizon. He had seen travellers up there. Early one morning, indeed just as the sun was rising. They had talked to him. Twenty years before them, he might have used the same language. Twenty years ago, he wasn't sure. They were. Somers-Barclay was talking. Leonard tuned in, reluctantly.

'. . . and we still have no idea who he is.'

Somers-Barclay made failure sound triumphal. He would do well. Leonard turned. No longer smiling.

'Was.'

'Oh. Right, sir. That's right. Who he *was*.'

A uniformed woman sergeant smiled. Her head bent over a pile of statements. Forms MG 09. Forms MG 11. So many prefixes before nothing to report. Leonard thought she had a nice neck. Wisps escaping from severely combed and bunned dark hair. He wondered if sergeants were supposed to have pretty necks.

'Anything in that lot?'

Instinctively she knew he was talking to her. Her expression was serious. Her eyes dark and not quite serious.

'No, sir. Except the woman who found him.'

'Did she find him?'

Somers-Barclay was quick.

'Inasmuch as she was the first to see him there. I mean, she didn't actually go in. She saw him through the grille.'

Too quick. The woman's voice was not local. Neutral. London? She was speaking to Leonard.

'Begging your pardon, sir. We don't actually know that she found him.'

Somers-Barclay had not learned.

'Well, let's put it this way. No one else did.'

Too quick.

Leonard let her make her point.

'What I mean is, sir, all we know is that she was the person who reported the body. It doesn't follow that she was the first to see him there.'

Ray Lane came in. He was eating a hamburger. He should not have been. His cholesterol was high sevens. The doctor had said fresh vegetables, no alcohol and plenty of exercise. The doctor was not a policeman. He nodded hello to a few of the team. He was popular. He got results. He was clean. He looked after his team. There were six inspectors at the Bath station. He was the only detective. He had been promoted to return to the city. Many people in the Central Police Station were pleased on both accounts. He smiled at Leonard, waved the hamburger.

'Sorry about this. Missed lunch. I heard about the gruesome stuff. Not straight up and down this one, is it?'

Leonard turned away. Stared beyond the spire.

'Where do they live when they're not outside the Pump Room?'

Lane wiped his fingers on a paper towel. He nodded to the hills.

'Not up there. They did. Most of them were shifted last year. But the main lot are here, in the borough. Thornbank Place, some of them. Hampton Row maybe.'

'Beckford Gardens. Some of the real nasties are there.'

Leonard looked at the bowed head. She was going through the statements.

'What do you mean by real nasties?'

She looked up. Not quickly. Even gracefully. Her neck was quite long. She was sure of herself. Not intimidated by seniority. Not arrogant. Just sure.

'The crusty kids are predictable. They come here via Glastonbury. They're harmless enough. Just like that way of life, I suppose.'

Somers-Barclay, his smile the smile of a patronizing primary-school teacher, cut in.

'Of course, sir, they think they've found the answer to society.'

Leonard ignored him.

'Go on.'

Her gaze had not left his.

'But then you have the nasties. They're not kids. Some of them would have been bikers in the old days. They're into anything they can get their hands on.'

'Drugs?'

She shook her head.

'Some of them do soft stuff. No, most of it's booze. Usually stolen. They can get away on a cider bottle – some of them.'

'Then, why "nasty"?'

She shrugged. She had said enough in senior company. Lane continued for her.

'They're into blades. Some of them may even be carrying. They had one over at Pilton who did his girl with a hatchet. She was a strong kid. She didn't go down first chop. Took some determination. Very sticky. But he did it. None of this finishing-second stuff. He stuck her and kept on doing it. That one was from here. Yes?'

The girl nodded. Lane continued.

'And they steal from each other. The kids Jack's talking about wouldn't. Right?'

Jack? Leonard supposed Jacqueline. She did not look like a Jacqueline. The telephone at her desk rang and she answered. Somers-Barclay had fetched coffee from the filter machine.

There had not been one before. Somers-Barclay had organized it. He had that sort of attention for that sort of detail. Leonard moved away just as the hand was stretched in his direction with the fresh polystyrene beaker. Lane said thank you and took the cup to save Somers-Barclay's embarrassment. Beneath the Hackett suit and designer tan, the Sergeant was a good policeman. Anyway, Lane knew a fast-track promotion prospect when he saw one.

He might have said something to Leonard, but just then Stainger appeared in the doorway.

'Got a moment, James?'

He did not wait for an answer and Leonard followed him along the corridor and into the Superintendent's corner room. Stainger was standing in the centre of the office, his thumb and index finger to his square chin.

'We have a problem.'

Leonard was taller than Stainger. He looked at his boots. They were dull. Matt brown. Not dirty. He did not answer. Stainger looked sideways at him, waiting to be asked. Leonard did not. Stainger slapped his hands to his sides.

'The Chief Constable's suggesting we might need help.'

'It's always useful to have a few more door-bangers on the ground, especially if it drags on.'

Stainger shook his head as he continued.

'No, no, no. Not that sort of help. We'll get that as a matter of course. The PSU will fill us up. That's what Support Units are for. It's this Task Force stuff. All ready to leap into action. Or so they claim. No, that'll come up with the rations.'

'What, then?'

'He's talking about a senior officer. A superintendent. Some-one to take over from you.'

Leonard said nothing. Stainger waved him to a chair. Leonard leant against the bookcase.

'It's not personal, you know, James. Nothing personal. You know the system. Perhaps you don't. Anyway, they've got four of the buggers at headquarters.'

'What do you want?'

Stainger was caught between bureaucratic stools. He wanted a quick conclusion to the affair. He also wanted an in-house result. But he was far from stupid in these matters.

'Put someone with a bit more rank on this and we can get all the resources we need. And another thing, if we don't ask for help and it turns nasty, then we're, I'm, in the clag. Savvy?'

Leonard understood. He didn't see the problem. But he was the man who had been given the job of reviewing procedures. He knew the form. The investigation was too young for them to be drafting-in heavy artillery. Tomorrow if there was no end in sight. Yes. Tomorrow if there was trouble in sight. Yes. He looked at the wall clock. The city was closing down for the day. The police were not. Why today?

'Did he say why?'

'No. He was only doing his job. Reassuring, I suppose. Offering us, me, reassurance.'

'Anything else I should know?'

Leonard's voice was quiet. Not timid. Stainger eyed him. A slight figure. Incongruous in these surroundings. Different. The force did not like officers to be different. He wondered who cut Leonard's bubbling, curly, almost red hair. Certainly not the Italian at the bottom of Milsom Street who knew how to disguise a policeman as a football manager. Anything else he should know? Yes.

'Apparently, James, apparently, mind you, there's pressure.'

Leonard said nothing. Waited. Stainger liked his officers to pick up their cues. Leonard wrote his own lines. Stainger sighed and sat down.

'I understand that there's pressure from the Bath mafia to get this one out of the way. They want a result. Pronto.'

Leonard nodded. He did not understand at all. But he nodded.

'What sort of result?'

'An early arrest, as the Press Office would say.'

'*Any* arrest?'

Stainger's shrug said it all. Leonard would not get an answer, but he asked anyway.

'Who is putting on the pressure? And why?'

The Superintendent looked at the slowly blinking eyes behind the clear, unsmudged frames. He had no answer. None that he could give Leonard.

'You've got until this time tomorrow and then we go nuclear.'

Nine

The sun had more or less given up for the day. But the daylight was broad and the pavements warm. Leonard sat by the Pump Room. The fire-eater was there but his brands were doused and rolled in their sacking beside him. Up from the gloss-black doors, a jerky youth and his girlfriend were doing their best with 'The Entrance of the Queen of Sheba'. A German filmed them on his camcorder and his daughter dropped a pound coin in one of the plushly lined violin cases, then turned to smile at the camera.

A couple of fluffy pups rolled and chewed, but without any enthusiasm, and an impossibly thin figure in greased black rags tugged at their string leads. The group around the seat said little. One of them, an older man with a ponytail to his waist, laughed to himself, but no one took up his cackle. The fire-eater stretched his bare, dirty strong arms and his chain-hung waistcoat gaped over his concave stomach. He relaxed and smiled at Leonard.

'Got any change?'

Leonard had not expected the man to speak. The face was open. Clean beneath the grime of his time. The smile friendly. The breath foul yet the gums pink. Leonard said nothing. The man was still smiling.

'Don't need much. Just for tonight.'

Leonard wondered.

'And tomorrow?'

'Try again.'

Leonard nodded at the rolled sacking.

'And today?'

'OK. But I need to pay people.'

'What people?'

'People.'

'Friends?'

'Sometimes. You know how it is.'

Leonard raised his eyebrows.

'Do I?'

The man laughed. It was friendly enough. Wise even.

'Course. Mr Policemen know everything.'

'You're sure?'

The fire-eater ran an eye along the stretch of Leonard's tweeds. The brown boots on their heels. The green socks.

'We see you around. Saw you this morning.'

He laughed again. One or two of the others turned. Nodded. Smiled. Friendly enough. Leonard slipped off his spectacles. Polished with his silk handkerchief.

'Who was he?'

The man laughed. This time, no humour. Instead he picked up his sacking and wandered off beneath the arches opposite to sit on the steps with his friends. As he leaned against his bag, he looked back at Leonard. But only once. The bag. Leonard wondered again about the bag. Why no bag?

In the wine bar the prices were up. Summer prices for people who came once, sipped in the cool of the cellar and then left for another city. Leonard sipped and filled in two of the gaps in the crossword. The barman topped up Leonard's glass. Did not charge. It was his way of protecting his regulars. Leonard nodded his thanks. Sipped again.

'Anyone saying anything?'

The barman shrugged.

'To me? Why should they?'

'To each other.'

'I don't hear anything, if that's what you mean.'

'It is what I mean.'

The cellar bar was fashionable with people who knew. In the winter evenings, it was a place to rub shoulders. In the summer, movers and shakers picked at their taramasalata and swigged Frascati. People who knew and people who thought they knew, and people who heard what others knew and thought, were to be found in the bar. Sometimes they gathered in the dank back room beneath the George Street pavement, but never in the garden with its bumpy lawn and late pear tree. That was for lunchtimes and dawdlers. In the garden, you never saw who came, who left. People who wanted to know or be known needed to see and be seen. The bar was best.

The barman was smiling. He was friendly. Knew Leonard, although not by name. Didn't mind him filling in one or two clues. Leonard never added more than two answers. A long time ago, a very correct inspector had told everything.

'Always leave something for the next man, James. Always.'

He always did. He looked up. The voice was confident. The smile dazzling. Somers-Barclay had known where to find him. Leonard nodded at the barman, but the tall glass had appeared. The barman was already unscrewing a fresh bottle of mineral water. He knew Somers-Barclay. Everyone knew Somers-Barclay. Somers-Barclay saw to that.

'Well, sir, a little progress, even if it is negative. As far as we can tell, our friend isn't in Pirsy.'

Leonard did not say anything. Just blinked. Somers-Barclay took the silence as confusion.

'Pirsy, sir. Photographic Image Retrieval System. You know, sir, the computer.'

Sir did know. He nodded.

'Why?'

'Presumably because he's never been nicked.'

The police jargon jarred his rich accent. Somers-Barclay looked at the blackboard. He was peckish. But he wouldn't eat. One meal a day. That would come later. The young doctor. A jolly dinner somewhere quite smart. Afterwards Calvados and rum truffles at his flat. Her brother had once mentioned her passion for both. Somers-Barclay remembered. He wondered if it would be cool enough for the log-effect gas fire. He hoped so. Leonard watched the other man's face. It was as groomed and barbered as a ceremonial prince's. The blond hair bleached and streaked naturally by the summer. The soft three-buttoned suit discreetly cut for an expensive boardroom. Lane was right to humour him. Somers-Barclay was on a quick track. One day, he'd be Lane's boss. Never Leonard's. Leonard stood away from the bar.

'I thought you had to have a name before you could get anywhere with that thing.'

'Pirsy? Right. But some people have pretty good memories. One of the girls worked on it for three months. She was part of the catalogue team.'

'And you asked her to go through it?'

Somers-Barclay smiled. He had not. The girl had done it off her own bat. But there was no need to tell Leonard. She had scored too many points that afternoon.

'Mind you, sir, if we can get any idea of a name, then it'll be worth checking.'

'As long as his record's in this area.'

The smile almost went. Almost.

'Right.'

Somers-Barclay knew everyone. Leonard tried him.

'Tell me about this PR woman. Patsy Bush?'

The Sergeant looked surprised. Was surprised.

'Is she in this one?'

'Maybe. Tell me.'

'Longest legs in Bath. Thirty-two. Australian. Melbourne. Good family. Gold. Whyalla ship-building. Broken Hill mining. Grandfather won the Melbourne Cup. Father's dead. She's an only child. Master's degree from UCLA, communications and journalism.'

Leonard wondered why Somers-Barclay knew all this.

'What's she doing in Bath? Sounds as if she's on the wrong continent.'

'She knows people. She was in New York doing an art history course. Someone else was there and told her to apply when the job came up. She got it.'

'When?'

'A year ago.'

'You know a lot about her.'

Somers-Barclay moved in some of her circles. When he did, he could not take his eyes off her. Only his incredible vanity saved him from infatuation. He fiddled with his signet ring. Yes, he knew quite a lot about her. Leonard pressed on.

'Who are these friends of hers? Influential. Mm?'

The Sergeant might have told him but at the moment he was looking over Leonard's head and through the window onto the street stairs. The legs were long. Maybe the longest in Bath. She paused at the doorway. Not to make a grand entrance. But to see who was there. Somers-Barclay raised a hand and she smiled. Leonard thought there was a great deal of social smiling in Bath. Perhaps that was because he rarely tried it himself. She sat at the bar and crossed one leg over the other. Leonard thought Somers-Barclay, on this occasion, knew what he was talking about. She did not wait for introductions.

'I hear you were looking for me.'

Leonard remembered the slow youth.

'How did you know it was me?'

She could have been dramatic and glanced him up and down. She could have joked about the suit. She did not. The eyes were as direct as the rest of her.

'You left your name. How can I help?'

While she waited for an answer, she took a small gold cigarette case from her bag. Somers-Barclay was at her side, a slim Dunhill lighter having appeared in his hand, seemingly from nowhere. Somers-Barclay did not smoke. Had never smoked. Patsy Bush might have smiled her thanks to the gallant officer. If she did not, Somers-Barclay could only believe that she had. If she did, Leonard had not seen her. He removed his spectacles. Breathed a film on the inside of the lenses and polished. He squinted. She was just in focus.

'Who is putting pressure on us?'

Patsy Bush did not play innocent. It was not her style. The accent was long-ago Australian. More at home in Nappa than Barossa Valley.

'Whoever it was who was killed. I'd have thought that obvious.'

'Who in the city?'

'Everyone with interests. I'd have thought that also obvious.'

'So it's bad for business. That's the answer.'

'One of them. Yes.'

Somers-Barclay could sense showdown. He thought that quite a bad idea.

'What the Inspector means, Patsy, is –'

She ran over him.

'You see, Mr Leonard, we're on your side. Don't see it as an attack on the police. Or you personally. Some poor man gets killed. Justice says find the killer.'

'And people who think they're more important than justice tell us to produce a publicly acceptable result and quickly.'

'No, Mr Leonard. The people you talk about are the ones justice is all about. There's no special pressure. Sure, it's bad for business, if that's what you're thinking. But that's up front. Sure it makes my job harder. That's up front too. We had twelve high-powered guys from the US at the Bath Spa today. They love the city. They should. It's a fine city. They've got a multi-million-dollar programme that'll feed into Bath for the next five years. They got the big treatment, I can tell you. Everything but the dancing girls. But d'you want to hear the numero uno question they had? Do you?'

Leonard slipped on his spectacles.

'You know what they asked your boss? "Tell us, chief," they said, "is it safe to come here?"'

'Come on, Patsy, you know it is.'

For the first time she acknowledged Somers-Barclay's part in the conversation.

'I know it is. You know it is. You've just got to be damn sure you can throw in your part to convince them that it is.'

There was a silence. Suddenly she relaxed. Her smile was as dazzling as anything Somers-Barclay had tried all day, but twice as real.

'Look. I came in here for a drink. It's been one of those days.'

But she had a pay-off for Leonard.

'Let me tell you something. Don't look for bodies in the establishment cupboard. You've got yourself a real one. Be satisfied with that.'

Ten

Leonard left the wine bar and walked up the hill and into Woods for a glass. Selsey was laying off bets wherever he could. He really did not want to be a racehorse owner. Leonard had asked about the Bath mafia. Selsey had said everyone was the Bath mafia, or thought they were. He had left, saying that he might drop by later. But wouldn't.

Two officers were guarding the Cross bath. Portable lights were already on. Shadows from the simple black rail by the pool were thrown across the badly repaired walls. The water steamed and gushed like a burst standpipe. A few people stood by the yellow tapes. They did not expect to see anything. Or did they? Leonard wondered how a live man could have been brought to such a public place and then so brutally murdered without anyone seeing. Had he been unconcious at the time? Drugged? Dead?

Leonard's head was down. His mind full of thoughts that zipped from one cell to another, ringing urgent bells.

He might have walked for an hour. Sometimes the same streets and alleys. He did not walk to clear his mind, but to fill it. Leonard liked jumbling his mind with ideas and chance. He left others to arrange the evidence and clues to that evidence. An admirer had assumed that Leonard must like crosswords. Was good at them. Wrong. Most people seemed wrong about most things when they thought about Leonard. He never quite saw the fascination with crosswords. If you were good at them, then why bother? If you were not? Then why bother? Leonard avoided frustrations. Problems were to be resolved. Best dealt with in the course of his time. Not theirs.

He looked up. At first not recognizing where he was. A back street. Empty. It was all but dark. Melincourt. Melincourt? His jumbling crossword mind picked a memory. There had been a novel. Someone called Sarcastic? Why had Harriet Bowles chosen Melincourt? What did it say about her?

He stared into the window as if the solution, even the clue, he needed might be disguised in the marbled and leather-edged covers of day books and diaries, particular envelopes, parchments and notepads. He had not expected the door to open. He grunted surprise. She smiled. A friendly native. The end of the day. Her white shirt still fresh. As soft as a favourite pillow.

'Just looking? If it's the TV licence, I don't have one.'

Leonard said something like hello and found himself inside and through to a tiny back-room with a small rug-covered sofa. A horsehair armchair. Her whisky was on the Georgian table. Harriet Bowles picked up another glass.

'Same again?'

He nodded and looked about as she poured from a decanter. The walk were dark green which made the room seem smaller than it was. A couple of engravings. Mostly seascapes.

'They were my husband's.'

She handed him the glass. The whisky was Islay. She hadn't asked him about water. There was none.

'Were?'

She sat at the table. She looked cool, yet a thin sweater was draped about her shoulders and loosely tied. Comfortable in the tall-backed green leather chair.

'Cheers. He's dead.'

He raised his glass in salute.

'Oh.'

'Something like that.'

He noticed the music. Had not before. It came from two small speakers, barely audible.

'You like opera?'

'Yes. I like musicals.'

'Not the same thing.'

'The acting's just as bad.'

Her laugh was light. Relaxed. She would not have a career in PR.

'OK. Try again. Is this official?'

It was Leonard's turn to smile. The whisky was good. He shook his head.

'I was passing. Not even that, really.'

'No, you weren't. You weren't passing at all. You were looking in the window.'

'I was wandering. I saw the light.'

She did not say hallelujah. She nodded to a sheet of figures from a computer.

'That we all should.'

'Times are hard?'

'No, no. They've been that. Now they're worse.'

'Everyone in this city talks money.'

She sipped and put down her glass. She looked the sort of person who knew how to put down a glass. Didn't mind too much about rings on the table.

'Not quite. Everyone in business talks money. But that's what people in business do. That's what business is.'

'Then why aren't you selling soap powder? Everyone needs it.'

'Because Waitrose is cheaper. OK. You're right. I do this because I want to.'

She stretched and yawned. The shirt moved with her. Cuddly. He had forgotten the word. There had been something. A rag bear? Maybe. Most of those things he had blocked out long ago.

'Sorry. It's been a long day. But then so has yours. Yes?'

Leonard did not feel he had to say anything. Her glasses were buried in her hair. Yes, comfortable.

'How long have you lived in Bath?'

'For ever. I was born here. Father was Navy. The old Admiralty took over the Empire Hotel in '39. After the war they refused to give it back. So he came here in '60. I arrived, well, later.'

She was not shy about her age. She liked innocent games.

'So you know everyone.'

'No. I know quite a few.'

'Was your husband Navy?'

'Good lord, no. He thought they were a bunch of poofters. We met in London. He was doing his law conversion course. He came to meet my parents. Loved it here and got a partnership.'

'That easy.'

'For some.'

'Special handshakes?'

'I never asked.'

'I see.'

'Very conventional.'

'And then?'

'And then he jumped out of a plane.'

Leonard sipped. Blinked.

'I don't see.'

'Don't worry. Wasn't that dramatic. Mind you, if he had been the it's-all-too-much-for-me type, he certainly wouldn't have joined the queue on Clifton suspension bridge. No, I'm afraid he joined dad's army. You know? The Territorials. A real action man.'

'So it was an accident?'

'Of course. Not with the TA. Certainly not with his lot. They were real cloak-and-dagger. At the weekends anyway. Rest of the time, just a bunch of plonkers playing cowboys-and-Indians with reverse balaclavas on their heads instead of feathers.'

'What happened?'

'He was off doing some charity jump. He was on his second jump. Leapt out like the damned fool he was. Thing opened according to plan. But for the first time in his life Giles did not land on his feet. They think he had a blackout. Next thing, I get the "terribly sorry, Mrs Bowles" visit from your lot.'

'When was this?'

'About ten years ago.'

'About?'

'You mean death's a bit more precise than that?'

He shrugged. He did mean that.

She got up. She was tall and the cotton trousers very thin. She did not ask. Simply poured more into his glass.

'Why am I telling you this?'

Leonard did not know. Why should he?

'I asked about the pictures.'

'You didn't.'

'You saw me looking. It's the same thing.'

She was back in her chair. It was big enough to curl her legs beneath her. When she did she leaned forward. She saw him looking at her open shirt. She did not mind. Might have been annoyed. She was not. Funny-looking man. Not harmless. No. Not funny. Amusing. There weren't many who were. Not when you were a widow. That's when you got the

Available label. Ask any man. The more married they were, the more they were doing you a favour. Ask any man. Yes. This one was all right.

'So you haven't caught your murderer?'

'No.'

'Will you?'

Cynical? He thought not.

'Yes.'

'Because there's heaps of evidence or because you always do?'

'No. That's the Mounties.'

'So why will you?'

'I will.'

'If they let you.'

He put down his glass and wiped his lips with his handkerchief.

'Who they?'

'Oh, lots of theys in this city.'

'But it's a straightforward murder.'

'Really? Sorry. You're the policeman. But I thought straightforward murders were done by families, lovers and boyfriends.'

'Mm.'

'He had all three, did he?'

Leonard settled further back in the down pillows. She went with down pillows. He wondered if he'd read that somewhere.

'Which is why we shall get there.'

'As I said, if they let you in.'

'There aren't many vested interests in a vagrant. That's usually why they're vagrants.'

'Vagrants are wanderers, aren't they? Isn't that where it comes from? *Vagabundus* or something?'

'So gathers no moss.'

'But covers a lot of ground.'

She was enjoying herself. He was tired. He looked at the wall above her head. A small silver frame. A man. Husband?

The shadow from the lamp didn't help. Next to it, but in the light, a man-of-war. A ship of the line belching broadside.

'And Bath's big guns rule the waves. One unknown scavenger causes so much distress. I don't see why.'

'It's happened before. Ten, twelve, years ago. I can't really remember. Up in Rainbow Woods.'

'A traveller?'

'In those days I think they still called them hippies.'

Leonard had not heard. It had not been mentioned.

'So.'

'Bath is a gossipy city. The OK people lunch, cocktail and dine with the OK people. It's so full of gossip, you'd think the whole of Lansdown lived in a telephone box.'

'What were they saying?'

'Then? That's the point. Nothing. Oh, the usual boneheads and pearls did, except that a hippie didn't count for a row of petrol coupons. But the real people. Nothing. Nothing said at all.'

'Who were the real people?'

'Same as now. The ones who own the city.'

'Perhaps a traveller was not important enough. They weren't bothered.'

She laughed. Sipped.

'Wrong. The fact that they didn't gossip meant they were bothered.'

'The Bath Image.'

'Maybe.'

'Just as today.'

'One dead hippie doesn't turn Milsom Street into the Shankill.'

'What happened ten years ago?'

'You're the policeman.'

Leonard glanced at his watch. Harriet Bowles yawned and stretched to order.

'Go on. Off you go. Time for bed. For me anyway.'

She stood. She was his height. He had been right. Pretty eyes. Amusing. There weren't many.

Eleven

The morning sun brightened the dull room. It now had an official sign on the door. MAJOR INCIDENT ROOM. It said that people should knock. She thought that was daft. This was a police station. Anyone who had business there did not have to knock. Anyone who did not have business there did not go in.

She had been duty sergeant. A uniformed inspector was running the show. She was co-ordinating information. She liked the job. She liked pulling together information. Looking for the odd man out. Looking for what others missed. Some in the canteen moaned about the drudgery of routine. They wanted more to happen all the time. They trained you to run up and down stairs. To push crowds back. To ask questions. To live up to the telly image. Then they told you it was all routine. Routine inquiries often meant getting nowhere. It also meant never knowing if your bit was going to fit a result. And, when you got one, you might never hear what happened to the villain. Funny job. She loved the painstaking piecing together of unlikely data. She liked sending them off in directions they'd never thought of. It hardly happened. It had been her turn, her shift, for the changeover briefing. Still not much. There was no ID. No one had suggested a name. Not even a nickname. Statements from travellers and crusties showed very little that suggested motives for the murder. But there were small things. Nothing yet that made sense. But she knew they would. But not yet.

Leonard was standing by the window.

'He must have had a name. Have we tried the helping hands? What about the chapel? Next door. They must have called him something.'

She was at her files and clipboard. She now had a desk-top screen in front of her. She heard his question. Knew it was not directed at anyone. Thinking aloud. She knew it was OK to answer.

'Not necessarily, sir. Sometimes there's good reason for these people to keep to themselves, even when they're in a group.'

He remembered. A banging door. Always someone else's blanket. Someone else's rag toy. When someone else had done. It was best to be alone in a group. He believed her. He understood.

'Anyone say they knew him?'

She scanned her notes. He heard a laugh. Across the room, Somers-Barclay was running a comb through his blond locks. Half crouched. Using a bookcase door as a poor mirror.

'Three of them, sir.'

She handed him notes.

Somers-Barclay, beaming, was at his elbow. More poly-styrene cups.

'Morning, sir. Coffee?'

Leonard ignored the cup.

'What do you know about a vagrant murder? About ten years ago. Rainbow Wood?'

Somers-Barclay had not stammered as a child.

'Er. Er. Um, er, er . . . Nothing, sir.'

The coffee did not quite spill. Not quite. Leonard turned to the desk.

'Sergeant?'

Embarrassed. Her voice was quiet. Somers-Barclay was losing his smile. She had no use for enemies.

'His name was Pete. Person or persons unknown.'

Leonard nodded his thanks to her and left the room. Somers-Barclay had lost his smile. His orthodontist would have been furious.

On his way out through Lost Property he met Stainger coming in.

'Anything?'

'Maybe.'

'Enough for a result?'

Leonard sighed. Shook his head. Stainger raised his eyebrows. His expression said it was inevitable.

'I'll have to let them in, you know.'

'Fine. There's no need, but fine.'

'No choice, James. If anything goes wrong they'll want to know why I didn't call for help before then. Savvy?'

'Who will it be?'

Stainger shrugged. He would rather not have had help. It was routine. It was procedure. He should not have worried. Policing was not a game. He had nothing to prove. But he still wanted to. It would have been good to tie it up.

'Who knows. Probably Superintendent Marsh. Come across him? Nice man. Good organization man.'

Leonard was humming. In tune. No tune anyone had heard.

'Why wait until noon?'

'Because I said I would.'

Leonard half-raised a hand. Then stopped. Stainger was going through the door. Leonard wondered.

'By the way, what happened to the one they called Pete?'

Stainger stopped. Turned. He looked genuinely mystified.

'Pete who?'

Leonard didn't know who.

'Ten years ago. Rainbow Wood.'

Stainger stared at him. The eyes were expressionless.

'I'd forgotten all about that. No idea.'

Leonard did not believe him.

In the centre of the city, Leonard talked to the straggling travellers. They did not mind. Did not mind the attention. Were not frightened of the police. They had done nothing. The three names he had from the uniformed sergeant were useless. No one knew them. They said. He asked ten, fifteen, of them. They were relaxed. They did not know. They said. He did not believe them.

Across the way from the abbey, the fire-eater was feeling

good. He had a large crowd in a square about him. He made it look more dangerous than it was. But he would not make much. They watched. They gasped. They applauded. And, when he was done, most of them did what most of them always did. They drifted away. No need for eye contact. Backing off into the crowd. Tugging the toddlers. No need for money in the outstretched hat. A free show. Only a crusty.

A minor canon, steel-grey hair and angular and slit-eyed through metal-framed glasses, watched with distaste. Leonard hummed and nodded.

'Colourful.'

The Canon looked through Leonard's eyes as if some explanation of such a crass remark might be impressed on the back of the stranger's sockets.

'Hopeless.'

'I thought there was always hope.'

'For few of these people. They don't want hope. They avoid it, you know. We can stretch out our hands. Offer them our hopes in their comfort. But they . . .'

He shook his head in sadness. Maybe anger. Maybe frustration. Maybe not in charity. Leonard finished the sentiment.

'Scorn?'

The priest nodded slowly. That was the word.

'Yes. Scorn. That's it.'

'Why?'

'They do not need our society. We let them be.'

'And they annoy us.'

The priest thought about it. Yes, he supposed they did.

'But then we are so easily annoyed. We continue to dislike those who mock our ways. They only need us when winter comes.'

'Not all of them.'

The priest thought about that, as well.

'That is because Samaritans are institutionalized. That's what they don't like. Our institutions. Some simply say no. Not even no thank you. The ones who say thank you are worse. To tell us politely that we are wrong is hurtful, you see.'

'Some of them come to a terrible end.'

'The poor fellow yesterday? Oh yes. Terrible business. Terrible business. But one has to ask if it were but inevitable.'

Leonard was back polishing his spectacles. The sun had brought smiles to the tourists. Leonard liked that. He often wondered how people on holiday could look so serious. Maybe it was something to do with six cities in five days. The Canon should have had a rosary in Santa Croce. Leonard finished polishing.

'The way of all that sort of flesh?'

'Why not? It is uncharitable to think so, but such a precarious life must encourage chances of a terrible end to it.'

'Especially in Bath?'

The priest shook his head.

'No, not especially in Bath. But there is an irony, is there not? This is the city of elegance?'

'Did you know him?'

The Canon looked amazed.

'I? Why on earth would you think that? Certainly not.'

'You see them. You may be closer than many.'

'Why do you ask?'

Leonard dabbed at his dry lips with his silk handkerchief.

'I'm a policeman. I need to know.'

The priest shuffled, his well-brushed cheap shoes making little sound. He looked up.

'Then you must ask his friends.'

Leonard looked over to the porch of the Pump Room where the unwashed sprawled in the way of any who might think they could ignore them. He heard the Canon bid him good day and murmured a response, but, as in so much liturgy, the Church had gone and was already out of earshot.

The fire-eater had done. The act over. The crowd was breaking up as quickly as it had gathered. He grinned at

Leonard and shook his head. A few coppers in the flat and all-but-ignored bag.

'They only watch to see if I torch me fucking self. Know that? That's what they want, you know. Set fire to me fucking self. Then some bastard would steal the lot while I roasted. Know that?'

Leonard knew that he was probably right. The Canon's elegant society was one in which crash victims were robbed while they waited for ambulances.

'Tell me. You know him? The one who died?'

The fire-eater bobbed his head. This was another dead. Why not? He knew him.

'He travelled with us sometimes.'

'Why didn't you say so yesterday?'

'That was yesterday.'

'What was his name?'

'The Piccolo man.'

'What does that mean?'

'Whatever you want it to mean. Everything does.'

'Everyone has a name.'

'Only because someone gave them one.'

'What was his?'

'Never said.'

'You never asked?'

'You asked mine?'

'I'm not travelling with you.'

'But you never.'

Leonard smiled. The fire-eater laughed.

'See? See what I mean?'

He finished wrapping and collecting and tucked the dirty sacking beneath his bare arm. He started to go, then stopped.

'She knows.'

Leonard swung round. A girl was across the abbey yard. Turning the corner. Going away. He caught sight of a mongrel pup trailing after. Then she was gone.

'Sure?'

The fire-eater was also going. Still laughing. He called over his shoulder.

'In this business. *Sure?*'

Leonard walked quickly across the flagstones. A powdered and bewigged figure in eighteenth-century satin was shrilling a baroque recorder to an almost empty yard. Another empty hat. Leonard almost ran, but did not. He never did. He could hear the fire-eater laughing. Playing a game. He dodged a mother and her pushchair and ducked into the passage the girl had taken. Nothing. She was gone. He tried the alleys and the lanes. The arcade. She had disappeared.

Twelve

Selsey was on the telephone. He waved a hand and reached for a bottle. Leonard looked at the stationmaster's wall clock and raised his eyebrows. Selsey shrugged. Put the bottle back in the rack. Leonard smiled at one of the girls, the one he always smiled at, said that coffee would be fine and watched her walk away as he always watched her walk away. She knew. She always did. There were some who could not keep their eyes from her legs when they were ordering, no matter how much they tried and whoever they were with. There were some, including the women, who wondered what sort of girl this was. She did not mind. The skirt and the thinnest camisole said that. She liked Leonard. He was not a toucher.

'Do you remember anything about a killing? Ten years ago?'

Selsey did not. Not even a whisper of memory. He had other matters on his mind. Four-legged matters.

'You haven't asked me.'

Leonard looked puzzled.

'Asked you what?'

'About my problem. You know. The flaming horse.'

'I'm sorry. What's happened?'

'Don't ask me.'

The pause was eye contact. Then they both laughed. Leonard did not laugh often. He did now with a freedom that only comes with being with friends. It did not matter that nothing was particularly humorous. Selsey was an imp. A rounded one. But an imp. The girl brought coffee. She smiled at Leonard. Not professionally. Just smiled. She could without him getting the wrong idea. Selsey was talking about his pending disaster. That's how he saw it.

'You know how sure this fella is? Go on. You know?'

Leonard shook his head.

'Well, I'll tell you. He reckons Talal – you know the fella?'

'The Arab?'

'The same. He reckons Talal has already offered him a quarter of a million. A quarter of a million. Can you believe that? A quarter. Of course, he'll have to sell.'

'Doesn't that get you off the hook?'

Selsey ran his hand through his thick brown hair. Clearly it did not.

'I'm in for a horse I haven't even seen. For all I know, the damn thing is probably out there even at this very moment pulling for the Express Dairy. You know that, do you?'

Leonard stirred his coffee. Heard Selsey out. There was a pause, not for breath but commiseration. Leonard slipped in.

'It was a traveller.'

'What was? Oh, your man. Ten years ago. Maybe. Maybe there was something. But you're the police fella. Shouldn't you know?'

'I'm more interested in what people remember.'

'What sort of people?'

'Same ones who don't like this one.'

Selsey leaned back and spooned brown sugar into his coffee.

'You'll never hear that from them. They'll give to charity – as long as everyone knows.'

Leonard still did not really know who they were. Always they. Always the people on the inside. They. But who were *they*? Selsey held out his hand, palm up, and started to tick off his fingers.

'One, they don't wear badges. Two, they've been here a long time. Three, they've got money. Proper money.'

'To burn?'

'To buy. Buy anything and anyone. Four, they only know each other.'

Leonard looked up from his cup. Took off his spectacles. Started to polish. Blinking in time to his question.

'What does "only know each other" mean?'

'They're so inside that no one outside really matters. Money doesn't matter. It's taken for granted. Not even considered. So what do they trade in? Let me tell you, James my lad. They trade in influence. It's the strongest currency in the world.'

His hand was still outstretched. Leonard stopped polishing.

'And five?'

Selsey closed his hand.

'There is no five. But, but if there were to be, then Montague James would know what it was.'

Leonard slipped the wire arms over his ears.

'Who he?'

'He's the one person who knows everything.'

'Why?'

'Because there always is one person who does. He does.'

When Leonard returned to Manvers Street, the police station felt overcrowded. He was heading for the Murder Room when Lane called along the corridor.

'The boss is looking for you. The cavalry's here.'

'How many?'

Lane grinned.

'Enough to use up every overtime docket in this place. He wants to see you.'

The man with Stainger was tall, thin, humourless. His name was Marsh. Superintendent Marsh. He did not shake hands. He showed an inch of crisp white cuff and oval gold links.

His hair was as short as a friar's, his stare as stainless as a confessor's.

Superintendent Marsh was one of four senior officers based at police headquarters. There was nothing demeaning about calling in Headquarters. As Stainger had said, there would have been problems if they had not. Now everyone knew that the murder of the traveller was officially a mystery. It was not a predictable investigation. It was not one which could pull together three or four suspects and evidence enough to reassure the Crown Prosecution Service that a conviction was as near certain as it could ever be. Stainger sensed Marsh's displeasure with Leonard's appearance. Policemen were a mixed bunch. Especially CID. They dressed casually. Up and down. But, to another policeman, even the most undercover officer might just as well have worn regulation boots and a helmet. Policemen were like prostitutes: they sensed which game people played. Didn't have to be told.

Marsh was thrown by Leonard. Stainger had said he was unconventional, in appearance, not method. Marsh did not like the unconventional. He had a fear of CID becoming elitist, living in a fantasy world. He had applauded the idea of CID being pulled back into uniform every so often. He did not like them getting in a rut. Ruts led away from the main highway of policework. Marsh lived on the main highway and had become a senior officer at a very young age. Leonard was not only from another force, he might just as well have been from another world for all Marsh could see. Stainger's soft brogue came through in his reassurance and almost, for him, jolliness.

'You'll stay on this, James. The files will wait.'

Leonard nodded.

'I expect close liaison.'

Of course Marsh did. He meant that he did not want Leonard stepping out of line. Leonard did not intend to.

'I'll carry on as before. If that's all right with you, sir?'

Marsh did not quite ask what 'as before' meant, but considering the short time the investigation had been under way he wasn't quite sure what answer, if any, he would have got to his question. Instead he pulled out a hardbacked chair from the conference table.

'You'd better fill me in and we can get on with it.'

He smiled although neither of the other men noticed. Marsh gave little away.

The briefing did not take long. Leonard left the room with half a smile on his lips and half a tune on his mind. He had forgotten to mention the question in his mind about the murder in Rainbow Wood. Or had he?

Leonard was on his way out when he met the policewoman on the backstairs landing.

'Tell me, Sergeant. What happened to the traveller. Ten years ago?'

'Pete, sir?'

He nodded. There was a trace of lipstick. Not obvious. She looked thoughtful, trying to remember what she had read.

'I wasn't in the job then, sir, but I've read about it. I seem to remember it was a stabbing.'

'What sort of stabbing?'

She shook her head. But not because she didn't know.

'It was all a bit nasty. Throat cut and, er, well, he had his, er, his penis cut off.'

Not simply another murder.

'Do we know why?'

'Lots of guesses, sir, but no. Nothing for sure. The whole thing didn't come to much. There were some ideas that he might have been involved in drugs. I think when anything like this happens with these people everyone immediately says it must be drugs. But there was no evidence and, of course, no one was ever caught.'

Leonard was even more interested.

'Why "of course"?'

'Well, not *of course*. I simply mean that, if it had been down to someone we knew, you know, sir, a result, then we'd know more about it.'

Leonard looked at his watch. There was a visit he needed to make. But it would have to wait.

'No arrest? No one went down?'

'No, sir.'

'So the file's not closed?'

'Well, yes it is and no it isn't. As far as I know. Officially it's open but . . .'

'Realistically it isn't.'

'Yes, sir.'

The girl was intelligent. Girl? She was almost petite for a police officer. She looked more like a girl than a woman. But then, who was he to know? She was waiting. Wanting to go her way. Not wanting to offend.

'Tell me, Sergeant, where is the file? Still here?'

She nodded.

He followed her down the scuffed stairs until they were in the basement area. He was lost. Six months in Bath and he had no idea this warren existed. She led on and into a long and narrow room with rows of tall steel lockers. Blue nylon kit bags. A neat changing room. But not empty while the team played its heart out. Characterless. Unfriendly. No mascots left on a wall hook. No smells. No discarded socks. It was not a game. It was here that civilians became police officers became civilians. He tripped on a bench, rubbed his shin. She didn't stop. Like a white rabbit with silver chevrons on the shoulders of her white summer blouse, she was late for an important date and was already disappearing through a door. Beyond it, he paused. A skittle alley. Beneath the streets of Bath? She smiled.

'Big in this part of the world, sir. You're not a pub without a skittle alley, you know.'

He shook his head. He had not known. Then they were off again. A mini-gymnasium with benches and weights and pulleys and mats. And then a carpenter's shop with shelves and clamps. But no tools. Couldn't leave anything lying around. A carpenters' watch area. And then, as if an afterthought, another room and rows of shelves. Buff files with huge black numbers. Dates. Here was the record of Bath police. Crimes and offences. Villains and offenders. Year by year by deed. She walked on and round a corner before stopping. She was reading off the dates.

'Eighty-seven, eighty-six, eighty-five, eighty . . . Here we are, sir. Somewhere here.'

Ten years gone. Ten years waiting to be reopened. She could not reach. Leonard pulled down the whole section of files. They carried them back into the workshop and started to sift through on the scarred bench. It took half an hour. The dates were there. The files neatly arranged. The chronology perfect but for one reference. The file on Rainbow Wood was missing.

Thirteen

The editor's desk faced the wall. It was a desk from another age of journalism. Wooden. Built for partners. Now bare but for an already yellowing copy of some past edition of the *Chronicle* and a silently flickering mini television. Peter Dover was a survivor in an age of electronics. Instant reporting. Portable telephones. On-the-spot, 'as-I-stand-here' journalism. The *Chronicle* wasn't about that sort of reporting. His paper was part of the community. It was about Bath. If it happened in the city and its scuffed edges, then it would be in the *Chronicle*. Mostly. Some things never got there because of space. Some things never got there because even he would never know about them. He wandered in and out of the city's society but did not kid himself. He was the editor.

A journalist. A journalist was someone who met the most illustrious people under the most humiliating circumstances. Who'd said that? An American. It usually was an American.

Nowadays, they said all the best things. That's where the language was. Not the stilted style he had to follow. Trying to be grammatically correct yet graphically exciting. But things had changed. Even in a decade.

Dover looked down at the paper in front of him. The report had been big on the day. Big on the second day. By the following, it had almost disappeared. By the Friday it had. The headline-writer had done well. A tight four columns. You had to be clever to get the message in that space. People thought you made it up. Said what you wanted to say and then fitted it to the paper. No way. He remembered his own days as a sub. Scribbling dozens of would-be headlines. Counting the letters to see if they'd fit over one, two, three, even four, columns. This one had been a perfect headline. It had said it all. It had fitted. Two lines. No gaps. Squared off and eye-catching. A good headline.

Police probe throatcut
murder in lovers' wood

The editor grinned inwardly. Probe. What a wonderfully evocative word. Probe. Said it all. Matched easily with the others in the unwritten style book of if-all-fails headlines for tabloid sub-editors. Probe. New Move. Row. Rumpus.

Just imagine, he thought. NEW MOVE IN POLICE ROW RUMPUS. Now that would sell a few extra copies. He came back to the text of the story. It was nothing like as good as the headline.

Police probe throatcut
murder in lovers' wood

by

Steven Reece

A HIPPIE was found dead in Rainbow Wood early this morning. Police said the body was of a man in his early twenties.

Sources close to the investigation confirmed that the man may have had his throat cut.

Police sealed off the area, a well-known beauty spot overlooking Bath.

Locals say that Rainbow Wood is popular with courting couples.

And there was speculation that the hippie may have come from the pop festival taking place this week near Glastonbury.

Detective Inspector Ralph Stainger of Bath CID said that it was too early to give the cause of death.

And he refused to comment on speculation that drugs were found near the body.

He said the police were following a number of leads and were confident of an early arrest.

Local resident and parish councillor Major Dickie Jackson said that the council had warned the authorities about hippies using the woods. He claimed that the police had ignored the warning.

Major Jackson said the parish council would be demanding extra police patrols in the area.

There was a knock. His secretary put her head round the door. 'Inspector Leonard's here.'

Leonard had left the policewoman searching the rest of the files. He did not believe she would find anything. Had said so. In the MIR, Somers-Barclay had been all smiles and concern. Smiles because he always smiled if he could. Concern because he did not want to lose Leonard. Superintendent Marsh had his own doggie from headquarters. Somers-Barclay did not like to be kept at a distance from the power centre. He was only too keen to go below and help the uniformed sergeant in her search, but instead Leonard told him to get on to the coroner's officer. The investigation file might be missing, but the coroner's officer would have something. Presumably the coroner had returned a verdict of death by person or persons unknown. Somers-Barclay, eager to please, picked up the telephone. Leonard shook his head.

'Go down and see him. Never telephone if you can talk face to face. People tell you things with eye contact even if they don't say anything. Understand?'

Somers-Barclay understood everything that might further his career. He was on his way out, when he stopped. Somers-Barclay's ideas were few and far between unless they concerned social and career climbing.

'Just a thought, sir. The *Chronicle* editor. He'd have something in his back numbers, wouldn't he? Just a thought.'

He waited. It was worth it. Leonard smiled.

'Not a bad one. What's his name?'

'Dover, sir. Peter Dover.'

As he headed for the stairs, Somers-Barclay's smile was genuine.

Leonard was shown into the oblong room. There were office chairs along the wall opposite the window and a green plant which would have been best left in the Seychelles. Dover's handshake was firm. Honest. No knuckles bent. No probing index finger. He offered Leonard a seat, made pleasantries, did not ask why the policeman wanted to see the cuttings, and handed him a photocopy. Leonard read it. Four or five times.

When he finished, Dover gave him a single sheet with the follow-up stories. There wasn't much.

As Leonard read, Dover watched. So this was the mystery inspector He could see why he was a mystery. If he had seen him coming out of the police station himself he wouldn't have guessed him to be a policeman. And the boots. His grandfather had worn boots like that. If someone had told Dover that Leonard was on the philosophy faculty at Bristol University, or even that he was the new artistic director of the Theatre Royal, then he would have believed it. Leonard was looking at him. Suddenly. The head had not moved. But the stare gave the impression of penetrating his speculation.

'Who was Steven Reece?'

Dover leaned back and smoothed his striped shirt over his stomach.

'Reece? Just before my time. Senior reporter. It was one of the last stories he did, apparently.'

'What happened to him? Fleet Street?'

'No. In fact it was, by all accounts, a bit of a surprise. He was a good lad, or so I'm told. Young. Sharp. In fact he was the first Oxford trainee we'd had down here. But he suddenly decided that journalism wasn't for him.'

'Before your time. But you knew him?'

'Not then of course. But I've met him a few times since.'

'So he's still in Bath?'

A burglar alarm was going off across the street. Dover looked out of the window. An elaborate eighteenth-century window on the second floor opposite, starved of sun. It was double-glazed. The alarm was noisy. He smiled.

'Not young Reece. London. He was offered a job in PR. Plenty of money. That was that.'

'When exactly?'

'About three or four weeks after that murder.'

'But you said it was his last story.'

'So I did. So I did. So it was. Oh, he wrote the odd leader column. But it was. My predecessor was his patron, I suppose you'd call it. Reece apparently believed there was something behind it. You know, something more than just a hippie murder. Anyway, he was allowed to snoop about. But, you know, the *Chronicle*'s not really in the business of investigative journalism. We investigate, but staff is limited, funds are limited and there's enough to do without spending all the budget on one big story that may never come to anything.'

'Too much to lose?'

Dover laughed. He made a quiet noise when he did. But he laughed all the same.

'No. Nothing so sinister. I'm telling you the truth. We don't have the staff. Nor the money. Come to that, we don't have those sorts of stories in Bath.'

'Reece thought so.'

'Not necessarily. Don't forget, Inspector, young Reece was a high-flying graduate trainee who came here to get experience, show us what he could do, make a name for himself. You have the same sort of fast-track people yourself, don't you?'

Leonard thought of Somers-Barclay. The looks. The upper second from Oxford. Or was it? He remembered the pretty doctor. Cambridge. The signet ring. The confidence. The ambition. He knew what the editor was talking about.

'So what happened?'

'Nothing. Or, as far as I know, nothing. Apparently he spent every waking hour on the story. And then one day he came in and said that he was leaving.'

'To go into PR?'

'So the story goes. Right. Funny that. Most journalists, the good ones anyway, have a deep suspicion of PROs. Some of them despise them. Don't trust them. Good journalists start from the point that PROs are selling something, which they are.'

'You mean, Steven Reece sold out?'

'No. Not at all. Just fancied his chances. And, as I say, for a fat salary and all the expenses he could spend.'

Leonard looked down at the cutting. Perhaps it had nothing to do with the murder in the bath. Perhaps. But then he had, for the moment at least, nothing more.

'What made him go? Just the money?'

'Maybe. I wasn't here, remember.'

'Do you have a number for him?'

Dover shook his head.

'Not me. But I could probably find you one. But why don't you call his boss? He lives here in Bath.'

'I thought you said Reece was in London.'

'So he is. And New York. And anywhere else they have airports, or so I'm told. But try London. That's the group headquarters of the holding company, the name of which escapes me. But someone out there will remember.'

He nodded in the direction of the door leading to the *Chronicle*'s newsroom. He reached for his pad and scribbled a name.

'Here you go, Inspector. Try him if you can get through. He's more ex-directory than Martin Boorman. But he was the guy who offered young Reece the job.'

The paper was lined and yellow. The name was Montague James.

Fourteen

A little light lunch taken, Montague James strolled in the gardens. The flagstones were kempt. Brushed. The man at his side was stout. Baggy moleskin trousers and heavy corrugated-sole shoes. As they walked, they talked. Soft voices. Best not overheard. A gardener clipped at an already clipped hedge and a boy snipped at a perfectly snipped lawn. Not the man's idea. His wife's. Liked things tidy. Liked seeing people with things to do. Especially the hired help.

James raised a hand towards the terrace, where his wife was stretched beneath a wide shade on a floral-covered sun-lounger. She smiled. But the small glass of white wine with lunch she had allowed her complexion and the little something extra after lunch had been comforting and she only vaguely saw the figures. The other man was grunting under his breath. His voice was as gruff as he was bluff.

'I can't see what the fuss is about. No one cares a sod for a crusty. It'll come to nothing.'

They paused. James was expressionless. Precise. In command.

'There is no fuss, dear boy. There may be. If there should be, I want to make sure that everyone who is concerned remains so. It was a silly, an extraordinarily silly, mistake. There was no need.'

'Course there bloody well was. He was ... well, you sodding well know what the fucker was up to.'

Montague James sucked his teeth. He disliked profanity. Quite unnecessary. Distasteful. Could he really have been at school with this man? Even worse, they were related, albeit distantly.

'I make my point clearly, I trust. Whatever the reason and whatever the decision, the execution of that decision was not only melodramatic, it drew attention. Quite unnecessarily so. You lost control. I will not have it otherwise.'

'It's done.'

'Without my agreement.'

The other man turned to look directly at James. When he spoke, it sounded like a drinker's worst morning.

'Oh. I see. That's what we're about, is it now? Christ. You and Pontius Pilate together.'

'I merely make the point that I was not consulted and if I had been I would never have agreed.'

'Really?'

'Certainly I would never have agreed to the way it was handled. If indeed it was at all.'

'I suppose you would have wanted closed bids in an envelope by the first of the month. Winners read about it in the *Times* personal column.'

'You miss my point.'

They walked on. The gardener clipped in five-four time and the boy thought carnal thoughts that, to become deeds, would have to wait until darkness and the sinking of six pints of Butcombe.

On the terrace, one of the sons appeared from the French doors. He had a cold lager in one hand and offered it to Hilary James. She smiled no thank you. He was a big, strong boy in his early twenties. He looked down at her almost bare thigh. The light breeze from the valley had lifted the white lawn of her most summery dress. He gulped at the cold beer. She was a bit old, he thought. But a better bet than some of the little tarts in the village. Put your hand up their skirts and they wanted the banns read next week. She would not complain. She hadn't. He could not see her eyes behind her dark glasses. But he knew her. He'd seen her eyes. Watched her after lunch when she'd gone into her dreams. Liked to see pain, this one. Liked it in others. Liked to watch pain. He rubbed a forefinger and thumb. She watched. He knew what was behind those dark glasses. He knew what she was thinking. Knew the way she moved. He finished the beer and bent to leave the glass on the iron table at her side. A few white dregs of foam slid down the sides. She could have touched him. She wanted to. The bleached hair on his arm. The crudeness of the ragged scar that ran from elbow to wrist. She sniffed his summer sweat. She knew why he stood in front of her like that. She didn't mind. Wished he'd stood longer. But he turned and she watched him go. Watched the stride of muscular thighs. The strong buttocks in tight and faded jeans. She watched the easy way he swung into the Land-Rover and the brutality as he churned the wheels and gears out of the drive, across the cattle grid and away along the dusty lane. Hilary James had an enormous desire to be in a shower. Instead, she closed her eyes and waited for her master.

Montague James watched the dust in the distance.

'He's dangerous. This time he's gone too far.'

The other man looked away when he spoke.

'A mistake, that's all. A mistake. How they got him, I don't know.'

'I expect you to.'

The man looked into the other's face. The sun was strong. He shaded his eyes.

'Then don't. Because I don't.'

Montague James looked at his watch. Time to go.

'All I wish to say is that you must make it clear to everyone that nothing must be done to encourage this investigation.'

'Come off it, Monty. We're hardly likely to turn up with written sodding statements. Are we now?'

'I'm talking about caution. I'm also talking about the right people knowing that it is in their best interests that the whole matter be left to rest. When in doubt, do nothing and nothing will be done.'

The other man grinned. Rubbed a stubby hand across his chest.

'What about Friday?'

'No more Fridays. A Feast Day and nothing more.'

Fifteen

A pigeon had messed on Leonard's bicycle. He was rubbing at the leather saddle when Stainger appeared in the car park. The Superintendent nodded.

'Well, if that's all that shits on you, then it'll be a fine day for it'

Leonard tried a laugh. It was silent and did not come very far. Stainger was going in, heading for the small corner door. Leonard waited, then called, softly.

'What happened to Peter? Rainbow Wood.'

Stainger stopped tapping the door code and walked back. Slowly.

'What you mean? What happened?'

'Just that. What happened?'

Stainger was a couple of feet away. He leaned against the rusting car and fiddled with the broken wing mirror.

'Did anything have to happen? It was ten years ago. Eleven?'

'Ten.'

'Well, then. I don't see the connection.'

Leonard watched the June sun dry and smudge the dirty saddle. He looked up at the older man. The eyes were level. Waiting. Firm. Not cautious. Just firm. Leonard carried on rubbing the saddle as he spoke.

'Coincidence. There's usually a connection in coincidence. That's what makes it a coincidence.'

Stainger sighed.

'Not this time, James. Not this time. OK, I grant you that they were both crusties but that's as far as it goes.'

'Three unsolved murders in ten years. Two of them travellers. I'd say that goes a long way. And of course –'

'And, of course, I was the investigating officer. OK. But it's hardly bingo. Full house.'

Leonard sighed. Looked about the car park. It was covered in the dust of abandoned vehicles. A hopeless place. Crimes and offences awaiting attention. Like most things they did. Inconclusive. He tried again.

'And you never had any idea who it was?'

Stainger spun the wing mirror in its rusting and peeling socket. Did not look up.

'A few. But nothing came together. We pulled in the usual people. And a few more. But, for my money, it was down to the pop festival. Glastonbury.'

'Pilton.'

'OK. But it's the same thing. The festival had finished a couple of days before. I reckon whoever it was was gone before we even found the poor bastard. Probably pissing on Stonehenge when the whistle went.'

Stainger patted the crumpled wing as he might have patted a favourite labrador. End of statement. He started to wander off. Leonard had not finished.

'What about this man James? Montague James.'

Stainger turned.

'What the hell's he got to do with it?'

Leonard shrugged. He was not sure. Except for the fact that Montague James kept cropping up. Stainger laughed. It came out as a dimissive sound. He did not like his officers treading on dangerous ground. For the moment at least, James Boswell Hodge Leonard was one of his officers.

'Montague James is one of those people who come up everywhere. He's like a board game in this city. Everything you get into, every move you make, if you look into it you'll land on Go To Montague James. Every town has one. This town's got half a dozen. There isn't one with a regular name, so that makes it more obvious because they even have unforgettable labels. Montague James is one of the Colours of Bath. So, what's your theory?'

Leonard did not have one. Just two facts.

'In the first couple of hours people were telling me that the Bath mafia wanted this kept quiet. Bad for business.'

'They always do.'

Leonard ignored him. Continued.

'And then his name came up when I asked about Rainbow Wood.'

'Who brought it up?'

'Dover. The *Chronicle* editor.'

'He's a hack.'

'Doesn't make him wrong. He happened to mention the name. There was a reporter on the *Chronicle*. Steven Reece.'

Stainger nodded.

'I remember. Cocky little bugger. Trying to make a name for himself. Made himself a pest instead. Seemingly, he thought there was some conspiracy theory. Some great cover-up.'

'Was there?'

'Don't be daft, James. Course not. There was nothing at all. That was the problem. Nothing at all. But what's he got to do with Montague James?'

'James gave him a job as a PR man in his London office.'

'Did he now? So?'

'So nothing much except it's another coincidence.'

This time Stainger's laugh was louder. More assured. Stronger ground.

'Let me tell you something. The fact that he gives this reporter a job is unstartling fact of the week. Montague James is one of those people who has so many fingers in so many pies that, if you went to the bottom of the pile in Companies House, you'd probably find even the Queen was on the payroll of M. James Inc.'

'He owns a lot.'

'And he owns a lot of people. Not through pay-offs. He owns them the way mandarins own people. Influence.'

'Someone else said that.'

'Then he was right. Just remember that.'

Leonard watched Stainger go. He watched him tap in the door code. He watched him shut the corner door after him without looking back. Dismissed. Leonard rolled up the damp rag and tucked it into his canvas saddle bag. He looked up at the Murder Room window. Somers-Barclay was looking down. He smiled, or Leonard supposed that he did. He wondered how much of a name Somers-Barclay was trying to make.

The journey to Melincourt took a few minutes. He pedalled slowly, avoided the slopes and free-wheeled past the leather-goods shop that was forever holding a Final Reductions Closing Down Sale, past the old hospital that had been curing back aches and pains since Brunel was a boy and braked to look into the corner window of the shop from which he bought shirts. The owner saw him. Waved. Leonard thought a lot of people in Bath waved. A lot of people except the folks who lived on the hill. No one waved in Royal Crescent. No one waved in Lansdown. Everything was done behind drawn curtains.

In Melincourt he waited while a grumpy man in a bad-tempered plaid jacket worked out the cost of marbled envelopes, repeatedly demanding to know why Harriet Bowles would not take his dollars. The man was caught between his determination to bargain and the difficulty he had in being stern with this woman who could make a half-buttoned thin cotton shirt his gran'pappy would have worn look pretty damn special. She continued to smile, which made him even grumpier. Leonard was tempted to interrupt. To ask if he had a disbelieving sister and whether they had ever found their way to Royal Crescent. At last, the man was satisfied and almost smiled when Harriet wished him a nice day. Leonard said that he hoped he wasn't interrupting her.

'Not at all. I was going to call or leave a message with Selsey.'

Leonard put down an elegant dip pen and looked up.

'How do you dust this lot?'

She raised her eyebrows.

'What lot?'

He waved a hand about the shop cluttered with tiny boxes, scrolls, paper packs, nib holders, nib boxes, nib slides, pots and trays of pens and pencils, address books. A picture-book study. A balanced catalogue. Designer chaos.

'This.'

From a large vase of dried flowers Harriet pulled a well-disguised feather duster. They both smiled. Didn't bother to laugh.

'Tea?'

She did not wait for him and he followed into the rear room.

'Tell me more about Montague James.'

'More than what?'

'More than you've told me.'

'I've told you almost nothing.'

'Which is what everyone does. Everyone says Montague James this, Montague James that. He's influential. He is part of the Bath mafia. But no one tells me anything.'

'He is elegant. Fifty. Lives in Royal Crescent, two floors of it, which makes him even more special. Has a wife called Hilary who is a non-practising nymphomaniac. No children, of course.'

'Why "of course"?'

'He would find them disgusting.'

'And his wife?'

'He would find them disgusting.'

'Who are his friends?'

'He has none. A lot of people would like to think they are his friends. But they're not. Montague James would find friendship unnecessary. His life is divided into those things which are necessary and those which are not.'

Leonard sipped his tea. Hilary Bowles smiled. Amused. She waited for the obvious question. It came.

'How do you know all this?'

She straightened her spine in the tall chair. He found the movement disturbing. For a moment. Then not.

'That's all anyone really knows. Anyone, that is, who has thought about it. Giles knew him.'

'Your husband?'

She nodded. Finished her tea.

'They were on a couple of committees together. The Bath Festival, for example.'

'So you know him?'

'I know what I've told you. Now you tell me why you want to know all this. You got me down as a copper's nark or something?'

He did not mind her taunting. He shrugged. Took off his spectacles and started to polish, blinking into the middle distance as he did. Not looking at her.

'I'm not sure.'

She put down her cup and saucer on the desk.

'I thought policemen just got on with routine inquiries and things. I thought this disconnected thinking was strictly academe.'

'I don't think we're going to get anywhere.'

'Why're you telling me?'

He didn't know the answer and so did not answer. The wire arms went over his ears and she came back into focus. She was looking down at her desk diary.

'What're you doing at seven tomorrow evening?c

He shrugged.

'Good. There's a reception. Art in 21st-century Bath or something. I'll take you.'

'Do I need 21st-century art lessons?'

'None of us does. But come anyway. Montague James is chairman of the exhibition committee. It's about time you met him.'

Sixteen

By the time Leonard got back to Manvers Street it was long past closing time but not yet dark. Somers-Barclay had left a note that he would be helping Superintendent Marsh in the morning and hoped that was OK by Leonard. It had not taken long. There was a second note from the ambitious sergeant. Seventeen bags and holdalls had been picked up from corners, alleys, skips and waste sites. None seemed to be connected to the dead man. But he had sent them to the laboratory for second opinions. There was another note to call the Screaming Skull.

Leonard dialled the number and got an answer machine with a message as spare as Griffiths.

He looked about the second floor. Almost empty. It was late for most people, even a murder team. He remembered

Stainger's opinion about levels of investigation. If a kiddie had been murdered, the place would have been humming. A traveller? In Stainger's book, a black bin-liner was all that was needed to tidy up this case. Marsh's too? Leonard stretched. Yawned.

The duty sergeant returned with coffee. Somers-Barclay had already moved the filter machine to Superintendent Marsh's temporary room. Unasked, the sergeant had brought two. Leonard did not want it. He knew it tasted awful. He smiled. Said thanks. Took it. Asked how long the sergeant had been in Bath. Heard about the children. Had he heard of this man Montague James? The sergeant had not. Somers-Barclay would know. Somers-Barclay made a point of knowing anyone who drove a Roller. He made even more effort if that someone had someone to drive it for him.

By the time the coffee was finished, Leonard knew about Bath rugby, Somerset cricket, problems of infants' schooling in Weston and houses that were sinking into old stone tunnels up on Combe Down. But he was no closer to knowing why a traveller had been sadistically murdered and left in a public and ancient place in what was supposed to be a grand and genteel city. The next day, the sergeant would tell his colleagues that the DI wasn't such a bad bloke after all. But, after all, did not solve murders.

He left the police station and for a moment stood by the Methodist Chapel steps. There were six of them. Down and out in Bath. Leonard wondered how the strictly technicolor Patsy Bush coped with this doorway. Not in the tourist guide but on the main road to Bath Spa station. InterCity poverty. One hugged a cider bottle. Thin rugby shorts and a huge coat. None speaking to the others. One speaking to himself. Leonard sat on the steps and the one with the bottle paused. But not for long. The bottle went back to the foul lips and the dirtiest hand wiped at a sore-covered mouth.

'You want a fuckin' taste? Then get yer fuckin' own, cowboy.

That's a fact, yer know. That's a fuckin' fact.' He looked about him. 'Fuckin' fact.'

The others were not interested. He tugged at his army greatcoat and slipped the bottle inside the flapped pocket. But he never took his hand from it. He pulled his trainered feet under him and pouched his flimsily covered crotch with his other hand. Leonard stared. The man looked away. Shivered. But it was not cold.

'Get yer own. Get yer fuckin' own. That's a fuckin' fact, cowboy. A fuckin' fact. Yer hear me?'

Leonard's voice was soft. Not menacing. Soft.

'Don't need it. Got mine.'

'Get yer fuckin' own. That's a fuckin' fact.'

'You hear about the killing?'

No one said anything. Leonard pressed on.

'Sad. Very sad. A nice lad. No trouble to anyone. Sad.'

'Fuck off.'

'What d'you have to tell me?'

'Fuck off.'

'Best tell me. If you don't, I'll tell everyone you did.'

The greatcoat shifted. Leonard could smell the stench of urine. He tried again.

'He was doing no harm. Was he now? Nothing at all. Nice man. Nothing at all. All wrong.'

The drunk moaned. But did not grumble. Not now. Leonard dropped his voice to a whisper. He was close to the old man. Closer to the stench.

'All wrong. All wrong, wasn't it? Something to tell me, have you?'

A seeping trickle ran from beneath the coat and over the edge of the step. The man was moaning. Rocking. His head buried deeper into the khaki collar.

'Get us all fuckin' done. You will. Shouldn't talk about it. Get us fuckin' done, you will. Fuck off. Get yer own.'

Leonard looked at the others. One of them, no more than eighteen, was grinning, then laughing and pointing.

'Fucking pissing himself again. Fucking doing it.'

The others looked at the closed chapel door. The man pulled the coat above his head. His misery gurgled incoherently in the folds once fit for heroes.

Leonard left. They knew something. They would not tell.

It was muggy in the city. He walked slowly. Wondering about the fouled steps. What those people could know. Something. But what? Just because they were outcasts did not mean they were part of the same society. Not travellers. These ones were sadder. They didn't know they had a choice. Maybe once they had known, but not now. Choice was all too long ago. Not even a memory. The stragglers and down-and-outs on the chapel steps were not the fire-eaters and buskers, the beggars and mongrel-kickers of the Pump Room porch. Just as Bath had its breadline at the foot of Bathwick and its groaning tables on Lansdown, so the vagrants shuffled into tribes of their own freedoms and miseries.

Time for home. He had turned the corner of the narrow lane. Above him the towering walls of Bath stone and blank windows. Doorways with their slits of flat numbers and bells. Their black-painted railings. Hanging baskets of fuchsia. Few sounds except his. The sturdiness not of his tread but the strong leather of his boots and the tight tap of the metal blakies in their heels. At first, there was no noise. Just a sixth sense. He carried on, wishing for a shop window and a reflection, or good reason to stop and glance. The painted doors and shuttered windows said private, not for peeping, and he continued, but listening. Then he was sure. He paused. So did the noise. Footsteps. Maybe. But in unison. It was close to midnight, but Bath was no village. Others lived and never slept. He stopped again. Elaborately looked at his pocket watch beneath the street lamp. A step. Then nothing. He carried on. Listening. Not looking back. He thought of turning back. Confrontation. He did not.

When he reached the iron gate leading down to his basement flat he turned. Quickly. There was, for a split second, a figure by a railing. Then it was gone. Gone into a porch. A shifted shadow. He left the gate open and took his time down the stone steps. Took more time opening the door. Switched on the outside light that flooded the tiny courtyard. Went in. Left ajar the door. He was being followed. He knew that. Didn't know why. But he knew who.

Seventeen

It was cool in the flat and he eased off his brown boots and socks in the hall and padded barefoot to the kitchen. He left his jacket and waistcoat on the patchwork sofa, then fetched glasses and white wine. For a moment he listened. There was something. Then nothing. He opened the doors onto the garden and slumped into the cushions of the slatted chair by the sundial where Johnson had slept and waited all day. The cat curled and purred on the cushion by his shoulder and Leonard sipped his wine and listened.

He heard the mongrel just as Johnson did. The cat's claws dug into the cushion and then he was gone to the safety of the wall overlooking the river. Through half-closed eyes, Leonard waited and watched. And then she was standing in the doorway.

He said nothing. She said nothing. A slight figure in black cotton clutching a purple ragbag to her chest and holding a limp string that ended about the neck of a brown-and-black pup. He could see her eyes flicking from wall to wall, to the garden shed, to the overlooking window. Ready to turn. To run. Just as she had run through the side-streets and alleys to the echo of the whistler's baroque trill and the fire-eater's mockery. Leonard sipped. Continued to watch. Continued to wait. Said nothing. Did not need to. She had chosen to come here.

The girl looked behind her. Into the square living room with its unframed canvases and smoked-glass Sappho watching from an ebony plinth. Then into the garden once more. Leonard waved a hand at the other chair. She walked close to the wall and then came to the chair from behind, all the time eyes darting and spotting. When she sat it was on the edge. A governess at her first interview. She searched his face. Couldn't see the freckles in the half-light. Wondered about the curly hair. The green braces with exaggerated leather tabs to the green buttons at the waistband. His bare feet. Bony. Long-toed. Surgically white. He said nothing. Careful not to smile. Careful not to frighten.

It took time. She sat quite still, never letting go the bag. The pup fell quickly asleep. Johnson had gone. Leonard held out his glass. She shook her head. He poured more for himself. Sipped. Filled another glass and left it. She was thin but her face was as soft and as round as a novitiate's. A silver stud. Pinching and mean in one nostril. Her shaved head was not defiant but had its own sexuality, as dark as her eyes. As dark as her black Indian-cotton shift.

'What's your name?'

Leonard was surprised. He had not expected her to speak first. The accent was there. A strong accent.

'James.'

Her head moved up and down. Not a nod, but knowingly, as if she had guessed and had been right.

'You're a policeman, isn't it? A policeman here?'

He nodded. Dublin?

'That's right. How did you know?'

He saw her eyes shift. The question had come too early. She looked away to the door. He dropped his voice.

'There's no one else. Promise.'

She looked back.

'You don't have to.'

'Thought you would want to know.'

'I do. But you don't have to promise. Nothing's a promise.'

He knew that.

'What's your name?'

'Josie.'

There was a defiance in her voice, daring him to say it wasn't. He didn't. Maybe it wasn't Josie. Didn't matter. He had four names. None of them mattered. Given him by an institution. Names mattered when they came from parents. Then only the parents mattered. He knew. It didn't matter.

'Hello, Josie.'

She smiled. Her teeth were dirty. The gums too red.

'Hello.'

Then she stopped smiling. Perhaps remembered. More time. More saying nothing.

'He was my friend.'

Leonard felt a tingle inside. It should have been something more sophisticated. It was not. A tingle. At last. He said nothing. Smiled. Hoped it would look as if he understood. Looked kindly into her eyes. Wanted her to find in his eyes everything she had to have. Reassurance. Better than words to tell her it was all right. She was looking down. Stroking the soft purple bag. A comfort. A gentle pillow. Gently fingering the oh-so-soft fold of grubby rag.

'Proper friend.'

'That's nice.'

She looked up to see if he might be mocking. It had not been in his voice. But she knew about voices. His eyes were all right. Safe. She nodded slowly.

'He was beautiful. He looked after me. Never let them touch me.'

Leonard wanted to ask 'Who.' They? Who? Did not.

'That's what proper friends do, Josie. You trusted him.'

'I did. I did. All the time.'

'Tell me about him, Josie.'

'He was kind. Not like some of them. Didn't want me for, well, you know.'

He knew. Said nothing. Let her go on.

'Some of them did. They all did. Then he came and

wouldn't let them no more. He was beautiful. Looked after me. He was . . .'

She paused. Looking across the small garden to the cherry tree as if he might be there. He wasn't. He was in the Screaming Skull's freezer. She didn't know that. Leonard did. She tried again.

'He was . . .'

'Your friend.'

'Yes.'

'What was his name?'

Leonard held his breath. He wondered if that would be it. When she spoke, she smiled.

'Nothing.'

'Sometimes?'

'Sometimes Piccolo.'

Had the fire-eater said Piccolo? He couldn't remember.

'Sure?'

'Yeh. Had to be. That's what he was. He played. Know? Piccolo.'

She held the bag to her thin body.

'And Piccolo was your friend.'

She swayed. A meditation. Leonard waited, not sure where to go next. He wanted to hold the spell. Needed to wait for her. He removed his spectacles and she watched while he rubbed them on his tie. She watched his eyes. The sockets were deep. The eyes green. They frightened her. She wished he'd put on his glasses. She looked away. Waited. She heard his voice but did not look at his face. Not at first. Didn't answer. She heard it again. It was gentle. She relaxed. The glasses were back on and he was taking something from the wooden box. Then he took a match and lit the funnelled end. Puffed. Inhaled. He handed it to her. She shook her head.

'Don't do it now.'

'Did Piccolo?'

'No. He was clean. Gentle.'

Leonard drew deeply, lay back, eyes closed.

'Where did he come from?'

'Long way. I don't know. I didn't have to, really. It wasn't important, you know.'

'He never mentioned anything like that?'

'Like what?'

'Where he came from.'

She wondered. Looked at the grass and then at Leonard.

'He didn't have to. Some of them did. But usually they made it up anyway. Piccolo didn't make anything up. He was just real. He was now. You understand?'

Leonard wasn't sure he did. But he nodded.

'When did you meet him?'

'Six weeks ago. Maybe a month. Maybe two.'

'You're not sure?'

'No. Nothing's sure, is it?'

'Was it warm? Wet? Cold?'

'What?'

'When you met.'

She could not remember. Even though she lived in the rain, the snow, the sun, the light and the dark, she could not remember. It was important. But only to Leonard. Again.

'Where did you meet him?'

'By the church. Where everyone meets.'

'Which church?'

She looked surprised. Everyone knew.

'Glastonbury, of course. He just turned up one day. We were sitting, some of us, in front of the church. You know? On the grass.'

So it had not been raining. Not snowing. Not too cold. Maybe she was right. One month. Six weeks. Not much more. Or just a nice day. He waited and then he listened as she talked, sometimes stopping, sometimes smiling, sometimes sad, and Leonard began to know a man called Piccolo.

Glastonbury. He didn't understand. So she told him. Glastonbury had, over the years, become a gathering place for travellers and hangers-on. Its Arthurian claims, its mystical romance, had attracted the communities and soft traders who fed the hopes and half-beliefs of mostly young drop-outs and would-be drop-outs. Unlicensed vans, old coaches converted with stoves and blackened chimneys, bedsits for four, in the summer, hedges for even more. Bead-threaders and crystal-gazers. Asian trinkets and transcendental soundtracks to levitate the soul if not the body. Exotic and sometimes cruel substances to magnify abstract understandings and line pockets of dealers had completed Glastonbury's reputation. And above it all the Tor, at which the saint had stopped on his way from Ireland, or so legend claimed.

They had been sprawled in front of the church, talking of nothing. Then Piccolo had come. Sat beside her. A quiet man. Long lashes she thought beautiful. His cheekbones jutted not from hunger but grace. And, when they got up to go, she went with him.

'Where?'

'Nowhere. We just went.'

'But you must have gone somewhere.'

'There were lots of places. Someone usually had a room. Or we moved on. Sometimes there was a van. That was nice.'

Leonard watched her closely. It had been nice.

'Always in Glastonbury?'

'For a time. Then we came here.'

'Bath?'

She nodded. Looked surprised. Where else?

'Why here?'

'He knew people. Piccolo did.'

'Who?'

She tugged at the ragbag. The pup nuzzled her bare foot.

'Don't know.'

Leonard smoked. A last time.

'You ever see them? The people he knew?'

She knew what he meant. She had. She shook her shaven

head. Looked up from the pup. Smiled. Maybe she was beautiful. Maybe everyone was.

'No. Not me.'

'But Piccolo did.'

The pup was rolling on its back. Labrador in the ancestry? A bit of Springer there? It wanted to play. She rubbed its belly. It nipped her and she pulled her hand back. A finger to her mouth. Smiled.

'He saw them a time and sometimes he was away.'

'I don't understand.'

'Well, sometimes he would go off. Maybe two, sometimes three, days.'

'Off where?'

'I tell you, I don't know.'

She wanted to please. Always she had wanted to please.

'Promise. I don't know.'

It was very dark. But still warm. Even hot. Moths flew about the porch light. He looked across. She was waiting. She had come to help, he could see that. Her friend. But she did not know how.

'How do you know he went to see people? He tell you?'

'Just used to say that he had to go.'

'Then how do you know he did?'

'He wouldn't lie. He never lied. Sometimes I asked him things and, if he didn't want to say, then he'd say nothing at all. Wouldn't lie. Understand?'

He did. He nodded. He was about to ask again. To pin her down now that she was more confident and so was he. But she got there first.

'I know he'd been somewhere good. Always he'd been somewhere good.'

Leonard smiled. Warm. Even warmer. He nodded. Waited. She told him.

'Had to be somewhere special. He was always clean when he came back.'

'You mean washed?'

'No. Not washed. That's easy. The chapel, they let you do that there. Lots of places do. No, this was different. This was proper clean. Clean like he was used to before.'

'Before when?'

'Where he was before.'

'How do you know?'

'You do know. Some people come from good places. Good places. Good families. Big families. You do know.'

'The way they speak?'

'Not like you.'

'Like what?'

'Like he wanted to be.'

'Think, Josie, what did his voice, his accent, remind you of? What did it sound like?'

'Everything.'

'But he might have been something special.'

She laughed. Josie had long stripped accents to the raw. They meant nothing. You could get those anywhere you wanted. No. There was something else. Wasn't important. So, she didn't say.

'Clean. That was important.'

'What sort of clean do you mean, Josie?'

'He'd be gone a day, two days, sometimes three. Then, when he came back, you could tell. He was washed all over. Everywhere. You understand? When you go to the places, you know, the chapel and like, well, you don't get everything clean. Not even the ones with the baths. Not everything.'

He did not understand. It didn't matter. She was smiling again. Remembering.

'His hair was nice. Not soap nice, like the chapel places. Shampoo. Expensive. Made his hair fluffy. Then his nails were done. You can't get your nails done. The hands don't get clean. It's the skin. Has to grow away before you can.'

'And Piccolo's was clean?'

'Beautiful. And the nails had been done.'

'Scrubbed?'

'And done. With a board. You know, they didn't look broken no more. And the smell. Gone, it had. People can tell the smell. You can see them sniff. They hold their breath. It's funny. At first. Then, well, then it's not. Mostly it's the hair. It's in there. You can't get rid of that smell. But he came back. Different smell. And his clothes. Same things, but they'd be done. Washed properly.'

She looked about her. Rubbed at the pup, then tugged at the long widow's weeds. She looked at the door and cocked her head in its direction.

'You got a shower?'

Leonard nodded.

She stood. Looked down.

'He wasn't there, you know. He came from the hill. They brought him.'

'Who did?'

But she was gone. She was gone a long time. He heard the water from the machine. Heard the shower many times. The pup had come to him. Sniffed at his feet, then his ankles, then his trouser legs. From the safety of her wall, Johnson watched, disapprovingly. Leonard wondered what else the girl knew. She and Piccolo had met on the green in front of the church. They had left Glastonbury and come to Bath. When? He needed to find out. But, according to the fire-eater, they had only come in with the crowd who had been bussed out for the Royal Visit Amen, as Lane called it. He still did not know who had decided to move them on for that one day. He needed to check. So either the fire-eater was wrong, or lying, or Josie was. Or, they had kept themselves to themselves. But why? Was that likely? She had said Piccolo protected her from the others. What others? And what protection? Protection from what? What did they do or threaten to do to her? When she had said she'd been protected, Leonard had guessed. But he did not know. He needed to.

The pup stood up, yapped and scampered to the door. She was standing beneath the light. Wrapped in a white bath towel. Her neck seemed longer out of the black shift. A Celtic arrogance. She came towards him. Almost a gracefulness in her cleanliness. Almost. She sighed with deep satisfaction as she sat astride the slatted garden chair. The bottom of the towel parted to the tops of her thighs. But not erotically. She rubbed at her head. The thick hair in her armpits damp. Untouched. Skinny arms bruised. Elbows pointed and savagely red. Her thighs scratched, and bitten by insects. Her knees like the knuckles of a hacked and jointed carcass. Her legs unshaven. Her toes bent and the nails picked and torn. Clean, but the grime lay deeper than a shower could reach.

They sat while she dried and he heard the furious spin of the machine from the stone-floored kitchen. When he spoke, his voice was quiet. Hushed. He wondered if the spell had gone.

'Tell me, Josie, you're really sure you don't know where he went?'

She stretched. The towel never moved on her thin frame. She moved her head from side to side. Sleepy.

'Was it always to the same place?'

'I think so.'

'Why do you think so?'

She did not know why. She just thought so.

'Did he say it was?'

'No.'

'Then why do you think so?'

'I don't know. I just got the idea. It was always the same time. In the evening. And then suddenly he would say he was going and then, well, he'd go.'

Leonard believed she must know more, even if she didn't know that she did.

'Think hard, Josie. Why did Piccolo go? Do you know that?'

She looked at him. Then at the wooden box. So she did lie. Leonard gave her the box and watched while she fumbled with a match. She sucked deeply, her eyes closed, and passed it to him. They said nothing, then again it was Josie, not Leonard.

'He said one day everyone would know.'

'Know what?'

Her head was back and she spoke to the stars.

'Just would know. Everyone would know, just like the Piccolo man.'

The tingle. The barely-to-touch tingle. His voice a whisper.

'But he was the Piccolo man.'

She smiled. Miles away.

'Come on, Josie. Piccolo was your friend, right?'

'Mm.'

'Was he the Piccolo man? Is that it?'

'No. Not Piccolo man. He was Piccolo.'

'Who was the Piccolo man, Josie?'

She moaned softly. He stroked her head. He did not understand. He heard the rambling from her head. He could not work with ramblings.

'Tell me again, Josie. Help me. Piccolo was your friend. Right?'

'Mm.'

She was a long way away.

'Was the Piccolo man someone else?'

'Mm.'

'Who was he, Josie?'

'Bolt.'

'Who was Bolt? Was Piccolo Bolt?'

'No. He was Piccolo. I told you that. Piccolo said he knew and soon everyone would know.'

'Who knew, Josie? Who?'

'That's what he used to say. Always used to say it. Bolt knew. That was it. Always, Bolt knew.'

Bolt. At last. A name.

Eighteen

The next morning, Leonard's immediate problem was that he did not know what to do with Josie. She was a witness. There were procedures. Simple police procedures. Investigating officers were not expected to become personally involved in material witness. Keeping Josie in his flat was against procedures, if for no other reason than, if the case ever went to court, any second-rate brief would demolish her credibility by insinuating that she was personally involved with one of the murder team. But Leonard believed she needed protection.

Late in the night, when he had cradled her as he would a child, she had told him how she and Piccolo had kept away from most of the travellers, sweet walkers from Glastonbury and especially the small vicious gang of drop-outs. She knew more than she realized. But for the time being she knew enough to be frightened. Isolated. She didn't want to be back on the streets. Where else was she to go? Safe houses did not exist for her. Social Services would not get involved. And, if she knew more, then Leonard believed she was in danger.

Stainger had suggested that the murderer was probably far away and would disappear into the community of crusties just as had been the case ten years before. Leonard's instincts told him that the murderer was still in or around the city. Also, he believed it possible there was a connection with the Rainbow Wood killing. He did not know why. Instinct again. The very correct inspector he'd known would have told him to ignore instincts and stick to policework. Policework got arrests. Policework got the right arrests. That meant bodies the Crown Prosecution Service would run with. That meant convictions.

Leonard knew all about policework, routine and teamwork. Applauded each one of them. Yet Leonard had lived his early and lonely life obeying instincts to survive. He had survived.

Not the cruelty of others. There was no need. There was little in the home. Maybe less than in the lives of the outsiders, which he and the other boys never quite understood. But instincts helped him survive the buzzes and taunts in his head. Night after night he would dream of grotesque faces rushing at him. Gaping and silently screaming mouths. Swooping as if he were trapped in a fairground's hall of mirrors. And, when he woke, he would carry those visions along corridors. He was frightened when sent to the cupboard for brooms, believing that when he opened the spotless door the faces would be there. When he was older, they told him they were visions of parents he had never known. It was 'only natural', they had said. When he was older, he still dreamed. They were there. Still in every cupboard. In Florence, he once confessed to a friend that he was afraid of the dark. The friend, a nun, said that was because he was God-fearing. Leonard longed for such simplicity in his own beliefs. Until then, he trusted in instincts.

So, he had left Josie sleepy and wrapped in one of his nightshirts in the spare bedroom, the pup already at home on this new-sprung luxury. He had told her not to answer the telephone, nor the door. And, like a child, she had said she would not. It was a solemn moment of concern and trust in that concern.

He arrived in Manvers Street shortly after eight o'clock, checked that his bicycle was where he had left it and was trying to remember the door code when a voice behind him came to his rescue.

'26–26–43–STAR 3.'

He did not recognize her at first. The face, yes. But the clothes. He had only seen her in uniform. Policemen get used to uniforms. Out of them, they change shape. Army officers, he thought, still look like army officers whatever they're wearing because their civilian clothes conform to a common pattern. Even the labrador. Another uniform. Not policemen and especially not policewomen. She was wearing a loose smock and trainers. He opened the door for both of them.

'Day off?'

'No, sir. It's all-change day. My two years are up. As from midnight last night I transferred to CID.'

'Really?'

She nodded, beamed. Very pleased.

'I'm supposed to be over at Avonmouth. RCS. But the boss said I may as well stay until this one's over – after all, the RCS would have probably sent me back anyway. It is a regional crime, in a way.'

It wasn't. But Leonard wasn't arguing. They were in the doorway and two uniformed constables came by. Across the yard he could see Stainger arriving in one of the three priority parking bays.

Leonard wanted her on her own for ten minutes and he did not want to get caught in the Major Incident Room routine. Not yet. Something about Sergeant Jack had puzzled him and it was time for the answers. But first he had something to do.

'Look, Sergeant, give me five minutes, will you? I'll see you in the canteen. Mine's without sugar.'

He did not wait for an answer. His sense of theatre was about to be cosseted. Marsh was in the Major Incident Room when Leonard arrived. The look he got suggested that he should have been there before him. Leonard did not mind. Somers-Barclay got the same look from him. Marsh had a gaunt mind. It pierced his speech, his mannerisms. His voice would have served a Victorian tutor. His stare, a Stasi interrogator. His white cuffs were as starched as his collar, as his sense of duty.

'We seem to have proceeded with difficulty, Inspector. With cumbersome wit.'

Stainger had arrived behind Leonard in time to hear Marsh and to be embarrassed. The rest of the room had fallen silent. Marsh's sigh of exasperation could have been a death rattle.

None could ignore it. Few had the courage to look on the lifeless throat. From the window, Somers-Barclay staged a quiet cough.

Leonard ignored both senior officers and went to the blackboard. He took a fresh yellow stick of chalk, broke it in half and wrote in large capitals across the top.

PICCOLO

Then, without looking back at the silent room and seemingly unaware of the tension, he wrote another name beneath the first.

BOLT?

Done, he laid the chalk, so precisely, in the board's rack, dusted his hands and turned to the room. Then, with the theatricality of a confident don, he added to the moment by removing his spectacles, rubbing them on his green silk handkerchief, putting them back on and replacing the handkerchief in his top pocket. After that, his voice should have boomed, or snaked through the trail of the superintendent's. Instead, Leonard's voice was as it always was. The voice of a quiet satirist.

'The murdered man was known as Piccolo. That may not be his given name. But he was known to his closest friends in this city as Piccolo. Mean anything to anyone?'

There was much headshaking. It meant something to a middle-aged constable with a broad Somerset accent.

'Probably pretty obvious, sir.'

'Go on.'

'Well, sir. Piccolo is, well, Piccolo. Some of these crusties give themselves names. Some of them do things, sir. My guess, this one played the whistle, sir. You know? The piccolo?'

Leonard nodded his thanks.

'Precisely. Which is why I'm saying we may not know his real name. But we do know what he was called. By some at least.'

Marsh's voice came through the murmurings and the answered telephones.

'Bolt? What is this Bolt?'

Leonard did not look at Marsh. He addressed the whole room.

'Bolt is a Don't Know. It's the name of someone who may be involved. It was a name Piccolo knew and a name Piccolo repeated. Questions?'

Stainger was about to speak. Marsh did.

'Are we to know the source of these names?'

The whole room, including the constable hanging onto a call, turned to the blackboard. Leonard blinked.

'One of the travellers. That's all I can say for the moment.'

Somers-Barclay, his eye on Marsh's expression, kept the laughter from his comment but there was enough scepticism, he hoped, to impress Superintendent Marsh.

'With respect, sir, are crusties reliable sources?'

Stainger was looking at the ground. Marsh at Leonard. Somers-Barclay at Marsh. Leonard's voice was just tighter than it had been. Just right.

'No source is reliable, Sergeant, until so proven.'

He walked away from the board. The drama done. The rest of the room knew what to do. Lane was the duty inspector. He had them doing it inside two minutes. Marsh had gone. Somers-Barclay with him. Stainger walked along the corridor with Leonard. They paused outside the superintendent's room. He did not smile.

'This is good stuff, is it, James?'

Leonard was looking at his shoes. The hummed aria avoiding a crescendo. He nodded, his head bobbing in time to the music, to the rise and fall of his brown heels.

'Four-star.'

'What about Bolt?'

Leonard looked up. Odd question.

'Why?'

'I don't understand Bolt. You put Piccolo on top and question-marked Bolt. But Bolt's a name. Piccolo? Well, it could be anything.'

'Yes.'

'Do I need to know your source on this?'

The hum was back. The bobbing head.

'Not yet, sir.'

'OK. Nice one. So far. Just watch your back.'

He was gone almost as he said it. Leonard looked back along the corridor to the office door behind which Marsh had bivouacked his raiders. He would watch his back.

The room at the top of the building was almost empty. A lanky ginger-haired constable, more absorbed in the menu than in his cholesterol count, was the only other officer in the canteen. Steak Pie. Spanish Quiche. Pasties. Chicken Curry With Rice. All £2.10.

Sergeant Jack was in the corner with two coffees. She was stirring sugar into hers and he wiped his spectacles.

'What's Jack? Jacqueline?'

'Jack.'

'What?'

'Jack, sir. Sergeant Jack, sir.'

He slipped on his specs.

'What's the first bit?'

'Madeleine.'

'Oh.'

She smiled. He slipped off his jacket and hung it over the back of the chair next to him. It was hot in the canteen, but the waistcoat stayed buttoned.

'My mother taught French.'

'Fond memories.'

'I hope not.'

He sipped. The coffee was better than in most canteens.

'Tell me. What happened about Rainbow Wood?'

'Nothing. Everything's gone. Our files. Coroner's. The lot.'

'Gone where?'

She shrugged. The hair was still in a severe bun, but a fewa strands were here and there. The ginger constable kept glancing over and dribbled fried egg down his chin when he saw Leonard eyeing him. She would have the effect on most men. Leonard looked back.

'Is that unusual here? Is there a use-by date on the files, then they're off to the burner?'

'On some. But not –'

'On unsolved murders.'

'No, sir.'

Something had been puzzling him. The unanswered questions.

'Tell me. How did you remember his name when no one else did? And how do you seem to know so much about it and the travellers? You can't have been here that long.'

'I haven't. I was still a student then. Coincidence, really. I did criminology.'

'A degree? Where? Bristol?'

'No, sir. Teeside. It's a poly. Or was. It was the only place I could get into that did it. I did my dissertation on violence against vagrants in affluent societies. This was my home, so I did it here. The living's easy at home.'

'But there was nothing available on Rainbow Wood, surely?'

She finished her coffee and pushed her cup away.

'Right. But I had a friend who knew something about it.'

'Boyfriend?'

He wasn't sure why he had asked. She was. They all did. Whoever they were.

'At the time.'

'How did he know about it?'

'He was a reporter on the local rag. He knew as much as anyone. Which wasn't much.'

'On Teeside?'

'No. Here. In fact he was the one who called him Peter.'

'Was this Steven Reece?'

He was quiet, this inspector. But he knew things others did not. Others who had been about for longer.

'That's right. I met him in London. He'd got out of journalism.'

'Gone into PR.'

'You knew him, sir?'

Leonard shook his head. But he wanted to.

'D'you still see him?'

'No. Not him. He was already getting into Armani and poser phones even when I knew him. Not my style. Anyway, there were other complications.'

Leonard did not ask what they were. But he still wanted to meet Reece.

'Did he ever mention someone or something called the Piccolo man?'

'Not that I can remember. Don't forget it was ten years back.'

'Where would I find him now? Discreetly.'

'Until a year ago, which was the last time I heard from him, he was in Docklands. A converted warehouse with his Jacuzzi, a passion for harpsichord music and a nice young man called Warren.'

Leonard looked puzzled.

'Warren?'

She was laughing but only with her eyes.

'It's called coming out, sir.'

'I see.'

'He's not hard to find. His office is in Covent Garden.'

Leonard had an idea.

'Somers-Barclay seems to have got himself involved in the, er, in the more administrative side of this investigation. How would you feel if I asked for you to give me a hand?'

'Fine. It'll beat door-knocking.'

'OK. Now leave that to me.'

He was scribbling with a pencil stub on a page of a tiny notebook. He tore out the sheet and handed it to her.

'That's my home number. And my address. Why don't you

get yourself an away day to London and look up your old friend?'

'And then what? I mean, sir, what's it got to do with, well, this present case?'

Leonard took his pocket watch and peered at it. Things to be done.

'I'm not sure. But I want to know everything he can remember. I want to know why he thinks nothing much appeared in his paper and, most of all, I want to know if he thinks there were those who tried to kill off the story. If there were people, I want to know who they were.'

'So you do think there's a connection.'

'Not yet. But there might be. And just one more question for him, I want to know how he got his job.'

'That bit's easy, sir. I can tell you that. There's a man called Montague James.'

Leonard was nodding.

'Sorry, sir. You know that, don't you?'

'Yes. I know James offered him a job, but I don't know the circumstances of the offer. Had he known him long? Did it come out of the blue? Did he turn it down? Were there any pressures on him?'

She looked up at the clock.

'That's a lot for a casual call on an old friend, sir.'

'I'll leave that to you. This is official, but then, like most things on this one, it isn't.'

Leonard got up. He had an appointment on the ground floor. They were walking through the club room, with its shuttered bar and caricatures of former officers, when something the sergeant said stopped him.

'What was that you said about Peter and Reece? About him giving him the name. Was it ever confirmed?'

'The hippie, sir? No. No one knew his name, or at least I've never seen it on a file. No, sir, Peter was a name one of the other hippies suggested. It didn't come to anything. Wasn't even true. But Steven, in the best tradition of tabloids, called him Peter.'

Two officers were coming along the corridor. Casually dressed. Each carrying small bags, one of them a towelling tracksuit top. They smiled their good mornings and turned into the doorway where Leonard was leaning against the wall. It led to a sauna. She was waiting.

'Listen, Sergeant, I want you to ask him one question above all others. Did he ever really know the name of the hippie?'

'Wouldn't it be in newspaper cuttings if he had?'

He was nodding, going away along the corridor. His voice came back to her as a mumble through an almost inaudibly hummed and unidentifiable baritone.

'It wasn't. But if he did know, why wasn't it? Mm?'

He turned. He'd remembered she hadn't been at the morning meeting.

'Oh, and check the MIR blackboard. A couple of good names for your friend.'

Nineteen

The room below was narrow. Very little furniture other than a couple of steel frame chairs and a long table against the left-hand wall. On the table was a computer. On the door the notice said PIRSY. Photographic Image Retrieval System. The heavily built constable at the screen was sweating. His short-sleeved white uniform shirt was already damp. He eyed Leonard in his tweed waistcoat with something approaching disbelief.

'Morning, sir. 'Nother scorcher.'

Leonard dabbed at his lips with a silk handkerchief in sympathy.

'To hell with the formers, eh?'

The constable, whose detested brother-in-law fanned the

other side of Radstock, laughed, his head rocking in undisguised agreement.

'Have to wash their Volvos with slurry.'

'Which is how they can afford them, eh?'

The constable put even more into it this time and the coroner's officer, passing on his way to claim yet another DOA from the Bath United Hospital, smiled. Harry would have made a good fairground barker. Harry was nodding his approval of any remark against the farming community and, by implication, the brother-in-law, especially when it came from a senior officer. This one was all right, Harry would tell them in the club later that day. Got his head screwed on, even if he don't look it.

'What can I do you for, sir? Lovely fresh villains? Ram-raiders to order?'

Leonard pointed to the machine and tucked his jacket under his arm. The computer was new to him. He had seen similar systems before, but this one, as far as he knew, was restricted to the immediate area.

'How far does that thing go back?'

The constable liked being asked questions. Showed not everyone knew everything as they would have you believe.

'Depends what's been put in, you know, sir. Computers are OK and that, but they're not Lassie the Wonder Dog. They won't do everything. Fact is, sir, computers will only tell you what you or someone else has put in. You got me, sir?'

'Ten years back?'

'Could be, sir, could be. You give me a name or a crime and I'll fetch you a photo of the blighter if we got one on record, and in some cases I can give you a whole album of blighters who got similar previous. As long as it's on our patch. Otherwise you have to go into the National Computer. You got me, sir?'

Leonard nodded. Enough humouring. He had a name.

'Try Bolt.'

'That a name, is it, sir?'

'Yes. B-O-L-T. Bolt.'

The constable knew his system. He tapped in a four-figure code as a password. It was the same number as that on his shoulder tabs. Always was. The colour monitor did everything but wish him a nice day. He then went into surnames. There were two Bolts. Brothers. Reg and Brian. From their pictures, which were better than anything that had ever come from a photo-booth, they were almost twins. The DOB column said they were fourteen months apart. The constable was reciting their form.

'GBH, ABH. Taking and driving away. Receiving. Receiving again. And what's this? Oh, I like this one, Causing An Affray. Haven't heard one of those for some time. Well, sir, you've got yourself a couple of likely lads.'

'Addresses?'

'Here we go, sir.'

He read them off.

'Mind you, sir, young Reg won't be giving much bother. Look there, sir.'

The constable pointed to the information column.

'They got him in Shepton.'

'Shepton prison.'

'Not the prettiest cage in the world, sir. But then he's not the prettiest parrot, is he, sir?'

Leonard made another weak joke about farmers, got a guffaw of thanks for his trouble from Harry and in turn nodded his thanks and headed for the trophy-cum-conference room, which had been taken over by Marsh. The Superintendent was not there, which suited Leonard. He saw Lane, who was running the MIR for the moment, and told him that he was borrowing Sergeant Jack for a couple of days. Lane rubbed the end of his beaten nose and grinned.

'Didn't take long, did it?'

'Any problems?'

'No, no. Just that every two-pip willy's been trying to get a leg over that one since she arrived.'

Leonard smiled.

'You can tell the troops she's in safe hands.'

Lane did not make the obvious comment. He did, however, point his pencil along the corridor.

'Bit of advice, Jimbo. Marsh likes to know what everyone's doing.'

'I'll have routine inquiries written on the door.'

'You'll have to do better than that. Just a bit of advice, that's all. Just watch . . .'

'My back?'

'And your balls. He's a balls specialist.'

The telephone on Lane's desk burbled and Leonard looked at the spare one. The line light was blank. Vacant. He wondered how Josie was. For the moment, he'd forgotten all about her. He had thought of telling Lane. He trusted Lane. He'd thought of telephoning but remembered that he'd told her not to answer. He would anyway. She would recognize his voice on the answer machine. He dialled his private number. It was engaged. He redialled. Engaged. He did not wait for Lane to finish his call. He headed for the door and leapt the backstairs two at a time.

It took him ten minutes. The front door was open. Josie had gone.

He could smell the soap and the steam from the shower. The towel she had used was damp. The light in the spare bedroom was on and the nightshirt she had worn was folded on the pillow. She had not bothered about a plate, and the stale flakes from yesterday's croissants were scattered across the wooden draining board. He could smell her. But she had gone. So had the spare key from the dresser.

Twenty

He saw the fire-eater by the Pump Room. He hadn't seen Josie. Or said he hadn't. He laughed when Leonard asked him about the Piccolo man.

'Means nothing, friend.'

'You mentioned it.'

'You think I did.'

'I know you did.'

'Then be content. You know something you did not. I'm not a jigsaw.'

He was wandering off towards a sniggering group on the bench. It was not good to be seen to be talking to policemen.

The nearest of the addresses Harry had come up with was not far away. A shabby street. Once smart but never grand. On one side a Christadelphian hall. Still waiting, but only the bailiff coming. The Percy Boys Club. Shuttered. He ignored two teenagers easing the locked door of an old Golf GTi and found what he was looking for. Peeling where it had been painted. Black where it was damp. There were eight bells by the door. He tried the number that should have been the younger Bolt's. He tried above and below. He was about to give up when the door opened and a thin youth in jeans and sweat-stained T-shirt came out. His head down. Dank hair. Leonard put his foot in the gap before the youth could close it.

'You know someone called Bolt?'

The youth shook his head. Did not reply. Walked on. No hurry. Ignored him.

The stairway stank. Mildew, urine, tossed wrappers, cans and spilled dustbins – a cheap place to rent. Health inspectors did not spend much time in this part of the city. The Christadelphians across the way had chosen well. Flat Four had a padlock as well as a Yale. The padlock was secure although there were signs that it had been forced a few times. The door was on a landing and Leonard looked down into the patch of grass and rubble below. The syringe count was enough to start a bottle bank. It was the view of The Roman City of Aquae Sulis that somehow escaped the Leicas. He banged on the other door. Flat Five. He heard a noise, then nothing. Banged again. Same noise and then the door opened to a crack. The chain looked feeble.

The woman was in her twenties and ugly. She had spots where there should have been dimples. There was a gap where most people had top teeth. She did not say anything. Just looked. Leonard did his best to smile without sharing her halitosis.

'I'm looking for Brian. D'you know him?'

She nodded.

'Did.'

'He lives over there, doesn't he?'

She followed his eye to the padlocked door.

'Did.'

'Not any more?'

'No.'

'Do you know where I can find him?'

She closed the door. He did not see any point banging his head against it. Instead he made for the street. He would have liked a shower. As he walked he could smell the stairwell in his clothes, his hair, his hands where he had tried the padlocked door. He walked with head bent and deep in thought. He wondered about Bolt. Was there a connection? Was it a common name? Why hadn't he checked the obvious?

Sergeant Jack had gone. The ginger-haired constable was in the MIR updating contact numbers on the blackboard at the far end. He still had dried egg yolk on his chin. Leonard took him to one side, told him what he wanted and then went along to see Marsh. He was out. Stainger wasn't.

'Seen these?'

The Superintendent tossed across a sheaf of statements. MG

9, an updated witness list, with MG 11, statements. Leonard eyed them coldly. He would get to the gates and St Peter, and Stainger, standing behind him, would want Leonard to fill out an MG file. Stainger believed in files.

'Ten officers have been through most of those crusties with a fine-tooth comb. And they could do with it. Nothing. Most of what they say is made up. It's bullshit. Ten officers. That's twenty-five per cent of our strength on this one, James, and all bullshit.'

'Some of them know something. I've talked to them. They're frightened. Some of them.'

'Look, James, I've known these bastards for years. They're frightened of anything that pays a day's work and may be investigating their benefit claims. You know why they have so many bloody dogs? Go on. D'you know?'

Leonard gazed at the ceiling. He knew what was coming. He'd let Stainger burn out.

'Well, I'll tell you, James. They try to get the DSS to pay them an allowance to feed the damned things. That's the strength of these bastards, James.'

'They still could know something.'

'And you think that would bring a smile to the CPS?'

Leonard knew that nothing brought a smile to the Crown Prosecution Service other than a scene-of-crime confession before twenty reliable, non-constabulary witnesses and the murder weapon in one hand and a guilty plea in the other. But Stainger had not finished.

'Put them in the box and a halfwit straight out of law school would have them thrown out in ten seconds as unreliable witnesses. Forget them, James. Whoever your Bolt is, whatever he is, you'll have to seek him out yourself. This is Bath, not Hill Street Blues.'

Outside it was worse than hot. The traffic fumes hung over the city and the local radio station had attempted to fry an egg on the stones in front of the abbey. They had not succeeded but, when Leonard walked by, the too-cheerful presenter, complete with headphones that kept slipping and inane comments which did not, was drawing a bigger crowd than the buskers. Leonard tugged at his waistcoat, looked at his pocket watch and headed for Woods.

The restaurant was packed and Leonard was heading out again when Selsey came in. He had a grin on his face and concern in his eyes.

'You do realize, James lad, that you're looking at a mined man. You realize that, don't you?'

'Horse troubles?'

Selsey bobbed his head and took Leonard's arm, sat him at his usual corner table in the window and within thirty seconds was pouring Chablis.

'I've got more in bets on than the overdraft on this place.'

'Is that wise?'

'Course it isn't wise. But . . .'

Selsey's smile reached his eyes.

'You're going to have to come with me. To the course. We'll have a bottle or two and then see this through like men.'

'You never go to flat races.'

'That's why we've got to be brave.'

Leonard sipped. Relaxed. Eyed Selsey over his glass.

'Ever hear of a man called Bolt?'

'Didn't he do something in the films or some such thing?'

'Not that one. This one lives or lived in Bath. You don't know the name around here?'

The waitress with the small bottom and the short skirt had taken an order at the next table. Selsey tapped the table. Anyone else would have been ignored or scolded. Selsey wasn't rude. Erratic. Eccentric. Never rude.

'Know someone called Bolt?'

She shook her head.

'Ask the police. They know everything.'

She made for the kitchen and the already-fraught lunchtime chef. Selsey shrugged.

'There you are. Mind you, you could try your friend.'

'Who's that?'

'The wonderful Mrs Bowles. She knows everyone. Mind you, she says she doesn't, but she does.'

'If you don't know, why should she?'

'Ah, James lad, you no savvy. I think I know everyone and maybe everyone thinks they know me. But we're both wrong. H. Bowles, widow of this parish, is a name kleptomaniac. You know there are people she's never heard of but she knows them. She flits through the social scene of this city and everyone tells her something.'

'Why?'

'Because she's not available. She's supposed to be because she's on her own. This city doesn't understand that.'

'Wives do.'

'Bit of a social philosopher, is it?'

'No. When you're on your own, you think you know what other people are thinking. It's called being sensitive to moods and nuances.'

Selsey finished his wine.

'I wouldn't know. I'm a happily married man. And simple.'

He stood up.

'I even dribble to prove it.'

He walked to the bar and came back with the telephone directory. Plonked it in front of Leonard.

'So simple, I stick to the obvious. There you are, James lad. Bolt. It'll be under B.'

He smiled, waved a hand and headed for the kitchens. There were forty-two Bolts in the directory – each of them law-abiding.

Twenty-One

In the police station, there was an afternoon air that the investigation had come to a standstill. The arrival of Superintendent Marsh had added a different authority. It was a good system. Cope. Get the investigation going. When it is clear there will not be an early arrest, then bring in artillery. New questions. Needled pride. It works. But inside twenty-four hours it was clear that even Marsh's crown and rank on the head of the investigation's wiring diagram was not going to bring forward mislaid witnesses, angles that had been forgotten, evidence overlooked. Already the MIR was piled with files and reports. The computer screen was dancing with names, addresses, MG numbers, cross-references and columns of completed inquiries.

The lady who worked in Customs and Excise had been questioned and re-questioned. She had been jogging to work. Doctor's orders, or so she said. All the way from the other side of Sion Hill, along Church Street, Brock Street, down the hill. She had, as she always did, rested by the Cross Bath to get her breath. Early in the morning, but one or two of her colleagues (she was quite senior) got in very early in the summer (and away early for school pick-up and swimming in the afternoon). She rested so as not to arrive at the office in a state of near-collapse. Appearances, you know. Especially in her position (at her age, thought Somers-Barclay, who had questioned her). She had been standing, hands on hips, deep-breathing and counting her pulse and sightlessly facing the black grille in the wall of the bath. It was not for some seconds that she saw, or noticed, the body. She had peered through the railing, thought it maybe nothing more than a drunk and had gone on to work, washed, changed into office clothes, thought about it some more and dutifully called the police. She didn't really want to get involved. But she recognized her duty.

The bag Leonard believed existed remained a heading on a blank file. Bags had been found. One in suspicious circumstances. That had been exploded by an ever-cautious squad more concerned with terrorism than police evidence. Missing Persons had come up with nothing to link the body with their files and there was no evidence that he would ever be indentified.

Four hundred and thirteen people had been interviewed. Nothing had come of those interviews that would justify four hundred and thirteen report forms other than the necessary elimination process.

Forty-eight officers had each worked twelve hours a day. Some of them more. The desk officers had co-ordinated more criminal evidence in less than a week than the whole district would normally pull together inside six months. The result: an unidentified body remain tagged, sliced open, stitched up and bagged in one of what the Screaming Skull called his ice trays. That afternoon in Manvers Street, the most productive activity in the MIR could have been pencil sharpening and reading the *Chronicle's* headline. According to the paper, there was no new move in police probe. Shorthand, but about right. In Lane's words to Leonard, the inquiry was dead in the water.

Stainger was bogged down in committee reports and restructuring proposals. But, when he saw Leonard in the corridor, he wanted to talk the whole case through. To Leonard's mind, corridors were for whispered plotting not quiet discussion. The one point he raised, Stainger tossed aside.

'You're obsessed by that Rainbow Wood affair. Seemingly you've been off on your own on this one. It won't do, James. I don't know what your previous masters thought, but, I can tell you, I'm in the business of structured policework. Teamwork. Leave the Lone Ranger stuff to the box, will you?'

'But what if there's a connection?'

'Then it will show up through this inquiry. Not by reopening something that came to nothing in the first place and which would be even more impossible now. Ten years ago we knew sod all about sod all. We still don't.'

'Coincidence.'

'No. Fact. The chances are that Rainbow Wood was a family affair. Personally I think this one was. But thinking's no damned good to the CPS. If we get a nick, then it's got to have more boxes of evidence than you can shake a stick at. You know that. I know that. Everyone knows that. I don't want a nose poke on this one, James. I've already had the Chief Constable taking an interest. As if I hadn't enough to do.'

The door slammed. Leonard leaned against the wall wondering why the Chief Constable would be taking a direct interest. It certainly was not a novelty. There had been three murders during the past ten days in Bristol alone. But then Bath was not Bristol. The cage-rattling was pretty predictable. Leonard was not about to give up on the Rainbow Wood killing.

He wondered how Sergeant Jack was getting on.

He tried the coroner's officer. He was out. His downstairs office telephone was covered with yellow stickers. Everyone wanted the coroner's officer. Leonard did what he always did when he wanted to think, to move on from a blocked investigation; he went for a walk. Perhaps he hadn't intended to find himself in Westgate Street. But he did anyway and after a quick inquiry at the desk of the *Chronicle* he was ushered up to Dover's office.

The editor waved him to a chair and carried on talking to a tall, slim girl. The city edition had just gone. They were discussing the next day's prospectus. She was writing a leader on law and order in the city and kept eyeing Leonard. She would have liked to have talked to him. She did not. As she went, Dover's secretary, a lady who had seen it all before, arrived with the tea. Dover sipped, watched Leonard rubbing at his spectacles and waited.

'I saw your headline this morning.'

'It was accurate. You haven't a clue who killed him.'

'I also read the bit about there being no connection with Rainbow Wood. Who said that?'

Dover put down his tea and picked up the city edition. There were only two editions each day. To him, this was the one that mattered. It was the one which always got response from readers, especially those who thought they mattered more than others. The story was on the front page. Just five paragraphs and that had been a struggle. No new moves. Maybe no probes. But still worth page one.

'Presumably your people.'

'You asked them?'

'I don't know. I haven't spoken to the reporter.'

He did know. The morning meeting shortly after seven-thirty had produced a line from the news editor. She had been at a reception. 'A senior officer', as she liked to describe her source, had raised the point that, if there was any suggestion that there was a connection with the murder ten years ago, then it was a false connection. When she mentioned this at Dover's news conference meeting, he recognized it for what it was. Someone trying to tell them something. Senior officers did not make casual remarks during a murder inquiry. Maybe the *Chronicle* was being used. For the moment he did not mind. He would find out later. Maybe. And maybe, if he did, then that would be the real story. Leonard finished cleaning his spectacles. Slipped them on.

'Between you and me, I'd like to know.'

'Like to? Or need to know?'

'Both.'

Leonard was gazing across the room, through the window at the stained glass on the other side of the road. He was humming, madrigally, beneath his breath. Dover stretched his large frame and clasped his hands behind his head.

'Tell me why. Between you and me, you understand.'

'I think there may be a connection. I think also that it is unlikely that we will ever find the evidence to take the connection to court. But, if I do find it, then I might find out who killed both or, more likely, who killed this one.'

'But you're suggesting that there are two investigations going.'

Leonard blinked.

'I'm not suggesting anything. I simply don't want anyone else to be killed.'

'You think someone else might be?'

'Until a murderer is caught, that is always possible.'

'Likely?'

'Possible.'

Dover turned to the centre drawer in the old wooden desk. He took an envelope and shook cuttings on his desk.

'Rainbow Wood. Mostly young Reece's stuff. You know what I find odd? Reece was very thorough. But there's no mention of what happened to the body.'

'A knife. All very nasty.'

Dover shook his head.

'Didn't mean that. What happened to the body once your lot had given up.'

'Officially, we haven't.'

'You know what I mean.'

'Normally . . .'

Leonard paused. He was about to say that in normal circumstances, if there were ever normal circumstances in a murder, and after a reasonable time, the coroner would have released the body to relatives for burial or even cremation.

'But it wasn't normal, was it? You never found out who dunnit nor who he was. So, if you didn't know who he was, then there was no one to claim him.'

Leonard was back with his unidentifiable madrigal.

'It doesn't work that way. Not necessarily.'

'I suppose your files will show you. But, well, there you are. I thought it odd. That one sentence or par that would have been a line under the investigation.'

Leonard looked across the room. The cuttings were photocopies.

'Is there any chance that you could let me have a copy of Reece's cuttings?'

Dover smiled. He did not do business with the police. He would never have handed over unpublished material. He would never have told the police things he had heard in confidence. He was not a policeman. He was an editor, an impartial one. Dover wanted to keep it that way. But these cuttings were what the paper's lawyers would have described as being in the public domain. Leonard could have gone to the central library and maybe found them. Anyway, it was always nice to know that a policeman owed you. He took a similar envelope from the still-open drawer. He had taken the copies himself. He would rather that the rest of the staff did not know what he was doing. He handed the buff envelope to Leonard.

'Here. Thought they might be useful. Between you and me?'

Twenty-Two

There was no news from Sergeant Jack. He had told no one about her trip to London. The MIR had only one message. The Home Office pathologist, Griffiths the Screaming Skull, had left a third message. Would Inspector Leonard do him the honour of returning his flaming calls? The constable at the other end of the line enjoyed the verbatim message. Leonard had forgotten. He dialled a Cardiff number. Cursed. Made another call. Griffiths was at the hospital in Bath that day. Leonard left the phone-booth in Kingsmead Square and picked up a taxi. Ten minutes later he was in the mortuary gallery waiting for Griffiths to finish with the innards of some poor unfortunate who'd keeled over on a zebra crossing.

Washed up, the Screaming Skull was in no better mood. In spite of his reputation, he valued the lives of others.

'Bloody gracious of you to show up, Leonard. Bloody gracious.'

'I'm sorry, I got your first message and I called you back. But, well, it slipped my mind.'

'You might at least have the decency to come up with a dramatic excuse.'

Griffiths wasn't smiling. But he might have done if persuaded.

'If you really want to know, I was waiting for the Test Match score.'

'That's all right, then.'

He was persuaded. He pulled a pink file from a pending tray and opened it like a schoolmaster reviewing a recalcitrant's term. Ran a silver propelling-pencil tip down neatly word-processed paragraphs and looked up.

'Here it is. Your friend was full of heroin. Thought you should know.'

Leonard was surprised but did not insult Griffiths by asking if he were sure. Of course he was. It was not the sort of thing to have doubts about. But, at the start, there had been little sign of heroin. His question threw the pathologist.

'Self-injected?'

A pulse in the bald dome went from an easygoing sixty to sixty-four. Not much. Enough.

'Why do you ask?'

'My information was that he wasn't a user.'

Griffiths turned a page, found another paragraph. He sat back in the plastic hospital chair. The dark eyebrows – apart from tufts in the flared nostrils, the only visible hair on his skull – twitched.

'Could be. Could be. The arms were bruised. Bit punctured. But they weren't old ones. He certainly doesn't appear to have been a greenkeeper. Not much spiking.'

'So he could have been.'

'Stuffed? I don't know.'

'Don't know or can't say?'

'Amounts to the same thing. What I do know is there was enough in him to give him a street value per kilo.'

Leonard was thinking of another name. Another mystery.

'Were you here ten years ago?'

The Screaming Skull snorted. Closed the file in front of

him. Tapped with the silver pencil. Tapped out his response. Ta-tay. Ta ta ta-tay. Ta.

'Aha. The long-gone crusty. Yes?'

Leonard nodded. Wondered why Griffiths had not raised it himself. Wasn't his job to do so? Most Home Office pathologists stuck to their jobs.

'Rainbow Wood. Remember?'

The skull shook.

'No. But I know about it. There were four of us covering this area in those days. I was in Cardiff then. Always have been, you see. I came over at the tail end.'

'Was there something special about it? To make you remember.'

'No. Simply an unsolved murder. Except for one up at Lansdown, that's not something that happens in this smarmy place.'

'You don't like it here.'

'Don't I?'

'It didn't sound that way.'

'Maybe. Too bland, you see. Oh, people trot out the isn't-it-lovely stuff. But once you've seen one crescent, once you've seen one bit of Bath stone held together by a mortgage, then you've seen it all. I've sliced more interesting thighs.'

Leonard looked at the closed file. Griffiths was in no hurry.

'What happened to the body?'

'Dog food.'

'What's that mean?'

'We got rid of it. At least, the coroner did.'

'It was here?'

The eyes rolled beneath the bushy brows and disappeared for a moment.

'Well, there's only so much room in the deep-freeze.'

'What happened?'

Griffiths turned down the corners of his mouth. He knew, but so what?

'From memory, you people never established who he was. Right?'

Leonard nodded. The Screaming Skull shrugged. Obvious, was it not?

'Well, that meant there was no one to release the body to. You know? No grieving loved ones and all that shit. Anyway, see, as the poor bugger had been stuck and had a murder sign on the end of his toe, well, the coroner had to hang on to him. But you can only do that for so long.'

'So you kept him in the trays?'

Griffiths got up. Headed for the door. He talked as he led Leonard through the back corridor and a door marked bluntly that admittance was strictly limited to authorized personnel.

'Not the trays, Inspector. You can only do that for so long. We get about eight hundred stiff ones through here every year. We're not bus conductors, you know, boy. No use shouting "move along there, room for one more on top" because there isn't and anyway, they can't hear you, now can they?'

They reached the end of a long narrow room. It was cold. Griffiths opened the lid of a large chest freezer.

'No, you see, Mr Leonard, we keep our long-term guests in these.'

He opened the lid. Inside, three frosted black bags. Griffiths reached down and unzipped the top one as a valet might a suit-carrier. The face was colourless. Frozen. Crude stitches where Griffiths's saw had removed the top of the skull.

'Now, look at this poor sod. Been here too long. About time we sent her home. Trouble is, Inspector, as far as you people tell us, she has no home to go to. Maybe that's why she came this way in the first place.'

He grinned at Leonard. It was not one of his best grins. Not much enthusiasm in it.

'She'll be going out to tender, as they say in these modern times, as soon as the coroner can find his pen. And that's what happened to your Rainbow Wood friend.'

'When was that?'

'Five years ago.'

'So you kept him five years?'

'Arithmetic your strong point, Mr Leonard?'

'Where did he go?'

'Now that is a good question. You see, I was interested. Casually, you understand. So I thought I'd look at the file. Nothing of the sleuth in me. I'm interested in the guts. I'm interested to know what people have been eating before they die. Tells you a great deal. Can even tell you where they have been. Some little bastard's got king prawn biriani churning away, then you can bet he hasn't been to McDonald's for his last fish supper. See?'

Leonard said nothing. Waited.

'Well, I looked up his file and tell me what?'

'There wasn't one.'

Griffiths paused. Peered at the unblinking eyes behind the rimless spectacles.

'Exactly, Inspector. Gone. And, when I asked, no one knew. Something to do with computer transfer, they said.'

'And was it?'

Griffiths zipped up the body bag. Closed the lid. Shrugged.

'So they said. Thought you'd like to know.'

Griffiths saw him to the door and paused with his hand on the brass fitting.

'Oh by the by, Inspector. I had one of the forensic kiddy-winks in last evening. I've finished the final on our friend. Just a small thing. He had sheep's wool under his nails. Not much. But enough. Both hands.'

'What d'you mean by sheep's wool? Most of it is. Dyed.'

The great dome shook from side to side. The thin lip came over the upper gum. Almost a smile. His friends would have said it was one.

'Long strands.'

'A sweater? At this time of year?'

'Crusties take cold quicker than most of us.'

'What about a jacket?'

Griffiths shrugged.

'Not knowing, Mr Leonard. Not knowing. But, and only but, what about those sheepskin rugs people used to have?'

'Likely?'

'There may have been bits of grit in this. But there was so little, I'm not sure we could go into court with anything stronger than that.'

Leonard blinked. Opened the door himself.

'We've got a body. Or, at least, you have. And that's about it. Doesn't look as if we'll be bothering a judge for some time.'

Leonard was using the public telephone when he saw Somers-Barclay's friend. He was surprised when she smiled. They had never been introduced. Her voice was easygoing.

'Don't tell me you've found another one.'

He put down the telephone. There were no messages.

'Another what?'

'Body, of course. Nick tells me it's tying up the whole police station.'

Nick? So that was his name. It would be. He'd never bothered to find out. Never heard anyone call him by his first name. Odd.

'Investigations like this do. Tell me, how's the cardiac-arrest business?'

'Healthy. Why, feeling faint?'

He ignored her mischief, but could not ignore her eyes. Leonard believed junior hospital doctors looked sleepless, baggy-eyed, hung-over. She sparkled. He wondered what she was on.

'Tell me, how long do your records go back?'

'Since they were computerized, not very long at all. And they're confidential so, as far as you're concerned, they don't go back at all.'

'Why d'you say that?'

'Because you're a policeman. Policemen never ask anything without an ulterior motive.'

She laughed.

'Don't worry, doctors are the same. And, anyway, Nick already asked. 'Bye.'

'Wait a minute. One thing you can tell me. Were all the files put on computer?'

'I don't know. Presumably there might have been a bit of a sort-out, but the important ones, or the unresolved ones, would have been. Why?'

Leonard ignored the question.

'What would have happened to any file that was dumped?'

'I really don't know. I save lives not rain forests. But anything that was dumped would go into the incinerator. Anything confidential that isn't shredded does.'

He had another question. But her bleeper went. She smiled, excused herself and headed for a grey telephone on the wall by the main entrance. He did not wait.

Leonard found a cab on the hospital rank and sat back as it mournfully trailed three coachloads of tourists towards the city. On the paths, mothers pushed prams, a crocodile of infants waited to cross and grandparents just waited. Normal people. Normal lives. Normal dying. He felt glum. Most of what he thought he knew was worthless. An obscenely murdered man found in a Roman bath by a jogging Customs and Excise office worker. The buskers, the beggars, the mongrel-tuggers had said nothing. The drunk had shivered in fear. The door hangings, the reams of statements, the dug-out informers had shaken not a leaf of information. The mighty, the movers, the shakers, all had whispered let it be. Only Josie had known his name. But now she too had gone. Where? He didn't know this city. The people who did said nothing.

Suddenly he sat up. Of course! He called out to the driver, paid him off and walked back along the way they had come.

Staring from the taxi window, Leonard had been in a half-daze as he tried to clear his mind. Somewhere he had seen something that clicked, but the taxi had been a hundred and fifty yards on before he realized why. He was now standing in front of it. Goldings. Monumental Masons & Funeral Directors.

If a coroner released a body, someone had to bury it or arrange a cremation. The local authority might well do what other councils did with unclaimed or unnamed bodies. In years gone by, thought Leonard, they were known as paupers' graves. Now there were certain arrangements for incineration. Discreetly burn the cadaver. Satisfy the death certificate and the coroner's release form. When Sergeant Jack got back, he would have her check the registrar's office. But, for the moment, Leonard was off on his own. If he were right, it just might be the case that the body was not cremated. If he were right, it was because someone had deliberately not claimed it. But that someone might just want to have one of the dead remembered. Someone somewhere always knew someone.

A Person Unknown file meant nothing more than that the person was unknown to those trying to identify the body. To someone, the chances were that the body was known.

Twenty-Three

Leonard walked into the yard. It was stacked with cut blocks and sand-coloured arches and mullions waiting to be linked in some folly of urban grandeur. An ear-muffed and goggled man, slicing through soft Bath stone, took no notice of Leonard as he walked through to the inner yard. Marble slabs were stacked along one wall. Polished pink. Polished grey. Polished white. All polished and waiting for the names of those who would never see them.

A woman came out of the low-windowed office. She was in her thirties. Small. Sturdy. Jeans much laundered beneath the dust. A T-shirt brilliantly white against the tan and stone dust of her arms.

'Can I help?'

Leonard showed her his identity card. She bent her head.

Looked at it as if there were as many forgeries as fifty-pound notes. He wondered if the freckles were real or designer dust. She twitched her nose and smiled. They were real.

'I'm trying to find some information about a local-authority burial. About five years ago.'

She cocked her head to one side.

'Mr Robert isn't here now. Out at the crem.'

She looked back through the office window at a round wooden-framed wall clock.

'Should be back in half an hour or so. He's got another one in an hour. So he'd better get a shift on.'

She chuckled. She did not expect him to see the connection. He had but did not laugh. He said he would come back. She was going back into the office when she turned.

'Wait a minute. When did you say?'

'I don't know the exact date, but about five years ago. It would have been the council.'

The head was once again on one side.

'I wonder. You sure it was council? We had a burial about then that was a bit odd. Was on the parish but then someone came up with a cheque that didn't bounce and we scratched a slab for him.'

'A what?'

'A nice headstone.'

'Who paid?'

'I'm not sure of the details – you'll have to ask Mr Robert. But I think it was something like someone paying on behalf of someone else.'

Leonard wondered who. Who would pay for a pauper's grave? Who would play agent? The woman was wandering off. Busy. Lots of dying, even in high summer. But why should she remember?

'Oh that? Easy peasy. It was my first job. I did graphic art at the poly. Couldn't get a job that paid. Then I came here on some government scheme for six months. And I stayed. Anyway, the first job Mr Robert let me loose on was this.

Simple bit of stone. Nothing fancy. But it was a first for both of us.'

'Both of you? Who else?'

'The poor drongo in the box, of course. Sorry. Bad taste. Haven't lost anyone, have you?'

Leonard shook his head. Impatient.

'No. No. Tell me, do you know who actually paid the cheque?'

'Sorry. I was just chipping. You'll have to ask Mr Robert. It'll be in the book somewhere.'

Leonard nodded as if he understood. He would have liked to see the book. He wouldn't ask this woman to let him in. He did not want to foul things for her. Business details were ever confidential unless approached from the right angle. There were few transactions more confidential than those conducted in an undertaker's parlour.

'I don't suppose you can remember what was on the headstone?'

She nodded.

'Course I can, more or less. Don't forget, this was the first time I'd ever chipped one for real. Black slate. Gold letters. Could have been an executive-built four-bedroom two-bathroom house sign. You know them?'

Leonard did not sigh. He would have liked to.

'So you do remember it. For sure?'

'Course. It's like your first time, well, you know what I mean. You'll at least remember his name. Wasn't hard, but it was all mine. And it was all a bit odd, or so I thought at the time. But then, in this business, there's a fine line between in Loving Memory and Dear Departed.'

'What was odd?'

'The words. For a start there was no Christian name, or first name or whatever they're supposed to be nowadays. Then there was no age. You normally get an age, or the year they were born and the year they died. You know?'

Leonard wanted to hurry her. She would not be. He tried.

'Yes. 1884 to 1926. That sort of thing.'

She had opened a small tin of thinly hand-rolled cigarettes. Now she was searching in her jeans, and nodding. She found what she was looking for. A creased book of matches. She tried two or three before lighting the brown liquorice paper. The smell of Golden Virginia was sweet in the warm afternoon. Leonard had taken off his spectacles. The green handkerchief was at work.

'What, eh? What exactly did it say?'

The woman blew two sharp streams of smoke down her nostrils. Picked an end of tobacco from her tongue. She closed her eyes as if reading for the poetry adjudicator.

'As I say, odd. Just said "The merry-go-round has slow'd now".'

She puffed again. Opened her eyes.

'Is that all?'

'Mm. That was it.' The smoke came out in wisps as she spoke. 'Except the name and the date.'

'Go on.'

'Bolt. 1989.'

She drew deeply. But the rollings had gone out.

Leonard had waited for Mr Robert and the empty hearse. But the waiting became too long. He promised to come back and headed for the graveyard.

He needed to see the cemetery's plot book but there was no one in the lodge. The door was locked. The day's doings were clearly at the crematorium. He walked the rows, ignoring the family tombs, the winged angels, the Celtic crosses, the dirtied crucifix. A gardener was of little help and explained that he kept the verges and the paths and not the past. It took time. But, eventually, there it was. Not tucked away in an embarrassed corner of the burial ground, but almost lost between green marble in memory of Helen who was Missed

By All and Edward Arthur Goodmayes, yet another Only Beloved Son.

The dark slate had weathered. The letters bold as ever. He read the inscription. Just as the woman had said. He read it again. Just as she had said. He read once more. Or was it just as she had said? Almost, but no, it was not. And there was one other point he had not expected. A small posy. Quite fresh. In a vase, not a jam jar.

Twenty-Four

It was early evening before Leonard got back to his flat. The answerphone had nothing to say except a hurried message from Sergeant Jack. Leonard did not want a hurried message from Sergeant Jack. He wanted a slow message from Josie. For the moment, Jack would have to do.

'Hi. It's me, sir. Bingo. We're meeting for tea. Savoy, four o'clock. Don't worry. Is this on expenses? Call you later.'

He scraped some brill into a stainless-steel dish and watched as a crouched Johnson picked at her dinner.

'What d'you think? Savoy a bit obvious?'

Johnson switched her tail. She did not care to be interrupted at supper

'A real sophisticat would have said Browns? Yes?'

If this Browns could do a sensible bit of brill, why not Browns indeed.

'On the other hand, if you're trying to impress an ex-girlfriend, especially one up from the provinces . . .?'

Why folk bothered to go up from the provinces and risk goodness knows what, Johnson was not quite clear and so continued to chew in near-silence.

Leonard switched back the answer machine and went into the bathroom. The hot water was harsh. He needed it. He wanted to know where he went from here. He did not know. He wondered about Josie. Why had she gone? She must have believed him when he said she was in danger. He should have handed her to the District. Should have told someone. Perhaps after that morning's dramatic announcement he should have confided in Stainger. Like most of his life, there were more shoulds than dids.

He opened his mouth, letting the powerjets bang against his lips and fill his throat. He spat out the water and turned off the tap. For a moment he stood staring at a form in the steamed mirror. Slim. Tallish. He supposed it was him. Nothing more to see. He wondered about the image as he began to slowly scourge his damp body on the rough towelling. What had changed? He knew what had changed him and closed his eyes, hummed seconds of nonsense into the tiny bathroom as he refused to remember. Refused to let the cruelty, the viciousness, the slaughter, the weeping, the misery come into his eyes. It was not long enough ago. Never would be. There had been talk of counselling. Not for him, for the victims who had survived. He had been a victim who had not.

In the distance he heard the telephone. Three rings. Click. *Josie*. He dropped the towel and ran into the sitting-room. *Say something. Don't go. Don't hang up. I'm here.* It was not Josie. Harriet's voice was easygoing. Amused. Almost as if she could see his nakedness. But mostly his urgency.

'Listen, Poirot, where are you? Don't forget it's culture night. Seven o'clock in the hut. Kick-off's seven-thirty. Don't stand me up. Don't forget it's black tie. Don't spit. It's charity. Byeee.'

The wretched machine snorted its contempt for a human who had obeyed its instructions and furiously spun back the message. Clicked again. Blinked its green warning light. Waited patiently for another sucker.

Leonard arrived at the Guildhall at five past seven. Harriet Bowles arrived at seven minutes past. Not for the first time Leonard envied females. They could wear whatever they liked.

Men could not without the branding most of them would not want.

'You look, er, well, very nice.'

'Why thank you, kind sir. My, you do a lil ol' country girl a right honour indeed. And, if I may say so, what a pleasure to see a gen'lem'n in such fine duds.'

'Simpsons via Oxfam.'

They both laughed. But he thought he was right. Soft black. The thinnest of straps. Not at all summer. Quite stunning. A waitress offered a tray. They both took orange juice. Both had been there before. June nights and warm champagne. The perils of charity recitals and balls.

The recital was predictable and unexceptional. 'The Trout'. A fish supper. Leonard remembered the Screaming Skull's cynicism. His attempt to throw Leonard. Everyone was trying that.

By the interval it was too hot. This time the orange juice was cold. Leonard tried the champagne. It was sparkling burgundy, at best. And, if it was, at its worst. Leonard put it to one side and took the orange juice Harriet handed him. The approaching voice came through like a dean's chastising an illicit gathering of his chapter.

'Harriet, my dear. Quite ravishing. Succulent.'

Montague James offered his cheek for a kiss. He was not at all put off when it was ignored. He eyed Leonard, did not offer a hand.

'Aha. Our great detective. I hear you are new to Bath.'

Leonard experienced the same sense of contempt he had once felt on first meeting a particularly arrogant lawyer. The lawyer later committed suicide. Leonard had felt no remorse.

Montague James was too perfectly groomed. His white dinner jacket was so perfectly tailored that he could not possibly have been carrying even the thinnest of credit cards, the slimmest of fountain pens, the tiniest of keys. Montague James had no need of those things. His word was his credit, his signature unnecessary and no door remained closed to him. Leonard started to answer and was distracted as Harriet murmured that she would see him later and wandered off to talk to Selsey. Selsey was tapping the *Chronicle* editor on the chest. The racing saga was obviously getting on top of him. By the looks of it, on top of Dover as well. Montague James smiled with the sincerity of a Presidential candidate.

'I didn't know policemen at my level were noticed.'

'But, my dear Mr Leonard. So modest. Of course you are noticed. I was saying to the Chief Constable only this evening how pleased we all are to know that an officer of your reputation is handling this unfortunate affair.'

'We are? Who we, Mr James?'

'Oh dear, Mr Leonard, so suspicious. This will never do. We are not the royal we. No. No, never. Or, rather, hardly ever. No, Mr Leonard, we are those who care for our city. A fine city, don't you think?'

'I do. So who are those who care for it?'

'Like-minded souls. Simple and no more than that. We find ourselves on this committee and that sub-committee. In this huddle and that discussion. But plot as we may, Mr Leonard, we do so on behalf of the city.'

'And you care about the death of a traveller?'

Montague James gave a long sniff. A sniff so powerful that he lifted his shoulders to finish it with grace.

'Frankly, Mr Leonard, I must be honest with you. No. I might try, but I could not bring myself to say that I cared one wit for the death of a traveller. I cannot identify with such creatures, so why pretend that I should mourn one's passing?'

'But you care about the investigation?'

Montague James took a glass from a pausing waitress and handed it to Leonard with one hand while removing his half-empty glass with the other. It was done and the waitress gone before Leonard realized what had happened.

'Now that, Inspector, is quite another matter. Of course we care, even the royal we cares in particular. You see, my dear, violent death ill becomes this city. In modern times, of course.'

'You mean it interferes with the image and therefore business.'

'Do I mean that? Perhaps I might. More reasonably and socially acceptable, Inspector, I mean that I do not like to see this city scared. And, before you doubt that it is, let me tell you it is so. Which is why an early arrest, as they used to say, is desirable – and, if not, well, some recognition that the dastardly fellow will be far gone and therefore it's best not to prolong the suspense by prolonging the investigation.'

Leonard was blinking. The rate quite high. He looked across at Harriet. Selsey had gathered more mourners to his plight.

'Such a beautiful girl.'

James could have been in Regency fig. He needed only to affect an eyeglass. Leonard did not answer.

'Such a pity about her husband. But then he did play with extremely dangerous friends.'

'Wasn't it a parachute accident? Something to do with charity?'

'An accident? Ah yes. An accident in such a state was inevitable, I imagine. And charity, you say? Mm. My dear Inspector, charity? Ah me, on these occasions there's always some beneficiary. Mm?'

Somewhere a bell was calling them back to the recital. James started to drift away, then paused.

'Inspector, you are a man with questions. Some I may be able to answer. Others, no. But I may set your mind nearly, if not neatly, at rest. I wonder if you would do me the honour of calling on me. Tomorrow. Six-thirty – p.m., of course.'

The amused laugh was just perceptible. He glided towards the door with slight nods towards left and right, where real or imagined gave slight bows in return.

They had suffered the rest of the recital. Leonard had switched off his mind to the music and wondered about Montague James, especially his remark about Harriet's husband. Harriet had thought him absorbed and had sat wondering why. She felt tetchy. The audience's applause had been absurd.

A scruffy performance had deserved nothing more than polite acknowledgement, not three bows. Even then, it had been the musicians who had had the grace to bow out. Now Leonard and Harriet were walking up Milsom Street, he wondering if Selsey would be back to find them a table, and she wondering why she might be so attracted to this curious orphan who hummed tunelessly to himself and who when he smiled appeared to have suddenly understood the universe.

'Well? What d'you think?'

He did not answer – not immediately. They paused to peer in a half-lit department-store window. Shop windows, almost any shop window, held a fascination for Leonard. He loved displays and, at the sight of tinselled and snowflaked windows, could almost believe in Christmas. Harriet tried again.

'Well?'

'The music? Sight reading's a very adventuresome thing during a recital.'

'You're too charitable. It was dreadful. No, I was wondering about the main attraction, or so he would think. Montague James. Isn't he smooth?'

'Slippery.'

'Greasy.'

'Not to be taken internally.'

'Nor lightly. So you did not like him?'

They had walked on and were standing opposite the wine bar. He wondered if Somers-Barclay were down there. He wouldn't mind knowing what was going on back at the ranch. He shrugged.

'I don't think he expects to be liked. Admired maybe, but not liked. He invited me for drinks.'

'You'll go.'

'Will I?'

'Of course. You're a policeman.'

She took his arm as they crossed the top road and he followed her down the stone steps. It was busy but Somers-Barclay was not there. The PR lady was. She greeted them a little too loudly and then went back to her quiet conversation with the rugby international who was fantasizing over what she might be wearing beneath her flimsy wrapover skirt. Leonard took a bottle of white wine and two glasses through to the small cellar room beneath the pavement. They were almost alone.

'He knew who I was.'

'He knows who everyone is.'

'Even policemen?'

'Especially policemen.'

Leonard poured.

'Tell me, was your husband a friend of his?'

She sipped. Put down her glass. Picked it up. Sipped again.

'Giles? First names.'

'But not a friend?'

'It doesn't follow. Why?'

'James suggested he knew him quite well.'

She looked away. Even in the summer evening heat, she managed to shiver. He stood, took off his dinner jacket, and she put it over her bare shoulders. Yet her smile was wary.

'Thanks. What did he say?'

It was Leonard's turn to sip for time.

'Not much, but he implied that your husband had some odd friends and that his accident wasn't quite an accident.'

'And you believed him?'

Leonard shook his head. He did not like this. But he wanted to know.

'No. I'm simply telling you what he said.'

She tried a laugh. It did not quite work.

'You haven't. You've implied. Not told. Come on, Poirot, you'll have to do better.'

Leonard sighed.

'OK. What he actually said, or so I remember, was that an accident in such a state was inevitable. What he meant by "such a state" I didn't know.'

'But you want to.'

'No. It has nothing to do with me.'

'But you bothered to mention it. Always on duty. That's what they say, isn't it?'

'Who "they"?'

He could see her face tightening. Even beneath the summer tan, the colour rising. He wished the conversation had never started. Too often, Leonard knew, he lacked a sense of social diplomacy, which he mistakenly believed was nothing more than a behaviour reserved for other people's dinner parties.

'Perhaps the same "they" who might wonder why you bothered to mention it.'

'No, Harriet. I did not bother to mention it. I mentioned it, but I made no special effort. Who your husband's friends were and the circumstances of his death are no business of mine.'

He was about to change the subject. To suggest supper at Woods. But she was on her feet, his jacket in his lap.

'I'm sorry, Mr Leonard. Thank you for the drink. I really must go.'

She did. Leonard was left holding his jacket and contemplating three quarters of a bottle of warming white white.

Twenty-Five

Madeleine Jack returned on the last train that night from London. She had called Inspector Leonard from Paddington and he had said that she should stop by if she wished. Within fifteen minutes of leaving the station, Madeleine Jack was sitting on Leonard's sofa watching him while he opened a new bottle of Calvados and polished two glasses.

In Manvers Street, they wondered about him. He did not look like a policeman. Not a modern one, at least. She wondered about the nineteen-forties or-fifties. Maybe that was his era. He should have had a droopy moustache and a trilby. He was tall, but slightly stooped before his time. He was slim, but not athletically. An Oxbridge don? No. His spectacles did not give him a donnish personality. He had that with or without the spectacles. Yet there was a strength in that personality which encouraged the rumours of dark events before his arrival in the West Country. He handed her the Calvados and she smiled more than thanks.

'What's funny?'

'Sorry, sir. It's, well, the natty stuff. Didn't know this was a formal interview.'

He looked down at the very correct patent-leather shoes and the black trousers. The dinner jacket and tie had long gone. His smile was warm. A couple of hours earlier it would not have been. He had not intended to upset Harriet Bowles. Now, he was back on firmer ground. Leonard understood investigations because his mind constantly analysed even the most innocent events. He would wonder at the sequence of even the most predictable events, such as the changing of traffic lights. The perfection of a soufflé. The imperfection of a truant. The cause of political disbelief. The misunderstanding of social contradictions. A police investigation was all these things and more.

Now he sat opposite and smiled once more as Johnson appeared from the open garden door and jumped on to Madeleine Jack's lap, gave the tiniest of clawing, narrowed her eyes to a contented slit and settled for a nap.

'So? Tell me all.'

Sergeant Jack sipped at the Calvados and stroked Johnson's thick fur as she talked.

She had telephoned Reece from Bath and a secretary had said that he was in a meeting and could he get back to her? Madeleine had said no. She established that there was a spare moment that afternoon in Reece's diary and told the secretary to keep it clear. The secretary pointed out that only Mr Reece could decide that. Madeleine Jack simply told the secretary that, unless he was organizing the second crossing of the Red Sea, the PR man would keep it free when she told him that

Madeleine would be in London at three-thirty. She had been right. They had been close.

'Who suggested the Savoy?'

'He did. Why?'

'A favourite haunt of his?'

'It's never unimpressive. To Steven anyway.'

'To you?'

She shrugged. She didn't see the point, but did not say so.

'Is he rich?'

'He behaves as if he is. He was always a dresser. But he's doing well and it's a business where you have to be, or at least pretend to be, top of the range. Don't you think?'

Leonard nodded. He supposed so.

'From what you say, he seems to have done well in a short space of time.'

'I wouldn't say that, sir. He was already doing quite a lot of freelance PR work when he was here. Working on the *Chronicle*, he had a lot of contacts. So he was . . .'

'Already running.'

'Right. And don't forget he's just the right age to come good. A lot of his university friends went into business in London. Quite a few of them are now in red-braces management jobs. So the old boy thing rules. OK.'

Leonard sipped and stared at the ceiling. Trying to imagine the life of Reece. Trying to think ahead. To see if they were both wasting their time on him.

'OK. What did you find out?'

'One, it really was Montague James who gave him the job. Two, it came out of the blue. Three, it was an offer he couldn't refuse. Four, and this is the most important bit, sir, he knew far more about the Rainbow Wood murder than he ever wrote.'

Leonard held up his hand. There was plenty of the night left. He wanted to start at the beginning.

'Let's start at one. Did he say why Montague James gave him the job?'

'He says that he was doing bits and pieces for him in Bath. Nothing to do with James's companies. Charity work, festivals, exhibitions. That sort of thing. And mostly for nothing.'

'Why nothing? That doesn't sound like your man.'

'Oh, it does. I knew more or less about that when we were together, remember.'

Leonard had almost forgotten.

'Go on.'

'Well, for a start Steven was really interested in local things. He liked getting involved. Made him feel a bit important, but he wasn't daft. He made quite a lot of contacts. By getting involved in the fashionable charity and arty world in Bath, within six months he knew more people who mattered in the city than the whole newsroom put together.'

'So not all altruism.'

'But not all two-faced.'

There was a spark of loyalty and affection for Reece in her voice. Leonard wondered how deep it went and if Reece knew. Or cared.

'But at what stage did Montague James give him the job in London?'

'I think when Steven was getting on to something about Rainbow Wood.'

'He told you that?'

'No, sir. He was quite evasive in the charming way he has. That's why I only think it was then. Steven's one of those people who wants to tell you everything. When he's evasive he's about as subtle as hiccups.'

'You do know him well, don't you?'

Madeleine Jack almost blushed.

'As much as his partner would allow.'

'I'd forgotten.'

'Nice boy. A lawyer. But nice.'

'What did he say happened?'

'Steven?'

'Mm.'

Madeleine Jack sipped and closed her eyes. She could see Steven Reece in his white shirt and dark-blue tropical suit. The tan as even as his teeth. The signet ring. The Pangbourne tie. She still wasn't sure how much of the story he had told was Steven and how much was fact and she wasn't even sure if he knew himself. After all, he was still Steven Reece.

'He said that the *Chronicle* had more or less dropped the story but he had carried on by himself.'

Leonard interrupted.

'Dropped? Why? Banned it?'

'No. I don't think so. There simply wasn't much more to go on and there were other things happening. He says, *says*, mind you, sir, that he had started to get close to a connection the hippie had with people in Bath. And that was when James offered him the job.'

'To shut him up?'

She shook her head. Sipped. Johnson shifted her claws.

'He says not. He says it was coincidence. He says that James's company was opening up two new offices. One in New York and one in Brussels. He wanted someone to handle what he called corporate affairs.'

'What sort of offices?'

'According to Steven, he's in the business of cultural tour operations, which is mega bucks. But, at that stage, Steven's interests were in James's other business, negotiating intellectual property rights.'

'I see.'

He did. Leonard had spent part of his law studies looking at who owns what of an idea and how it can be registered, stolen and exploited. It seemed so appropriate for Montague James to be in that business.

'And, Steven says, the business was being expanded at the time. It wasn't contrived.'

'You asked him?'

'Sure. He knows why I'm interested.'

'What did he say?'

'To begin with, he said I should steer clear.'

'He say why?'

'He said something about the whole thing being complicated and too easily misunderstood.'

'And you said what to that?'

'Nothing.'

Leonard wanted to know more about the warning. Warning? Threat? How fine a line. He needed to know. He doubted that Madeleine Jack would know. For the moment, he wanted to know how Steven Reece had got the job with Montague James.

'He said that instead of employing him, as I thought he had, James encouraged him to set up his own PR agency and then gave him the contract to handle the London end of public affairs. He still is.'

Leonard thought it was probably true. What it did not explain was why James had chosen a relatively inexperienced man like Reece to run what could have been a delicate and costly end of an international organization.

'Right. Now tell me about four.'

'Sir?'

Leonard got up and trickled Calvados into her glass. Johnson did not stir.

'You said he knew more about Rainbow Wood than he had written.'

'Oh, right. Well, according to him, he had spoken to most of the hippies around here at the time, and in those days there weren't that many, and very few of them knew Bolt. And . . .'

'Bolt?'

'Yes. One of the names on the blackboard this morning. You told me to look. That's the point, sir. That's what he knew most of all. According to Steven, the dead man's name was Bolt.'

Leonard's sigh was a hissing of breath not of exasperation. So there was a connection. He had been right.

'Tell me, how did he know?'

'I don't know, sir. He wouldn't say.'

'Why?'

'He said that he found out by an enormous piece of luck. In fact, he hadn't meant to tell me. It came out when he was describing the man and what had happened. It was then that he clammed up.'

'No indication at all?'

'None, sir. Mind you, he's a bit of a Walter Mitty. He could have made it up. After all, there's no record, is there?'

'No. He didn't. It was Bolt. Or I'm as certain as I can be. But, tell me, why did he come up with this name Pete, or Peter?'

Madeleine Jack looked away. It was a silly story. She wanted to get it right.

'Well, according to him, this hippie, Bolt, had almost no possessions, but in his pocket there'd been some sort of flute or pipe. And, well, Steven being a bit sharp, came up with this name, Peter. Peter the Piper or something. Daft as that, really.'

'Flute? Piccolo?'

'He didn't say.'

Leonard paced the room. Johnson eyed him, then settled back on the sergeant's lap. Leonard stopped and pointed his glass at her.

'But we don't know where the name Bolt came from?'

'He said someone told him. Slipped out.'

'And we don't know who.'

'No, sir. Just one thing, sir, where did you get the name from?'

He would have told her. He wanted to tell her. But, just then, a key turned in the front door. They both looked surprised. Madeleine Jack looked at the wall clock. Two in the morning. The hall door hadn't been closed and Josie walked into the room as if she were completely at home. Johnson leapt for the open garden door and the pup hardly tugged at the dirty string.

'Oh hello, James. Been out. Mind if I have a shower?'

And, without waiting for an answer, Josie let the string drop, tossed her cotton bag onto the sofa and started to pull the black shift over her head as she wandered in the direction of the small corridor and the bathroom.

Leonard had started to say something and then had stopped. Sergeant Jack, expressionless, quietly put down her glass.

'It's late, sir. I'll be getting along, if you don't mind.'

'Let me explain.'

'No need, sir. I'll see you in the morning. Good night, sir. Thank you for the drink.'

Twenty-Six

Leonard sat in the garden. He sat in the shadow from the sitting-room light and by the wall where Johnson sat. Johnson watched the river and the pup watched the French doors. Josie came when she was ready. A towel rubbing at her head. His soft shirt from her pillow where he had left it. She sat on the patch of grass, leaned against his legs and rubbed at the pup's belly. They sat for a long time until she was ready for him to speak.

'Where did you go?'

She hummed as he might have. Not hearing. He tried again.

'What did you do?'

She raised her hand and he took from her the rolled and smoking paper.

'Saw people.'

'Which people?'

'People.'

The night was still. Not really dark, not really black. Tomorrow, the longest day. He smoked and said nothing. Waited. The pup nipped.

'Nice people?'

'I don't know.'

'Which people?'

'People who knew Piccolo.'

Leonard stroked her shoulder. She snuggled further against his leg.

'Travelling people?'

He could feel her head move slowly from side to side. No. Not travellers.

'Who, then?'

'People who knew him.'

Leonard's voice was soft. The whisper of a lover.

'Tell me, Josie. How did you you know who they were?'

'Didn't.'

She reached up her hand. He felt her draw deeply. He waited. She would tell him now.

'I saw one of them once. Piccolo used to go. Just come back to me and say he had to go. Remember how I told you? Remember?'

He remembered. He said so. She went on.

'So, one day I follows a bit. He goes down the car park. Pod...?'

'Podium.'

'That's it. Podium. That's where he goes. I see them. That's how I knew. Then when I was by the abbey, well, same person.'

'And you recognized him.'

Of course she recognized him.

'What did he look like?'

'Cool.'

'Your cool? My cool?'

She giggled. A slow throaty giggle. Playing with her own visions.

'Rich.'

'Big rich? Clothes?'

'Big. Big. Like his car.'

'What sort of car, Josie?'

'Same as the one in the Podium. Big. Piccolo said it was a Roller. He'd know.'

She was holding his leg. A child by his hearth. He waited, stroking. Josie needed to see what she was thinking. She needed pictures. Pictures someone else had drawn by being there. Then she could colour them for him. Leonard understood.

'Tell me, Josie, where did you see him?'

'Where they said.'

'Who said?'

'When they phoned. Here.'

He remembered the engaged line. She must have switched the answer machine off. He closed his eyes. Listened carefully to what she said. Yes. But more than that. To her voice.

'They said I should come and see them.'

He listened. Could hear her remembering through the cloud where she lived.

'Did they say why?'

'Said Piccolo would have like it.'

'You believed them?'

The head-shaking was more urgent. Of course she had not. She knew. Of course she did.

'Never. How could he? He would have said. Told me he would have. Right? Didn't, did he?'

He knew. He had to be sure.

'Who, Josie? Who would have said?'

The voice was whispered.

'Piccolo, of course. He always told me to stay away. So I did.'

'But you saw them. How could you see them, Josie, if you did what Piccolo told you?'

She nipped at the end of the paper cone and sucked. Nearly done.

'I went. But they didn't see me. Didn't let them. They were waiting. He was, anyway. But they didn't get a look at me. Piccolo said no. See? I was hiding. Like Piccolo told me.'

'I see, Josie. I see. Now tell me. What happened?'

'Nothing. He was waiting. Then nothing. Just went off in the car. Straight off. Like before. You know, in the Podium.'

'That's where you went to, Josie?'

She nodded.

'Where they always went. Piccolo and him.'

'The man?'

'Yes.'

For a moment, Leonard was surprised that Josie could be so direct as to give a simple affirmative. To her, yes and no were complicated because they were commitments. Josie did not understand commitments but she knew they came to nothing. Maybe cruel nothing.

'You sure you don't know who he is?'

She was sure. But to Josie that did not matter. She had been to see. He was still there. Piccolo was not. But Dancer was. He would know.

Leonard's mind clicked over.

'Who is Dancer, Josie?'

'You know him.'

'Do I?'

'Course you do. You know, Dancer. The fire-eater. Dancer. Everyone knows that.'

'Josie, you sure you don't know him?'

'Really sure. Piccolo told me keep away.'

'That's what he said, was it?'

'Right. Said it was a merry-go-round. Said I should keep off. So I did, didn't I.'

She rose in one motion, stretched and took off the shirt. She smiled down at him. Turned. Trailing the shirt, she wandered into the flat. He heard the drains run from the shower once more. So much to wash away.

Twenty-Seven

In the morning he left her. She promised she would not go. Again. She had seen what she wanted to see. It no longer mattered if he believed her. Belief was irrelevant. Nothing was important, therefore nothing was a lie.

As he closed the front door, Leonard could hear the forecaster. It would be hotter. Too hot for fire-eating. He popped a hayfever tablet in his mouth and gulped. He hated them. By late morning he had more or less given up. He had tried the usual haunts. In front of the Pump Room. In the precinct by the bus station. The buskers, the jugglers, the joss-stick sellers, the bead girl, the pavement artists gathered within yards of each other. You soon ran into the same chorus, the same flute with the same cassette backing. Like the Bath stone buildings, everything on the streets of the city was much the same as it had been yesterday.

Leonard checked into Manvers Street. Nothing. Sergeant Jack was not in. She had left a message. She was checking out the telephone list of Bolts. She would be back by the afternoon. Lane mentioned the coroner's hearing. It was in hand. The coroner's officer downstairs had assured him that it would be adjourned. Leonard was about to go out again, when Lane muttered under his breath.

'What's up with the dashing nice sergeant, then?'

Leonard took off his spectacles. Polished.

'I haven't seen her this morning. You tell me.'

'Well, our bright-as-a-button fast-lane officer is very dull and slow. What have you done to her?'

'Nothing. She was in London all day yesterday. On this. Got back late. Perhaps she's just tired.'

'Young Summertime-Barclay Card gave her one of his dazzling ones and she told him to go screw himself.'

'Maybe she knows something we don't.'

Lane heard the monotones. They were obviously spreading.

'OK, OK. Just thought I'd mention it. Thought I'd warn you. Last thing you need is a hormonal sergeant on the firm.'

'Thanks. I'll keep an eye on her.'

Lane nodded and wandered back into the MIR. He suspected that the last thing Sergeant Jack would stand for was someone keeping an eye on her.

Leonard had hoped she would be there. He needed to explain to Madeleine Jack. He should have explained Josie to Lane. Again, he had not. Sergeant Jack had made it clear that she suspected Josie was someone too special. But then why not? The important point for Leonard was that Sergeant Jack did not know who Josie was. He was going to have to present her as a witness. He left a note for her to meet him in Woods if she came back by two o'clock and went out through the Lost Property door. He saw Stainger crossing the street. He waved a hand in salute rather than greeting and kept going. Superintendents did not shout in public after retreating officers. Leonard kept on going.

On the car-park corner the cider drunk was resting. The greatcoat still stinking. Still buttoned.

'Where's Dancer?'

The drunk leered. The red gums of a Cuddalore crone.

'Clever one, that. Know that?'

'Where?'

The arm swept a befuddled horizon and he nearly fell.

'Hidin' in the fuckin' yard. Everyone's in the fuckin' yard.'

'Which yard?'

But the cider man wanted nothing more than the price of a bottle and cursed the policeman when he walked on.

An hour later, hot and fed up with searching for Dancer, Leonard was leaning against the wall, talking to the canon, still minor, still angular and accusing through steel-rimmed glasses. He had not seen the fire-eater and hoped not to.

'I heartily support the thought that too many beggars are a

product of our leniency. Not our lack of compassion. The city has more than its share.'

Heartily? Leonard wondered that the canon would do or feel anything heartily.

'Tell me, would anyone feel strongly enough about the travellers to . . .'

'Murder one of them?'

'Yes.'

'Of course. That is the nature of passion. It is a degree. Therefore it has extremes. Therefore the answer is always yes, whatever the question.'

'Who would feel so strongly?'

'Ah, that I do not know. Most passions are hidden unless collectively expressed or, more usually, kept secret between consenting *aficionados*. You should know that, you're a policeman.'

Leonard was surprised.

'How do you know?'

'You mentioned it.'

Leonard had not remembered doing so.

'And you remembered.'

The priest's hand fluttered.

'Who remembers? But yes, some of my colleagues discussed the, ah, unfortunate event. Sadness is a great conversation-maker.'

He tried a smile. It was never going to come to much. It had been a long time.

'So you see, Mr . . .?'

'James Leonard.'

'Ah yes, that was it. So you see, Mr Leonard, you now have a reputation, if only among the Chapter, which in its modest way is a caring group. Now, I must go.'

'Caring enough to discuss a murder investigation and even the investigating officer?'

'No, Mr Leonard, idle enough to gossip.'

He left, briskly and short-stepping towards the abbey. As

he did he pointed, shaking his finger like a marquee-rigger directing operations. Leonard followed the wagging sign. Dancer. The fire-eater. Dancer saw Leonard leaning against the warm wall, started to veer in another direction but laughed and came to where the policeman waited.

'Heard you were looking for me.'

'You seem to have dropped out of sight.'

'In a meeting. Know how it is? Got a couple of big deals upcoming. Poser phone was on the blink. Had to handle the biz myself. Which reminds me. Got a coin? Left the Ferrari on a meter.'

They both laughed. The fire-eater put his sacks between his legs and fished a grubby soft pack from his waistband. He blew smoke like a dragon snorting and looked about, wondering who was watching this meeting.

'So? What's the prob?'

'What happened to Piccolo's bag?'

'Roll?'

'All right. What happened to his roll?'

'Good question.'

'Good answer is?'

'Don't know. Bad one is also don't know.'

'Which one's yours?'

'Both. That it? Brill. 'Bye.'

Dancer picked up his sacks. But Leonard touched his arm. For a second or two, Dancer looked at the freckled hand against his strong bare skin. Gave a cocky shrug. Put down the sacks. Leonard dropped his hand.

'I hear you knew Piccolo's friends.'

The fire-eater's eyes were now darting furiously. The company of a policeman was not the natural habitat for Dancer. Never had been, although a few desk sergeants in central London would have queried that.

'No way.'

'Not so. What I hear is true.'

'No way.'

'I hear there was one with a large motor car. Maybe a Roller. Who?'

'Don't remember.'

'Even in this city there can't be many Rolls-Royces, so perhaps you can.'

'I'm no good at cars.'

'Unless you're wiring one?'

Leonard was way off. Dancer had been picked up and charged on many occasions. Maybe zealousness. Maybe incomplete evidence. Maybe innocence. Dancer had never been convicted. He turned. Looked Leonard full in the face. Confidence. Fear. For a moment they came together. Strength.

'Look, chief, bleed in someone else's bucket. OK? I not only know nothing but I'm alive to prove it. Piccolo was a guy. Not mine. He had a couple of friends. Maybe a couple of specials. That was his business. OK?'

'Until he was killed. Then it became mine.'

'You signed up for the helmet. Not me.'

Leonard threw another dart.

'Did you know Bolt?'

The blank look was real enough. Dancer may not have known him, but the question was wrong. Leonard tried again.

'Who did?'

'Just one. Then 'bye time. OK. It won't do you any good. He did.'

'Who?'

'The Piccolo man.'

'Bolt? He knew Bolt? How?'

But Dancer was gathering his bundle.

'Ask Josie. She's yours now. Ask his lady. She knows.'

Twenty-Eight

He was about finished, when Madeleine Jack arrived. She was not cheerful. The linen suit was cut for a speech day and her hair was swept back in a hacking bun. No hairnet. But no nonsense. Leonard was sitting in his window seat, with a wedge of Somerset brie. He pointed to some wine. She shook her head. She did not sit down.

'You were looking for me, sir.'

Leonard dropped his napkin on his plate. Pointed to the seat. The atmosphere was not relaxed. Observing them from across the room, Selsey thought it not the best time to explain the latest on his horse-owning dilemma.

'About last night . . .'

Madeleine Jack raised her eyebrows. Leonard really was getting the treatment.

'There's absolutely no need, sir.'

'Sergeant, there is. The person you saw last night . . .'

He paused, removed his spectacles, held them to the light and polished.

'Sir, really.'

'Is the key witness in this murder.'

She blinked.

'Oh.'

'She is the one person who knew who he was. She is also the person who supplied the name of the man murdered in Rainbow Wood.'

He slipped the wire arms over his ears. Sipped at his wine and once again offered to fill the second glass at the table. This time Madeleine Jack did not say no. Said nothing at all. Sat down. He filled her glass with the last of the Chablis.

'So, now you begin to know that last night was not what you might have easily thought it to be.'

'It was late.'

'It was.'

Her embarrassed smile as she picked up her glass was a relief to Leonard.

'How long have you had her? I mean, sorry, sir, how long has she been there?'

Leonard managed a smile of his own. He told her the story

of Josie's arrival. Of her disappearance and the reason Josie had given him.

'And she definitely doesn't know these people?'

He shook his head.

'She may be lying, but I think not. Piccolo apparently warned her. And the way he did ties with something else I've come across. He told her to keep off the merry-go-round. Now, listen to this . . .'

He stopped. She was looking at him with mouth wide open like some ham thespian discovering what the bloodstained butler had done.

'What?'

'The merry-go-round. Is that what she actually said?'

He nodded. Slowly. 'Go on.'

'Well, Steven warned me. I told you.'

'You said he told you to steer clear. There was more?'

'No. But it was the same expression you've used. His exact words were: "Stay out of this one; that's one merry-go-round you don't need."'

Leonard had not seen Harriet Bowles come in. She was leaving before he noticed her. The waitress came over. Smiling. She was doing that more. She gave him a grey-blue envelope. It was from Harriet. Almost an apology. She understood that some people were never off duty. Leonard tucked the card back in the envelope and looked across to where Harriet Bowles had gone. He hoped that she really did understand. He thought it had been a heavy twelve hours of misunderstandings. One was reasonable. Two? Clumsy.

They walked down the hill and paused on the pavement at George Street. A dark-haired estate agent was going into his corner office. He smiled at Madeleine Jack and, as he passed, said hello. She explained she had bought her flat through him. Leonard was glad she wanted to explain. It meant, he hoped, that they were again on talking, and not just speaking, terms.

By the time they got to his flat, he had told her almost

everything he knew. He had mentioned the cemetery again, but not the detail of the inscription. He was not yet sure. He needed to be sure.

Josie was in the garden. She was still in the soft shirt. Leonard introduced them. He explained that Madeleine was an old friend as well as a colleague and that she was helping him to find who had done such terrible things to Piccolo. The more he explained, the more Josie seemed to drift. Time to leave the two women. Leonard had thought Madeleine Jack might free more from Josie's memory. The sergeant thought it unlikely. Josie had learned to trust him. Leonard told Jack to stick with it and left them.

Leonard got back to Manvers Street and picked through the list of forty-two known and unknown Bolts she had left on his desk. There was nothing special. Most were accounted for. There was no indication of what he was looking for. It was unlikely from her pencilled notes that the man murdered in Rainbow Wood had lived locally, nor that he had had relatives in the area. It was not a well-managed conclusion, but for the moment it would do.

He went through to the MIR and got himself updated. Still no belongings recovered. Nothing on Bolt other than two missing persons. One was female, the other was the son of a hardly known Irish peer. Leonard looked over Lane's shoulder.

'When was that?'

'Nine months ago.'

For a moment, Leonard had wondered. Nine months ago? Nine years too late. This was not Leonard's Bolt.

Back in his office, Leonard ignored a message that Stainger wanted to see him. Not urgent. But pronto would be soon enough. Instead he looked across at the empty desk and wondered how Madeleine Jack might be getting on. He tapped his fingers in silent frustration. He would have liked to telephone the flat. Anything yet? He did not. Instead he made a brief call to Harriet Bowles. He thanked her for the card. Her voice was businesslike.

He said that she should not have been shy at lunchtime. Should have joined them.

'You were involved.'

'Sergeant Jack? You should have come over to say hello. You'd like her.'

'Is there a reason why I should expect to?'

He said goodbye as diplomatically as he could. He felt a little sad. He had other things on his mind. Which was when the telephone rang. It was Somers-Barclay.

'Just brought in an interesting one, sir.'

'Where are you?'

'Downstairs. In the Custody Suite.'

'Who? What?'

'Gent by the name of Bolt, sir. DI Lane said to inform you.'

Leonard dropped the telephone receiver on its hook. Stood. Straightened his waistcoat and walked to the head of the stairs. Bolt was dead. He knew that. But what if there had been more than one Bolt? What if another Bolt had known? What if Piccolo had been right? Bolt knew? Josie not concerned with tenses? He thought not. Josie repeated Piccolo verbatim. Right tense. But wrong?

The Custody Suite was the smart name for the cells. Somers-Barclay was waiting in the anteroom to the low corridor.

'Picked him up in King Street, sir.'

'Why?'

Somers-Barclay looked confused.

'He was one of the Bolts you'd asked about. One of the brothers on Pirsy. And, er, sir, we had some bother with him.'

Leonard nodded and picked up the sheet. The address was right.

'Which means?'

'DC Hancock and I . . . Well, sir, we'd been knocking on the door and –'

'Was it padlocked?'

'Yes, sir. How did you know?'

'If it was padlocked, why knock?'

'He could have had another way in and out. The padlock could have been a blind, sir.'

Leonard had not thought of that. Somers-Barclay had. Instinctively. Leonard took off his spectacles. Hurred on the clear lenses. Polished.

'Go on.'

'Well, sir, the next thing the other door opened and out he came at enormous speed. My goodness, yes.'

'What other door?'

'The flat, sir. He was in the opposite flat.'

Leonard remembered. The stinking landing. The ugly woman.

'Number Five.'

'Right. You knew?'

No. Leonard had not known. The chain on the door. He had been there all the time. Simple. Now it did not matter.

'What happened?'

'Well, sir, as I say, he suddenly appeared. Surprised us. DC Hancock went for him and, well –'

'You mean hit him?'

'Hancock, sir? Oh no. He tried to grab him. Bolt pushed him down the stairs. I'm afraid Hancock's up at the quack, sir. Shoulder's a frightful mess.'

'And Bolt?'

'Oh, he's all right, sir. I managed to get him in the street.'

Leonard glanced at the block letters on the form Bolt had been shown.

YOU HAVE A RIGHT TO:
1. SPEAK TO AN INDEPENDENT SOLICITOR FREE OF CHARGE.
2. HAVE SOMEONE TOLD THAT YOU HAVE BEEN ARRESTED.
3. CONSULT A COPY OF THE CODES OF PRACTICE COVERING POLICE POWERS AND PROCEDURES. YOU MAY DO ANY OF THESE THINGS NOW, BUT IF YOU DO

Have a nice day. He knew it off by heart. So, probably, did
Bolt.

'Where is he?'

Somers-Barclay, less certain of himself now, led Leonard to
the second door on the left. Grey steel. Heavy. Scratched.
Mainly at the bottom. A good kick did wonders for cocky
visitors. The custodian was standing by. Leonard shook his
head and instead looked through the spy hole. The distorted
vision told him all he wanted to know. The tall, almost empty
room. The alcove with the plain white lavatory bowl. No
seat. The high bottled windows leading nowhere. The innocence soon showed. As an old hand had once remarked to
him, 'They don't call it the slammer for nothing.' The anteroom to despair, the very correct inspector had said. Bolt sat
on the blue plastic-covered bunk, opposite the door. He was
in the corner. One leg up to his chin. The other straight out.
Doing nothing. Staring. No more than a youth. Skinny in his
thin dirty T-shirt. Probably the same one he'd been wearing
when he passed Leonard going out of the front door. Brian
Bolt. Leonard could see it now. Hadn't on the day. Somers-
Barclay had. On the day it had been important. Not any
more.

Leonard turned from the door. Somers-Barclay was fiddling
with his gold bracelet. Leonard made for the stairs. Somers-
Barclay was confused. Especially in front of the custodian.

'Sir?'

Leonard turned.

'Wrong Bolt.'

Twenty-Nine

Wrong Bolt. But what about the original? Leonard had business with a funeral director. The woman was rolling another cigarette when he arrived at the yard. She licked the paper, stuck it down and cocked a thumb at the office.

Mr Robert was not Mr Robert. He was Mr Golding. Mr Robert Golding, the son of the deceased founder. But, in the way of all mustiness, affection as well as affectation, he had become Mr Robert when he joined the firm and had remained so. In *per memoriam*. He stood quietly when Leonard came in. Attentive. A portly figure. 'Well nourished' was how the Screaming Skull would have described him to the coroner. Black, militarily cut and Brylcreemed hair. Parted in the middle. His smile was professionally done. Concern. Not jovial. Mr Robert did not take a drink except on cold and frosty mornings. Then just a tot. Then more toothpaste. The dead were indifferent. The living were not.

'Inspector Leonard, is it not?'

Leonard was surprised. The girl had been thorough. He nodded. For good measure he showed Mr Robert his warrant card. There was a new picture. Better than Bolt's on the computer screen.

'I need to know who paid for the burial and headstone of someone called Bolt. Five years ago.'

Mr Robert did not offer a seat. Leonard was in no distress. Was unlikely to faint. Did not need the few moments sitting down that allowed the bereaved to compose themselves. And this would not take long.

'So I understand. Well, Mr Leonard, I'm afraid I cannot be of any help to you. I was told that you required such information and of course I immediately consulted our records.'

Of course. Leonard's raised eyebrow was the question.

'I regret to say that the information is not to hand.'

'You don't keep records that far back?'

Mr Robert's back straightened. A sensed insult?

'My! But surely we do. We began in 1805. The very day of the great battle. Trafalgar, you know? I am proud to say that our records have been used on more than one occasion by eminent historians. A veritable social history of our famous city.'

Leonard nodded.

'So what's the problem?'

He wrung his hands. Very professional.

'I have looked. The simple system of entry could not be astray. There is no double-filing. It simply must have slipped the mind of our clerk. Her only mistake in forty years. A small detail. Yet, so inconvenient.'

Leonard looked to the mirrored wall. The inner office. Perhaps the clerk was watching.

'Do you mind if I speak to your clerk?'

The professional smile was back. This time one of condolence.

'I'm afraid she is no longer with us.'

Undertakerspeak? Mr Robert caught his question before he asked it.

'That is, she has retired. Forty years is a long time, you know, Mr Leonard.'

Leonard looked at the director's eyes. Liquorice centres. Nothing but black compassion for his plight.

'I wonder if you would give me her address.'

Mr Robert bowed his head. So sad. So sorry, so sad.

'I'm afraid she has left the district. They retired away. I believe Scotland. She was.'

'Was what?'

'Scotch. Or is it Scottish? I'm never sure.'

'Isn't it odd that after forty years you don't know where she went to? Christmas cards?'

'Mrs Gordon was quite independent, Inspector.'

'Pension?'

'I would have thought so.'

'But not through Goldings?'

'Inspector, please! We are tiny. And, as I said, Mrs Gordon was quite independent. I believe her husband's company provided for them. Rather well.'

'What company was that?'

Mr Robert had slipped. Nearly.

'I do not quite remember. It may have been the Civil Service. Then again . . .'

'It might not.'

Leonard walked to the window. The woman was changing the head on a buffing machine, squinting through cigarette smoke as she did.

'Your colleague said that the cheque for Bolt's headstone may have come through a third party. To disguise the origin of the money.'

'Something similar is not uncommon.'

'But you cannot remember who gave you the cheque? A receipt wasn't needed?'

'I seem to remember that it was not a charity. Not a fund. An individual and a covering note.'

'And the inscription?'

'That too.'

Leonard turned back into the room. He could smell the man's odourless breath. Expressionless. Anonymous. Always anonymous. Intrusion on grief was never permissible. Pall-bearers and bodies. Unseen actors. Voices off in the minds of mourners. Mr Robert could handle Leonard. They both knew that.

'Mr Golding, I am conducting a murder inquiry. If there is the slightest way in which you believe you could answer even part of my question, then you should do so.'

'Of course.'

'There is always the risk of obstructing the police in their inquiries. It is not something to be taken lightly. Do I make myself perfectly clear?'

'I assure you, Inspector, there is no way in which I can help you. As much as I would care to, of course. Sadly, I am not in a position to help you. I hope you understand.'

Leonard understood. He left the yard. The girl saw him go. Did not wave. Did not smile. Mr Robert would be watching. Leonard did not understand.

He ignored a cab looking for a ride into the city but saw little of the way he walked back until he reached Queen Square. He turned down towards the Theatre Royal and then into a side-street. Harriet Bowles was locking up. It was gone six.

'Thanks for your note.'

'You've already said that.'

He looked down at his boots.

'Right. Anyway, thanks. You were probably right. Being off duty in the middle of a murder is not simple.'

She touched his arm.

'Come on, Poirot, I'll buy you that drink.'

He shook his head. He was sorry. He would have liked her company.

'I'm due at the Montague Jameses.'

'Not pleasure, I hope. Come on, I walk that way.'

The traffic had eased. A coach the shape of Europe was unloading plaid baggage and checkered Americans into the Francis Hotel. The courier was reciting from her scarlet clip-board, knowing she would have to do so again. The Americans were listening only to themselves. One of them spotted Leonard. Another planet. Certainly another continent. The suit. He just had to have one like that. The tour had been worth it after all. He nudged his companion. But the other man was watching the gentle sway of Harriet's breasts. The shirt was thin. He only just moved aside to let Leonard and Harriet through. She instinctively folded her arms, her raffia basket in the crook. They said nothing until they were on the corner of Gay Street and waiting for a gap in the traffic.

'Know anything about Goldings?'

'The funeral people?'

'Mm.'

'Only the hard way.'

He had forgotten her husband.

'What about Robert Golding?'

'I've meet him. He gives me the creeps, but then I suppose that's an occupational hazard for him.'

'Where've you met him?'

'Friends of the Abbey. Couple of things like that. He has a very big rep. And not just in Bath. Throughout Europe. There was a piece about him in the *Chronicle*.'

'What sort of rep?'

'Embalming. Apparently he could make a drunk look like a saint.'

'And does?'

'Being Bath, he gets a lot of practice.'

She shivered. It was warm.

Across in the centre of The Circus, language students lounged on the grass and a passing matron looked on with annoyance. They were unpopular. But they were paying her a lot of money for her apartments. She supposed there was a tolerance factor that would compensate for their rudeness. There was. It was eight hundred a month – each. The going rate was six hundred.

They both kept straight faces until the matron was gone by.

'People in this city don't like change, do they?'

Harriet laughed at him.

'Come on, brains. No one who has got it made likes change. Especially in a place like this. That's why they've bought in. Go out into the boondocks. There isn't a village in England which hasn't got its well-off newcomers all trying to preserve the quaint atmosphere. They'd have the yokels in smocks given half the chance.'

'And Bath's no different?'

'I've told you. Bath is a Nob Hill. The folks who live on it own it. Make changes, dirty it up and you've attacked what they think they stand for. Hell's teeth, they've even got a by-law here which says every building, even new ones, has to be built in Bath stone. No, Poirot. Change comes out as threatening behaviour. They don't go for it.'

'Enough to kill?'

Harriet Bowles stopped.

'No, James. Not enough to kill. If they did, four fifths of the population would be in Robert Golding's parlour. You can take conspiracies too far.'

'Sorry.'

'Mind you, why don't you try this one on Montague James? Ask him why a report on vagrants by the Town Centre management office was never published. And, while you're about it, ask him who suggested that they should be bussed out of Bath before our Royals arrived at the abbey.'

'How do you know about this?'

'Business is quiet, James. When it's this quiet, traders call each other up to say that business is quiet. And, as the Town Centre management thing can't succeed without their co-operation, then they know what's going on. The next best thing to banking the day's takings is gossiping. So, I do know. Ask him.'

'He knows?'

'Poirot, Poirot, Poirot. Have you understood nothing? It's Montague James giving you dwinkiepoos. This is no lager lout. When it comes to knowing, our Montague makes Thomas Aquinas look like the Vicar of Bray.'

Leonard smiled. She made him smile. He wished that he were going to the wine bar. With Harriet Bowles. She gave him a sisterly peck on the cheek.

'As you said, never off duty. 'Bye. I'll see you under the gallows. Don't forget the corkscrew.'

She smiled. Went. Another woman who would not look back.

Thirty

The Filipino girl opened the door. Her English was not precise. But she needed only to understand commands. Self-expression was best left to the way in which she zealously performed her duties. She therefore said nothing. She led Leonard to the drawing-room doors, knocked, opened both and stood aside as he entered. The room was furnished with just a sufficient touch of vulgarity to make it interesting. At the tall windows, the blue Chinese silk curtains hung in perfect folds. They were tied back with matching and tasselled bands. Beyond the windows, a panorama. Bath observed.

Montague James stood at the hearth. Above the mantel a gilt eighteenth-century mirror exaggerated the already generous length and breadth of the room. He cut an elegant pose. Tall. Slim in black trousers and a white silk dinner jacket. Double-breasted and waisted. Not the same jacket of the previous evening. In his hand, a tall flute of pink champagne.

'Welcome.'

Only then did the pose break. Almost by magic, the Filipino girl offered Leonard a similar glass from a lacquered tray. There was a hardly noticeable nod from James and she withdrew, backwards. Leonard raised his glass, but did not drink. If James noticed he said nothing. He walked to the windows and spread a beckoning arm.

'The finest view from any drawing-room in Bath. Don't you think?'

'I don't know many drawing-rooms in Bath. But I'll take your word for it.'

'Oh but, my dear fellow, you should. I most certainly do know many drawing-rooms in the city. What I say is true. Is it not majestic?'

'Impressive.'

'And majesty is not always? Ah yes. A point to be taken.

But it has a depth and an elegance rarely found in our cities. Even the grubby parts have that wonderful seediness which suggests that they have fallen on hard times rather than have never had anything but squalor.'

'Is that true?'

'Of course it is not. No, no, no, my dear Leonard, whatever next? Cities are like whores. No matter how much paint applied by the rough trade, it is no more than that.'

'And, no matter how good the accents and designer labels, the high-class whore is still nothing but a whore.'

'Yes, 'tis a pity. How clever, Mr Leonard. How very witty.'

'Not really.'

'No. I suppose not. Mr Leonard, you are a very serious man.'

'I disapprove of murder, if that's what you mean.'

'Oh, I know perfectly what I mean. I mean you are very serious. Not without a sense of humour, but like all serious people you are careful how you use it. Yes?'

Leonard did not answer. He sipped.

'And quite rightly, Inspector, you take this inquiry without any humour.'

'Why did you buy Steven Reece when you did?'

It was Montague James's turn to sip. He slipped his hand inside the breast of his dinner jacket. No. Not elegant, thought Leonard. Yes, imperialistic. The cough was discreet and affected.

'That is a very direct question.'

'You invited me here for answers. Or so I remember. I thought the niceties done.'

'Niceties are never done, Inspector. Never. Now, where were we?'

'I was at Reece. You were about to be.'

'Reece? Why did I buy him? Because he was a bargain.'

'You needed a bargain?'

'One is always attracted to something which is even better than value for money. Reece was just that. At the time I needed a Reece. He was, as you put it, Mr Leonard, a good buy. Still is, as a matter of fact.'

'And convenient.'

'Now or then?'

'Then.'

'I suppose so. Inspector, you do not think me a fool and certainly not foolish. You are far too intelligent for that. So let me give you the answer to the obvious question. I assume you have been asking elsewhere. In fact I know you have.'

'How so?'

'Because I make it my business to know most things and because others know it is my business, so they tell me.'

'You buy information.'

'And pay promptly. Does that shock you? It shouldn't. It is business. I am in business.'

'You bought Reece because he was digging too deeply into the Rainbow Wood murder.'

'Are you asking me or telling me?'

Leonard looked about the room. It was sufficient answer for James.

'Question: did I buy Reece to take him away from that ghastly murder?'

'Wrong question.'

'Nonsense. Answer: yes, I did. Satisfied?'

He poured more champagne. The ice bucket was silver and held two unopened bottles.

'Why?'

'Because he had discovered something others had not but was making more out of it than was there.'

'He was getting warm.'

'How very 1950s, Inspector. "Getting warm". Oh, I do like that. Was he? No, I don't think so. If he had been, I'm sure all would have been well.'

'For you?'

'Most certainly.'

'Then why stop him?'

Montague James moved back to the window and seated himself in one curve of a love seat. He bent a wrist and Leonard sat in the other half. Neither man turned his body, nor his head. James faced the city. Leonard, the tall ivory doors. Montague James drew breath.

'Ten years ago, Inspector, I was about to bring off an important business transaction. My, yes. How important. It is no secret. It is now done. I had always, always, avoided the leisure industry. Tedious people, low margins, but above all, Inspector, subject to every known capriciousness. But the year before that sad creature was done for in Rainbow Wood I had been approached by an American friend. I spent a year at Harvard, you know.'

Leonard did not. He was not surprised. But Montague James's tone suggested that he might, just might, be telling the truth.

'I did not know.'

'Of course not, Inspector. Of course not. We met at Harvard Business School. He was rich. I came from richness but was not. He was a lawyer. We went into intellectual property rights. Lucrative, but long-term. Then he had an idea.'

Leonard shifted. James showed a little anger.

'Inspector, I would ask you to listen. To pay attention, as my nanny would have said. I am telling you this so that you understand. You may then go and do as you please, but not with me.'

'Go on.'

James sipped the tiniest sip and inclined his head.

'Thank you. I shall. Now, among the alumni of American colleges are rich old men and women. They are dreadful culture vultures. They spend their retirement, and goodness knows how much money, digesting culture. They take culture as they take sedatives and laxatives – with morbid regularity. My friend's idea was simple. We would put together, in Europe, the highest-class history summer schools there had ever been. Art History in Florence. Musical History in Salzburg and

Vienna. The Tsars in St Petersburg – not Moscow, you note, Inspector, but St Petersburg. Just think.'

Leonard was thinking. Bath?

'Why Bath?'

'Aha. Yes indeed, why Bath? Because I was here, partly. I had something of the organization. Bath had Celts, Romans, but, above all else, Bath had Regency history. But it had something else. Ideas?'

'Quaintness?'

'Oh no. These are proper culture vultures. They are suspicious of quaintness. They devour libraries before they travel. They know more than their lecturers. They seek value for their dollars, but most of all for their fast-failing minds.'

'So why Bath?'

'Because it was safe. Americans do not travel well. Noisily. Irritably. Certainly not well. They have weekly bulletins in their magazines of dangerous places. Social unrest in, say, Bonn means, in American eyes, that it is practically a war zone. More than that, the hero, or should I say heroine, of the American world was at the time in England.'

'Ten years ago? You mean Thatcher?'

'Of course I do. Mrs Thatcher, as she then was, bless her, was even more admired in the United States than she was in Finchley and Surbiton. Remember, Mr Leonard, she had single-handedly just won the Falklands War. President Reagan was discovering Star Wars and all sorts of fantasies and, however ludicrous his ideas, the great lady was the only Western leader supporting him. They loved her. Adored her. She was what the Grand Old Party understood. She played very big indeed in Main Street, Wisconsin.'

'So they loved the UK. But I still don't see why Bath.'

'We offered the ideal place for the experiment. Remember, we were not talking about the usual folk. We were after high-denomination notes. We set up a summer school on Regency culture. Twenty-five thousand dollars a head.'

Leonard whistled. He was believing James.

'Exactly, Inspector. An impossible amount. But it would work. Has done. How? American colleges are so much better organized than ours. They have wonderful lists of the rich and damned and the very rich and the thrice damned. All old members of their colleges. All persuadable. Ten million dollars for the new college theatre? Name it after the fattest benefactor and you may even get the whole lot on one cheque. Yes, Mr Leonard. That, as Mr Punch would have said, is the way to do it.'

'And your friend had access to these lists?'

'Absolutely. Absolutely. Only blue chips need apply.'

Montague James poured more champagne and passed the nearly empty bottle across the curved arm to Leonard.

'And?'

'And, Inspector, we put together the highest-quality lecture list. We arranged to rent the most sumptuous house-cum-hotel at Ston Easton. And, with that list, we had one hundred names inside four weeks. Your arithmetic will tell you the rest.'

'More than three million dollars.'

Montague James raised his glass in fiscal memory. Leonard turned to look at the smiling profile.

'And then you had a murder.'

'No, Mr Leonard, not a murder. A gruesome murder of a vagrant.'

'But no one in the United States would hear about that.'

'Absolutely. But for one thing. Young Reece was very ambitious. He was, and I suspect is even more so, an opportunist. He was an avid money-maker. He became what I think is called a stringer?'

Leonard nodded. Every policeman knows them. Journalists – usually provincial ones – who string, or act as freelance correspondents for magazines and papers in places they don't keep staff men.

'Who was he stringing for? The nationals?'

'Why, of course. But he had found a lucrative outlet in the

North Americas. He started writing features for magazines and some newspapers. Just as we love to read the front-line garbage from America, so it appears that many Americans like to read about quaint Europe. Reece was a good marketing man. He did his research. He found his way into influential magazines and then a couple of the big city papers. His audience was enormous. That same audience, Mr Leonard, which reads the little travel warning paragraphs.'

Leonard drained his glass.

'OK. I buy all this. But a traveller's murder in Bath will not make headlines in America. Especially America. Even their own murders don't make headlines.'

'But they do if they're abroad. They are particularly sensitive to their fellow-Americans being slain, I believe they use that phrase, when they're overseas. And particularly if there is too a story that the murder is unresolved. That, under the pen of an enterprising and dollar-hungry stringer, may easily turn into a killer stalking Americans.'

Leonard stretched out his legs. This was getting ridiculous. It was time to say so.

'OK, Mr James. As I say, I buy all this. Except for one thing. The man killed in Rainbow Wood was a refugee from the Glastonbury pop festival. This was hardly a serial killer looking for American passport-holders coming off the six-fifteen from Paddington.'

'You forget, Inspector, or do not listen. I told you that young Reece had discovered one factor unknown to others, including the constabulary, and, as far as I know, still unknown. And he sold it for all he was worth. And they bought it for all it was worth.'

'Tell me.'

'The man killed in Rainbow Wood was an American.'

The telephone burbled. Montague James excused himself and went across to something early French and picked up the gilt handset. He listened rather than spoke and Leonard thought perhaps it was not for his benefit, but that James was the sort of man who would rarely trust his thoughts to such an insecure instrument as a telephone.

Leonard got up and stood gazing across Bath. Thinking of James's explanation. The detail was remarkable. He could believe James. He remembered the paranoia that had caused Americans to cancel trips to London during the Gulf War for fear of being killed by Iraq's one-hundred-mile-range Scud missiles.

So a series of newspaper and magazine articles about the unexplained death of an American, especially when it was being hyped by an imaginative journalist, would be just the thing to put off culture-craving septuagenarians. Thirty thousand dollars was a lot to pay for the privilege of making three black-bordered paragraphs in the *Boston Globe* and a name mention on CNN.

Montague James had finished. He smiled the smile of the satisfied. Leonard put down his half-empty glass on the lacquered tray.

'So you bought Reece to stop him selling Murder Inc tales to New York wire services?'

'Exactly that.'

'He says it was a real job.'

'Oh, my dear Mr Leonard, so it was. So it was. I support charities. But I am not one myself.'

'Tell me, how did you know he was doing this?'

'My partner. He was most distressed. Transatlantic telephone calls, Inspector. Most distressed. The little rascal, Reece that is, was actually getting his name on the nonsense.'

Leonard was about to ask him more when the doors opened. Hilary James stood framed like a Hollywood Oscar winner. The smile was pearly white. So was the dress, what there was of it. It was definitely summer.

'My dear. Your timing, impeccable.'

The phrase passed his lips as a perfect glissando. Each note blending, yet each note a character of its own. As James went to take her hand, Leonard noticed for the first time the short paces he took. The exquisite pointing of the steps. He led her to where Leonard was standing and when he let go her hand it fluttered to her side.

'My darling. This is Inspector Leonard. He's a policeman. Now you must give him a little drink and entertain him because I must be perfectly rude and leave.'

Leonard shuffled as policemen are expected to in these situations.

'I must be . . .'

But James's hand was up. His eyebrows would hear nothing of Leonard leaving. He really was like an exceedingly tall dancing master.

'No. Not at all. Do stay. Hilary is to leave shortly. But finish your champagne. One must always finish champagne.'

And he was gone. The doors closed quietly behind him.

Hilary James walked from her hips. The white silk did the rest.

'Do have some champagne, Mr Leonard.'

She was for enough away for him to have to look at her. Close enough to make sure he missed nothing. Leonard could not make out what was going on. His instinct said he was being set up. He heard the front door close. That was no reassurance. He said no more champagne thank you very much. She looked at the ice bucket.

'There should be mineral water in there. Would you, please?'

There was. The bottle was dark blue. The water was still. He poured it into a champagne flute and she kept her hand over his when he handed it to her.

'Are you really an inspector?'

'Yes. There's nothing remarkable in that, surely?'

'Of course not. I don't think I've met one. Do you have a name?'

'James Leonard.'

'Jimmy?'

'I don't think so.'

'Good. I don't like shortening names.'

She took her hand away and sat, then relaxed into the deep sofa. Crossing her legs took time. It really was summer.

'Your husband was telling me about Steven Reece.'

'Who?'

'Steven Reece. He was a journalist here.'

'Was her?'

'He worked for your husband. Still does.'

'Do you work for my husband, James?'

'No, I'm a policeman.'

She patted the sofa for him to sit. He sat opposite. Maybe a mistake. She recrossed her legs. Took her time again. She was well practised. He wondered how many times she had rehearsed. She'd lost count. Why not? She'd been rehearsing since she was fourteen.

'Of course you are. But that doesn't mean you can't have business interests. A lot of people work for my husband. You must know that.'

'Other policemen?'

'I really don't know. You must ask him.'

'You must meet them.'

'I meet so many people. But then, I am the perfect wife. I remember only what pleases my husband.'

'Why?'

'Because that way I remain his wife.'

Leonard blinked. Rubbed his fingers. There had been a lot of champagne.

'Don't look so surprised, James. I enjoy everything I do. Everything.'

She wriggled in the soft leather sofa. Leonard looked away. She laughed.

'Don't you? Or are policemen not supposed to enjoy themselves?'

Leonard did not answer. He took out his pocket watch. Stood.

'I'm very sorry, Mrs James, but I'm afraid I must be going. It's been very nice meeting you.'

For a moment, Hilary James looked worried. The eyes moved too quickly to the mantel clock and back to him. So, the masque was not yet played.

'But you simply cannot. I won't hear of it.'

She was holding her glass out to him. She hadn't touched it. He took it and put it back on the table. She got up. Another performance. She took him by the arm.

'We're going to a party.'

She was standing very close. He wondered how the whites of her eyes were so spotless. He shook his head.

'That's very thoughtful of you, Mrs James, but I'm afraid I'm working.'

'That's twice you've been afraid in twenty seconds. You must stop it, James, otherwise you will make me feel quite horrid. Anyway you must not be rude. I have to go and I need someone to take me. You will do, perfectly.'

She leaned forward. He started to protest. The champagne had had its fun. The protest did not have much feeling.

'I really should be getting on.'

'Nonsense, James. If I have to go, you can come. It's one of those arty bashes. I'm not arty. Are you? Of course you are. I can see it in your eyes. Anyway, James, you'll meet lots of nice people and you can put on your serious voice and get all gruff and say simply loads of people are helping with your inquiries.'

She took his hand and for a split second brushed it against her breast. Laughed and led him to the front door. The Filipino was waiting. So was the dark-green Rolls-Royce, the driver standing with the rear door open. There was no sign of Montague James.

Thirty-One

Leonard did not like parties. He never knew where to hide. He did not understand small talk. In a gin-cheered throng, he was hopeless. He was soft-voiced. For him, speaking over a crowd was almost impossible. He had tried circulating. But he never had the confidence to believe that, as everyone had been invited, then everyone had to have something in common. Other than duty parties, professional gatherings, Leonard never really understood why he had been invited. He never understood why he was the only person who did not know everyone.

Once, he had tried very hard. He'd accepted an invitation for early drinks and late supper given by a prominent city solicitor. A lady he hardly knew. Hiding in a corner, he found a kindred spirit clutching a warm and smudged glass of white wine. Like two expatriates marooned by a minor revolution, they had fled the gathering to a nearby pub. On their fourth round, Leonard's fellow escapee confessed he was the husband of the hostess. Leonard turned down subsequent invitations.

But this was different. This was work. This was his way into a group in which, he believed, someone held the solution to one murder, maybe two.

The Minerva Gallery was in a tall, thin private house in Lansdown. The rooms were white. The floors polished elm. The ceilings high and made to look higher by the stainless-steel spiral staircase to the galleried landing. Canvases decorated every wall. Lots of space in between and above and below. Some very large. None very small. Others were suspended from the upper floor and into the middle of the room by scarlet chains. At first glance, none of the people were off the streets. This was expensive viewing. No one looked poor. No point in inviting the poor to a preview. The Minerva expected gold cards, often and very nicely took platinum. Leonard blinked. He was on his own once more.

As soon as they arrived, Hilary James had parked him. Told him to stay put until she returned from something she called 'you-know-where'. He supposed that he did. So, James Leonard watched the crowd. Felt the old fears. Watched the people watching the pictures watching the people. Some peered, stared, leaned back. Others glanced up and down, mentally calculating canvas area in pounds sterling per square metre or space to be filled above mantels. Others went through a ritual of distant viewing, close viewing, a search of the catalogue, then a slow bending motion to examine artist's name, title and price. None gawped.

Leonard was standing by an alcove. In front of him, a slash of magenta, bleached blue and bobbled pitch. A square of cream card at the foot of the painting claimed it was *Express Dream*. No one else was looking at it. Leonard looked again. A simpering youth, in white silk pyjamas, offered him his tray of smoked-blue glasses. Leonard took one sip. Still Soave after fine champagne. He put the glass on a catalogue table and returned to the painting.

'Hi. Pretty dreadful, ain't it?'

The accent was London. The figure, rotund. A yellow shirt and bottle-green cotton trousers. The face, broad. The stubble, black and grey half a week onward. The eyes, mostly drunk. The breath, yesterday's.

'I think I like it. In fact I *do*.'

The man shook his head. Burped.

Then I'll tell you something for nothing. You're either a connoisseur or a fuckin' idiot.'

'Does one follow the other?'

'Like it enough to buy it?'

'Yes, but no.'

'So you don't like it that much. Seven hundred. Pretty reasonable.'

'No, I do like it that much. But I don't have anywhere to hang it and I don't have that sort of money.'

The man was looking at the canvas. As if for the first time. His head was tucked into his throat and he was moving his upper body back and forth. An elaborate focusing exercise. The tumbler he was holding started to spill. It was whisky.

'What d'you like about it?'

'It has strength.'

'What does that mean?'

Leonard smiled his best. Took off his spectacles, started to polish.

'What I say. Strong use of colours. Strong idea. Don't know about the title, but that doesn't matter. Anyway, what do you think?'

The man looked at him suspiciously.

'Sure you're not buying it?'

'Sure.'

The man ran a thick finger beneath the buttoned neck of his shirt. Sighed.

'Then I'll tell you what I think. It's fuckin' rubbish. But then I know what I'm talking about. I painted the fuckin' thing.'

Leonard stooped as he slipped on his spectacles. The artist saved him the effort.

'Jules Benedict.'

He was scratching his belly. By the sound of it, it was very hairy. Or very spotty. To Leonard, he did not look like a Jules. Nor even a Benedict.

'Well, Mr Benedict, I think you're very wrong.'

Benedict took a drink. Waved a chunky arm at a gaggle of backs across the room.

'Tell them, sunshine. Tell them. They need a rumour before they'll buy anything over three-fifty or anything under three grand. You have to do a whisper job on them.'

Leonard looked blank. Jules Benedict looked at his drink. Decided not yet. Maybe it was the only whisky in the gallery.

'Talk it up. Whisper that it's undervalued, or that JBs have started selling big in the Smoke.'

'And have they?'

The artist gave him a long watery bloodshot look.

'Have they buggery. One or two, but by the time the fuckin' gallery's got into you you're pushed to come out with half the catalogue price.'

He shuffled nearer. Put his hand on Leonard's sleeve.

'Listen. Perhaps we can do something privately. Meet you halfway on the gallery price and mine? Yeah?'

Leonard looked down at his boots, then into the man's eyes.

'Maybe. Tell me, who are all these people who won't buy your paintings?'

Benedict peered.

'Tossers.'

'Because they won't buy your genius?'

'Because they're tossers.'

Leonard watched the rest of the room as Benedict continued. The women sculptured or interesting, the men predictable and, when they were not, then mainly too old for their clothes.

'Most of them? Nice enough. I'll give 'em that. Nice enough. Nice enough by themselves. Put them together? Well, they're tossers.'

'And they're often together.'

Benedict nodded with the seriousness of a serious drinker.

'Course. If you're in with this lot, really in, in the inner circle, then Bath's too small. Lunch with someone and you're sitting next to someone you're having dinner with. Screw someone's wife and her old man's giving your ex one. You get stoned, they're all right. Don't, and you'll want to piss in their pockets.'

'Is there much of that?'

'Pissing?'

'Getting stoned.'

'You down from London or something? Bristol?'

'No. But I've only been here a couple of months.'

Benedict wagged his finger.

'So you're looking for some, are you?'

'I was wondering.'

'I'd guess half that lot's screwing around.'

'Doing drugs?'

'Bit. Mostly nothing to frighten the fuckin' parson.'

'Mostly means not all.'

Benedict stood back.

'Now that, mate, is not for the likes of you and me. That is very private in this town. And it ain't money. No way. That's private.'

'Just drugs?'

'Why you interested?'

Leonard smiled, shrugged. Nice guy. Naive. Just down from who-knows-where.

'Surprised, that's all. Bath is, well . . .'

'Nice? Nothing exciting happens outside the Rec?'

'Well, isn't that true?'

'Ah, mate, the black art of the truth game. What's your name?'

'Leonard.'

'Well, let me tell you something, Len, this place is no different from any other smart city. There's lots of money. There's lots of bored money.'

He smiled. Friendly. Harmless. *Express Dreams* forgotten. Swaying just enough to go with the yellow shirt.

'You see, Len. Let them do it. Let them do it. As the lady said, as long as they don't frighten the horses, so what?'

Leonard nodded. Chums. He did his best with the smile of dawning.

'Horses. That reminds me. Ever heard of something called the merry-go-round?'

Benedict was about to drink. Changed his mind. He was a little bit more sober than before Leonard's question. He nodded at the tweeds.

'You a critic, Len?'

'No.'

'What line you in, then?'

'Does it matter?'

'It just did.'

'Why?'

'Cos there's nothing about fuckin' merry-go-rounds on the tourist map. Come on, Len, what's your line of country?'

'I'm a policeman.'

The artist started to chuckle. It began as a rumble somewhere in his belly. It grew and the canary corduroy shuddered. It reached his throat and it was a roar. It reached his mouth, a bellow. Leonard found himself smiling, then laughing. Jules Benedict rubbed at his eyes with his sleeve.

'Well, well, well. Let me tell you something, Len: if I were you, in future I'd stick to the 'ello, 'ello, 'ello routine.'

'And the merry-go-round?'

'Never heard you, mate. Never heard you.'

Hilary James appeared. She floated in from the corridor which presumably led to 'you-know-where'. She clung to his arm as if he were a bargain.

'James darling, I'm so sorry. But you've met the most wonderful man in the whole room. How clever you are. Jules, you're drinking whisky.'

Benedict was openly surprised.

'Well, mate, you really are getting warm.'

Hilary James looked from one to the other. She did not care to be left out of private conversations.

'Now, Jules, what are you saying?'

The artist scratched his arm this time. The whisky slopped this time.

'When you want me to give you one, darling, you just give me a bell. OK?'

He wandered off in the direction of an oriental-looking woman in a turquoise silk smock. They stood side by side, Benedict caressing the woman's buttocks, heads on one side in front of a still life. He looked back for a moment to where they were standing. But he looked only at James Leonard.

It was noisy. Hilary James whispered very close to his ear.

'My first promise delivered. These are Bath's beautiful people.'

It was not that noisy.

'Your friends?'

'I don't have friends. Friends are too demanding. I have people I know. That way no one is offended when I am bored.'

'I'll remember that.'

'James! You're sulking and we hardly know each other. How wonderful.'

Leonard wondered how long he was going to have to keep up the charade.

'Tell me, Mrs James . . .'

She put a finger over his lips.

'That's very naughty. *Hilary*'

'Tell me, Hilary, what is the merry-go-round?'

He might just as well have asked if she wore odour-eaters. He tried again.

'Merry-go-round?'

'Montague said you were intelligent, James. Let's not waste time talking about things I don't understand.'

'Don't know, or don't understand?'

'I know nothing, James. I'm a tourist. I don't really care either. Merry-go-rounds are things in fairs. I never go to fairs. Never. So I do not know. OK?'

She was about to move on, her arm through his, and he tightened his grip and stopped her.

'Tell me. Why did your husband want me to come here?'

'Did he especially? I thought you might care to come. Anyway, I get bored coming to these things by myself. Some of your species are so suggestive. Let us say I brought my own policeman. Or rather my husband's.'

Leonard let it pass. He wasn't going to be tripped by this woman.

Two fashionably bored-looking males were heading in their direction. Like an accomplished ballroom dancer, Hilary turned Leonard and glided with him to a group standing in front of a long, unframed canvas. The males took the hint. A little sulkily perhaps, but the shorter one gave the other a comforting touch of the cheek and they drifted arm in arm to admire what appeared to be a stainless-steel jagged totem pole.

Hilary James saw Leonard watching them.

'Silly boys. They just wanted to ask me where I got my dress. They always do. D'you like it? You haven't said so.'

'Yes. It's, er, very fetching.'

'Fetching!'

She had a pretty laugh. Real.

'Is that the wrong word?'

'Oh dear, James. Of course it isn't. It's not one of *my* words. But it's nice. I shall use it in future. Why is it fetching? What does "fetching" mean?'

'Sort of attractive.'

'Only sort of?'

'Very.'

'it's very soft.'

She ran her fingers across her breasts.

'Feel.'

And then she laughed again and moved away. As she did, he followed. They stopped at a small group. The painting was unframed. Tall. Thick black and green tropical foliage. In the foreground a near-lifesize figure of a young woman. Lithe. Oiled. Crouched. Snarling at the artist. Arms outstretched and fingers curled as she backed away. A snake hanging about her neck, its fangs bared to defend her, its tail brushing a long brown nipple.

Hilary James dug her nails into his bicep. Her voice was a whisper.

'Isn't it magical?'

Leonard moved slightly to pull away his arm, but her grip tightened.

'*Jungle Cat.*'

'What?'

He turned with his question. She was staring straight ahead. A film of moisture on her upper lip, her voice still a whisper.

'*Jungle Cat*. That's what it's called. Can't you see it? Doesn't it excite you?'

Leonard said nothing. The face was not the face of a human. It was not the face of a cat. The artist had taken the model's face and had started to dissolve it into the wild lines of a puma. A human cat. The body could only be erotic. The face threatened. The eyes of *Jungle Cat* were shrieking at him. Daring him. This was her jungle. Her darkness. The body was on the move. Retreating. The claws ready to rip at the artist if he came closer. He? A woman was standing by his side. Hilary James was introducing her.

'Norma. This is James. He's too lost for words. We all are. It's wonderful. You know it is.'

She did not put out a hand. She was small. Eurasian. A silk turquoise smock. The eyes were laughing quietly.

'You like it?'

'Yours?'

Hilary's hand was still on his arm.

'Of course, James. Don't you think she's wonderful? Now, Norma, you must tell me, who is she?'

'She's *Jungle Cat*. Does she have to be anyone but herself?'

Hilary pretended to pout. She was probably quite good at the real thing.

'But we must meet.'

'You have.'

'Norma, you're being naughty. Of course we haven't. Is she local?'

Leonard ignored them. Watched the *Jungle Cat* watching him. He was mesmerized but didn't understand. It was not the nakedness. Nor the blatant sexuality. The snake was real. Too real. Somewhere inside he wanted to shout No! The eyes were inhuman. He stared back.

Norma turned to him. When she smiled, her eyes were soft. Her teeth tiny and sharp against her scented skin.

'Do you have a helmet outside?'

He grinned.

'No. I'm a detective.'

'And what do you detect?'

He looked about them. There were more people than when he had arrived. Hilary had gone. He wondered where.

'Bath society buying for its walk.'

'Wrong. Bath society saying they'll buy.'

An accent he could not place. Partly American? No. Did not matter. He turned back to the painting. On the title card, there was a small round sticker.

'You've sold this.'

'It has a notoriety value. Or will do.'

'Why?'

'They want to know who the model is. They think she's erotic. Sexy. Real. It's a great fantasy. It was already sold before this.'

'Who bought it?'

'No, no. That too is part of the mystery.'

'Or part of the hype.'

'Why not? It'll be talked about for a while and then maybe it will become a mystery. More than likely it'll become a bore.'

'Then what?'

She smiled. She tucked her hands into big sleeves. Swayed as she spoke.

'Do you always ask lots of questions? Of course, I was forgetting, you're a policeman.'

'Benedict told you. Why?'

Her eyes were oval. Dark.

'You made him laugh. He liked you.'

'I asked him about the merry-go-round. That didn't make him laugh.'

'Is that important?'

'The merry-go-round? Could be. If I knew what it was.'

'Why not *is*?'

Leonard searched her face for her reason. Eyes still soft. No longer amused. Not frightened.

'Tell me about it. What is it?'

He might not have spoken. She was looking at his face. She touched his chin.

'Would you sit for me?'

'No.'

'Tomorrow. Here. Eleven o'clock.'

'No.'

'I think you should. I want to show you something. Eleven o'clock.'

She took his hand. Then left him standing before *Jungle Cat*. Her nails were very long.

Thirty-Two

It was late. The place was a mess. China mugs, their cartoons and logos stained with the runs of foul coffee. The half-finished crossword covered with the scabs of an abandoned cheeseburger. The sweat of men too long on their feet, too tired to go home. Stainger paused at the door of the Incident Room and disliked it all. One or two officers twitched where they slouched, but none felt the need to look busy, to break into activity that had long been discarded. Only Somers-Barclay responded true to form. His shirt was crisp, his hair shampooed that very evening. His cufflinks, once his grandfather's, gleamed.

'Coffee, sir?'

He was offering the glass jug from Marsh's room. Stainger shook his head. He wanted a result. He wasn't going to get it from a funnel of mountain blend. He had just come from a meeting in Bristol. The Chief Constable wanted to know how the investigation was going. Marsh had said it was a matter of time. Stainger wondered if his colleague was thinking in light years. The Chief Constable had been quite specific. They did not have the resources to chase this one indefinitely. If a result appeared unlikely, then it was best not to mess about. Stainger had said why not give it forty-eight hours and then scale down the inquiry? The Chief Constable wanted to know why it was necessary to wait so long. Keep it open, but don't tie up a third of Bath's overstretched force on something that was unlikely to come to anything. Stainger was not inclined to agree but guessed he might have to.

The team in front of him had more or less come to the end of the normal inquiries. The megabytes of information were in and had been cross-matched. There wasn't much. Marsh was leading from the front, which was good. But no one, including Marsh, appeared to know where they were going. That couldn't be allowed to last. He looked across at Sergeant Jack. She was comparing files and handwritten reports. So much for modern information technology, he thought.

'Well? Anything?'

He knew the answer before he asked the question. If there had been anything new he'd have been told. The briefings had been empty. Lane had shaken his head in the corridor five minutes before. But he wanted to hear it from them. Heads were shaking. Shoulders shrugging. Somers-Barclay, ever on the fast track, had a spin of his own.

'Still pressing on, sir. Nothing yet. But still *en avant*, you know.'

'No, I don't know.'

Sergeant Jack had not looked up. He wanted everyone on this.

'Maddy?'

She smiled. Stainger was the only one in the job who called her that. She tossed her pencil on the pad. Leaned back and stretched. It cheered up most of the men.

'Just one thing, sir. There really might be a connection between Rainbow Wood and this one.'

Somers-Barclay's sniff was obvious. Stainger's annoyance nearly so. But there was nothing else.

'This Inspector Leonard's idea?'

Sergeant Jack heard alarm bells.

'Not entirely, sir. It is, for example, perfectly true that the

Rainbow Wood files are missing. But one thing's certain, the name of the man killed ten years ago was Bolt.'

'Are we sure?'

'Yes, sir, as near as we can be.'

Somers-Barclay produced one of his flaws.

'Surely, sir, we've got to be closer than "as near as we can be". Anyway, even if it's true, so what? It doesn't prove there's a connection.'

Stainger's answer was to raise an eyebrow in Madeleine Jack's direction. She knew the connection, but laying it out in full would drop Leonard in Stainger's cage. She did not want that. She looked at her notes. Then, pointedly ignoring Somers-Barclay's leer, at Stainger.

'With respect, sir, the link between the two murders is that the someone who knew Piccolo is the someone who knew the name of the man in Rainbow Wood.'

Stainger folded his arms.

'Who is this someone?'

This is what Madeleine Jack had tried to avoid. If she told Stainger, then Josie would be blown. If that happened, so would Leonard. She took the dangerous way out.

'It's one of Dl Leonard's marks.'

Stainger's stare picked up a grade of intensity.

'And, as a result of Dl Leonard's lead, I've checked it out with my own source. He confirms independently.'

She sat back. There was silence. Somers-Barclay did not say anything because he knew more about protocol than the Earl Marshal of All England himself and was not fool enough to jump in where Stainger might first tread. Stainger did not say anything because it was obvious that Leonard should have fleshed out his source's evidence and that it should be available to the whole investigation. Stainger would never say anything against any senior officer in front of juniors. The voice from the doorway did it for them all. Lane had come back with a nearly fresh cheeseburger. He took a bite. The green pickle squelched and oozed over his fingers.

'Seems to me, boss, that maybe it's time we have this mark in here. I imagine Jimbo's on to that one, don't you?'

At that moment, James Leonard was not on to anything. He had left the Minerva Gallery just in time to see the green Rolls-Royce pulling away. Hilary James saw him, but gave no sign. Montague James was sitting beside her and did not look his way. Jules Benedict was on the step in front of him. He did not recognize Leonard. Not at first. By the state of him, Benedict's mind was as slurred as his speech.

'Oh, it's . . . it's you. You. Whatsitsname.'

Leonard waved. Started down the slope towards Lansdown Crescent. But Jules Benedict had other ideas.

'Oi! Oi! Len. Oi!'

Leonard turned. He tried a smile. He wanted a quiet evening. He looked at his watch. Light still. Nine-forty. A quiet evening. What was left of it. He had questions for Josie. Had she known Norma? Benedict? Any of them? Had Piccolo? But the evening didn't happen that way.

Benedict said he fancied a drink. Leonard said that he had an appointment. Benedict said he was off to the merry-go-round, was he? Leonard fell for it.

They found a pub at the bottom of Camden. Everyone seemed to know Benedict. As the evening went on, it was clear that Benedict knew everyone in Bath – or everyone who used the pub. It was also clear that Benedict was going through what he called 'this week's fuckin' crisis'. Norma had told him he couldn't use the gallery. Too many insults. Too much booze. Too many friends who stole everything that moved. But, especially, too much booze. Norma, according to the drunken artist, was a bitch. Yes, she had told him to go to hell. Benedict was not impressed. He was already there.

They had left the pub and now, on the rickety pavement, with the night air attacking him from all angles, Benedict's eyes were weeping with self-pity and more whisky than

Leonard could afford. It was a gruesome combination. Also, a very vulnerable one. Benedict stumbled. Did not fall. But he would. When he did, Leonard wanted to be there, to hear what he had to say. He propped him against the railing and searched George Street for a cab. Like policemen, never a cab when you wanted one, Leonard thought.

He heard the muttering and struggling gait and looked back to see Benedict along the street and stumbling down the steep stone steps of the wine bar. Leonard still believed Benedict in his present state might be vulnerable to Norma's scorn and therefore would tell him things he needed to hear. He caught up with him as Benedict was lurching into one of the arched and dimly lit alcoves into which coal was once poured from the elegantly cast covers in the George Street pavements. Benedict demanded more light. Leonard gave him a large whisky. Benedict forgot the light.

'So fuckin' Len's a fuckin' copper. Well, well, well. And, and you sly old bastard, you're giving La James one.'

Leonard raised his glass in salute. Said nothing. Benedict clinked his tumbler against Leonard's soda water. Lots of ice and lemon. Benedict drank a lot of the whisky.

'Bet she goes like a rattler, don't she?'

He did not notice Leonard's silence. Perhaps Benedict preferred to give answers to his questions. He then got the ones he wanted.

'Bet she does. Bet she does. I tell you something, Len, that woman's got a fine pair, a fine pair. And an arse. I tell you, Len, normally it's only people like me who put arses like that on women. You get a model and you have to do the arse yourself. Most of them have got slack botties. Dropsy. One last week. Great up front. Behind. Sags away!'

It came out like a deckhand's roar. And he had not finished.

'Got a crease where it ended and the leg started. Could have posted a letter in it.'

He tried to light a cigarette. Fumbled with the packet. Then the bookmatches. Then he coughed. The deep inhaling would get him before the whisky that night. He was holding the tumbler and the cigarette in the same hand. He pulled on the cigarette. Not a drop spilled. He was almost gone, but not out. He'd done this before. Alcoholic brinkmanship was his pastime. He drew a curve with his free hand.

'But La James? Not her. Never wears anything underneath. You can tell, you know.'

Leonard sipped his soda water. It was time to break in. To keep Benedict warm.

'You would know, Jules. Or so I imagine.'

'Imagine? Me? Not just imagine, Len. Oh no. I'm an arse man myself. You? You an arse man, Lennie?'

Leonard looked away. Benedict's stare was urgent. He needed reassurance.

'Anyway, Len, don't have to believe me. You just ask Norma. Now there's a nice little botty for you. And it's oriental, you know, Lennie. Not known for their bottles, are they? Most of them flat as a Gideon Bible.'

'Why should Norma know?'

'They're like that. Aren't they?'

'Like what?'

Benedict, with some difficulty, crossed his fingers.

'Like that, Len. Very close. And if anyone would know it would have to be Norma. Have to be. 'Cept your good self of course, Lennie. 'Cept your good self.'

He slumped further into the corner. The small wrought-iron table shifted. The glass specimen vase toppled. The water ran to the floor. The carnation was left stranded. Leonard put the vase on the next table. Benedict flicked at his wet leg as if brushing cigarette ash. He dropped the cigarette. Looked at it. Not much focus. It kept moving. Maybe two of them. It smouldered. He kicked at it and it doused in the pool of water.

'How close, Jules?'

Benedict's chin was on his chest.

'What?'

'Norma and Hilary. How close?'

'We're just good friends, she told the *Express*. Jush good friends.'

Leonard watched the tumbler slipping. Reached for it. But his reflexes were not as quick as the artist's instincts. Benedict opened his eyes and raised the glass to his lips. When he spoke, his voice clouded in the tumbler.

'All part of the rich tapeshtry, Lennie. Life's rich fuckin' tapeshtry. All part of the merry-go-round, ain't it?'

Leonard waited. Wanted to ask. Needed to hold back. The pause took ages. Then Benedict struggled up, leaned on the wobbling table. Continued.

'Place hasn't really changed, you know, Bath, you know? Hasn't changed. You know about that Hadrian?'

'The Roman?'

'Fuckin' right the Roman. Not just your high-street version. *The* Hadrian. The emperor one. Know about him? Know what he did?'

Leonard shook his head.

'He stopped all the fuckin'. That's what he did. Those Romans used to get in the baths here, right?

Leonard waited.

'Course they did, Len. Everyone knows that. And I tell you something, Len, when you got no clothes on, it's pretty hard to impress anyone how much dosh you got. So the Romans, well, they'd count oily girls. Bloke used to lie by the bath and if he had, say, four birds oiling him, then he was a cat. If he had half a dozen of the little darlings, then he was a fat cat.'

He slumped again. Exhausted.

'What's this got to do with . . .'

Benedict waved his arms, spilling his whisky, bewildered by Leonard's ignorance.

'Lennie. Everyone, and I mean everyone, knows. They weren't washing each other. They were giving each other one. Sho . . . sho along comes Hadrian, a right prick. What does he do? One wave of the staff and up goes the notice. No more mixed bathing. End of public orgies.'

'I still don't see what this has to do with Norma and Hilary James.'

'Because, my old son, Hadrian still rules. Right?'

Leonard supposed so.

'But Norma, Hilary and all their darling friends are still into it.'

The slump was almost complete. Even Benedict was having trouble with the dregs in the glass. Leonard watched the artist's breathing, the hands, the eyes trying to hold on to today. It was time.

'The merry-go-round?'

Benedict's head went up and down. Very, very slowly as his eyelids closed. The sound came out as a running-down gramophone.

'Right, Len. Right. That's what I was telling you. They're on the merry-go-round. All very private. Top people bonkin', Len. Fat fuckin' cats only. Take care, Len. Bad news. Bad, bad news.'

The last syllables slipped away from the tongue. Thickly, quietly, unknowingly. The gramophone done.

Thirty-Three

It was one in the morning. Leonard had called a cab. The first two taxi offices had refused. One of them said to try an ambulance. Benedict had fallen down a couple of times. The bleeding from the nose did not help. The third took him. The driver had heard the radio conversation between control and the reluctant cabbies. He turned out to be the artist's brother-in-law. Or had been. Leonard was puzzled.

'I hadn't realized he was married.'

'Old Jim? Well, he's not, is he? Not now, he's not. My sister got wise to him. She's got herself a farmer over Godney way. Much better than this one.'

'Jim? You mean Jules.'

The driver had laughed.

'Jules! Jim. Jim Robson.'

The taximan looked into the back. The snoring, rotting lump was smiling in some fantasy.

'Well, you can't blame the old sod really. Whoever heard of anyone buying a picture from a Jim Robson?'

The driver was gone. Still laughing as Leonard made his way down the hill wondering what was in a name. Maybe Monet sounded ordinary in French. Norma? Didn't sound like an artist. Perhaps it was. Instead of walking down Milsom Street with its expensive windows and hanging baskets, he crossed the square and then the back streets which would lead him to the bath. No tapes. No duty policeman. Blue sheeting had been tied over the inside of the grille and Leonard pictured the inside.

Was there something obvious they had overlooked? The pool with the centre plume of opaque hot water. Strong, steaming, forced from the Mendips through miles of limestone. The narrow stone terrace. Rickety enough for the utility black iron railing. Plants in the wall. Some contrived. Some wayward. Nothing there. He walked to the other side of the walled pool. There was now a padlocked chain across the wooden entrance. The horse had gone which way? He went back to the grille. Nothing. From behind him, a door opened and then closed. He heard the tumbling of the deadlocks. High heels. A pause. Then that slight Australian accent.

'Oh it's you, Inspector. You gave me a bit of a fright.'

Patsy Bush walked across the echoing street to where he stood looking at the bath.

'Sorry. Working late?'

She shook her head. The hair, bobbed and expensively cut, moved like a matador's cape.

'A late, a too-late, supper. So I'm picking up notes for a breakfast meeting tomorrow. What about you? Still chasing phantoms?'

She was businesslike but, he felt, laughing at him. She

knew the system. She knew the system was winning. There was so little to go on, the city almost might not have had a murder. Leonard was losing patience with the city.

'Phantoms don't put pokers up the rectums of travellers.'

'You're not very subtle, Inspector.'

I'm a policeman, not a sauce chef.'

They fell into step towards the empty shopping precinct. He glanced at her.

'D'you mind a couple of questions?'

'You chatting me up?'

'At this time of the morning?'

Her laugh echoed. The hand to the mouth like a naughty schoolgirl. Leonard thought her too smart to have ever been caught. Maybe too smart to have been naughty. She was dressed for a smart reception or dinner. Not a hair nor a move out of place.

'Tell me, Miss Bush, what happened to your report on vagrancy in the city?'

'Did anything happen to it?'

'I'm asking you.'

'Sorry, Mr Leonard, you've got the wrong colony. It wasn't mine. Came out of Town Management.'

'But it was covered up?'

'Right.'

Leonard was surprised by Patsy Bush's candour.

'Why?'

'Bad for business. Obvious, I would have thought. It's a big problem. Last Christmas, for example, we had more beggars than shoppers. Bath isn't a breadline, Inspector. Publicity of the problem wouldn't send them back to Glastonbury. But it would make the park'n'ride redundant.'

They stopped across from the Pump Room's black doors. Inside, the deep chandelier was unlit. In the porch, two travellers lay on flattened cartons. She shrugged in their direction.

'It's a problem. We cope the best we can. People come here to spend not to give hand-outs. Especially at Christmas and festivals. Cruel, but that's the size of it. If they don't come, the city dies, the problem is bigger. So, no cover-up, Mr Leonard, simply a strategic decision not to give it wide circulation.'

'At whose instigation?'

'Consensus.'

'And who chairs that particular committee?'

She smiled. Not much, but she did. She was tired. She put out her hand. It was cool, the grip firm. Honest. The formality surprised him.

"Night, Mr Leonard. See you around.'

'Who?'

She stopped a few feet away.

'Ask his wife. 'Night.'

Leonard watched her go. Tall. An easy swing. The girl most likely to succeed. Untouchable. He wandered through the arches and by the abbey and then through a back lane and turned right into Manvers Street.

There was no one in the Major Incident Room. He thought about phoning Josie. She would be asleep. Leave her that way. He'd be back in ten minutes. He went into Marsh's sanctum, put a hand on the coffee machine. Warm, nearly hot. He poured coffee into a plastic cup, sipped and left the nearly full cup on the sill. He could see a light under Stainger's door, but he did not knock. In his own room, stickers told him that while he was out the world and his brother had tried to get him. He picked up three. Dover had called. No message, just a number. Leonard assumed it was the *Chronicle*'s. He looked at his watch. One-forty-five. There'd be no one there. Mrs Bowles had called. No message. The third was a brown envelope. Internal. No stamp. Just addressed: *Inspector Leonard. Personal.* Inside, a single sheet of paper. The handwriting finishing-school regular, the bottoms of the letters flat as if written above a ruler.

Sir,
Thought you should know. There's
talk of asking you to bring in Josie. I haven't
mentioned her, but they know you have a
contact linking both murders. I'll be at home
about eleven-thirty.

Sgt Jack.

The warning was enough, but he was grateful. Grateful enough not to disturb her. Instead, he shredded the letter. Switched off the light. Walked downstairs and let himself out.

The cider drunk had gone. But his bottle was there. Not rolled. Upright and to attention. A patrol car came through from the bus station. It slowed, the driver peered, waved, and it headed on past the police station, towards the city centre. Leonard turned back and went past the car park. The drunk was in the corner by Dukes Place. He would not be there long. Normally he was bedded down by ten. He had a plaster. When he saw Leonard he turned his head. A child pretending what he could not see was not there.

'Got yourself a knock.'

The drunk was clutching a paper bag. He put a dirty finger to his forehead. His expression was one of discovery. Maybe remembering. It couldn't have been long. The plaster was clean. The eye was going to be blue.

'No, I haven't.'

'Fall over?'

'So I did. Fuck off.'

Leonard crouched on the wall ledge beside the man. He could see the lip. Split. A cold sore, possibly, but more likely caused by a heavy ring. He put a pound coin on the ground between them. He knew what the old fool would buy with it. Didn't much care.

'Fall over?'

'Yes.'

But this time he did not tell Leonard to go. His nose was

dripping. Leonard wondered if it would hit the coin. It would be a pity. It was heads up.

'Who hit you?'

'Fuck off.'

Leonard put down the second coin.

'Who?'

'Don't know.'

He was shivering again. The third coin went down. The drunk clutched the bag and slid his fingers along the pavement. Leonard moved the three coins just out of reach.

'Don't know.'

'They tell you anything?'

He watched as Leonard very slowly, with his boot, moved the coins towards him. When he spoke, the drunk was almost in a trance. Could have been an engraver explaining his art to a silent apprentice.

'Said not to speak to you, that's what. Fuck off.'

'Who said?'

The spell was broken. The drunk rolled, scrabbled to his feet, clutching the paper bag. Dragged his lame foot and away to the bottom of the car park. Leonard did not really mind. He'd blown it. The drunk probably did not even know who they had been. If anyone at all. Might even have been kids having fun. They did sometimes. He waited. He knew the man was watching. He walked away. Left the money.

He dawdled. Thinking. He half-expected to see a light in Melincourt. Didn't know why. Didn't even know why he should have gone that way. It was not on his way home. Harriet Bowles lived nowhere near her shop. He wasn't thinking or perhaps he was and that was why he was on such a detour. He thought about Norma. What had she meant? 'I want to show you something.' Really? Just a ploy? Eleven o'clock. Forget it.

As he approached his flat, Leonard sensed, rather than saw, something wrong. He was coming from the Pulteney end of the road. The gloss-black railings smartly painted that spring by the management company sparkled in the light from the standards. He could see from some distance that the iron gate was open. Nothing odd. Postman usually shut it, but this was June. Maybe the relief man was on. Maybe circulars. Nothing strange. Just instinct.

For a few seconds, Leonard stood at the top of the stone steps. The dustbin, even in the shadows, was undisturbed. The bay tree still safely padlocked in its tub by the doorway. It was the door. Not closed. Not wide open. Just not closed. Maybe too hot. Maybe Josie had opened it for a draught. Josie would not know about through-draughts. He remembered the patrol car. Back-up? For what? Maybe nothing. He had no radio. Nearest phone box? By the pub. Forget it.

Boots were not good for tiptoe policing. He held the side-rail to lift some of his weight. The right boot creaked. He'd not noticed before. At the door, he looked at the jamb. Nothing forced. No need. Anyone who watched television knew how to do it. A small pane above the handle had been taken out. Glass-cutter and suction pad. Left against the wall awaiting the glazier. Very tidy. Odd. He could hear the drain and the shower. He thought of calling out. Didn't.

Leonard stepped onto the coir doormat. Listened again. He wanted to call her name. Did not. The light in the hall was out. At the far end of the long inner corridor he could see into the open bathroom. The thick white plastic shower curtain was pulled-to and undisturbed. As he went towards the open bathroom door he knew instinctively that there was no one in the side-rooms. But he stopped at each door frame. Checked. Sitting-room. Empty. The glass doors to the garden were right back. He could see Johnson puffed and waiting on the wall overlooking the river. Spare bedroom. Check. Empty. The pillows still soft. Hardly disturbed. His shirt, still soft. Hardly disturbed. He wondered about the kitchen through the living-room. Dismissed it. Too late. He was too late. He knew that now. He edged into the small bathroom, looking over his shoulder as he did. Nervous. He was a policeman. Of course he was nervous. He had been there. Frightened. Of course. The hole in the curtain was in the middle and big enough. Josie was sitting facing him on the tiled floor of the shower. The water ran cold over her lap. She was very thin. Very thin. Her chest had been blown away.

Leonard reached in and switched off the shower. Nothing moved. He heard a clank as the over-run system recovered from his yank on the shower-lever. But nothing moved. Josie did not move. Not now.

He went into the sitting-room and picked up the telephone. Dialled. Said enough. He re-dialled. Sergeant Jack took three rings to answer. He told her what she needed to know. She said she would be over. She had not been asleep. As he put down the telephone, there was a noise. Nothing much. A scratching. The kitchen. He had not checked the kitchen. Leonard picked up the smoked-glass Sappho and held it in front of him. Another scratch. Then a whimper. A pup's whimper. He opened the kitchen door and picked up the mongrel and went into the garden and sat in the long chair to wait.

He sat, staring. Remembering other times. Bad times. He could feel her against his leg. He understood grief for the first time. Johnson jumped from the wall and, somewhere in Leonard's reactive system, an eye marked the spot. A purple ragbag. Josie's purple ragbag. By the wall, in the shadow, where Johnson washed one raised paw, ignoring the pup.

Leonard picked up the bag. Took it inside and pulled things onto the table. There would be a search. Best to look first. A cloth begging rag with a few coins. One of them an outdated fivepenny piece. Even beggars got cheated in the city. A few beads. A headband. An orange and green woven purse. No money inside that. Just bits of paper. Her passport to social security. There were other odds and ends, but nothing that couldn't wait. At the bottom of the bag he could feel another cloth. He laid it on the table with the rest. Just two things. A small silver piccolo. A small thin booklet. A passport. An

American passport. Inside, the explanation. It was Bolt's passport. The face was the face of the dead man in the bath. But
the name was not Piccolo. The document had no doubts. The
bearer who was entitled to all the protection of the state
which declared In God We Trust was Richard L. Bolt.

Leonard, his head back, blinking at the obvious, tapped out
his morsed thoughts. At last. The connection. He flicked
through the back and empty pages. A carefully creased piece
of shiny magazine paper was between the back cover and the
last page. It was carefully cut from what looked like an estate
agent's advertisement. Not a house for sale, but perhaps an
apartment. He blinked and held the wrinkled and small coloured illustration. Only one picture. Cleverly shot by someone
who knew what sold apartments. It was taken in a room,
enough of which showed its elegance and beyond which was
a magnificent view of the city of Bath.

Thirty-Four

Madeleine Jack arrived two minutes before everyone and his
brother. She really had not been asleep. He told her everything
she needed to know. She was covered. He would take it from
there. She nodded and very quietly, very thoroughly, went
through each room. On the dresser, something caught her eye.
Something open. She closed it and put it in her shoulder-bag.

Marsh most definitely had been asleep. So had Stainger.
Marsh was bad-tempered. Stainger was in the way but wanted
to see for himself. Somers-Barclay had been on a bleeper, as
Marsh's doggy. If he felt any annoyance at having been disturbed during the most thorough cardiac examination he had
ever experienced, he showed no sign. And, somehow, he was
freshly shaved. No one else was. But then he was Somers-
Barclay. The Screaming Skull was the last to arrive, but that
was two and a half hours later. All the way from Cardiff. All
very unusual, but then this was all very unusual.

By seven-fifteen in the morning, Leonard had briefed both Stainger and Marsh in the former's office. The Assistant Chief Constable had been informed. The head of public affairs had been told as much as could be told and was on his way over to Bath.

The duty sub-editor at the *Chronicle* had checked the morning recorded message from police headquarters and was about to tell the editor's seven-forty news conference that there was nothing much of interest overnight. The deputy arrived as she was about to speak, apologized for being late and asked what all the police fuss and hardware was doing at the end of Dukes Place. Peter Dover had flexed his hands but not picked up his direct line. Do not interfere. Direct where necessary. The second clenching and unclenching and the duty news editor had excused herself and gone back to her desk. In three minutes she was back to say that a body had been found in an apartment. Cause of death unknown. Person unknown. Nothing more to tell anyone. A statement from Bath District police could be expected later in the day.

By eight o'clock, a news photographer had been diverted from a delayed railway commuter story, a freelance crew from HTV and staff men from the BBC studio in Bristol had arrived at the end of the road.

By twenty past eight, Peter Dover had closed both his office doors and dialled Stainger. The woman at the other end was very sorry but the Superintendent was in a meeting. Yes, she would ask him to call back. Could she tell the Superintendent what it was about? Dover told her that he was sure Mr Stainger knew. She did not actually say have a nice day, but she might nearly have done.

Stainger really was in a meeting. Or on his way to one. He had taken three telephone calls. This one was from the ACC. Along his corridor, the Major Incident Room had been cleared. The debris black-bagged. The blackboards wiped, redrawn with major information in yellow. There was plenty of space. Sergeant Jack was standing by the board, chalk and telescopic lecture pointer ready. Leonard was polishing his spectacles. Marsh arrived. Somers-Barclay closed the door, handed Marsh coffee. Marsh said no. Somers-Barclay smiled. Marsh coughed. He looked about the room with all the gravity of a grumpy privy councillor announcing the death of the monarch to courtiers. Only Marsh was still tetchy. He had shaved. He had cut himself. On a buckled foil of his electric razor. Superintendent Marsh was out of many sorts. He did not say so. His tone did. He looked older than yesterday morning when he had approved a gentle scaling down of the investigation.

'Right, listen out. Most of you know or think you know what's happened during the night. I'm going to give you an outline. Then Inspector Leonard will fill in what you most certainly will not know. At least I sincerely hope he will. A woman called Josephine Webster was found dead at two-forty-five this morning. The address is on the board.'

He half-turned. Sergeant Jack tapped the blackboard. The whole room knew whose address it was. Marsh was coughing.

'Death, was, according to the ME, by a single gunshot wound. Probably from a twelve-bore. No weapon found. No witnesses thus far. The flat above is empty. The one next door, people away. Holidays.'

There was a general shifting of chairs as Stainger entered the room. He had been talking to one of the Assistant Chief Constables. The Chief Constable was demanding answers. With him was the head of public affairs. Stainger made an unobtrusive don't-get-up motion with his hand. No one had been about to.

'I will leave Inspector Leonard to explain why there are certain connections with the death of what was, until the early hours of this morning, our current investigation. But let me make a couple of general points.'

He coughed once more. Those who new Marsh well knew also that this was no summer bug. Superintendent Marsh was a nervous speaker, especially when he was angry and unsure of his ground. For the moment he was both of those things – in spite of Leonard's private briefing little more than an hour before. Another sharp, mean cough, and he continued.

'This was a premeditated. Signs of forced entry. Start thinking a pro. Secondly, the dead woman was a material witness to an existing investigation. Start thinking bigger involvement. Thirdly, this took place in the flat of one of your colleagues. The circumstances, don't dare think about them. We have someone who is willing to kill, possibly, possibly, mind you, to suppress evidence and a witness. He, or she, is willing to blow someone away with a shotgun. Each one of you, before you leave this room, even for a pee, is going to go over everything you've gone over before. You're going to make yourselves aware of every aspect of evidence, suggestion, lead and possible lead of both these cases. And then you are all going to pull finger and hit the phones, streets and contacts. I want every favour called in. Understood?'

There was a general murmuring and nodding. Marsh stared about the room. Last Christmas Day he had become a grandfather. He adored his granddaughter. He had perfected chin--tickling and goochy-goochy. None of the officers looking at his expression now would have believed it.

'Questions.'

It was a snapped defiance. Lane's voice, from by the window, was almost lazy in contrast.

'One point, sir. What about Rainbow Wood? I know this has been raised before, but it seems we have a connection to explore between all three.'

There was a silence. Leonard was polishing his spectacles. Holding them up to the light. Polishing again. Blinking. Marsh felt Stainger watching him. Leonard had been too right on too many things. Unconventional. But right. Marsh nodded.

'Would you like to take that one?'

Lane nodded. He already had. Marsh turned to Leonard. Leonard slipped his spectacles on and blinked at the faces turned towards him. His briefing was short. They had expected something from *Crime Monthly*. But at the end of it they knew what they needed to know. Lane noticed that Leonard did not say when Josie had turned up. He did not raise it.

The name of the dead man in Rainbow Wood, we believe, was Bolt. The man found in the Cross Bath, Richard L Bolt. We have reason to believe they were both Americans. We have no evidence that they were related, but the suggestion is obvious.

'Richard Bolt was twenty-two years and ten months of age. His birthplace is given as Boston. He had arrived in the UK last August on a multiple visa.'

Leonard paused and someone asked if the passport could be a forgery. Someone else's passport? Leonard said he did not know. The US Embassy had been notified, but nothing had come down the line. The computers were awake, but few people were. Washington was five hours behind.

'Sir? Are we sure the Rainbow Wood killing was Bolt?'

It was Somers-Barclay. He looked pleased with himself. But he did most of the time. Leonard turned to Madeleine Jack. She closed her pointer and looked straight at Somers-Barclay's patronizing smile.

'There's an MG 9 on the file. It's in there. The evidence is uncorroborated. It comes from one Steven Reece. He was a reporter on the *Chronicle* at the time of Rainbow Wood. He was the one who raised the name Bolt.'

Marsh grumped. Sniffed.

'Why did we not know this before?'

Sergeant Jack stood her ground.

'Some of it we did, sir. It was not read as significant.'

Marsh looked at Leonard. Looked at Stainger. Leonard continued, but not for long.

He told them about the missing files. The gravestone. The curious story of the missing memory of the undertaker and the missing clerk. He told them that the word 'merry-go-round' appeared to spark but no one said why. He told them about Dancer. He told them about Josie. He told them she had come to him with information and he had protected her. No one asked why. They knew that Stainger and Marsh would have done that Leonard blinked. He told them about his meeting with Montague James. He did not tell them about his meeting with Montague James's wife. Nor about Jules Benedict. Nor about Norma. Nor that he was going to keep his appointment at her studio. Nor did he tell them about the advertisement someone had cut from *Country Life*. He did not know why he did not tell them. He did not do so.

Leonard summed up and looked about for questions. There weren't many. Most of them were answered by Sergeant Jack. Leonard was about to stand down when Somers-Barclay reminded everyone why he was a high-flyer.

'Excuse me, sir, may I ask just one question?'

Leonard blinked. Paused. Blinked. Somers-Barclay put on his gravest expression. Not a line.

'Well?'

It was Marsh who hurried him on.

'Well, sir. I've been back to Inspector Leonard's flat.'

'Come on, man.'

'Well, sir, the shower curtain is very thick. Much thicker than normal curtaining. I believe it is called industrial weight.'

Leonard nodded. It was. Much thicker. Like most things he bought, substantial.

'So what does that mean?'

'Well, sir, I turned on the shower again and looked at the target as a gunman would have seen it from the front door, then from about halfway along, then from about four or five paces and then up close.'

'And?'

'It's just, sir, that I don't believe the gunman would have seen the woman. The gunman would have only seen a figure, especially if the water were hot and steaming.'

There was a silence as Somers-Barclay's point sunk home. He was very good. Johns Hopkins did not after all take many one-year postgraduates, not even from Cambridge, unless they were very good. They had taken Somers-Barclay. He made his final point.

'You see, sir, I don't believe we have enough evidence to say that this woman was the intended victim. My question is obvious, sir.'

Stainger's voice was very quiet. Very Scottish.

'You mean, Nick, seemingly it's very possible that Inspector Leonard was the target?'

'Actually, sir, yes, I do.'

Thirty-Five

The raised voice in Stainger's office had not got any further than the outer room, which said more for the corner alcove entrance than it did for the decibels. But the shouting came not from Stainger, nor from Leonard. Marsh was all for suspending Leonard. 'Unpolicemanlike' was the word he kept using. Hiding a witness. Doing his own thing. Withholding a witness. Marsh's voice was sharp. Menacing. He paced Stainger's office, slightly bent. A tall black angle-poise lamp had taken human form. He spat words before him like zigs of electricity.

'If I had my way, you'd get such a kick up the arse you'd clear fifty feet over the Clifton suspension bridge. OK? Understood?'

Stainger started to interrupt. Stainger's voice quiet now as the other's had risen.

'There is one simple consideration.'

Marsh ignored him. Kept pacing. Stainger backed off. Tactically withdrew. He was senior, but he'd let Marsh burn out.

'This place was quiet. Bath is quiet. It minds its own bloody business. We gave you a simple, a simple, inquiry. Open and shut. OK? Understand? No witnesses. No great hopes. Keep it going. OK? Understand? All we have to do is wait and chummy'll be picked up. On something else. Somewhere else.

Who knows? All tied up, when no one's looking. And what did you do?'

Leonard blinked. Hummed somewhere deep below his breath. Slightly, ever so slightly, jigged his knee as if the hummings were setting his whole body through some aboriginal trance. Marsh's lightning crackled. Each phrase sparked, looking for a conductor.

'I tell you what you did. You got up noses. You off-pissed some extremely, extremely, nice people. You pick up some little scrubber. Right? Scrubber turns out to be a material witness, as they say. Next thing, we have got some sodding little Pol Pot running around the city, this city, with a sodding shooter.'

Stainger observed the pause. Counted to five. When he did speak, he was looking the fuming Marsh in the eye. Leonard kept out of it. Let Stainger hang in. He had the rank.

'I'm not sure I like anyone trying to murder one of my officers.'

Marsh shrugged indifference to the idea.

'Who says anyone did?'

'Somers-Barclay raised a good point.'

'Only a possibility.'

'Realistic.'

Marsh disagreed. Said so.

'Unlikely.'

Stainger disagreed. Said so.

'Possible, you said, which is not unlikely.'

Leonard squinted as the fencing masters of two different schools thrust and parried. Parry. Thrust.

Marsh, the calculating mind. The humourless lay preacher. Determined no faith should falter. Six days a week, a humourless policeman. Persistent in step. A text for every procedure. A believer. Sin, something to be conquered. Then punished. Marsh, a determined punisher. A joyful punisher.

Stainger, still in other men's country. The confident exile. The confident policeman. The discreet solver of crosswords.

225

The quiet professional. The steady tread. First along street. Then ascending the rank ladder. The believer in good. Good, something to cling to. Stainger, too, the believer. The believer in others.

Stainger asked the obvious question.

'Well, James. What do you think? This one had your name on it or the girl's?'

'My name? It missed.'

Marsh looked at Leonard. Nodded to Stainger and left. He closed the door with the consideration of a priest at a bereavement. Superintendent Marsh did not take rows into the corridors.

Stainger sighed.

'He's got a point.'

Leonard blinked. Removed his spectacles. Rubbed them on his green cotton tie. Stainger swung in his executive (superintendents and above) chair. When he spoke, it was over his shoulder as he eyed the manpower chart and its problems.

'But so have I. Young Nick may be right. Maybe they were after you. As we both know, that's different.'

He swung back to face Leonard. Sturdy forearms on his desk. Strong, thick fingers entwined in a mighty fist. He looked into Leonard's eyes. Without his spectacles, Leonard looked serious. Maybe sinister. Stainger did not know what the expression meant, nor whence it came. But, to Stainger, Leonard was not the slightly erratic, slightly professorial odd-ball that some of his colleagues thought. Stainger had never been allowed to see Leonard's Personal Report Folder 206 on whatever it was that he had been doing before the transfer. He had asked to. He was told that it was classified. That, to Stainger, said a lot. It had been classified by the Home Office. He had made some quiet inquiries with the station's two Special Branch officers. But, since their herograms from Chief Constable and London for their work in nailing a couple of IRA terrorists in a local quarry, they had been even more secretive. More independent. The truth was, they did inquire, for their own interests. They were told to pull in their necks. The 206 was not for their eyes. Best forget they'd ever asked.

Stainger was tapping his clean blotter.

'Why would they go at you? You've got something you didn't tell in there?'

He nodded in the direction of the Major Incident Room.

'Nothing worth killing me for.'

'Are you the best judge?'

'Are they?'

Stainger tapped his fingers. Could be.

'They think you have something, but are wrong. But, if the boy wonder's right and you were the target, you must have some idea. So give. I need to have something to protect you.'

'And to keep the ACC off your back.'

'And yours.'

Leonard liked Stainger. But gave nothing. Not yet.

'Try with a couple of ideas, James.'

'What did he mean by getting up people's noses?'

Stainger tried a half-smile. Almost worked.

'Some officers are very political. They hear about these things. Maybe a word from someone in his lodge. But there you are. You know about these things as much as I do. I sometimes think the whole damn force is on the square or whatever it is they do.'

'He's a Mason?'

'Grand and wondrous wizard probably.'

'So he would know people like Montague James?'

Stainger put up both hands. Sat back in his charcoal-grey moquette.

'Steady, James. Steady. You don't have to have hoofs to know Montague James.'

'The important point is not does the Superintendent know Montague James, but does James know him. There's a big difference.'

Stainger knew that. He wouldn't say so.

'I don't know what you're getting at. So don't get any closer. OK?'

'Hilary James asked me if I worked for him. She said a lot of people do.'

'I didn't hear you say that, James.'

Leonard stood. Went to the window. The abbey looked nearer than it was. He thought of the Minor Canon. Of Dancer smirking before him. Untouchable. So many prejudices. Montague James? Prejudice. Maybe. But too big to let them get in the way. Of what? A merry-go-round? He kept remembering the inscription, the merry-go-round is beginning to slow now. It was from a song. He'd played it years back. How did it go on? 'Have I been too long at the fair?' Had Bolt known it was time to get out? Or had someone else? Who had paid the cheque over? He turned back into the room. Stainger was waiting for him to speak.

'Tell me something. Why, in this place, has no one heard of the merry-go-round?'

'What merry-go-round?'

'Exactly.'

'Perhaps it doesn't exist.'

'Not at the level we work.'

Stainger was doodling. He was thinking. He thought that something as obscure could just be the sort of alleyway along which lay a contract on Leonard's life.

'And so?'

Now Leonard was pacing. But there was no electrical shorting and spitting this time.

'This city, as everyone keeps telling me, is quiet. Bit of ram-raiding, joy-riding, grievous and aggravated at chucking-out time, family and civil. Little bit of drugs, but nothing like Bristol. Right so far?'

Stainger nodded.

'Text book, James. Go on.'

'But supposing there is something much bigger going on. Why don't we know?'

'Because, James, it doesn't spill onto the streets. Doesn't frighten the dinner ladies.'

'And so we don't hear of it, until something does spill onto the streets.'

'James, none of my officers covers up anything.'

Leonard stared at him, turned away. If an officer did cover something, then how would Stainger know? Stainger tried again.

'If they do, it soon blows. You tried it with the girl.'

'That was different. Anyway, I didn't hold back on what I knew, only the source. She gave us Piccolo. She gave us Bolt. Sergeant Jack confirmed.'

'Why did she call him Piccolo? Wasn't that a blind? She had his passport. She must have known his name.'

Leonard shrugged. Stopped his pacing.

'Not necessarily. We don't know when she got his passport. And she wasn't the only one who called him Piccolo.'

'Odd, though, isn't it?'

'You wouldn't say that about Benedictines and Carmelites. Same ritual. Take a habit, take a name.'

He flopped into the seat opposite Stainger's desk. He was nodding slowly. Trying to keep his thought train moving.

'Let's forget the name game. The big question is the merry-go-round.'

Stainger blew through his nostrils. He was willing to go so far. The merry-go-round hypothesis was unproven as far as he was concerned. He started to say so, but Leonard was voice to his thoughts.

'Question: If the merry-go-round is tied in with this, if the merry-go-round is organized and hidden from the dinner ladies, why murder? In public. Why street level? Why bring it to our attention?'

'Answer?'

Leonard got up. Shook his head.

'I'm not sure.'

'Which is a hell of a lot better than I don't know.'

'It may be.'

Leonard nodded his thanks. He too closed the door with care. He never slammed loyalty in the face.

Thirty-Six

The green Rolls-Royce sped by a slow-moving feed lorry up the hill from Farrington Gurney. Montague James was alone. He was in a hurry. The snaking Mendip road before him was empty except for a tractor. James did not notice passing it. He was thinking. He was thinking about carelessness. Montague James abhorred carelessness. He was impatient with clutter. Once, at a small family gathering in Wells, he had asked a second cousin why she allowed her children to play with more than one toy at a time. Montague James never allowed himself more than one plaything at a time. He regarded his life as quite satisfactory. The present circumstances were not satifactory. There had been carelessness. There had been clutter.

He braked as the road twisted and descended and he swung right, along the lane, by the church and then the track and then the farmhouse. The man was waiting. As they walked along the mown lines of the lawn, the son watched from behind the curtain of an upstairs bedroom. He rubbed at his scarred arm and sneered at the scene below. It was not his fault. But he knew that it would be seen that way. He also knew that there was nothing anyone, even they, even the high and mighty James, could do.

Montague James listened as the man gurgled his explanation and reasoning. The matter was out of hand, but there was nothing to be done about that. James paused and closed his eyes in a slow blink of deep disapproval.

'After all this time, it would not be at all unreasonable to be told how such an unacceptable mistake could have come about.'

The other man scratched at his arm. Heat rash, he supposed. Nervousness did not help.

'He wasn't to know. He didn't have much time. I asked him.'

'My dear fellow, you're not supposed to ask. You are supposed to tell. What's more, you're supposed to tell in such an unequivocal manner that the lunatic doesn't make mistakes.'

'There was a decision. He took it. That's all.'

'That is all? I hope to God it is. This time last week, nothing. Now we can't step from our drawing-rooms without tripping over the constabulary. And, may I ask, whose decision was it?'

'He reckoned –'

'Reckoned! You do not blow someone in half with a great gun simply because you reckoned. The boy is an imbecile. An imbecile.'

'He could have been dangerous.'

'Yes, he could. Thanks to the damn fool, he remains dangerous. But the fact remains that it was wrong. There is no control. We are in the business of other ways of life. This is not the dreadful underworld. And, for heaven's sake, what's this business of the man in the car park?'

'He was dangerous.'

'According to you, the whole world is dangerous. But we don't go around beating up vagrants. Didn't the fool realize what he was doing?

'He was frightened.'

'Frightened! My God. He is six foot six and the man's a drunkard. How could he have been frightened?'

'It's all right for you. You didn't have to do any of this.'

'If it wasn't for the idiot child, none of this would have been necessary in the first place.'

They stopped. Faced each other. Montague James unrepentant but annoyed with himself for having betrayed his normally impeccable manners. The other man angry. Angry but subdued. James was right. His son had fouled up. But, yet, he was his son. James continued walking. Got to the edge of the lawn. Stopped. Stared across the valley to the village below. A spire. A pub, squat and spreading. A row of council houses. A farmyard scarred by galvanized tin. As he gazed, Montague James thought through the problem. There had to be action. Or, rather, there had to be no further action.

His wife would be given the task of discovering how far the investigations had got. Yes, Hilary would enjoy it. Yet, there was one other piece of business. He retraced his steps. The other man had waited. Watching. Scratching. Once he had glanced to the upstairs window. It was open in the sunlight. Searching for breeze. He met his son's eyes. They were arrogant. Cruel. His son. Montague James looked to the window. The son had gone.

'He must go. Is there not family in Ireland?'

The man nodded, Sligo. A big family. An unpainted rambling house with uncomplicated rambling people.

'He could go there. But does he have to? It might look odd.'

'What about his brothers?'

'They're fine.'

'Then he must go. He hasn't the wit to keep his mouth closed once it's opened by that filthy ale he swills. The chances are that no one will link him. I assume there isn't anything you haven't told me. He didn't leave anything around, did her?'

'No. Don't think so. He's not such a fool as you think.'

'He most certainly is. Get him gone. Today will be soon enough. Drive him over to Bristol, or better still Swansea – I'll leave that to you. Ticket there. Then gone.'

The man scrubbed at his belly.

'What if he says no?'

'Then thrash him.'

Montague James was walking to his car. He got in. The driver's window was down. The man looked at him, hand on the sill.

'What next?'

'You're a churchwarden. Prayer might do it.'

'And in the meanwhile?'

Montague James turned the key in the walnut dashboard. Listened for the engine and looked into the steady eyes of the man.

'I would have thought that obvious. The merry-go-round is over.'

'Completely?'

'Unless you wish to spend a considerable length of time in prison, yes. It most certainly is.'

The driver's window slid up. Montague James drove off, mercifully at last, he thought, protected from the smell of sweat.

Thirty-Seven

The Minerva Gallery was bright and fresh. There was plenty of space and the smell of scented air conditioning. The youth who the night before had been burdened with the drinks tray and the need to simper was now surly and dressed in a silk blouse and white cotton surfer's shorts. When Leonard asked where he could find Norma, he sighed his best whatever-next sigh and pointed up the spiral staircase with a double-jointed finger.

Reaching the staircase meant passing the portrait of *Jungle Cat*. At five to eleven in the morning, the figure was less daunting. Leonard assumed it was the difference between a long day and a long night and maybe the difference between Montague James's Dom Pérignon the evening before and the embalming fluid which dripped from the MIR coffee-filter machine that morning. The morning hayfever tablet hadn't helped. He spent four minutes looking at the painting and one minute climbing the spiral staircase. He tapped on the green door at eleven o'clock precisely.

It was a tall room. Paintings stacked on the bare elm floor. On one side, skirting board to ceiling, north-facing windows. Norma was standing in front of a life-size canvas. She waved hello. Pointed to a high bar stool by the door and worked on.

Norma worked slowly. The near-finished painting had none of the savagery of *Jungle Cat*. The models were not quite twin brothers. Older, but only slightly so, than the pouting youth below. They were young. Unblemished. Naked and smeared with soft oil. The smell of beaches. They stood slightly turned from each other. One taller. Stronger. Eyes closed, head back, face raised ecstatically to the high ceiling. The other, a soft smile on his lips, was looking down, to where the older youth rested in his cupped hands. For fifteen minutes Norma worked without speaking. When she did, it was with a brush between her white teeth as she continued to paint.

'So you couldn't stay away.'

The night before, he had barely registered the accent. A slight sing-song; he had once heard it in Nawanagar. Not lisping. A slight trace of Welsh. He wondered how.

'I could, but I did not.'

She stood back and to one side. She looked at him and then at the canvas. Where *Jungle Cat* was menacing, this was soft. Dark-haired. Mediterranean. A trace of designer stubble. Hairless chests. Soon manly. It was not finished. She watched him looking. She was smiling. Mocking? Probably.

'They do something for you, don't they?'

The taller youth continued to gaze sightlessly at the ceiling. The other was now moving his heavily oiled hands very slowly. Caressing.

'Do they?'

She came up to him. Small, slim, beautiful. Teasing. Knowing. She touched him with her fingertips. She knew. She said so.

'Yes. They do.'

The youths hardly moved. But it was enough. He wanted

to watch. Instead he coughed. Leonard sneezed a lot until August, but never coughed.

'Don't let me stop you working.'

'Not very subtle. But then policemen are not known for their subtlety, are they?'

Not Welsh, the accent. Was it American after all? Surfin' Californian maybe?

'Nor are murderers.'

'Some are. The interesting ones.'

She was still close. Now not touching. She didn't have to. She had. She knew. He coughed half a question.

'You find murder interesting?'

'Of course. Death is the most interesting thing we know. It must be.'

'Isn't that the sort of obvious thing people said thirty years ago? Then it came under the heading "meaningful discussion". Didn't it?'

'Maybe. But it's true. Death is interesting. Everything else is unexceptional.'

Mocking him still. She turned back to the canvas. Raised a brush. Shook her head and clapped her hands. The youths, slowly and reluctantly, parted. She pointed to a door.

'An hour. No mess. OK?'

They waved hands at her. The way daughters do. Waist-high. The shorter of the two looked Leonard over. Smiled. Leonard said hello. Felt he had to. They giggled and floated towards the other room. Norma was sitting on the other bar stool and pouring fruit juice from an iced jug. She handed him a frosted glass. Crossed her legs. She was wearing a turquoise T-shirt. Nothing else. One leg was high over the other knee and she rubbed her foot against his thigh. He looked down. Her toes looked old. Curled. Calluses. Well-used to roads and tracks. The nails the same colour as the T-shirt. He sipped the juice.

'You said you had something to show me.'

'You said you'd sit for me.'

'I said I would not.'

'I was not convinced.'

She was eyeing him over the glass. Across the room, the younger model was peering around the door. Just half a face and a hand and a leg. She caught his eye, turned. Her look was sufficient to send the youth back to his brother.

'He likes you.'

Leonard looked into his glass. He hummed. *Desifinado*. She teased on.

'He's very sweet. His name's William.'

She was nibbing his thigh again. He shifted on the stool. But it made it worse. She enjoyed teasing. Teasing was boring if there was no response.

'Would you like to meet him?'

'No. No, thank you.'

'Are you sleeping with Hilly?'

Leonard's puzzled look was genuine. She laughed. Her laugh was genuine.

'Of course you're not. No one does. Not even pretty little Monty.'

'I really wouldn't know.'

'Come on, come on. Of course you would. You're a detective. You see behind people's faces. Isn't that it? Lotsa psycho courses for the cop who has everything?'

She moved her foot. Higher.

'And you? D'you have everything?'

'I'm more interested . . .'

'More interested in what? She had the hots for you last night. I could see. She nearly bit your ear off. She was so wet. Couldn't you tell? That's why she had to go.'

it was your painting. Not me.'

She laughed. Cynically.

'*Jungle Cat*. She would.'

Leonard was confused. Maybe it showed. Norma was enjoying herself.

'Dear Monty keeps her as a pet. Locks her up during the

daytime. She just lies there all day counting her diamonds and deciding which toy to use next. Which is a hard way to get laid if you're a nympho. Which she is in spades.'

'But she stays.'

'She's in love.'

'Really?'

'Really. Oh Chrissakes, not with him. She's in love with everything that comes with the deal. The apartment, the clothes, the platinum Amex card. The whole bit. And she's scared.'

'Of losing it? That's not unreasonable.'

'She's scared of getting cut.'

Leonard shook his head. He could believe it.

'By him?'

Norma slowed. Shrugged. Maybe. He'd enjoy it.

'Only because he'd do it better than the hired help. Funny people, Inspector, funny people.'

'So your friend Benedict was telling the truth.'

He could not see her expression. But for a moment she stopped work.

'He is not my friend. He wouldn't know the truth if it had wings and a harp. Jules is a slob, a phoney, and he's a drunk.'

'He speaks well of you.'

'Not any more. I've thrown him out.'

'I imagine a lot of people have done that.'

Norma turned to him.

'Then you'd be wrong. Most people wouldn't give him a chance. He's also a thief.'

'I see.'

'I did. He steals anything. Sells it for anything he can get. And he's a liar.'

Leonard knew what would come next. He said it for her.

'So anything he told me would be wrong.'

'No. Anything you believed would be wrong. But that's up to you to find out. He'll drink himself to death eventually. Hell, that'll be about the best thing he'll have done in years.'

'There's a lot of it about.'

'Death's OK. It fixes problems. And, when it comes up, you, well, you can stop handing out the shit. Right? No, Inspector, death's fine. It reminds you to do it now. Shall we?'

Leonard got up. The wet canvas glistened. He wanted to touch. Did not. He wondered why. Why *Jungle Cat*? Why the hopelessly erotic forms in front of him. Why was Norma telling him this? Why so morbidly in love with death? Maybe she sensed his thoughts.

'You really don't find death the most?'

He hummed. Paused. Took his time to answer. When he did, it was as he turned. The moment was quiet. His words thought through.

'No. I'm frightened of dying and sickened by violent death.'

'Isn't premeditated murder the ultimate sensation? The ultimate orgasm?'

She had closed her eyes. Sipping. Thinking. Remembering? He didn't say anything. She wasn't worth it. Anyway, he'd heard it all before. She wasn't put off.

'When you've done everything, then that's what's left. When you've lived your life, then it's time to die. Yes?'

The hum was deep in his throat. Barely reaching his lips.

'You know, when I lived in New York, snuffing was a gig. Right?'

'I don't understand.'

'Yes, you do.'

Her eyes were open. She scratched at her bare hip.

'Do I?'

'Forget it. Forget it.'

'You haven't.'

'I was there. OK?'

'Where?'

'New York? There were people. Some big people. Mega cats. They'd pay. So they did. There were people who could fix it. A few kids. Spaced out. You know?'

He nodded. He knew. He wanted her to tell him. He wanted to know why. Her eyes were closed again. Remembering.

'They'd get as much as they could use. For a few days. Then they'd get screwed. Every way. They were wild. Then, when everyone had done . . . Well, I guess that was the time.'

'For what?'

The eyes were tight. She spoke in rhythms. The same rhythms as she uncrossed her legs. Rubbing the insides of her thighs, her thumbs meeting at the top as her mind held out its technicolor images.

'Snuff time. Maybe a knife. Sometimes something a little more exotic.'

'Murder.'

'Private. No one to mind. No one to miss them. Who knew? Who cared? And everyone gets something. Couple of guys had a movie thing. They'd shoot the whole scene. Cool. Screwing, then snuffing. Good-quality stuff.'

'Sick.'

'You a doctor?'

'It's still sick.'

'Anything's possible in that town.'

'Where the low meet the lowest? Yes, that's possible.'

Her eyes were still. Not shut. Closed. Lids softly dropped. This was her special dream. A different trip. She smiled as she talked.

'But then there was Long Island. Very high-class stuff. Beautiful, beautiful people. Just doing it. Mmm. Just doing it.'

The eyes were open. The excitement was all hers. *Jungle Cat*. Leonard got down from the stool. He started to the door. Said nothing, just waved a hand without looking at her.

'You don't want the end of the story?'

He turned, his hand on the doorknob. Shook his head.

'I don't need anything from the top shelf today, thank you. I've got a problem with the real thing.'

She was coming towards him. Barefoot. Hands hanging loosely at her sides.

'I said I could help.'

'I'm not into fantasies. When someone gets murdered the first thing I have to do is fill out a form. That's very real.'

She smiled. Her hand was on his, over the doorknob.

'I made a promise. Last night. Remember.'

'It's why I came. No other reason.'

She took his hand and placed it flat against her.

'Sure?'

'Very.'

He wasn't. But it worked. She laughed.

'I see. Business before my pleasure.'

Norma, still holding his hand, led him to the corner room. The youths were entwined. She shooed them out. William whispered, '*Ciao*'. Giggled.

The room was not large. The roof sloped and a skylight was open. It was hot. Leonard was perspiring and he took off his spectacles. Norma was wiping her hands on a rag towel and when she handed it to him he could smell paint, oil and her body. She was bending over a rack of canvases. The T-shirt was at hip level. Jules Benedict was right. Perfect. She found the canvas she wanted, but for the moment left it in the stall. She turned. She knew. She faced him. Both hands, still oily, slowly massaging her buttocks. Smiling, but her voice quiet. Not provocative. No longer mocking.

'Do you know who they killed?'

'Who are "they"?'

She shook her head. Her silk hair going with it. It would not be that easy. 'Maybe that's not for me.'

'You know?'

'Maybe, because that's what most things are.'

'Look, Norma. I can do without the bohemian lore and goodly sayings. I'm looking at two murders, maybe three. Now what is it you have to show me?'

She looked surprised. Why not? She was.

'Three?'

'One ten years ago, that's my maybe. One in the bath and...'

He paused. One in the bath, now one in the shower. He could not take it. She was waiting.

'And?'

'And another one this morning. They're connected. Or at least I'm certain they are. So what is it?'

Norma smoothed her T-shirt. Held the middle of the hem and pulled it down. She was watching. Now, for the first time, uncertain. Leonard was rubbing his spectacles with his handkerchief, peering at her as he did so. Not really seeing. She felt a little frightened. Her voice was not so assured.

'You know who it was?'

'The one you're thinking about? Probably Richard Bolt. We think he was an American.'

'Not Piccolo?'

His look was sharp. She felt it sting. Fun time over. She let go the hem. Leonard was fed up.

'How did you know? There was nothing in the papers.'

'He sat for me.'

'Why?'

'I asked him to.'

'Why?'

'He was beautiful.'

'Where did you meet him?'

She did not answer. Looked over her shoulder to the empty couch where the youths had lain. The sickly smell of oil and their excitement was overpowering in the summer heat. She stretched to pull on the skylight rope. He was watching. Not bothering to see. She rubbed at her hands and looked at him from beneath her soft lashes.

'For the moment, let's just say that I did.'

'I need to know.'

'A party.'

Leonard drummed his fingers by his sides.

'He was a vagrant. He was not a natural for a *Hello* magazine interview.'

'Have it your own way. You asked.'

'Whose party?'

'I don't remember.'

She was lying. They both knew. For the moment, it did not matter.

'When was this?'

'Month back.'

'Where?'

'I'll have to think about that.'

'In case you're cut?'

She didn't reply. She bent into the slope of the roof and pulled a large canvas from the rack. He started to help but she shook her head. She put the painting on the easel and stood back. The light was good. So was the painting. It was Bolt all right. Almost an airbrushed photograph. Another nude. He was stretched over a boulder. His back arching into the stone's curve. One arm over his forehead. The other hanging, the fingers almost touching the ground. Coiled in the valley of his abdomen, a snake. Another snake. This time hooded. The head raised. The tail almost hidden in damp curls of dark hair. Ready to strike at where the vein stood proud.

Norma had found a cigarette. She drew deeply. Staring at the snake's head. Mesmerized. He waited. Let her be. It took minutes. Not seconds. When she turned, the cigarette had gone. Had been replaced. There was no smile. Just a whisper.

'There's something else.'

He knew there had to be. This was the edge. He wanted to look over.

'Go on.'

'He asked me to give it a title.'

'So?'

'People don't do that.'

She bit at her bottom lip. Leonard waited again. Then pushed.

'And did you?'

She didn't say anything. She tilted the canvas away from the easel. On the back, on the wooden stretcher, a simple inscription in black: *The merry-go-round.*

Leonard ran a finger over the inscription as a mourner might a tomb.

'Did he tell you what it meant?'

She put the cigarette in a giant china ashtray rescued from a pub's bar. Let it burn. When she smiled, it was without humour.

'I didn't ask.'

'Because you knew.'

'Because I thought I knew.'

He closed the door. Leaned against it. It could take more time. Best not be overheard.

'What was it?'

It did take time. When she told him, he did not want to believe her.

Thirty-Eight

Downstairs in the gallery the surly youth had brightened. He smiled. His eyebrows twitched just as he had practised. After all, this guy seemed to be on stroking terms with Norma. The youth smiled again. A warmer version. He wanted to keep his job. Leonard pointed to the maroon portable telephone. The youth asked him to help himself and, when Leonard made it clear the conversation would be private, pouted for a couple of seconds and wafted to the sunlit doorway.

Leonard made two telephone calls. He told Sergeant Jack to met him in thirty minutes. She said Stainger wanted him. The Superintendent picked up his telephone and was about to launch into a string of answer-me-now questions when Leonard stopped him in full flight.

'You serious, James?

'Absolutely.'

'This isn't the Met.'

'The procedure's the same.'

'It takes a light year.'

'How long would it take to set up?'

Stainger was back gazing at the wall. He did not have the authority to put through a direct request, but as district commander as well as senior officer in the station it would have to start with him. Not Marsh.

'The answer is I don't know. You're certain?'

It was Stainger's turn to wait for an answer. He waited.

'If I were, I wouldn't need it. But I'm sure enough to think it'll produce.'

'Straight?'

Leonard heard the formality in Stainger's tone. Leonard was asking Stainger to go out on a limb. Stainger would, if he believed in him. He would, because he did not like one of his officers being shot at – for real.

'Yes, sir. And, one other thing. I need an itemized list of his calls.'

Stainger relaxed. A little.

'That's the easy one. OK, James, I'll see what I can do. Now, while you're on . . .'

But he wasn't. The click told him that.

Leonard's second call took fifteen seconds. The voice at the other end did not ask questions. It just said yes.

The youth had closed the door. He'd done so not for any consideration of Leonard's privacy, but because Jules Benedict was trying to get in. The youth was not struggling with him. Didn't have to. Benedict was struggling with himself. He was having difficulty with the worn steps. There were only two, but he was having difficulty. Which made the youth's job as co-opted bouncer all that easier. He was telling Benedict that he was no longer welcome. That Norma had said to go away.

'What she say?'

'Fuck off.'

Benedict swayed, trying to focus on which one of the youth's mouths had made the offensive noise. The youth said it again and scampered in and slammed the door.

The artist's eyes were red. Piggy. His breath stank. A whisky, wine, lager and biriani morning sickness. The stains on last night's shirt were probably vomit. He belched in Leonard's face. Tried an apology and then lost interest.

'Jesus, I feel awful'

'You look worse than that.'

Benedict looked hurt. It was bad enough to feel as he did. But then he usually did at this time of the morning. It was just gone noon.

'She in?'

'Norma? I think so. She's in the studio.'

'Fuckin' whore.'

'She seems to think that times have changed.'

'Nothing's changed, Lennie. Fuck all's changed. I can tell you. She's a bitch.'

He staggered against the railings and sucked in air. Leonard said nothing. Benedict swung his head towards him. It was not a wise manoeuvre. The world spun. A centrifugal hang-over. The worst kind. Benedict clutched at the gold spikes of the black railings. One eye, perhaps the only one in commission, focused on Leonard with a mixture of dawning and suspicion.

'Still trying to string those little cherubs of hers, is she? Jesus, they're lovely. Almost fancy them meself.'

He swayed on the step and clutched his groin.

'Christ, Lennie, I need a piss.'

Leonard was about to move on. Benedict was not done.

'Little darlings are strictly high-class acts. Not my level. Like everyone in this place.'

'What sort of acts?'

Benedict belched again. His eyes watered.

'Command performances, ducky. That's what.'

He started for the door. From the side-window, the youth looked alarmed at the advancing figure. Leonard put a hand on his arm.

'Male whores?'

'On the game? Those two?'

His head went back. The laugh started all right, but the violent and sudden action was too much for him. He leaned over the black railings and threw up into the basement court-yard below. Leonard took a deep breath, then wished he hadn't. The sun-warmed stench was unrelenting. He waited. Benedict was hanging over the railings, spew dripping from his putrid lips. He didn't look up. Probably could not. His voice came in choking gasps.

'Rent boys? You stupid or something, Lennie? Command Performers, Lennie. Performers. They screw each other. Couple of hundred quid to watch the show.'

'Who watches, Jules?'

Benedict's shaggy head swivelled very slowly, leaving his body where it was almost comfortable. He held onto the railings with one hand, wiped the back of his fouled face with the other.

'High-class, Lennie. And I mean high. Understand?'

'Who?'

Benedict swung back to the railings. Tried to be sick. Couldn't.

'The lovely ladies, Lennie. All the lovely ladies. They love it, don't they? Does something for them. Hubbies watch the lesbos. Wifies watch the homos. Lovely stuff.'

This time he managed it. Leonard walked away. As he reached the corner, he could still hear the desperate retching on the steps. Hell, he thought, hath another fury. He was starting to believe Norma.

As Leonard was walking down the hill to Victoria Park, Peter Dover was reaching for his jacket. It was hotter than any day that June. But Dover never went out without his jacket just as he never went down to breakfast without shaving. He called from his door to the newsroom and the deputy came quickly. Dover was soft-spoken. Courteous. He never called unless it was urgent.

'I'm going out. We're going to need a late.'

'An extra edition or hold back the city?'

Dover nodded. His deputy had a good point. But holding for a quarter of an hour meant lost copies. Circulation was vital. Lost papers meant lost revenue. Lost papers meant explanations to advertisers who bought space based on the numbers of readers. Lost papers meant people didn't read that edition. No point in writing a dream front page for ghosts. Extra edition or hold the city? He'd do both.

'Hold it as long as you can. Then we'll have an extra one.'

Leonard had not said anything other than he had something for the *Chronicle*. For that day. The deputy scratched his head. He wasn't about to be told, so he would ask.

'What's up, doc?'

Dover took a tiny notebook from his top drawer and slipped it into his top pocket.

'I'm not sure. I had a call.'

He wasn't going to say who called. The deputy would not expect him to. Sources had to be protected. Dover never asked any of his reporters, 'Who?' Only, 'Are you sure?'

'Any clues?'

'Police. It's the murder. I can tell you that much. I think we're about to get a throat. So tell them we'll need special billboards.'

The deputy had things to organize. People to tell to stand by. The newsroom was computerized. But the pages had to be pasted up by hand.

'What about this thing this morning?'

'Could be. Nothing new on it?'

The deputy shook his head.

'Bugger all.'

'We'll see.'

'When will you be back?'

'Don't know.'

He was heading for the door. He stopped, picked up his mobile telephone and pointed to his large wooden desk.

'Stay in here. If I get stuck I'll call you on my private line.'

The deputy had another question. He should have been quicker. Dover was already heading down the narrow blue-glossed stairway.

He reached the park in five sweaty minutes and found Leonard where the policeman had said he would – stretched out on the grass. His tweed jacket was rolled and it cushioned his head. His hands were clasped over his waistcoated stomach like a contented poet's. Dover was not the sort of person to flake out in a public place during working hours. He sat. He was uncomfortable. Leonard did not look at him. He was staring at the heavens when he spoke.

'Need your help. OK?'

'Maybe. What sort of help?'

'What have you been getting from the press office on this thing?'

'Not much. Nothing to fill a notebook.'

'Do you know why?'

'No. You tell me.'

Leonard recrossed his ankles. While he waited for the detective to answer, Dover wondered why Leonard criss-crossed his brown boot laces. It wasn't important. Some people did, some people did not. It simply appealed to his sense of detail. He was still wondering when Leonard spoke.

'No one has been sure of what to say. There has been more, but it's all been speculation.'

'Iffy.'

'Probably.'

'So, what have you got to tell me?'

Leonard turned his head. He wasn't wearing his spectacles. Dover was a blur. A reliable one.

'We're working on new information that the murder in Rainbow Wood and the one in the baths are linked. You guessed that anyway. Now I'm telling you, it's so. Each victim had, we think, the same name. Bolt.'

'Related?'

'Don't know. But if not it's a macabre coincidence. We know the second one had a passport in that name. We do not yet know if that passport is genuine. Equally we have no reason to think it is not. We have nothing to identify the man in Rainbow Wood, other than the word of your former colleague.'

'Steve Reece?'

'Yes.'

'I didn't know that.'

Leonard ignored the implied question.

'The remains of someone, presumably Bolt, were buried in the city five years ago. We still have a problem with that. No one seems to know who paid for the funeral. But for the moment it's not important.'

Dover was looking at his watch. The city should have gone. They would be waiting for the extra edition. Time was getting tight. It sounded so when he spoke.

'I need to know what is. Without being rude, Inspector, like ten minutes ago.'

Leonard was back looking at the sky.

'You can say that police believe the murders are connected. You can say that the murder this morning was connected.'

Dover's mind did a double-take.

'That thing was a murder? You're telling me?

'I'm telling you.'

'I can use it?'

'Yes. I want you to.'

'And it's connected to the one in the baths and . . .'

'And Rainbow Wood.'

'Hell's teeth.'

'Something like that.'

'Who was it?'

'This morning?'

'Yeah.'

Leonard sighed. Felt sad. Proper sadness. A weariness of sadness.

'For the moment, I can't tell you that.'

'Next of kin?'

'Yes.'

It would do. Dover would understand.

'Anything at all?'

Leonard paused before replying.

'A woman.'

He closed his eyes. Thin. Scrubbed. Trusting. Leaning against his knee. Johnson satisfied. Approving from the safety of her wall. The softness of her pillow. A woman? He supposed so.

Dover looked at his watch. Took out his mobile telephone. He pulled an apologetic face.

'I'm sorry. There's not much time. Will this hold until tomorrow?'

Leonard raised himself. Leaned back on his elbows. Still a blur. Shook his head with the urgency of a schoolboy refusing linctus.

'No way. There's one other thing. It's the most important. You can say the police have a special lead. It has a codeword.'

Dover leant forward.

'Yes?'

'Merry-go-round.'

'That it? The codeword?'

Leonard nodded.

'Yes. Merry-go-round.'

'This a police codeword? Like Countryman, Bumble Bee or whatever?'

'I'm sorry. I've nothing more. Not today.'

Leonard got up. Dover looked up into the detective's face. Even in the sun it was tired. Sad.

'Just one thing, Mr Leonard. What's the attribution on this? You? Police spokesman? Sources?'

'Can't you just say it's understood?'

Dover nodded.

'OK. Just one more thing. Why are you telling me this?'

Leonard blinked. He was rubbing his spectacles. Same lenses. Same green silk handkerchief. He slipped the wire frames over his ears. Dover was in focus. Open. Reliable. Waiting for an answer.

'Why?'

'Yes. Why are you telling me?'

'I'm not.'

He bent. Picked up his jacket and trudged away. Dover watched for a few moments. Decision. He tapped his private number. The deputy's hand must have been hovering. Dover cleared his dry throat.

'It's me. I think we've got a goer here. Ready? Take this down.'

Thirty-Nine

The only service in the abbey was the straggle of tourists about their devotions to antiquity. An oriental posed for his wife's camera. A European camcorded the chancel. The Minor Canon winced and grumbled to himself. In some distant committee, colleagues rubbed their hands and blessed the building fund. Madeleine Jack was waiting for him in a side aisle. She was reading a simple inscription.

'So this is where the Bible and the sword meet. They've got more generals here than priests.'

He peered at the lettering.

Major General Thomas Nepean.

'He was a very devout man. India. Old family. A sapper.'

She wondered how he knew.

'Gospel's mightier than the sword and all that thing. Loads of heroes.'

Leonard shrugged.

'The only Coward buried here was a lacemaker.'

As they went from name to name, she found herself more interested in cameos of colonial history than the reason for their meeting. Leonard added a date, an aside. Death as far as the eye could read. Murder, for the moment, not to the front of their minds. Two friends in innocence. She fresh in light cotton and buckled sandals. He donnish in unsuitable tweed and brown boots. But not for long. He touched her arm. Something had bothered him. He remembered what it was.

'What happened to her dog?'

He looked anxious. She was pleased.

'I took him home.'

'Oh.'

'Someone had to. He'd have gone to the pound.'

'Maybe that would have been better.'

'I've called him Sid.' Her voice was soft. Caring. 'You can decide what to do with him when this is over.'

'That's the sort of thing they said in the war.'

'It's turned into that, sir. Hasn't it?'

He supposed that it had. Sid. An odd choice. He wondered if he would keep the pup. He felt a responsibility.

'I'm glad you took him. I'll . . . I'll come and get him, when, er . . .'

'When the blackout's lifted?'

He felt depressed. Too much killing. There had been the time before he came to Bath. Too much killing then. Leonard did not think of himself as an orphan. But there were moments like this, in places like this, when he had split-second understandings of being nothing and nobody. The only person he was was the person he had made. No one ever said to Leonard that he was just like his father, or his grandfather, or that he had his mother's eyes. No one knew. So he understood exiles. Understood Josie. He wondered if anyone cared if she were alive or dead. He would keep the pup.

Madeleine Jack sensed his gloom. She was talking. He tuned in very slowly, as if someone were turning up the gain on his old Cossor wireless. The valves warming. The mellowness of a dinner-jacketed announcer. It wasn't. It was Sergeant Jack.

'Superintendent Stainger said to tell you, first reaction is unlikely. What's that about, sir?'

Leonard said nothing. Stopped. Reset his time switch to the present. The brain clicked. She could sense that. She could see the eyes had not. He stood back from a large plaque. This time a full admiral.

'Well, well. Hargood. Didn't know he was here.'

Madeleine peered at the fuzzy inscription. Admiral Sir William Hargood had died in 1839.

'Special?'

'Well, he died in the year the first first-class county cricket club was formed.'

'Somerset?'

'Oh no. Sussex. And he commanded a ship at Trafalgar. So yes, special.'

She looked carefully at this strange inspector. Not a policeman to look at. Make a good friend. She rarely trusted. She might trust this one.

Leonard didn't notice her look. He was far away. Trying to remember the admiral's ship. *Belleisle?* Maybe. And here he was. In Bath. But why not? Landlocked. But a naval city all the same. And had not Nelson himself come here? Was not the tender Horatia baptised from the font? Had not the little and gallant sailor and his mistress denied the child was theirs, but promised to bring her up as their very own? Had not the crowds cheered? The arrogance of the powerful assuming even their most obvious lies to be believed. Two hundred years on. Nothing had changed. Arrogance begat murder.

'Stainger.'

She had not asked. Not her place. Not quite.

'Yes?'

'I asked him to fix a line on Montague James. I wanted an intercept on his home.'

'A tap?'

'Mm. Mm.'

'He's in this?'

'He could be.'

'If you want an intercept, it means you think there are others. D'you know who?'

Leonard knew some. Not all. He never would.

'The merry-go-round is coming together.'

'Marsh thinks you're out of your tree.'

He stopped. Looked at her.

'Really?'

'Really.'

He walked on.

'Have you heard of a painter called Norma?'

Jungle Cat.

'You've seen it?'

She shook her head.

'No, but I've heard about it. The story is that the model is the wife of one of Bath's finest.'

'So all we have to do is find a 38 D-cup with a tabby's head. Sounds simple.'

'It could be anyone.'

Leonard remembered the body. He remembered also the unfinished brothers. Norma painted faithfully. He did not think the figure could belong to almost anyone. But then, he thought to himself, he was a man.

'I think it's the artist.'

She was surprised.

'Does it matter?'

'Not really. Unless . . .'

He stopped again. Unless. Unless. Unless.

'Unless?'

He looked at her. What did the cool Sergeant Jack know? Guess?

'Unless it's part of this. She's got another picture. Bolt. Our Bolt. Not Rainbow Wood Bolt. She met him at a party. Or she says she did.'

'I wouldn't have thought he was on the white-wine-and-olives circuit. You sure?'

Leonard nodded. He was very sure.

'Very. She claims she met him at a party and asked him to sit. Perhaps "sit" isn't the right word.'

Madeleine Jack smiled.

'She has a reputation.'

'I can believe it.'

She looked at him. No. Not the Inspector. Surely he wasn't the type. At the same time . . . But he was talking again.

'I thought she was *Jungle Cat*. But supposing you're right. Supposing the model is someone's wife. Supposing she was someone else Norma picked up at a party. Another party. Hence the prospect of a scandal.'

'Not at all upstage-and-county Bath.'

'But it does start to tie in.'

They'd reached the south transept and stood before the mighty processional cross. Behind them, Waller lounged by his wife's marbled side. An earlier battle of Lansdown. Different from Leonard's.

'I can see saucy parties, sir, especially here. Bath's got a nice little coke ring running. And, if you want champagne and porn movies for afters, the folks do a thriving take-out service. But it's all private. Harmless.'

Leonard was surprised she knew so much.

'Who?'

'I'm not sure. Inspector Lane knows most of the numbers. Nothing to do with people who've come up in this one.'

'Who says?'

'I was co-ordinating everything for the first two days.

They're all discards. If your painter friend is a regular party goer, then maybe we can get somewhere. But, from what we know, she does her own thing.'

'When you were co-ordinating, are you certain there was never anything that mentioned merry-go-round?'

She nodded. She was certain, all right. She had heard Marsh telling Stainger that he thought Leonard was a nutter. He had told the boss that, if he heard another whisper of this merry-go-round nonsense, he'd get Leonard certified. So she had checked. Madeleine Jack trusted Leonard. She had met Josie. She knew Reece. She believed Leonard. So she had checked again. Nothing.

Leonard sneezed. Damned tablets. Useless. Maybe it was the musty abbey. He wiped his nose.

'She says that she went once. It was in the sticks. Maybe the Mendips.'

'Who took her?'

Leonard had asked that. Norma claimed she was stoned. Couldn't remember. He didn't believe her. But he wasn't about to arrest her for being maybe stoned.

'But she must have known who was there.'

He gazed at the high column in front of him. Norma had known. Wouldn't say.

'She claims the whole party was on video. There were a lot of people doing the sort of things others buy magazines for. Not the sort of video that gets to the British Board of Censors.'

Madeleine Jack was cynical.

'I would have thought that, with her rep, she wouldn't have bothered. By the look of some of her friends, she has permanent invites to very similar gigs. Anyway, why should she keep quiet?'

Something else Leonard had asked her. Over and over. Over and over, he had been given the same answer.

'She claims she was at a party upstairs in the gallery. Her gallery. There were a couple of people she didn't know.'

'At her own party?'

'This is Lansdown casual, not Sandringham family. Anyway, she claims that it was all pretty harmless, grass maybe, and one of them said he knew where there was something special. She says, she *says*, mind you, that they piled into his car.'

'But she lives here. She must know where they went.'

Leonard sighed. He remembered Norma, with her eyes closed, telling him about the journey. He gave Sergeant Jack the short version.

'As far as I could gather, she and the other guy were doing interesting things in the back. They weren't checking the road signs.'

'She actually said that?'

He shrugged.

'She enjoyed telling me.'

'Sounds right.'

'Must have been a big car. There was more than one of them. Anyway, according to Norma, the next thing she noticed, outside the car, was when they arrived.'

Madeleine Jack found herself wondering how the Inspector had reacted to the graphic description of the artist's journey. He was polishing those damned spectacles again.

'But she must have known people there.'

'She says not.'

'But she remembers meeting Bolt.'

'So she says.'

'And she didn't meet anyone else?'

'No. She also said that, even if she had known who they were, she couldn't tell me.'

'Threatened?'

'In an odd way, yes. Or, again, so she says. Very simple. Whoever they were, she needs their money. They buy her pictures. Keep the gallery going. Without the gallery she's nothing. She's painting the equivalent to elevator music. No great talent. But easy on the eye. And the bank balance. It's lucrative. She's not about to jump off the circuit.'

As he said it, he heard it. So did Madeleine Jack.

'Or, sir, the merry-go-round.'

His head bobbed in some dawning that had been there since that morning. But why had the painter shown him Bolt and the merry-go-round title?

'Maybe she loved him.'

Leonard looked to see if she were smirking. It wasn't in her voice. Nor her eyes.

'She said he was beautiful.'

'That's not the same thing.'

On the way out, Leonard dropped coins into the Restoration Fund box. It made up for his missed aims and oblations. At least he thought it did. Outside, the sun was enjoying the last days of June. Across the way, against the Pump Room railings, Dancer was talking to a group of buskers. Leonard wanted him. He touched Sergeant Jack on her bare arm. It was already warm from the afternoon.

'See if you can pull together some bodies. Somers-Barclay. Anyone you can find. Hit a few of the smarter bars. George's. Places like that. Put it about that we're looking for people on the merry-go-round. See if we can put up a few birds.'

She was looking at the ground. Pondering. When she looked up, her question was direct into his eyes.

'D'you get the feeling that we can't touch this one, sir? There's something about it. It's much bigger than a simple murder. We've known, or guessed, that right from day one.'

'Organized parties for the strictly invited like-minded is one thing. Sticking red-hot rods, or pokers or whatever they were, up someone's backside isn't exactly a party game.'

'It's more than that, sir. You keep coming back to Montague James. Right?'

Leonard nodded. She continued.

'He's not in the business of killing.'

'You know something I don't?'

'There's something about James. His style. Whatever he's got he's schemed for. But he's legit. We've been through his business friends. His money. We've a rough idea where it comes from and where it goes. I can't see Montague James being the sort of guy who'd risk anything. He's a schemer. Perhaps I'm being naive.'

'You're missing the most obvious point in all this. Let's take Bolt, or Piccolo, or whatever we're calling him. This wasn't hypnosis. Imagine how many it would have taken to hold him down.'

'Unless he was drugged.'

'The Screaming Skull said he was full of shit. But he wasn't sure if he was a regular user.'

'Which would tie in.' She looked away. Thinking he was right. 'But no one is saying anything, sir. No one is singing. No nightingale. No Berkeley Square.'

'No Berkeley Castle.'

'Sir?'

'Berkeley Castle, Sergeant. It's where Edward the Second was murdered – Bolt's murder was an action replay.'

Madeleine Jack shuddered in the warmth of the sun. Leonard raised an arm in farewell. A rough-tweed senator.

'Just one thing, sir. Meant to tell you earlier. I called Steven Reece today to see if he could remember anything more about Bolt. When I got him it was on his car phone.'

'So?'

'Well, it was all very odd. The reception was awful. Crackly. Kept fading. I said something about Bolt. And he said, "That didn't take you long."'

'Bolt? But he told you. When you went to see him.'

'No, sir, that's the point. The line was really bad. He thought I said Bowles, not Bolt.'

'You're sure?'

Leonard knew it was a stupid question. Of course she was sure.

'Absolutely. I'd asked him when it was that he first heard the name Bolt. That's when he said it. He said, "Bowles? That didn't take long." It seems odd, but that's the name of the girl in the paper place.'

'If the line was that bad, couldn't you have misheard?'

'No way.'

'What did he say about her?'

'Not her. Him. He was talking about her husband. The Fixer, he called him. When I asked him what he meant, he said forget it and rang off. I called back immediately but I got one of those intercepts. He'd switched off. Odd, don't you think, sir?'

Leonard looked across the yard. Dancer had gone. He'd wanted to talk to Dancer.

Forty

Leonard needed a drink. His hand did not shake. His mouth tasted respectable. His head was clear. No dog had bitten. But he needed a drink. He had a craving for cold, clear wine from a tall, thin-stemmed glass. And he wanted soft white bread with thin crisp crusts. Leonard wanted to be far from Bath. He wanted to sit at the small bar at the edge of a piazza and watch a little of the world in no hurry. Instead he walked. Quickly. Head down. Hands behind his back. As he walked, he thought.

He did not notice the crowded pavements of Milsom Street. He missed the half-smile of recognition from an American ancient emerging from Jollys' store. He didn't say hello when his bank manager, returning to Quiet Street, did. He would have walked straight across and in front of George Street's traffic if a hand had not grabbed his arm and a voice woken him.

'You ending it all? At this time of day yet?'

It was Harriet Bowles. A powder-blue shirt. Smiling.

'I need a drink. Come on.'

He took her arm and steered her in front of an oaf in a bronze Jaguar.

'Hey, steady, officer. I saved your life, remember?'

He kept walking. Up the steps and left towards the antiques market, and Woods.

She said no more. They were seated in the window, with the white wine poured, before he spoke.

'Your husband worked for Montague James.'

She did not smile.

'Not really. But, among others, I suppose yes. Why?'

He sipped the wine and nibbled broken baguette from the large white plate. It was not quite evening. Probably was, somewhere. Was in front of Santa Croce. He wished. But he was not there. He was here. And opposite someone involved. Someone he liked. 'Never like people' was his rule. He almost always kept to it. Almost always. Much better not to like. You could think the worst when you saw it and not feel bad about it. Like now. He hated being a policeman. He wanted to tell her that. But he didn't. Nor would he. Not yet. He sipped again. Leaned back in his chair.

'What do you mean, "not really"?'

Harriet had not touched her wine.

'Well, he acted for him occasionally, or so I think. But he wasn't retained. He wasn't employed.'

'They weren't friends.'

'Montague James doesn't have any. If he had, certainly Giles wouldn't have been one. Chalk and cheese. Come on, what's all this about?'

He sipped some more.

'One of my officers mentioned your husband's name.'

'He was a lawyer.'

'In connection with a murder. Ten years ago.'

Selsey came in. It was still early for him. Why not? It was going to be a long night. They were solid-booked from seven-thirty. He came across. Impish. Hands on both their shoulders.

'How do, children. All is good?'

Neither spoke. Selsey kept the smile. Backed off.

'Oh dear. See you later.'

He went to the table. Checked the bookings. Went to the counter. Checked the diary. Looked across. Silence still. Oh dear. Harriet sipped for show.

'What are you telling me?'

Leonard shrugged with his eyebrows. Polished his spectacles. He did not like this. Oh, for the Florentine piazza.

'I'm not sure. I promise. Not sure.'

'That makes it worse.'

She picked up the glass again. He waved a hand. Brushed away her point.

'Let me lay out a couple of things. Ten years ago a man was killed in Rainbow Wood. We both know about it. Right?'

She nodded.

'Steven Reece worked on that story for the *Chronicle*. He found out the name of the murdered man. Montague James was trying to bring together American business interests in this city. It was a very big business. Millions involved when millions were still millions. He told me as much himself.'

Her eyes showed impatience. He waited. He knew what she would say. So he let her say it.

'How very clever. But then he would be.'

'No one is above suspicion.'

'That must be a quote from somewhere.'

Leonard was looking at his glass. Waiting for her to let a little more steam go. But she had finished. For the moment. So, for the moment, he continued.

'Reece's investigation, by pure chance, hit a vein which the police never sniffed.'

'What's this to do with Giles?'

Leonard's head was down. Thinking it all through. How much to tell? How much did he really know?

'I'm coming to that. There is nothing to tie Montague James to the murder, only to the reaction. He bought off

Reece. For business reasons, he says. Nothing more. There's no evidence to suggest he isn't telling the truth. But . . .'

'But you don't believe him?'

'Oh, I do. I believe what he's told me. But I believe there's more he hasn't. Now we come to your husband. The same person who told us about the Rainbow Wood murder let slip that your husband was somehow connected. According to this person, he was called the Fixer.'

Harriet Bowles's glass went down quietly. Controlled.

'What is this, Inspector? A discarded manuscript from the Black Hand Gang?'

'I'm levelling. We have a witness who says your husband was involved with a murder. Indirectly, but, nevertheless, involved.'

'With murder? Giles was not connected with anything. Giles was a boy scout in long trousers. I've told you that.'

'We're told there was a connection and the only connection we have is Montague James. He's so damned obvious that I can't believe it. He may as well have waltzed through the Crescent in a butler's apron. If there's a connection, it's between your husband and Montague James. I need to know what it was.'

'It may not have been anything.'

Leonard had thought that through along Milsom Street. He had discarded the idea by The Savoy Tailors Guild.

'Did he keep records? Diaries? Notebooks?'

She didn't answer. She broke off a piece of bread. Chewed slowly. Her mother had always insisted on forty chews per morsel. With her mouth closed. Harriet Bowles suspected Leonard would not wait that long.

'Well? Did he?'

'What are you after?'

He looked out of the window. A normal world passing by. Not much of it. But normal. He longed to be normal. Looked back. She was watching him without expression. It saddened him. She was lightly tanned. But she looked tired. It was the eyes. She had not when they'd met. Him again. Always his damned fault. People who touched him burned. He pressed on.

'I'm not certain. But, if there is a connection between what happened in Rainbow Wood and the man killed in the bath, there may be a clue to it in something your husband wrote. Ten years ago.'

'If your informant is right and he was connected in the first place.'

'When we first met, you said they were on committees together.'

'The festival.'

'Right. Tell me, anything else? Anything at all?'

'Nothing. The rest was business. Don't ask me what. Giles never discussed it with me. I was just the memsahib. All I knew was that it was something to do with bonding. You know? Guaranteeing funding for the business.'

'The culture thing?'

'I think so.'

'Were did the money come from?'

'I don't know.'

Leonard took another sip. Blinked across the way. Selsey kept his distance.

'You didn't answer my question.'

'Diaries? Yes, there were a few. Still are, for that matter. I kept everything. They're in the shop. Exactly where I put them after the funeral,'

'Have you read them?'

Her smile was a memory. Her head moved slowly, side to side.

'Would *you* have?'

No. Diaries have other truths. Leonard would not have read them.

'I want you to. Will you?'

She rubbed at one eye. Pinched the bridge between them. Yes, tired. Of what? She rose. Yes, she was very tall.

Neither of them said goodbye. Selsey watched her go. He felt gloomy. He did not know why. But he was used to gloom. Maybe the Celt in him. He wanted to tell Leonard about the race. About the horse. He didn't. He half-waved and went to his kitchen. Woods was filling up.

Forty-One

Leonard picked up a copy of the *Chronicle* from the stand by Barclays Bank. Dover had done a good job. The front page was the only one that could be changed at such late notice. Dover would have put it there anyway. The main headline said it all.

CODEWORD CLUE
TO MURDER HUNT

It was exactly what Leonard wanted. Stainger had other ideas. He was standing in the middle of his office. He waved the *Chronicle* at Leonard. An-angry father facing his son with that quarter's telephone bill.

'What in hell's teeth is going on, James? What in hell's teeth?'

Leonard said nothing. Stainger was not a cussing man. A son of the Kirk. Stainger seethed. Threw the paper on his desk and sat down.

'You've got every available officer on the streets with this cock-and-bull story. They're looking stupid. First rule, James, first rule: if you make a threat, you've got to have the means to see it through. And the balls. And this?'

Stainger stabbed at the newspaper with a sturdy finger. He knew it was Leonard's doing. Leonard hadn't said yes to it, but they both knew.

'It's true.'

'James, it is not true. We don't know for certain what this merry-go-round thing is. The best so far is your imagination.'

Leonard blinked. Leaned against the wall. It was not imagination. Merry-go-round was everywhere.

'It's a ring. Drugs. The lot.'

'Who says? I'll tell you who. One spaced-out artist with a reputation for bouncing cheques, lies and husbands. You imagine the CPS's face if we dropped that file onto their desk. It's a Crown Prosecution Service, James, not something at the end of the Yellow Brick Road.'

'An unreliable witness.'

'She'd never see the court.'

Leonard knew. People told a policeman, then he had to go out and prove what he knew to be true. Sometimes he had to prove what he knew to be untrue. In the old days it was called fitting up. Today, times were more sophisticated. Policemen were more sophisticated. Villains still got themselves fitted up. But not by bright officers. That was the theory. Even if Stainger believed him, there was no way he could support Leonard. Not yet. Stainger, his ally.

'Look, James, I've had Marsh on to me. Now, I can handle Marsh by himself. But right now he's in a meeting with the ACC. Assistant Chief Constables, James, do not get mixed up at this stage unless someone has a grubby finger on the button of a mighty big fan and someone else has done a very smelly doo-doos. Understand?'

Leonard's blink rate increased. He did. That was the point of using Dover.

'I think we can flush them out.'

'Flush who out, James? Who?'

Stainger held up his hand and ticked off his points.

'Seemingly, the only people you've flushed out are Marsh, who is not exactly your number-one fan; the ACC who, incidentally, kicks with the same foot as Marsh, and the damned press office. Why weren't they told?'

'They're tossers. They wouldn't have handled this my way.'

'Who do you think you are? Alexander the Great? You're not. You're a busted chief inspector on my staff. You came here as an inspector in charge of wiring diagrams. You're now writing the local rag's front page and yourself and me into an early bath and a reduced pension.'

'Trying to find three murderers.'

'No, James. This is Bath. Not Hollywood. It's not down to you. This is a district. I've now got forty-seven officers all working very hard to get this one in the frame. Forty-seven out of a hundred and thirty-eight. That's big and that's busy. And they all know that, if they're going to succeed, they'll have to work together. It's not you. It's a team job. I don't need you writing your own scripts.'

'It'll work.'

'What do you expect? A couple of villains in Bristol will say, "Oh, look, seemingly that nice policeman in Bath seems to be on to us. Shall we steal a motor and toddle over and give ourselves up?" James, the people we're looking for probably don't even know the bloody *Chronicle* exists, never mind read it.'

Leonard was looking out of the window. He could see the cider drunk sitting on the wall. Maybe it was a better life down there. Even getting beaten up once a week was better. He wondered who had beaten him.

'I think the people I'm looking for will get to hear. I also think we don't have to go far to find out who they are.'

'And what do I tell the ACC and the press office?'

Leonard was at the door. He knew what he would tell them. He knew Stainger would not.

As Leonard was heading along the corridor in search of Sergeant Jack, Dancer was leaning against the Pump Room railings. Dancer was not a regular *Chronicle* reader. He did read the billboards. He begged some coins from passers-by and in ten minutes had the twenty-seven pennies for the extra edition plus more than enough for a hot pasty from the heat-and-chew shop. As he chewed, he read. Having read, Dancer rolled the paper into a truncheon and wandered in the direction of The Volunteer. The Minor Canon by the abbey door glared. Dancer smiled. Gave the priest the paper and fished in his pocket for change. Enough for one more pasty and one telephone call.

As Leonard was taking a call from Dancer, Montague James was sitting at the window admiring the evening view. His late mother, an Italian aristocrat (as were so many Italians his father knew), would have admired his silk jacket. If nothing else, it went with the gilt chair. She had taught him how to go so far and no further in all things (including his dressing). She would, of course, have particularly liked the green and red stripes, but not his expression. That suggested spite. Malice. His mother (as expressive and as flamboyant as any of her race) would have suggested that the English were best encouraged to be reserved. She would have preferred her son to keep his anger in the parenthesis of his temper and his Englishness for all to see.

The newspaper lay on the card table at his side, next to his hardly tasted lemon water. Not for the first time during the past week, Montague James felt that he was not entirely in control. He picked up the paper. Read, for the second time, what he had perfectly understood the first time. According to the paper the police knew about the merry-go-round. He had no reason to doubt the paper. He knew that anyway. What he did not understand was the timing. Montague James had been in his Gay Street office earlier in the day and had done what he always did when it was to hand, had read the *Chronicle*'s front page and opinion column.

James cared to know what the editor thought to be the most important news of the day and what he thought might be that day's most important issue in the city. Page One and the opinion column told him that. There had been no sign of this, this article, before lunch. And now this. Who had fed Dover? And why had it been held until the last moment? He shifted in the chair. It moved. It was, after all, not a reproduction. He sat still. Velvet-slippered feet together. Thought through the problem. A delicate yet over-decorated French carriage clock whirred and chimed the three quarters. It was time to put just a little more distance between himself and certain activities. For the moment.

Montague James stood, straightened his perfectly straight tie in the stately mantel mirror and for a second wondered if he might be using an excess of aftershave. Decided not.

His first telephone call was to Steven Reece. The simple task would be to pay him off. Montague James was not a fool. Reece's loyalty was to his large salary and generous expense accounts. He was good at what he did, but then so were most of his kind. Reece's lack of shame helped enormously. Montague James's understanding of Reece's character helped even more.

'Ah, Steven dear boy. What a pleasure to speak to you.'

James rarely found it a pleasure to speak to anyone. Few failed to bore him. Reece, however, did amuse him. It was a pleasure. The circumstances were not.

'I fear old wounds are opening. I would like you to visit the New York office. See if you can see opportunities to develop your public affairs.'

Reece was surprised. But he said of course he would go. When?

'There is an excellent flight to Paris tonight. Or so I seem to remember, my dear. You will be on that one. Go on to your Big Apple tomorrow.'

If Reece objected he did not say so. He did not mention the dinner parties to be cancelled, the hospitality box at Lord's to be handed over to someone else, the test drive in the new Porsche, nor the explaining to Warren. His partner had been pretty grotty recently. He hoped they weren't heading for a bust-up. This could do it. He wondered if he could swing an extra ticket for him. Montague James, as ever, was ahead of him. Knowing almost everything about his employees made life easier.

'And, Steven, why don't you take that nice young friend of yours with you. After all, you may be away some time and, well, one never wishes to rely on absence. Best take the heart with one on those occasions.'

He listened, but vaguely, to the expressions of gratitude from Reece and then dismissed him.

'I shall be in touch, Steven. Don't you be. Mm? 'Bye now.'

The second telephone call was to the farmhouse. He need not have bothered. The Land-Rover had left. Over the cattle grid. Right at the end of the lane. Out to Barrington Coombe. Onto the Bristol Road. Left into the airport. No bigger than a supermarket. But a plane, that evening to Dublin. The man would be home before nightfall. The son would be on his way to the rambling family house in Sligo and safety. Montague James's safety.

There was a light tap at the door and the Filipino maid entered. Montague James did not look. Did not speak. He believed that, if servants were worthwhile, they knew what to do and when to do it. No need to look. No need to speak. Conversation only confused and usurped proper household relationships. He glanced at the lemon water and inclined an eyebrow. The girl was about to leave the room. He found it necessary to speak.

'Ask Mrs James to come in.'

'She is walking, sir.'

'Nonsense. Mrs James does not walk. Anyway, I would have seen her.'

'No, sir. You in bath. She gone out. Walking. She said so. Back soon now.'

Montague James was put out. The Filipino closed the double doors. Montague James waited. While he did so, his wife was sipping sparkling water and watching Norma painting the brothers. Hilary James did not look much at the canvas.

James picked up the telephone, the same one he had used earlier, the one listed in his mother's name, and made a third call.

Forty-Two

There were two telephone calls for Leonard. The first from Montague James. The mackerel had not bothered to swim far and the *Chronicle*'s front page had hooked him. Or so Leonard imagined. Montague James's invitation had been pleasantly delivered. Nine o'clock that evening. At the flat. Time for a further word. It was James who had called Leonard. Or so James imagined.

The second mackerel had surprised Leonard. Dancer wanted to meet. When? Now's about right. There was a towpath at the back of Caroline Buildings. Quiet. By yourself. Dancer had heard the pause. Had told Leonard not to worry.

Leonard left the police station and cycled the long way by the Guildhall and the straight and gentle Pulteney. Ten minutes and he was there. He found the track rising by the side of the row of mostly rundown houses and the dried-out path alongside the canal. Dancer had a smile which was almost a leer. Not quite. But most people weren't quick enough to spot the difference. Leonard was indifferent. They walked as they talked. Dancer ambling. Bow-legged. Greasy leather waistcoat with tassels over bare brown arms and chest. Leonard pushing his Rudge. Trudging. Waistcoat buttoned over soft green cotton. His cycle clips green and about his ankles.

Dancer's opening made Leonard stop. He turned the front wheel towards the fire-eater. Blinked. Listened.

'Killing's done, you know. They done what they needed to.'

'Who has?'

'I'm moving on. Time for out. Right? It's all a bit nasty now. Thought you should know.'

'Who has? Who's done the killing, Dancer?'

'Didn't want anyone to think I'm doing a runner.'

'Dancer, tell me, who killed her? Who killed Josie?'

Dancer shook his head. Kept on telling Leonard what he wanted him to hear. Nothing more.

'Going north, while there's some sun. Edinburgh.'

Leonard walked on. The quick clicking of fat-tyred wheels noisy in the summer's near-deserted evening. A child kicked a rag ball and his mother murmured not to go too near the water. The soft sound of her voice carrying, easily, along the still path. Leonard and Dancer strolled at the evening's pace and talked of murder.

'Tell me why the killing's done. You must. To be sure.'

'Piccolo man knew about the merry-go-round. She knew about it. No one else. So no one else to be done. Right?'

The voice was a lame shout. The talk of a deaf man who'd once sung. Once articulate. Leonard could smell it. Spirit to drink or spirit to burn? He didn't know.

'You read about it?'

Dancer nodded. Time to tell. Then go.

'The Piccolo man got it.'

'The merry-go-round?'

'Right.'

'OK, Dancer. Tell me, what is the merry-go-round?'

'Don't know.'

'You must.'

'No way. I heard it said. The Piccolo man knew. Josie knew. He told her. No one else.'

'Piccolo was close?'

'Right. Piccolo. The Piccolo man. Always playing the pipe, that one. Made some change.'

'You going to tell me who he played for?'

It was Dancer's turn to look.

'Big people.'

'That's what everyone tells me. But which people? I need a name.'

'You got one.'

'James?'

'Maybe.'

'Come on. Help me, Dancer.'

'I heard things. The merry-go-round was something they had going. Piccolo busted in.'

'What does that mean?'

Dancer stopped. Leaned against the Wash House Lock bar. The wood was warm beneath his hands.

'Piccolo came one day. Played his pipe thing. Had a pitch. Then he asked around. Wanted to know about a merry-go-round. Everyone said he was a madman.'

Dancer laughed a Jamaican laugh when his hero hits a hundred. Leonard saw no humour.

'But he wasn't.'

'You know that?'

'You told him about the merry-go-round?'

Dancer smiled lots more.

'Me? No. No way. I didn't know. No one did.'

'So what happened?'

Dancer pushed himself off the wooden arm and they walked on. The mother looked at them. Waited for her son to catch up. Suspicious. Even in the evening's clear light.

'He went walking.'

'Piccolo did?'

'Right. He went. Then a few weeks back when you bussed us –'

Leonard broke in.

'I don't understand. Bussed. What does that mean?'

'Don't give me shit.'

'I promise. I don't.'

Dancer believed him.

'One morning. First thing. We get pulled and put on the bus. They drop us way out.'

'Who did?'

'You people.'

'Police?'

'No. Thomas Cook. Course it was the police. Told us they were moving us on.'

'That can't be true.'

'Oh no? It was true. It happened. Then we get to find out why. It was a warm-up act for the real thing. Right? When the great white queen blew in. They came again. Same bus. Same big smiles. They goes, "OK, you guys, split." They drop us same place. On the Shepton road.'

'I heard something.'

Dancer was back smiling.

'No big deal. Happens.'

'Where did Piccolo fit into this?'

Dancer spat into the water. It was the practised spit of an athlete. Or a fire-eater.

'First time they did it, we hang around for a while. But out there it's nowhere. Then maybe a day or two we're heading back. And there's the brother with that fine piccolo of his. He's wandered in. He's back.'

'D'you know where he'd been?'

'No. But Josie knew.'

'She didn't. I asked her.'

'She did. She told you. She told you about the limo.'

'In the Podium?'

Dancer said nothing. He was smiling to the heavens. Eyes closed. Nodding.

'She told you this?'

Still smiling. Still nodding. Leonard was getting impatient. He didn't want to be. Wouldn't work on Dancer.

'OK. So the people in the car were Piccolo's friends. Who were they?'

Dancer came down.

'That's for you to find out.'

'Josie said you knew about the car. She said you know about cars. What sort of car?'

'Clever policeperson. Clever one.'

'Well?'

'BRG. Roller.'

'Green Rolls?'

They'd reached the bend. They stopped. The towpath was empty.

'Mm. Mm.'

'You're sure?'

'Not in court. But yes.'

The smile had gone. The eyes softer. Sadder. The shoulders still strong, but not so arrogant. The swagger resting.

'Why d'you call me?'

'She was nice.'

'If you'd told me when I asked . . .'

Dancer said nothing. He knew. Leonard was not finished. Make him suffer. Not too much. Enough to remind him why he was telling.

'You knew about merry-go-round. She wouldn't have died, Dancer.'

Dancer banged his hands against his thighs. The amble had become a raw recruit's march. Legs wrong. Arms in unison. Banging in anger. Banging in frustration. All wrong. All wrong. Leonard backed off. Not too far. There had to be more to come.

'Did everyone know about merry-go-round?'

The man shook his head.

'No. No one.'

'Why you?'

'Piccolo told me.'

'So he never asked you. He told you. That right?'

Dancer nodded. That was right. Piccolo had needed to talk to someone. He'd talked to Dancer.

'Why you, Dancer?'

'He trusted me.'

'And Josie.'

'Not Josie. He didn't. He was sorry for her. Didn't trust her. Needed her. Needed to mix. Needed to go grey. OK?'

He looked at Leonard. The eyes sharp. The question in them important. Leonard had to understand. He wasn't responsible. Not him. Not Dancer. Dancer didn't kill her. Not him. Not Dancer. Down to Piccolo. He used Josie as cover. So she went when he wasn't there. Take her out. Take her out. Josie was not important to Piccolo. Only one thing was.

Leonard understood.

'It was my flat. My shower. They were after me. It could have been me in the shower.'

Dancer shook his head.

'Forget it. These people don't do for you people. That's bad news. Everyone knows that. You never see the movie? Cop-killers don't eat quiche. Know that for a fact. They wanted her. Just another traveller girl. No big deal. Never make a reliable witness. Best dig the hole now. Take her out. Take her out. Take her out. Take her out.'

The whine became a howl. He was staring into some distance of his own. Almost rambling. Smiling because that was the shape of his mouth. Scummed and crooked teeth. Tears from his own eyes.

'Take her out. Take her out. Take her. Take her.'

'And Piccolo?'

'Had to go.'

'Why, Dancer? Why the Piccolo man?'

Dancer did not answer. Just stared. But he'd heard. Leonard waited. Dancer came back. The eyes dried. Switched back to mocking. A mocking that was unreal.

'Piccolo? Come on, man. You know that. His brother. That's why.'

Leonard knew the answer. Didn't ask the question. Waited for the answer to come as he knew it would.

'Came to find his brother. Find who killed him.'

'In Rainbow Wood. Ten years ago. Bolt.'

Dancer did not answer. Leonard pushed.

'You knew he was Bolt, didn't you?'

'Just a brother.'

Dancer had said what he'd come to say. Leonard would not chase. Not now. He walked on. But Leonard had something more. He called. Softly.

'It's not done yet, Dancer. Killing's not done, you know.'

Dancer's walk was a saunter. He did not turn. Leonard's whisper was clear. Not to be missed.

'Not just Bolt, Dancer. Not just Josie. They've not done. There's one more who knows.'

Dancer didn't turn.

'Merry-go-round, Dancer. You knew. It's not done.'

Dancer didn't look back. There was no point.

Leonard peered at his pocket watch. Nine o'clock. He turned his bicycle and scooted it back the way they'd come. As he rode, one foot on the pedal, he was sensing not the peacefulness of the water and the warmth from the day's grass but the inside of a fine apartment. A magazine picture in his pocket taken from Joste's bag. He swung his right leg over the saddle and started to pedal. He was late for a date in a crescent.

Forty-Three

Shortly before nine, Montague James was driven away from the crescent in his green Rolls-Royce. Before leaving, he had given clear instructions to Hilary James. But not before he scolded her. His wife had arrived home quite flushed. Montague James assumed the weather responsible although it had cooled. She had gone straight to her room and the Filipino woman had run a full bath. By the time her husband caught up with her, Hilary was about to bathe.

'What on earth were you doing there? You were there last evening.'

'Norma's my friend.'

'Do not be ridiculous, my dear. It is quite inconceivable that you should have any. Women are jealous and men have but carnal ambitions for you. Out of the question.'

'Why must you always put me down?'

Montague James smiled.

'Why, whatever next? Of course I do not. I'm simply expressing a little distress that, when I needed you, you were not here.'

Hilary James sat sulkily on a white silk cushion on a china peacock throne. Her bath was waiting. The girl had tipped into it a few drops of oil. The scent rose in the steam. Montague James felt quite ill. He hoped it would not linger in his clothes. He spent a minute telling his wife what she had to do. He wanted to know what the Inspector knew about merry-go-round. He expected to return by midnight. When he did so, he expected to be told the answer to that which he had asked. Was he understood?

She nodded.

'Why should he tell me? He's a policeman.'

Montague James looked at the folds of silk clinging to the long form of his wife's body. He ran his finger over her shoulder, across her breast. He dug with his nails into the nipple so clear through the fine silk. Twisted. Smiled.

'I leave that to you, my darling. And I'm sure you will enjoy finding out. Within our understanding, of course.'

He did not say goodbye. That was unnecessary. The Filipino was at the door as he approached the hall. That was necessary. Montague James expected others to know his likes and dislikes. He did not expect them to understand them, indeed he preferred that they should not. But, above all, Montague James expected, and mostly got, obedience. The simplest way to obedience was through correct anticipation. It was quite necessary that the girl was there at the front door, just as it was quite necessary that his driver had the car door ready to open and air conditioning just right. The front door of the house closed as the car drew away. It would have been wrong to shut out her master should he have changed his mind and returned. In the bathroom, Hilary James sat where her husband had left her. Staring at the wall. Seeing nothing.

As a very serious, a more than usually thoughtful, Montague James was being driven across the high Mendip road, Leonard was chaining his bicycle to the crescent's railings. He put the key in his waistcoat pocket and headed for the shiny black door behind which the Filipino girl stood, anticipating his knock. It was fifteen minutes past nine o'clock. She showed him in, indicated the tray and left.

Leonard was standing in the drawing-room when Hilary James came in. He did not mind the white wrap loosely tied at the waist. He did not mind the revealing flare of the soft silk as she walked to greet him. He did not mind the hand which squeezed her greeting. He did not mind the flounce into the oversized sofa and the time it took to arrange the slippery silk. Leonard minded none of these things. Hilary James was performing for him. Promising what he knew she would never deliver. That was fine by Leonard. It meant he was getting warm.

'Montague is so sorry. He was called out at the last moment. So many committees, you know.'

'I didn't.'

'Oh but, James, you must know. The whole city is run by committees.'

'And your husband runs the committees.'

It took a second. Maybe two.

'You think so? He is very busy.'

Leonard looked across the city. Still light. But not much time. He walked towards the double doors.

'Well, I'm sorry I missed him. Perhaps he could call me when he has a moment.'

The alarm in Hilary James's eyes told Leonard enough. The

urgency in her voice confirmed it. She moved very quickly in the leather cushions.

'Oh please, don't go. Don't.'

Leonard was already opening the door. This was not in Montague James's script. Leonard turned. Wondering about his timing. It was fine. Just as hers had been at their first meeting. She was standing, legs slightly apart, with her back to the long window. The light was perfect. It poured through the thin wrap. Leonard's smile was one of sincere courteousness.

'But I have much to do, Mrs James. And I'm sure you have.'

'Hilary, please. Hilary. Montague said he would not be too long. Maybe an hour. Won't you have a drink? Yes, that's a good idea. Whisky?'

She did not wait for an answer. She poured from a decanter into a large crystal tumbler. It was a very generous whisky. She poured herself spring water over ice cubes. She sat in the middle of the white leather sofa and patted the cushion at her side. Leonard sat opposite. His sofa identical to hers. Much more comfortable. Just as last time.

Hilary James crossed one knee over the other. The wrap fell away. The legs would have sold the most expensive stockings. Once, they had. Back to the script. Leonard smiled. A friendly policeman.

'Tell me, Mrs James . . .'

'Hilary. Please.'

'Tell me, how well did you know Richard Bolt?'

The eyes were still. Register: nil. She sipped. Not for time. Relaxed.

'Who?'

'Richard Bolt.'

'I don't know anyone of that name. At least, I don't think I do. Should I?'

'I think you do. Or did.'

'What does he do?'

'For the moment, he lies in a tray in the mortuary ice box.'

'Oh. How horrid.'

'Yes. How horrid.'

He waited. Leonard spent a lot of his time waiting. He looked. Blinking. Waiting.

'I'm sorry, James, that's it, I'm afraid. I don't know the name at all.'

'Let me try again. How well did you know Piccolo?'

The shake of her head was a slow side to side. Not pondering. Not thinking. Telling Leonard the track was wrong. No Bolt. No Piccolo. Maybe she didn't. Maybe there was nothing in a name.

'He was the man murdered in the baths. Piccolo. His real name was Bolt. Richard Bolt. A particularly gruesome murder.'

The eyes flickered.

'Once more. Tell me, how well did you know him?'

'But I did not.'

This time the sip was measured. Theatrical.

'Your husband did.'

'Nonsense. He wouldn't.'

'Wouldn't what?'

'Well, frankly, know anyone like that.'

'He knew his brother.'

'Whose?'

'Bolt's. That was the man murdered in Rainbow Wood, ten years ago.'

'Ten years ago? I'd only just arrived in Bath.'

Distancing herself. Unsure. Reducing the options. But Leonard had seen it before. He wasn't going to be distracted. He would play along. Build her confidence. He needed her to have something to fall from.

'From where?'

She shrugged. Slightly. No exaggerated movement. It was enough for the wrap to do its stuff. Leonard looked at her face.

'Ten years ago? London? Paris? I was modelling.'

'What sort of modelling?'

'Photographic.'

Her expression was mischievous. For a moment, he liked her. He said nothing.

'Fashion, James. Fashion.'

He raised his eyebrows.

'There are other types, you know. OK, I got plenty of offers. I was once asked to do a *Playboy* centrefold. Can you believe it?'

He could. He did not say so.

'Did you?'

Her eyes were half-closed.

'Nearly. It was a long time ago. I was nineteen. I was flattered.'

'But you didn't?'

'Hadn't the guts. Or wasn't heading that way. Wasn't broke enough. Take your pick.'

Leonard had taken off his spectacles. Taken out his green handkerchief. Blinking.

'Which way were you heading?'

'James, that's a very personal question to ask a lady.'

'You have looks. You're not a feminist. You were in the business. That all makes it professional.'

She really did laugh this time.

'I like you, James.'

It wouldn't help her.

'So what happened?'

'I got a couple of parts in VLBs. You know? Very Low Budget movies. One of them had a club scene. I was one of the strippers in the background. All very mood stuff. Infrared lighting. No dialogue.'

'And the other one?'

She straightened her back. The wrap did the rest.

'I stood out, as they say. Same club. Same strip. Same movie, I suppose. I'm told it was big in Pensacola. Then I quit.'

'Getting chilly?'

282

'No. Too warm. One of the assistant directors was shooting porn movies. Big budgets. Classy. *Love Muscle Two, Three, Four* and more. Offered me five hundred dollars. That's when I went back to New York.'

It dawned on him. Had to be.

'And where you met Norma.'

Hilary James sat taller. The wrap had given up. She pulled the top back in place. The look of surprise was genuine. She'd never pretended to be that good an actress.

'She told you?'

'You both did.'

She shook her head. A silly little girl not understanding her transparency in front of a tired teacher whose stock in trade was transparent reasoning.

'She was lying. She always does.'

'Why should she?'

'You're a policeman. People like Norma always feel guilty.'

She shifted. Recrossed her legs. For Leonard's benefit. More smile. She held out her empty glass. Leonard refilled from the iced jug on the ornate table. She did not have to twist to face him as he came back. But she did. From the waist. Leonard went back to his sofa.

'People on the merry-go-round?'

Hilary James acted in accordance with her husband's stage directions. She touched the leather cushion at her side.

'Please come and sit here, James.'

'I'm fine here.'

'You're so formal. You make me frightened. Please.'

He'd play her game. But not by her rules. He took his time. Gazed out of the window. Refilled his glass without asking and sat down beside her. She took his hand. Gave it a squeeze. Let it rest lightly against her bare thigh. Smiled.

'You must be very hot. Why not take off your jacket?'

Leonard had thought she would have been able to do better than that.

'When did she do *Jungle Cat*?'

'How would I know?

Leonard let her see his eyes working slowly from her ankles, to her knees, along the the unmarked, childless thighs, to the tiny waist, to the firm breasts barely covered by the deep vee of the silk.

'It's very good. Has your husband seen it?'

'No. Should he?'

'He knows about it?'

'I doubt it. What are you saying, James?'

She knew.

'The body is very lifelike.'

'It did something for you?'

His smile was the nearest he could get to embarrassment without feeling it.

'I think so. It was perfect in every way, as far as I can tell.'

Hilary James shifted slightly. She was very good at it. The wrap dropped and for a moment her left breast was totally uncovered. Leonard stared. Said nothing. Hilary James pulled the wrap closer to her. But took her time. Perfect in every way. She pressed his hand. Gently. But his question was not in her script. His voice was soft. As gentle as her hand had been. But, still, wrong question.

'When did she talk you into it? After the party, was it? After the merry-go-round?'

She remembered the night. The moment. Then the next morning when Norma had called. Told her to come right over. When she arrived, Norma had taken her to the studio. Locked the door. Told her about *Jungle Cat*, that she, Hilary, had to be *Jungle Cat*. They'd smoked and talked about it. She had agreed. It had been easy. A little more grass. Easy. Norma had said did she mind if a friend watched as she worked. By then she did not. Norma had called him in from the small room at the end of the studio. It was him. Again. Norma had told her she wanted atmosphere. Told her to drop her light sundress where she stood. Told her to keep still. To keep her pose. To feel herself in the clearing. To smell the earth. The threat. To watch him as he swayed. Told her to watch him with her body. Not with her eyes. But she couldn't. She could remember every moment. Feel every moment. She could still hear Norma's soft voice calling that it was good. It was good. She knew there was a video camera. Didn't mind. Not then. Not later. Especially later. It was all there was left. She was rubbing Leonard's hand on her thigh. Didn't know. Didn't hear him at first. Then did.

'Tell me, Hilary, are you still on the merry-go-round? Still there?'

'What do you mean, James? Please.'

'Are you?'

She took her hand away.

'I'm telling you, James. Please, why are you being so horrid?'

'You in the audience? Or playing?'

'Stop being horrid.'

'You like watching, Hilary? Is that it? You like to feel it's you?'

'Don't.'

She raised the glass to her lips. Did not drink. He took it. Put it on the table in front of them. He put his hand above her knee. She looked down. Waiting. Very gently, Leonard started to stroke her leg. Very gently.

'Don't.'

'Because you like it, Hilary?'

Her voice was a whisper.

'Please, don't. Please.'

'But you wanted me to.'

'No.'

She put her hand over his but did not push him away. Instead left it there as he continued to stroke.

'You like this, Hilary?'

She breathed deeply.

'Very softly, Hilary. Very softly. Is that nice? Is it?'

Very slowly, in time with his hand, her head moved. Very softly.

'Is that what happens at the parties, Hilary? Is it?'

'I don't . . . I don't know what you mean.'

He moved his hand higher on her leg. He could feel the pressure of hers.

'Did he let you watch them?'

'Who?'

'Montague, Hilary. Montague. Is that what he let you do? Watch them?'

She said nothing. Her breathing had changed as he stroked her. It was answer enough.

'Who was there? Who did you watch?'

She had closed her eyes. Remembering. While his hand moved she had started to roll a fold of the soft leather cushion between her thumb and forefinger.

'The boys, Hilary, Norma's boys. They were there, weren't they? They were playing for you, weren't they?'

She uncrossed her legs. Knees just touching. But only just. He stroked with the flat of his hand across the top of her legs. The silk slipped away to her hips. She started to shake.

'Who else, Hilary? Who else?'

The whisper came through barely moving lips.

'I don't know.'

'Someone special for you, Hilary. Did they have someone special for you?'

He let his fingers fondle the inside of her thighs. She straightened. Arched. The silk parted.

'No.'

'Not for you?'

'No.'

'Someone to watch. Someone special?'

'Please.'

'Is that what you did, Hilary? Just someone to watch. Not touch. Someone special.'

'Please.'

'That's what you like, isn't it, Hilary. Someone all the time?

More and more. That's it, isn't it? Someone to touch you . . . here.'

She shuddered once. Then again.

'And then someone else. Always someone else, Hilary. Yes?'

Her hips moved to be nearer.

'Who was it, Hilary. Who?'

She moved again. Pushing herself closer to his hand.

'It was Richard, wasn't it, Hilary?'

Her whole body was heaving. Her breasts rising high. Her stomach sucked in.

'Tell me, Hilary. Say it, Hilary. Who was it? He was beautiful, wasn't he? He was beautiful for you, wasn't he? Beautiful for you?'

Her head nodded slowly, reliving each touch. Each moment.

'Tell me, Hilary. Tell me now.'

She moved further and he touched her. She gripped the leather between her fingers. Tightly. Her nails dug deeply into its pillowed softness.

'Tell me, Hilary. Tell me now.'

The whisper was hardly there.

'Richard.'

'Tell me again, Hilary. Who?'

'Richard.'

Hilary James wanted him. She closed her eyes again. She saw Richard. Tall, beautiful, strong arms. She saw the long, strong thighs. So alive still. Leonard pulled away.

She turned towards him. His face. Leonard had taken off his spectacles. His eyes. Horrid, horrid eyes boring into hers. No passion. No desire. Hard, cruel eyes. Uncompromising. Contemptuous. Ruthless. Horrid, horrid eyes.

'Please. James. Please.'

Leonard stood over her. Stared down with eyes that had watched a lifeless slab. Had watched a run-cold shower washing away the blood of a lifeless, helpless girl. Now watched her. Now she was frightened. Hilary James wanted to get away. Wanted to run. Wanted to be in her bathroom. The door locked. The water warm. Safe. She could not move. She did not know the answers he wanted. He probably knew that. She had started to cry. Oh God. Her eyes. Her eyes. What would they be like? Montague would see them.

'Who runs it, Hilary. Who?'

'I don't know. Don't. Please don't.'

'Because they'll kill you? Just like they killed Richard? Like they killed the girl? Is that why? Come on, Hilary. Tell me now. Who?'

'I don't know. I promise.'

'Your husband.'

'I promise I don't know.'

'Where, Hilary? Where is the merry-go-round?'

She was shaking again. This time tears. This time fear.

'Not here.'

'Where, Hilary? Where?'

'I can't tell you.'

Leonard was bending over her. She had gathered the white silk about her as best she could. It looked dirty. Crumpled. It wasn't. Versace didn't do that. Leonard bent lower. He spoke into her ear. As he did she stared ahead. Never so frightened.

'If you don't tell me, Hilary, you'll go to prison. You will. I promise. You will. You want that?'

She shook her head.

'You know what they do to people like you, Hilary? D'you know?'

Still the little girl. She didn't know. She would do.

'You're beautiful, Hilary. Beautiful. Prison's a bad place to be a beautiful woman. A woman who dreams. A woman who needs to be touched. To love, Hilary. Listen, Hilary, I'm going to tell you what they'll do to you. You hear?'

She heard. She said so. She listened as Leonard's voice spat venom. She heard every syllable.

'The dikes, Hilary. They'll share you. You know what they'll do? You'll be their free whore. They'll pass you around. They'll use you one at a time. They'll use you when they want to.

And then, when they want special favours, from outside. They'll fix you with the men. They'll charge for you, Hilary. They'll use you to feed their habits. That's what. And when they've finished, Hilary, and when you don't play, Hilary, they'll cut you. And they'll start cutting you here.'

Leonard jammed his hand between her still-open legs.

'Here, Hilary. That's where they'll start. So when you come out, there'll be nothing for anyone. They'll take everything, Hilary.'

And when he'd done she covered her ears with her hands.

He moved his lips right to her face. The malice in his voice spun her brain.

'Understand?'

She tried to say yes through her sobs. She couldn't. She believed him.

'Where, Hilary? Tell me where.'

'The, the, the farm.'

'What farm?'

'Church Farm.'

'Who, Hilary? Who?'

She shook her head. She wept on.

'I promise, I promise, I promise. I don't know. I don't, don't know.'

Leonard, for reasons he didn't quite understand, believed her. For reasons he understood even less, at that moment he felt sorry for her. The Filipino maid had not anticipated his going. He let himself out.

Forty-Four

Madeleine Jack was in the almost deserted MIR when Leonard arrived back at the police station. So was Somers-Barclay. He had drawn a blank in the wine bars and drinking clubs. She had drawn a blank with Norma.

'She spent most of her time telling me in the minutest

detail about what went on in the back of the car. She was winding me up.'

'Was she telling the truth?'

Madeleine Jack looked near to embarrassment. Leonard was pleased. He wasn't sure why, but he was.

'Maybe. She's got a pretty vivid imagination. She says there were two of them. We knew that anyway.'

'Which one was driving?'

'Both of them. According to her they swopped over – twice.'

'A lady of some stamina.'

'Appetite.'

Leonard hummed an untutored aria. Somers-Barclay ran a gentle hand over his hair. Leonard wondered what colour it became once the sun went in.

'If I may, sir, would you like me to see her?'

Neither Leonard nor Jack said anything. A constable, updating witness papers at a corner desk, smirked. Leonard stared at the blackboard.

'Check out the address and the owners and tenants of every Church Farm within a twenty-five-mile radius of here.'

Somers-Barclay looked put out. He was.

'There could be dozens. Every village in the country has a Church Farm.'

Leonard sighed.

'A twenty-five-mile radius.'

Madeleine Jack was at the coffee machine. She poured an extra cup for Somers-Barclay.

'Here you go, Nick, you're going to need this. And, don't forget, most Church Farms aren't church farms any longer. Private houses.'

The constable scribbled on another form and smirked at Somers-Barclay's discomfort. Leonard went to the board and chalked in large shaded capitals the name of the farmhouse. He pointed to the constable.

'You, too. I want everyone on this.'

The duty uniformed sergeant arrived back from the canteen.

'And you, Ed. We need soldiers. Loads of them.'

He tapped at the board.

'This farm, or house, is within easy driving distance of the city. At some time during the past few months, it was visited by Richard Bolt. We think it was the scene of very private parties and Bolt was at them. We think prominent people in this city were there. Now all this is we-think stuff. None of it is we-know. Understood?'

The other officers understood. Leonard continued, his soft, accentless voice with a new authority. They understood authority. Liked it.

'We believe there is a codeword, or a password, for what's been going on. It's Merry-go-round. You knew that. Now you know for sure. Now I know some people in this place have doubted the reasoning behind this, but for the next few hours we're going on it. Understood?'

Edwards the duty sergeant and the constable had no doubts. Movement. They understood movement. Liked it. Somers-Barclay was not about to air his doubts but wondered what would happen once Superintendent Marsh returned. Sergeant Jack had no doubts. Leonard walked from the board. Dusted chalk from his fingers.

Somers-Barclay almost asked Leonard if he were sure. Had the sense not to. Sergeant Jack did not think to.

'This from Mrs James, sir?'

Leonard nodded.

'*I Claudius* in spades.'

'And Montague James was running it?'

He shrugged. He wanted to say yes. But he didn't know. One thing at a time.

'When we get the names, I want you to match them with James. Anything. Committees. Societies. The usual stuff. Then check out any phone records. Call them up. Find out if they've got mobiles. Get the numbers, then check the company call record.'

The most sensitive job was for Sergeant Jack. Stainger had promised, but nothing had shown up.

'See if we can hurry up that print-out of James's calls for the past two years, especially the past quarter. I want everything on his itemized account.'

Somers-Barclay was already going through the farming list and checking addresses.

Sergeant Edwards was calling the canteen. He'd have three more officers inside two minutes.

The constable had dialled his first call to country police stations. The CBO would know every Church Farm on his patch. That's the sort of thing Community Beat Officers loved to know and no one ever asked them.

Leonard put a hand on Sergeant Jack's shoulder. It seemed a natural thing to do. There would not be a harassment complaint on Stainger's desk by the morning.

'Let's find this Church Farm. It may be a blank. It could be nothing more than a wild party, but I somehow don't think so. We need the owner. Could be behind the whole thing, as far as we know.'

'Or caretaker.'

'Have to be a pretty influential one.'

'If there's money in it, that could be enough. But I still don't see what Bolt has to do with it. And why kill him?'

Somers-Barclay looked up from his list.

'And why kill him in the Roman bath?'

Madeleine Jack had started to say something but stopped when Leonard held up his hand. He looked at Somers-Barclay for several seconds.

'Go on.'

'Sir?'

'You said why kill him in the bath?'

'Yes, sir.'

Leonard brought his hand down on the table. The force juddered a pile of brown files and they fell to the floor.

'Of course! Of course! Now I get it.'

Somers-Barclay did not. He looked from Leonard to Madeleine Jack then back to Leonard.

'Sir?'

'That's it. Of course! It's been so obvious. Now I understand.'

Somers-Barclay felt that if he'd turned a handle in Leonard's curious mind he should at least know what door had opened.

But Leonard was heading for the door. Madeleine Jack was looking when he turned.

'I'll be back in an hour.'

Dancer was not by the Pump Room. He was not at the back of the bus station. He was not in the cul-de-sac where travellers dossed beneath the railway arches. The dossers, the vagrants, the beggars, the travellers. The fragrant Georgian city. Leonard had almost given up. But there was one more place. There was an outside chance. Lane had once mentioned Bernie's place. He said Dancer went there to get away. The cider drunk had talked about the yard. Could be? This time?

He was not in the yard at the back of the Old Bristol Road furniture store. The light was on in the storeroom-cum-office-cum-bedsitter. Leonard banged on the door until the old man who grubbed a living from junk answered. Bernie had not seen Dancer. Not for a day or two. He cussed Leonard for waking him and went back to the rag pile that made out to be a bed. Leonard was glad to get away from the stench and believed him. Dancer had said he was travelling on. Maybe he had.

Leonard cycled away, the overpowering summer-dried rat-infested yard in his nostrils. Then, as his sense and memory of the dirty room connected, he stopped at the kerb. The grey duffle coat on a high-summer's evening. The rags. The baked-beans tin on the chipped enamel table. The wardrobe without doors stuffed with old newspapers. The scarred grey filing cabinet. Abandoned. Drawers open. Bits of unwashed clothing where once neatly filed letters and invoices had hung in order. The Victorian basin. Garishly painted and cracked. The sacking bundle on top. The Madonna and Child in a split gilt frame. The *sacking bundle* on top of the basin. The broken roll-top desk. The *sacking bundle*. The wooden washboard and split-cane chair. The *sacking bundle* carefully rolled atop the basin. Dancer the fire-eater. Dancer had not gone. Dancer was still in Bath. Josie had said Piccolo had known. Had said soon everyone would know. Dancer knew. Leonard now knew. He crossed the road, leaned his bicycle against the telephone box and made one telephone call. Dancer knew. Leonard knew.

Forty-Five

Woods was closed. It was late. The diners had dined. The lights were dimmed and Selsey was winding down at a corner table with a couple of the staff. The girl with the tight skirt unlocked the door for Leonard. Selsey was drinking. He gave a half-wave that eventually made it to a hail. Leonard sat at the table and the girl poured champagne into a fresh glass.

'I'm celebrating, dear lad. I'm rich.'

Selsey grinned. He did that more than he smiled. Politicians smiled. Selsey was never a politician. Leonard sipped.

'A winner?'

'No, Jim lad. A loser. A blessed loser. That genius of a horse lost by half the course. He scampered the first two furlongs like a co-respondent escaping down the backstairs with his shoes in one hand and his trousers over his arm. Not a stick of elegance in the beast. Not an ounce of breath for the run-in. The horse is a genius.'

'That good?'

'Is it good! Tell him, darling. Tell the man.'

The girl in the tight skirt was not a politician. But she smiled all the same. A proper smile.

'He loses. Right? So he doesn't have to buy the pony. Right?

And we can all get on with life. Pretend we're still running a restaurant instead of a nervous breakdown. Brilliant.'

She ruffled Selsey's hair and wandered off into the empty restaurant to cheer up the tables for the morning. Leonard's eyes followed her going. Selsey, relaxed, watched Leonard's stare.

'Shall I tell you something, Jim lad? I have customers who come in twice a week to do just that. Did you know that?'

'Do what?'

'Watch the little darling's bottom. Isn't it a wondrous thing? I love it. Shall I tell you that?'

His head was on his chest. Too heavy now. The day had been one of long celebration.

'Tell me something else, Selsey. Tell me about Harriet's husband.'

Selsey peered from beneath his black bushy eyebrows, his eyes screwed tight by his round and creased cheeks.

'The Bowles Boy? Tell you what?'

'He used to come here?'

'Of course. All the best people in Bath come here.'

'With Montague James.'

'So?'

'They were close?'

'Business. No one's close to that fella. Anyway, had to be business. Always went on James's card. Always.'

'When he wasn't with Harriet, when it was strictly business, who with? Apart from James.'

Selsey waved his glass from side to side. A comfortable don gently telling his protégé that his hypothesis simply would not do.

'Long time ago, Jim lad. Many moons. Too many moons.'

Leonard put down his hardly touched champagne. Selsey eyed the rejected wine with near-dismay. Leonard leaned across the table.

'Selsey, it's very, very important. I know about Montague James. There was someone else. There had to be.'

The other man grumbled in his cups. A gentle grumble for a day that was almost done.

'Mm. Maybe there was.'

'Whor?'

'I'm dreadful bad at names, Jim lad. Dreadful bad.'

Leonard was closer. Through the arch, the girl watched as she tidied. The smile gone. The policeman at work. A different man.

'Selsey, you must remember. We mustn't have any more death, Selsey. Please.'

Selsey looked up. Please? This was not Leonard the monosyllabic. This was not the off-beat who sat most lunchtimes at his window seat with lightly poached salmon and quails' eggs. This was not the eccentric whose eyes followed a heart-stopping short black skirt but whose hands never wandered. Whose lips never watered but after food.

'There was a fellow. Not now. But there was one.'

'With Bowles?'

'Mm.'

'With James?

'Mm.'

'Who?'

'The name's gone. It has, I promise. Gone. I'm not sure it was ever there.'

'Tell me about him.'

Selsey's glass was in his chins. He spoke with a low voice, muffled. But the thought was clear.

'Older fellow. Not much of the hair left. A done-well man.'

'What's that mean?'

'Done well. Done well. That's what some of them say. The farmers. They've done well at the table. Eaten well. That's what farmers tell you. Done well, they say. I thought a farmer. Always thought a farmer.'

'Why?'

'The hair. Farmers are mean on such things. Have their

hair cut. Barbers. Not hairdressers. Leave it a while. Fluffy round the neck. You know?'

He touched his hand to somewhere behind his ear.

'You know? Then we had the shoes. The shoes. Bramble cuts. Toe-caps big enough to boot a lad five lengths of the yard. Mm. A farmer all right.'

'He come in now?'

Selsey pondered. Almost forgetting to answer.

'No. Not for some time.'

Leonard's right hand was opening and closing with impatience. But he would not hurry Selsey. Would not. Then, did not have to.

'Chew Valley. That's where he did it, you know, Jim lad.'

'Did what? Farmed?'

'That's right now.'

Selsey sat up as if he'd remembered where he'd stashed the other bottle.

'Now I remember. Bowles and James were in one day. A January, it was. Oh, long time ago. The other fella calls and says they've got flooding out there and he can't make it. That's it, the Chew Valley.'

'You're sure?'

Selsey was once more deep in his chair. His legs straight out. Heels dug in. His glass on his chest. A sip or two coming. He grinned.

'No, Jim lad. Not sure. Never that. But, I tell you something, it's the best you've got.'

Forty-Six

Norma was wearing an unbuttoned white boiler suit and smoking a joint. Leonard had knocked. She had not been surprised to see the policeman. But few events surprised Norma.

Norma set her life clock against events. Her childhood had been a series of events which she hadn't recognized until she discovered the definition of a conventional upbringing. Her family were what she now described as Holland Park liberals. She had called her parents by their first names. Her father, prematurely grey curly-haired, had family money and reviewed opera and had had his youngest daughter baptised almost before her mother was out of labour. Her mother seemed to do a lot of social work. Her elder sister, Mimi, had lived on the top floor of the large house with her boyfriend. No one was embarrassed, except at first the boyfriend. Her father had encouraged him to call him George. Norma's first period had been discussed over Sunday lunch and George had said something like, 'Well done. That's out of the way, then,' and had gone off for the afternoon with what she later discovered was his mistress. It wasn't that her parents had hidden the affair. No one had bothered to mention it.

When she was eighteen, Norma had been raped. After an art-college party. She was not a virgin. Nor was she promiscuous. A heavy date that had turned into more than she had expected. She had waited for the trauma of that event to set her life in a different direction. She had read magazine articles. She had been counselled by her closest friend. No one else. Gradually it had dawned on her. She had enjoyed what had happened. She was no longer sure it had been rape. In a way she would never have tried to explain, Norma had gained a self-confidence which others imagined was already there. Others had been wrong. She now saw her life as a pleasurable event. She rarely got drunk, she often got stoned, she never used hard drugs, she often selected men for pleasure and discarded them with little pain. She drew few lines in her private life (although Jules Benedict was one) and therefore made few enemies (Jules Benedict was one). All this she told Leonard as they sat in the upstairs flat of the gallery sometime after one in the morning.

Why she told him, she wasn't sure. The easy time of the night and the gentle probing of the gentle policeman and the fact that she was quietly stoned: maybe those were the reasons. He had started by telling her that he knew where the farmhouse was. She had smiled. He had told her that Benedict had told him about the brothers and their exhibitions. She had smiled. He had told her that he knew Hilary James had been the model for *Jungle Cat*. She had smiled.

'You know so much. Why come here? You don't look like a gloating man.'

'I need to know what happened to Bolt.'

'You forget, I knew him when he was alive. My interest was his life, not his death.'

'You saw him killed.'

She sucked sweet-smelling smoke. Slowly, very slowly, shook her head.

'No. Wrong witness.'

'I don't think–'

Her laugh was short, sweet. Enough to interrupt him.

'Yes, you do. You're very clever. But so am I, Inspector. I break some laws, but none that matters. You people really don't mind if people have a little fun. As long as the curtains are drawn, who cares?'

'When there's murder, I care very much.'

'So you tell me. But that isn't true. When there is murder, you have to do something about it. When you do, you find people you don't like or, really and truly, don't much like. That's when you care. But the murder is not important to you. You have no self-righteousness that burns inside you to solve mere murder. You want to catch people who think they can get away with it. You want grand people. You want horrid people. But, if some poor man kills his wife when he finds she's been screwing his boss, well, Inspector, that's not your type of murder, is it? You like murder mysteries. It's the mystery you like.'

She poured Metaxas brandy from a long-stemmed bottle and so did he. It was now gone two o'clock and she wanted him.

'Tell me, where were you –'

'When the lights went out?'

'When they came on. I know where it was. By now, we know who owned the place. Now I want to know who was there.'

She sipped. Filled. Mellow.

'I told you. I don't know.'

'You do. There was a video. You knew them. They were customers. Some of them.'

'it was a good video.'

'You've seen it?'

She nodded. Teasing.

'Might have.'

'Where is it?'

'Somewhere.'

'Here?'

'You going to search me? Go on.'

She dribbled the soft brandy over her bare navel.

'Go on, search me.'

Leonard took off his spectacles. Rubbed. Another handkerchief. Still silk. Still green.

'I don't think you have it. I don't believe things like that go on general release.'

'A classical education, was it? Never heard of technology? Back-to-back dubbing?'

'Hilary?'

'I didn't say that.'

'I need to see it. Now.'

'Cool.'

Leonard replaced his spectacles. Squinted. She was smiling. A lazy smile. Very mellow.

'Very uncool. Evidence.'

'Won't help you.'

'Norma, I have to tell you, you are on a list. If we don't sort the person who wrote that list, you're done. There's nothing I can do to protect you except get whoever it is before they come here.'

'Don't be so dramatic. I'm no one. Harmless.'

'Not if they know you've got them on tape.'

'Why should they?'

'Word gets around.'

She didn't believe him. Norma stretched for the bottle.

'You're not very subtle.'

'Murder isn't.'

'You're even less convincing. No one's coming after me. There is no one. I am no one. I went to a party. I met a boy. He came here. I screwed him. I painted him. *Finito*. A regular day's work.'

'And you gave him Hilary James.'

'Bullshit.'

'Just as you gave her to your friends in New York.'

'Bullshit.'

Leonard got up. Took the bottle and poured for himself. Then the dregs for her.

'Not so, Norma. She's told me.'

'She wouldn't dare. You know what Monty baby'd do to her if he found out?'

'And to you?'

'Never.'

'Don't bet the ranch on it.'

Norma sniffed at the Greek brandy. Sipped what was left.

'He's too arrogant. He would never believe it.'

'Depends who told him.'

'You?'

Leonard looked at his watch. Wound it as he watched Norma's face show doubts. He slipped the timepiece into his waistcoat pocket and his barb into her confidence.

'My guess is that anyone who would do what they did to Bolt would have a lot of fun with you. Yes, I'd make sure he'd know.'

'You telling me Monty killed Richard?'

'No. I'm telling you that I need to know if he was there at the merry-go-round.'

She shivered. It was late. She still didn't believe him. Not quite.

'No.'

'Was her?'

'No.'

'Was her?'

'I did not see him.'

'There was more than one party?'

She nodded.

'You didn't tell me that before.'

'I told you enough. A few people going wild. Get drunk. Smoke a little. Everyone gets to do something. No one's disappointed. You know?'

'Everyone goes home with a piece of cake and a balloon.'

'Right. They break the rules, but not the law. Well, not too many.'

'So that's not the merry-go-round.'

Norma had buried her face in her arms. She wasn't weeping. Hiding.

'It's in another part of the house.'

'And?'

'I've never been in there. That's why those guys could take me. We never made it to the big one.'

'The merry-go-round.'

'Right.'

'But you've told me what happens.'

'I've told you. I've never been in.'

'But you know.'

'I heard.'

'Tell me more. Last time it was fun. It wasn't though, was it?'

Her whole torso said no. Leonard stood and put down his glass.

'OK. Play it your way.'

She looked up from her folded arms.

'What are you going to do?'

'What I said. Make sure James knows about Hilary.'

'You bastard. I don't believe you.'

'You should. I have nothing to lose. Bastards don't. You do. She comes here. You paint her. She's *Jungle Cat*. He's a very possessive man. Hilary is his property. Everyone tells me so. So, yes, I'll tell him.'

'You're a policeman.'

'Fine. I'll call him Sir when I tell him. Public servant. Remember?'

Her look had lost its confidence. She understood lies. She knew they were never far from her truth.

'You've no evidence.'

'James isn't interested in evidence. He's too suspicious of everyone, especially his wife. I'll tell him. He'll come for you. Or his friends will.'

'You're from another planet.'

She stared. Daring. But she knew. Leonard left his glass on the rubbed elm floor.

'The best bit's to come. We're going to pay Church Farm a visit. I'll make sure everyone knows you told us where to come. 'Bye.'

'They'd kill you.'

'No. They'd kill you. It'll be fun, remember? Death's fun? Isn't that what you told me? How about yours?'

Norma flew out of the long chair. Nails in front of her. Leonard held her off. But not far enough. Her bent fingers raked tramlines of torn skin down his cheek. She screamed violent oaths. Obscenities of hatred. Struggled until he threw her to the floor and lay across her screaming and panting half-naked body. When he thought her still, she spat in his face, her spittle stinging into the deep gouges. And then she sobbed.

Norma had never sobbed. It had never been necessary. And when she stopped she lay in his arms and she told him about George, her mother, her sister, about being raped. And Leonard listened and let her feed again on this strange narcotic of her childhood because he had not finished. He still did not know why.

They lay in silence and he pulled a rug over them both and she snuggled into his chest.

'There's one thing I don't understand, Norma, don't understand. Why did the merry-go-round stop for Richard?'

'It wasn't Hilary.'

'What wasn't?'

'The tape.'

'The video?'

He felt her barely perceptible nodding into his chest. He held her. Closer. Needed her to be reassured. He whispered the most important question of all.

'Who had the tape?'

'He did. Richaid He took one.'

'From the party?'

'No. From the other room. From the merry-go-round. He said there were three. He brought it here.'

'What was on it?'

She was silent. He remembered the drunken Benedict. The hatred spitting through the thick bile as he clung to the railings.

'The brothers?'

'More.'

'More than the party outside?'

Her voice was difficult to hear.

'Yes. Much more. Just kids really. Everything. They were doing everything.'

'And they found out?'

'Yes.'

'Who they?'

'The people watching.'

'They were taped? Is that why it was important? Because they're important?'

'Yes.'

'Who told them about the tape?'

Silence. The sobbing had returned. He felt no pity.

'You?'

She shook her head.

'Who?'

'She did.'

'Hilary?'

She said nothing.

'Norma, tell me, what was on that tape?'

'A kid.'

Yes, he knew.

'What happened to the kid?'

The whisper was miserable. Lost.

'Snuff.'

Leonard left the front door open. For one night, he'd had enough of women who tell the truth as if it were someone else's fault.

Forty-Seven

In Manvers Street police station, the incident room was working overtime. There had been a lull shortly after one o'clock. Someone had built a pyramid with dirty coffee-beakers. At about one-thirty, that same someone had knocked it over. The place was a mess. It stank of all-night. Leonard walked in holding an iodine pad to his torn cheek. Stainger stared. Sergeant Jack started to stand up and then didn't. Stainger looked again.

'What the hell's happened to you?'

Leonard dabbed at his scored face. The stain from the antiseptic made the wounds look as bad as they were.

'Long talons of the lawless.'

'What?'

'The Lady Norma. Don't worry. I'll live.'

'Not if Marsh has his way, you won't.'

Leonard went over to Sergeant Jack's desk.

'You all right, sir?'

He dabbed again. Nodded.

'Dancer?'

She shook her head.

'You sure you're all right?'

Stainger was angry as well as concerned.

'Course he is. You don't think Inspector Leonard bleeds, do you?'

Leonard ignored him. Tried again.

'Dancer?'

'Nothing. He could be anywhere.'

'His fire-sticks were in Bernie's hut. He wouldn't go far without those.'

'Nick's down there now.'

'By himself?'

She smiled.

'No way. The only place he goes by himself is the bathroom. Mostly.'

Leonard missed the joke. He wanted Dancer. If not in the yard, he wouldn't be far away.

'There are other places.'

'If he's still in Bath, well, he could be in a hundred places. The best we've got is ten pairs of eyes. Most of them are tired ones.'

Stainger was standing, hands on hips.

'Well?'

The advantage of being a senior officer was that he could ask 'Well?' The disadvantage was that he had to. Leonard liked Stainger. But not just then.

'Heard of snuff parties? Snuff movies?'

'Aye.'

'That's what we've got. Bolt knew. Dancer knows who killed Bolt. We've got Bolt in the morgue. We need Dancer before he's in there too. If I know Dancer's in this, so does whoever killed Bolt.'

Stainger coughed some authority into his voice. It was a quiet cough.

'What d'you mean "whoever"? Seemingly you've got this down to Montague James.'

Leonard took off his spectacles. He wanted Stainger to go away. He didn't want senior officers knocking down his thoughts. Not yet. He looked at Stainger as he rubbed the lenses. He was out of focus. Better that way.

'I didn't say that. I don't believe James would do anything at the crossroads. Not his bag. Anyway, you've seen the medical report. There must have been more than one person. But James is in the middle of it. Anyway, Forensic says the scene was clean.'

'What's that supposed to mean?'

'I'll tell you when I'm sure.'

Stainger scratched his head. He simply didn't like this sort of policework. Stainger liked procedures. Leonard liked other people to get on with procedures, as long as they didn't expect him to be there with a clipboard and Stainger's we-do-it-this-way checklist. There was a silence. It was tight. Madeleine Jack broke it.

'We think we've got the farmhouse.'

'Think?'

She was hurt by Leonard's sharp tone. It didn't show, but she was getting him off Stainger's hook. But Leonard knew and for a moment was sorry. He didn't say so.

'We've got eighteen hundred and twenty-one registered farms on this patch. Twenty-three of them, Church Farms. It took a couple of hours, you know.'

'Sorry.'

Madeleine Jack rushed on in case he changed his mind.

'The problem is that they're working farms. We weren't sure we were looking for a farmer. Could be a house without the farm. Twenty years ago it would have been a doddle. Lot of the farmhouses were sold off to green wellies from London.'

Her voice was husky. Sexy, it wasn't. Too little sleep and she'd started smoking again. Leonard blinked.

'But we think we've got it?'

'We've checked the local CBOs. If we rule out the tenants and the local roughs – you know, the sort of people James and his set wouldn't know from Adam – then we come down to a handful.'

'County.'

She nodded. Maybe they were.

'Where is it?'

She got up and he followed her to the wall map. The voice may have been tired, but she smelled fresh. Freesias? She was pointing.

'Here or here.'

There were two red pins. One on the edge of the Mendips south of the city. The other in the Chew Valley. She tapped the second one.

'Good.'

'Sir?'

'I saw Selsey. He thinks Chew's about right.'

Stainger wanted to know who Selsey was. Leonard ignored him. Madeleine Jack hurried by the silence.

'OK, if it is Chew Valley, then the local man says he thinks this one has a connection. Someone called Samson.'

'Why? Why not the other one?'

'You don't get too many Rollers in the Chew Valley. It's Volvo, BMW, Merc and 4-Wheeler country where he is. Rollers stand out. Especially green ones. Anyway they do if they've got a cherished plate and you're the local beat officer living in a Neighbourhood Watch Area with one of the highest rural crime rates in the county – and the lowest nick rate.'

'He's sure?'

'About the Roller? Absolutely.'

'And about the colour?'

'Green. Only time the local man's noticed it, it was on the lane going down to this Church Farm. Anyway, we checked the plate.'

Stainger was tapping a pencil on the map board.

'It's not an offence to have friends in the country and to

visit them. This is all coincidental. We shouldn't be at the mercy of coincidence.'

She looked at the wall clock. Four o'clock.

'At this time of the morning, sir, it's the best mercy we've got. Maybe a small one, but you know what they say.'

Stainger tried not to look grumpy. Leonard tried not to look pleased. She knew he was. Leonard vas on the move again.

'See you back here in an hour. We'll call on Mr Samson.'

'Five in the morning, sir?'

'Farmers get up early, don't they? Something to do with cows.'

'Right.'

'Oh, and get an intercept on his telephone. Now.'

'That could take time.'

'You've got an hour. The Superintendent will get the scribble on the chit for you. OK, sir?'

Leonard turned, went into his room, took his shaving kit from his bottom drawer and crossed the corridor and into the washroom. Leonard was taking off his tie, tucking his shirt collar into its neck, when Stainger came in.

'You look knackered, James. Here.'

Stainger put a tube of Germolene on the ledge. Leonard peered into the mirror. His eyes were red-rimmed. His curly ginger hair flattened. The cheek looked and felt awful. He needed a long hot shower, then sleep. Lots of blissful sleep. He put his spectacles into his waistcoat pocket and splashed water on his face.

'You going to tell me how you got that?'

'Norma, the painter. I pushed her. She went for me.'

'Shit.'

Leonard grinned into the mirror. It hurt.

'But it worked. She spilled.'

'Don't tell me she felt sorry for you.'

'No. For herself.'

Leonard rubbed shaving cream into the safe part of his jaw. Stainger threw the dirty iodine pad into the waste-bin.

'So what do we know from all these heroics?'

'Ten years ago an American called Bolt came to Bath to look up a woman he'd met in New York. Norma. They'd both been part of a pretty sick group. Greenwich Village. They were into very private parties. They'd tried everything, or thought they had.'

Leonard paused as he scraped at the mottled bristles under his chin. Stainger felt in his pockets for temptation. Found them, then searched for his lighter.

'Thought they had? What does that mean?'

Leonard ran the razor under his bottom lip. Muttered.

'The ultimate buzz. So they say. Snuff parties. Get a dead-- end Hispanic, say, drugged up to the eyeballs, go through all the sexual fantasies – but for real – then snuff.'

Leonard paused, holding the foam-covered razor away from his face, and gave Stainger a long look in the mirror. The eyes were hard. Stainger did not like those eyes.

'The poor little bastard would be killed. Preferably in the nastiest, the most perverted, way they could think of. And they had pretty imaginative minds.'

'This is true?'

Leonard threw the disposable razor into the basin and ran fresh water into his cupped hands. Nodded. It was true. He splashed it on his face and winced.

'The whole thing was filmed. The ultimate pornography.'

'They were doing it for money?'

'No. Kicks. But there was big money on top of it.'

Stainger leaned against the tiled wall. Lit the cigarette.

'And Bolt?'

'The younger Bolt had met Norma in New York and, I think, Hilary James.'

Stainger whistled through his teeth.

'She was in on this? Jesus!'

'Bolt came looking for somewhere to stay. But, by this time,

Hilary was Mrs James and Norma had cooled down. A little. He started bumming around and then put the arm on Hilary James.'

'"Pay up or I'll tell your husband."'

Leonard took a paper towel and dabbed carefully at his wet face.

'Something like that. I'm guessing, but it ties in with what I hear.'

'So she had him killed? I don't believe it. People don't. This is Bath, not New York. Hilary James is a bimbo. She's always been a bimbo. She was a bimbo before we had bimbos. She wouldn't know how to get the bathroom tap fixed, never mind a contract.'

He was right. Leonard knew that. Who, then? Norma had said Bolt had tried to blackmail Hilary James. Hilary James must have told someone. Would she have told her husband? He looked at Stainger. Steady Stainger. She'd have been too frightened to tell Montague James. But someone had known, or was Norma cleverer than Leonard thought? He finished buttoning his shirt. His face hurt like hell. It was clean but he felt dirty. He wanted a clean shirt. Clean air. Clean people. There weren't many in this job. Stainger dragged on the luxury of his Pall Mall. He'd given up years ago. His doctor brother had convinced him after their father had died. He allowed himself one pack per crisis.

'Tell me about this character Dancer. On the level?'

Leonard shrugged. Took another towel, wiped his chin and stuffed the soiled napkin into the overflowing bin. On the level? As much as anyone in this business.

'Dancer is smart. Or thinks he is. He knew about Bolt ten years ago. He knew that the man in the bath was Bolt's brother. I think he knows where he was killed.'

'But we know that.'

Leonard smeared the antiseptic cream from the tube. He now looked horrific. He stared at Stainger. No, Stainger did not like those eyes. He wished Leonard would cover them with his glasses. Leonard was leaning with both fists on the basin squinting at Stainger's reflection.

'We thought we did. We assumed we did. We were wrong. It was so bloody obvious, but we were wrong. Dancer knew the truth. He was not killed in Bath. Certainly not where he was found.'

'Where?'

'I don't know. But not there.'

'But why put him in there? After all, it's pretty public. And anyway you haven't explained why he was killed in the first place.'

Leonard gathered his shaving kit and opened the door. Stainger was annoyed.

'James. I said why put him in there? And why kill him?'

'I heard you.'

He slapped the tube of cream in Stainger's hand, nodded his thanks and let the door close behind him. He knew why. Let Stainger figure it out for himself. There was probably a procedure somewhere that would allow him to get there eventually.

Stainger threw his cigarette stub into the sink. He growled, and kicked at the nearest cubicle door. It swung open. It stank. The whole place stank.

Forty-Eight

Montague James returned late from Church Farm. He had given Samson his instructions. He trusted Samson to carry them out as best he could. He thought most things were under control but what James had not anticipated was the collapse of his wife.

He had instructed his wife to find out the state of Leonard's investigation. He regarded Leonard as interesting, but vulnerable to his wife's obvious attractions. He knew also that in times past his wife had used those same attractions to gain information for him and had done so without giving anything more than hope and disturbing dreams to her victims. Perhaps under stress Montague James had not recognized, or he had underestimated, Leonard's weaknesses and overestimated his wife's resilience. Whatever, it was a careless oversight and one which would be costly.

For the moment, though, he would behave according to his instincts. He really did not see any point in his wife's obvious sexuality if it could not be used to his advantage. Punishment was inevitable, and, while it lasted, enjoyable – to Montague James. Hilary James had understood. Had thought of leaving before her husband returned. She knew she could not bluff. But she knew that he would find her, have her found. That would be even worse.

When he returned, Leonard had not long gone. Hilary James was still distressed. The Filipino maid had not tried to comfort her. The woman sensed trouble and had gone to her room as soon as James had arrived home. The look on his wife's face told him everything. She might have been a good model. She had been a lousy actress.

She had no ability to lie, not convincingly. Not because Hilary James was transparently honest. She simply had no depth and, though sure of her beauty, no confidence in anything she did. Montague James had long believed that lack of confidence in either sex was pitiful, in a woman more so because without confidence the female of the species had no wit.

And so Montague James never even began to believe his wife when she said that she had not betrayed him. He did not believe her when she said that Leonard had threatened her. Certainly he did not believe her when she said that she had not been disloyal. Anyway, James believed her to be too stupid to be totally loyal. Total loyalty required a deviousness that her intellect and vanity made impossible.

'I told you to find out. What did he know?'
'Everything.'

'He could not have done.'

'I promise. He did.'

Her voice was weak. Her expression one of total fear. She saw his hand raised. Saw it sweeping towards her face. She could not move to avoid it. She stood still until the second strike. It was harder, and in the same place. She fell to the floor.

'Please, Montague. No. No. I promise. I promise.'

'What did you tell him?'

'Montague. Please. Nothing. I promise.'

'Slut.'

He kicked her hard in her uncovered ribs. She took a deep breath and cried out. The pain.

'What did you tell him?'

She could hardly speak. The pain was unbearable.

'I promise, nothing. Please.'

Montague James raised his heel over her face. She knew that he would. Her voice was all but inaudible. A whimper. His heel was steady over the bridge of her nose.

'What?'

'He knew about the parties.'

'Merry-go-round?'

She tried to speak. Couldn't. He kicked her again. This time, the other side.

'What did you tell him?'

'He knew about the farm. And, and . . .'

'And what?'

The whisper hardly reached him. But it did.

'And Richard. He knew about Richard.'

Montague James bent over her. For a moment she thought it was the end. All over. No more. But yet she knew that it was not. Not yet. The hand that reached towards her was clean, strong. The signet ring large, heavy, cruel gold. The fingers that grasped her hair were clean, sinewy, manicured. He dragged her crawling body across the deeply carpeted floor.

Into the square hall. Along the softly lit corridor and into her bedroom, and tore away her robe.

She cried, sobbed, begged. Montague James quite liked that. She bit into her lower lip until it bled as he tied her wrists to the white and gilt iron bedhead. She begged for mercy when he took the finest length of a fly-fisher's rod and stood over her. For a moment she stared in horrified silence as he raised the lime-green rod. And she screamed as he flayed and cut across her thighs and hips. She screeched in hopeless terror as the thin fibreglass wand slashed into her writhing belly and then across her flattened breasts. And, when he had done with her, he left her to bleed, went to his room, bathed, powdered and then slept soundly for the rest of the night.

Forty-Nine

Madeleine Jack slowed to cross the cattle grid. She needed to. Her car was not the sort to take kindly to spaced steel bars. It was the first time Leonard had been driven at high speed in an open-topped Alfa Romeo. It had been a safe but nevertheless frightening experience. Leonard frightened easily at five-thirty in the morning.

Two barking dogs appeared in the yard. One of them, a wolfhound of sorts, put its paws on the driver's door and barked into Sergeant Jack's face. She seemed more concerned about scratch marks on the dark-blue paintwork than any threat of throat wounds. The other dog, a border collie with one dark eye and the other almost white, crouched and snarled. The two police officers sat tight.

A man appeared at the back door. He was in his fifties, portly. Brown corduroy trousers and a city red-stripe shirt buttoned at the wrists. For a moment he eyed them and then from the back of his throat came a gurgle which belted into a throaty roar. The dogs had heard it before. They backed off. Leonard and Jack got out. But warily. The dogs were not done with them. When Leonard spoke he tried not to raise his voice.

'Mr Samson?'

The other man said nothing. Scratched at his arm. Then nodded. Leonard held up a warrant card. The man couldn't possibly read it from his distance, but it was something. Leonard smiled.

'I'm Inspector Leonard. Avon and Somerset police. This is Sergeant Jack. May we have a word?'

Leonard looked at the dogs between them and the man. For a moment, Leonard thought the man was going inside, but he'd turned to close the door before walking over to them. The wolfhound growled. The man did nothing to quieten the dog. He was stumpy. Looked up into Leonard's face, but not his eyes. It wasn't every day he met a detective, certainly not one who looked as if he'd gone three rounds with a Bengal tiger. Then he looked at Madeleine. It was a long, undressing look.

'About?'

'I understand you know a Mr Montague James.'

'Do your?'

The voice was still a gurgle. Dark tobacco and a deep-bowled and blackened pipe had done that over forty or so years.

'Yes, sir. I do. Mr James, he's a friend of yours.'

'Bit early in the morning to come all the way to tell me that, isn't it?'

Madeleine Jack did not smile. Not this morning. It wasn't her turn. She took over.

'We understand he's a frequent visitor.'

'What's the problem?'

Leonard was looking towards the open barn. A pick-up truck and a Land-Rover stood side by side. At the other end, a Mercedes saloon. No Rolls-Royce, but then he had not expected one. The house was stone, long, deep, with a covered way to a recent barn conversion at the back. He ran his eye along the upstairs windows. Some of them were open. He guessed maybe eight, maybe nine or ten, bedrooms. That big. Madeleine Jack was talking, which confused the man. He was used to male pecking orders.

'Not a problem. We need some answers. We're told you've got them.'

'What answers? Who's said anything about me?'

She ignored his demands. Threw another question. This time, a little more edge in her voice.

'You also know his wife. Hilary? Right?'

'I'm not sure I understand what this is all about.'

'I'm sure you do, Mr Samson. So if you'd just keep it simple? You know Mrs James?'

'Again, I'm not sure that my personal friendships have anything to do with you, young lady.'

'Once more. Do you know Montague James?'

'Well . . .'

'The local community beat officer has seen his vehicle, a green Rolls-Royce, visiting this house.'

'Then why are you fucking asking, if you know already?'

'Yes or no.'

'Yes.'

Samson turned to Leonard as if to appeal to reason. But Leonard was gazing at the house. No curtains had moved. But they were being watched. Leonard wanted to let the watchers know he knew.

'And Mrs James?'

'All right. All right. Yes. Yes. Yes. Satisfied?'

Samson rubbed his jaw. He'd yet to shave that morning. It didn't much show.

'We understand that Mr James and his wife are frequent guests at parties you hold here. They were described to us as special parties. For very adult adults. Is that right, sir?'

Leonard only slightly checked his eye wandering over the building. Madeleine Jack didn't waste time with the subtle approach. Stainger would have blown a gasket. Samson did.

317

'What the hell are you talking about?'

Leonard decided that it was time he got in. If she was playing the hard game, he had to be Mutt to her Jeff; or was it the other way round? He could never remember. The interrogation course had been light years away and seemed totally irrelevant in the quickly warming summer morning. He tried a smile. His face hurt. Instead, Leonard offered an understanding tone to his sergeant's abrasiveness.

'Well, it's this way, sir. We understand –'

Leonard hadn't guessed it would work so quickly.

'I wish you'd stop telling me you understand. If you understand so much, why the fuck are you asking me? Make myself clear?'

'Perfectly.'

Madeleine Jack's reply came out as three icy syllables in the fresh morning. Leonard smiled. He really could have been an art historian trying to calm a northern industrialist who's discovered that his one venture into culture has been a financial disaster.

'Of course, sir, and I appreciate your position. You see, Mr Samson, what Sergeant Jack is saying is that your name has come to our attention in the course of our inquiries and, naturally, we wanted to clear up any loose ends before they became misunderstandings. Now, sir, if you could just put us straight on a couple of points. First, and I promise it's simply a matter that has to be formally established, you do know Mr James, don't your?'

Samson looked at Leonard's blinking eyes. Pause. Blink. Pause. Blink. Pause. Blink. They set their own tempo to calm the landowner's fury.

'I know him. I suppose. I've said that.'

Sergeant Jack's tone hit him behind the knees.

'"Suppose" means you're not sure. You either do or you don't. Understand?'

'Look, young lady . . .'

'What Sergeant Jack means, sir, is that, well, Mr James is

rather well known. A man of some distinction, I'd imagine you'd call him. Not the sort of person you'd forget. Mm?'

'No. I suppose not. Yes, well, I suppose we are, er, sort of acquaintances.'

'Would that be business acquaintances, sir?'

'Social.'

'He comes to your parties? Is that what you mean?'

'No, I bloody don't, Sergeant whatever-your-name-is. Anyway, what parties?'

'Listen, Mr Samson, let's cut the charade, shall we? We have information that you've been holding parties involving solicited sex and narcotics on these premises for the past ten years. Savvy?'

Samson opened his mouth. Just a gurgle. He looked at Leonard. Leonard obliged.

'And quite honestly, sir, man to man, I can see that you and your friends may think that, *per se*, there's nothing wrong in these, shall we call them, gatherings?'

Sergeant Jack did not disguise her sneer nor the implication of her next question.

'All lads together, is it, Mr Samson? All fine till it went wrong? Right?'

Samson had rolled back one sleeve and was scratching again. Red scores of flesh where there had been tanned skin beneath the sandy curls on his forearms. He was about to speak, when Leonard's soft voice cut in.

'It's a difficult one, this, sir. Very difficult. You see, Sergeant Jack and I are investigating a murder. Maybe three murders. And, well, you see, sir, some of the footpaths lead to your lovely home.'

Samson's voice was croaky. He would have liked his pipe.

'I, er, I don't know what you mean.'

'Come now, sir, I'm sure you understand that, if you could help us, then we could sort any misunderstanding that may involve your good self. We just need to know about Mr James's involvement.'

'I told you, he's a friend. That's all.'

'It's a little more than that, isn't it, sir?'

'I'm not sure what you mean.'

Sergeant Jack leapt in before his husky breath was drawn.

'Look, he is or he isn't. Three people have been murdered, Samson. Your name's in the frame. Now I'm telling you. That doesn't add up to a maybe – not even if it is all boys together. Right?'

Samson had turned so that he didn't have to look at the belligerent Sergeant Jack. When James had arrived the previous evening, he had warned him it was the end of what James called, 'the arrangements'. But Montague James had also told him there was no evidence to make him panic. The boy was safely out of the way. There was no connection. James had promised. This Jack woman was something else. Leonard wasn't his friend in this, but at least he appeared sympathetic.

'You see, Inspector, maybe we have had some parties. But all innocent stuff. Consenting adults. Nothing more. You know how it is.'

Leonard blinked. He felt disgust for Samson. He wanted to nail him on the spot. But that wouldn't get him what he really wanted. Not yet. He did not smile, but he tried to show some understanding in his nod.

'Parties here, sir?'

'Yes. But nothing in them.'

'Just Mr James and his friends out from Bath?'

'Sometimes.'

Sergeant Jack's voice was sharp enough for Samson to turn. The eyes were blank. Without any hint of understanding.

'And Bolt.'

'What?'

'You heard me. Don't fuck about.'

The expletive knifed Samson's confidence. The yard girls swore like this. The tart in the pub did. When she'd been alive, his wife had. Sworn like a trooper. Mainly at horses and skiving grooms. This girl, woman, he supposed, was young, soft-faced. The eyes had warned him. But he'd been too busy lying to be ready. He started to speak. She stopped him. Wouldn't allow his hesitation. She said it again.

'Don't fuck about. Bolt. He came here. Didn't he?'

'I, I, er, I don't know what you're talking about.'

Leonard came to his rescue. His voice had an edge, but professionally. Not cruel like this bitch.

'You do know who we're talking about, don't you, sir? Richard Bolt? A young American gentleman?'

'I'm not sure I do.'

'Of course not, sir. But being an American, well, you probably don't see too many, do you, sir?'

'Never heard of him.'

'No, sir. Oh, that's a pity because we've lots of folk who think you have.'

'Then I tell you, Inspector, there's lots of fucking folk who are wrong.'

'Lying doesn't help. Bolt was butchered. He's been here. That means lots of folk are fucking right.'

Samson looked back at the house. The door remained closed. The dogs watching but not much interested. Leonard seemed to have lost interest as well. He had started to wander back to the car. Paused. A final friendly word.

'I tell you what, sir, you have a think about it. We'll come back later when you've had time to mull it over.'

He gave a slight nod. Almost a courtly bow and put his hand on the passenger door. Madeleine Jack swung her legs into the driver's well, not bothering to hide her bare thighs as she did so. Leonard, still smiling, looked across to Samson, who, confused, was tearing at his heat-prickled forearms.

'See what you can remember about young Bolt, won't you, sir? And, when we come back, maybe you can tell us all about the merry-go-round.'

'What d'you mean, come back?'

Leonard pretended not to have heard over the start-up of the Alfa Romeo and waved goodbye. Still trying to smile.

Sergeant Jack nearly reversed over the wolfhound. But only nearly. She watched in her mirror as the Spyder rumbled back across the cattle grid. Samson had not waited to see them go. He was already lumbering back to the house.

She drove slowly along the side-lane and took a look at Leonard. His head was back on the leather rest. Face burning and sore. Eyes closed.

'Well, sir?'

'Nice one, Sergeant. Nice one. I must say, you had me quite frightened. Don't tell me the nuns gave you ten out of ten for vocab.'

At the end of the line of woodland they slowed to a halt. Ray Lane was leaning against his black Ford. A similar vehicle was waiting behind, and a white Mercedes van was in the leafy lay-by, its sliding doors open in an attempt to give air to its cargo of constables. They were drinking tea from flasks. Lane wandered over. No hurry.

'Bingo, Jimbo?'

'We'll see. Give them half an hour unless they break. Then . . .'

'Do the business?'

Leonard allowed himself the first real smile of the morning. It hurt more than the pretend version.

'Yup. Then do the business.'

He waved and Madeleine Jack was about to pull away, when Lane tapped on the boot. With difficulty, Leonard twisted around. Lane was grinning.

'By the way, Jimbo, forgot to tell you, the lads love the make-up.'

Leonard felt his cheek and looked across to the transit van. The uniformed team were laughing. Probably the first sign of affection Leonard had seen from anyone at Manvers Street.

He could hear Madeleine Jack quietly laughing as they pulled away. He was pleased. But not about his cheek, and he cut out the pain with the thought of what was to come. By the time they were back in the city, Lane would have moved on Church Farm and Samson and his two sons would be on their way to Manvers Street to help Leonard with his inquiries while the vanload of officers and its two civilians went to work on the house. In the meanwhile, Samson would be encouraged to tug on the noose which Leonard hoped he had left for him.

Leonard closed his eyes again. He was tired. He needed sleep. He also needed to avoid the speed trial that Madeleine Jack seemed to be setting for herself and the Italian classic.

Fifty

Samson wasn't stupid. He was probably as smart as Leonard. Montague James most certainly was. When Leonard and Madeleine Jack got back to the Central Police Station, the telephone monitoring unit had reported in. Samson had made no calls to Montague James. Had received no calls. Had made no calls.

Leonard's cursing was silent. It was no less vehemently felt. He had been certain that Samson would have telephoned James. He'd been damned sure that Samson would have panicked. Montague James had been equally sure that Samson was inclined to panic and so he'd told him the night before to assume that his telephone was being tapped. He told him not to call the family in Ireland. Most importantly of all, not to call him, Montague James. The need for secrecy was the reason James had driven out to Church Farm and to make sure the rooms had been cleared. From now on, there must be no contact between the two, nor with anyone else involved.

Inspector Ray Lane brought in Samson and his two sons. They had arrived an hour after Leonard. They could have been taken into an interview room. Gentle probing. They weren't. It was too late for that. Instead they were driven down the side ramp of the police station and then bundled into the airlock – the small square hall between the back door and the secure door which led to the custody officers' counter and then the sightless cells. One by one they were pushed through the formality. Samson said nothing. One of his sons grinned the wet-lipped grin of a halfwit. The other son, the surly one, said nothing and wondered if they knew about his brother in Ireland.

The custody officer eyed Samson. He knew him. Had known him all his life. Brought up in the same village. His father had touched his cap to Samson's father. Had called his son Mr Oliver. So here was Mr Oliver. The officer's voice betrayed no recognition. But he took his time as he went through the routine of Form 8. The officer knew it by heart. He stared Samson in the face as he spoke.

'You have a right to speak to an independent solicitor free of charge; have someone told that you have been arrested; consult a copy of the codes of practice covering police powers and procedures. You may do any of these things, but, if you do not, you may still do so at any other time whilst detained at the police station.'

The blank stare from Samson and then his sons lasted all day.

Lane heard none of this. He was upstairs. Drinking undrinkable coffee. Confident. Leonard was humming under his breath. It had not worked. No running for the hills. No panic telephone calls. No blowing the whole ring. Leonard was very nervous. That telephone call. Samson was supposed to have made that telephone call. It was part of Leonard's plan. The monitors were in place. That had taken a lot of setting up. Short notice. But they'd been there. The half-hour gap between Leonard and Jack leaving and Lane going in. All planned.

Leonard wanted evidence on Samson. He needed to get back into Montague James. He needed something with which to confront him. Hilary James would not be enough. Leonard had made a mistake. He knew it. He should have taken her into safe custody. A basic mistake. He should have had everything she told him on tape. The recorded interview. Timed. Identified. Unquestionable proof. Stainger would have said 'basic procedures'. Stainger would have been right – again. Now, in the Major Incident Room, Stainger wanted to know everything. And he wanted to know it before Marsh got there.

The humourless Superintendent was already fuming. He had been told what was going on. Marsh had been at a Portishead headquarters group meeting all the previous day. Uncontactable unless really urgent, he had said. Very important man, Superintendent Marsh. Stainger had taken him at his word, especially at four-thirty in the morning. Now Stainger needed to know. Marsh was on his way over.

Everyone looked tired. They were. But not Sergeant Jack, who, in Stainger's opinion, was ridiculously young so couldn't possibly be tired, never mind look it. And there was Lane of course. Lane, he with a face that, even more so, looked as if it had been slept in, always looked tired. But now the adrenalin was working.

'It was all in the annexe. Out the back, through that covered bit. Purpose-built knocking shop, if you ask me. Wonder what detailed planning said about that. Very high-class stuff. Sofas, soft lights and this sodding great revolving bed in the middle. And you know what that daft bastard Samson said? Reckoned it was granny accommodation. Wish I had a gran like that.'

Stainger was po-faced.

'Nothing illegal in it. In court it will sound like a b. & b. set-up by the time some good brief's finished.'

'With three cine-cameras and a king-sized camcorder screen?'

'Still nothing illegal. Grannies are getting younger every day.'

'And the mirrors and cameras?'

'I'm telling you, Ray, nothing illegal. Very respectable therapists will swear in court that one man's pornography is another man's marital aids.'

'His wife's dead.'

Stainger lit his tenth cigarette of the dawn.

'I'm just telling everyone. We've got to put together the other half of this one. It's just one of the ends. OK, we've found the knocking-shop. That's good work. Well done, everyone. But your man's got to sing. Don't forget.'

Stainger looked over his shoulder to get Leonard's agreement. He'd been leaning against the cream filing cabinet. He was gone. He'd forgotten one of the ends.

The shop wasn't open. Too early. But Harriet Bowles was there. She'd been there all night. Gone straight from Woods to search out the diaries her husband had kept but she had never dared read. Now she had read them. She looked tired. Drawn. Drained. Saddened.

He took the coffee mug and dropped into the horsehair chair at the back of the shop. There was no hostility in her. There was nothing at all. Her voice was tired. The tiredness that comes from nothing mattering.

'You took your time. I expected you all night.'

'I'm sorry. We're almost there.'

'Almost is not very far.'

He sipped the coffee. Very hot. Very strong. It smelled nearly as good as it tasted. He nodded when she passed him his cognac in a silver thimble.

'Who did that to you?'

He felt the harsh rakes of Norma's fingernails.

'It's nothing.'

'She must have been angry.'

'She?'

'You're not very bright, Leonard. Whoever she was almost signed her name. Don't forget, I'm a woman.'

He had not. Now the wrong time to say so. He looked at her. Probably wouldn't be one again. He sipped and pressed on.

'I need to know what happened in Rainbow Wood. Why it happened.'

'I thought you knew that.'

'It's called evidence. There's a mile between what you know and what the court will buy.'

'Why Rainbow Wood?'

'It started it. Your husband knew about it.'

'Giles? Did he?'

'You do.'

'What else do I know?'

'What happened.'

'Wrong.'

'You know enough. I probably know most of the rest.'

'You assume too much, Inspector.'

The slow emphasis on his title hurt. Stung? Hurt. He liked her. But he was guessing why she didn't like him – any longer. If he were right, he could understand.

'You found the papers, didn't you?'

She sipped from her thimble. Took her time. When it came, it was only a start.

'They weren't lost.'

The humming was there. The spotless spectacles were being cleaned.

'Tell me.'

'Why?'

He slipped on the spectacles and stuffed the silk handkerchief into his sleeve.

'Because people are getting away with three murders.'

'People plural?'

'People plural.'

Harriet Bowles sighed. He was telling the truth. From her table drawer, she took a green square desk diary. Unopened, it lay on the leather top, her hand covering its gold lettering. G.D.S.B.

'Giles was a fool.'

'And he wrote it down.'

'Some.'

'Enough?'

'For what?'

'For you to think he was a fool.'

Another mistake. Clumsy mistake. Treading on her loyalties and now her memories. She wondered. He followed her gaze to a silver-framed photograph on the shelf. He'd noticed it before. But not seen it in the shadow. Now there was no shadow. He had wondered what Giles had looked like. He supposed he had wondered because, well, he'd wondered about her. About what she had, once upon a time, wanted in her prince. There he was. Bet he'd been a prefect. Head boy? Maybe not quite. Had read Biggies and then done it. An earnest face. Serious eyes. Unsmiling yet not miserable. Cheekbones. Short, dark hair. Straight parting. Intense. Breeding. Good bloodstock. By Mafeking out of Ladysmith. Leonard wondered how she could have loved him. Leonard reached for the diary. She shook her head.

'No.'

'Tell me.'

'Montague James knew what Giles did in the army.'

'I thought he was just a weekend soldier.'

'Sort of.'

He waited. She looked up. Defiance somewhere in her, yes, but not much.

'Before he did his law conversion, he'd taken a short-service commission in the army. You still could in those days. He was an ideal candidate. All hot and sweaty from university. Rowed. Fullback in the first fifteen. Opened the batting. Still managed to get an upper second. Well motivated. The army made him super-fit, showed him how to fire guns and things and jump out of planes. When he left, well, he signed up for the SAS.'

'TA? I didn't know . . .?

'Nor did I. But the answer's yes. There were two units, one in Leeds or somewhere, the other in Chelsea. Mm. Would be, wouldn't it? Twenty-Two or Twenty-Three Regiment or something, I really don't remember. I did know, but it was all silly and he told me to forget it. Anyway, it's not important.'

It would be. Leonard would need to see his army record. He didn't tell her.

'So he joined up again.'

'Right. And that was about it. He went off on exercises. Got dead tired and ate raw rabbits in the Brecon Beacons or somewhere horrid. Problem was, he started to believe it. He couldn't separate the two. Like a lot of them, had trouble deciding what he was. Soldier or lawyer. Man or superman. Everything in civilian life was tame.'

'How did Montague James know about this?'

She shifted the diary, but kept her hand on it.

'He doesn't say. But he did. Maybe the lodge.'

'Giles was a Mason?'

She smiled for the first time.

'Course he was.'

'They were in the same lodge? James and, er, Giles?'

She nodded. Leonard was finding the story easier to understand.

'So what does the diary say?'

She ran her index finger over his initials. Didn't say anything for a moment. When she did, it still sounded bizarre, but that was because she knew how the story finished. The sigh came as a prelude to a confession, yet not hers.

'James told Giles that he was looking for a couple of likely lads to act as bodyguards for one of the Americans in the culture deal. He wanted two who could take care of themselves, wouldn't have qualms if push came to more than shove, and two who wouldn't ask questions. Securicor need not apply.'

'What?'

She tapped the diary.

'That's how Giles described it.'

'And Giles supplied them?'

'Course he did. He only knew heroes.'

'This was?'

'Ten years ago.'

Leonard nodded. Perhaps too impatiently.

'I realize that. I meant, when was it in relation to the Rainbow Wood murder?'

'Two weeks before.'

'Where did Bolt fit in?'

'I don't know. Whoever he is, Giles called him Subject. That's it.'

'His name was Bolt. I promise.'

She shrugged. It really didn't matter. Not any more.

'OK. Call him what you like. Montague James said that Bolt was threatening his client. He claimed Bolt had followed the man from New York. Bolt was an American. Easy to believe.'

She wasn't looking at him but he nodded.

'And then?'

Harriet Bowles opened the diary where a gold silk ribbon marked the entry she wanted. She read it through in silence, her eyes no longer tearful. Just desperately sad. Then, she gave the book to Leonard. The writing was small, neat, but surprisingly juvenile. A page from a third-former's essay. But the content was beyond innocence.

23 July
It's gone horribly wrong. Complete balls-up. Subject at RV as planned. Warned him off. Bugger got stroppy. T says subject had knife. Should have been easy but T says he started shouting. T says C tried to shut him. Then T says he (T) went down and C went for subject in real time. T says C went berserk. Next thing, subject's got his head on wrong way round. No throat. No cock. Very wet.

Leonard looked up. Harriet Bowles was staring at the silver frame. He turned the page. The next entry was two days later.

25 July
Bloody nightmare. Can't believe it. C had him in boot

all yesterday. Last night did recce on R. Wood. 0130
dumped him. Poor bastard. Someone must find him. M says
no problem. Everyone clean. No connection. C and T
have off-poked. God knows where. I've told M don' t think
subject was a hitter. M says negative. He was. He said
what about knife? Maybe. I'm not sure. M tells me to stay
calm. What the f does he mean? He says it was an accident.
Tell that to the plods. M says no worry. No connection.
No plods.

26 July
   Harriet keeps asking me what's the matter? Told her
nervous about charity jump. Don't trust civilians up there.
Don't think she believes me. Why should she? She's
intelligent. Think she knows something's wrong. Why the
f did I sign for this one?

Leonard flipped through the rest of the pages. Blank. It was
the final entry.
   'When was the charity jump?'
   'The next day.'
   'I see.'
He hummed as he turned back the pages. He skimmed the
lines, but it was all there. The hand-picking of the TA soldiers.
Both out of work. The great adventure. Reliable men. M was
pleased. Promises of great things to come when the scheme
was up and running. But no names. Initials. No names.
   'T and C? M? Who are they?'
   'I don't know.'
Leonard could get a personnel list of all the men in Giles
Bowles's regiment. It would take time. But, given Bowles's
background, chances were that T and C were intials of sur-
names – even if they had been brother officers.
   'Nothing else in his other diaries?'
She shook her head. Finished her cognac. He blinked.
   'M for Montague. Must be.'

'M for Maupassant.'

'Or for murder.'

'It doesn't prove anything.'

'Not by itself. But it will.'

He got up. Put the thimble by hers. Held the diary under his arm. He put a hand on her shoulder. It was stiff.

'I'll need to keep this. Are there others?'

She opened the drawer and, without looking at Leonard, handed him two similar diaries, each with her husband's initials in the centre of the cover, the name of his law firm neatly along the bottom. Gold leaf. Blue chip.

'There's something there about his involvement with James. Not much, but it gives an idea of how much the business deals were worth.'

Leonard took the books and then his hand from her shoulder. His voice was soft. He really did care.

'Just one point. Who organized the charity jump?'

'It was for a hospice. Why?'

'No. Who organized it? Who else was in the plane?'

Harriet looked up. Fear in her eyes. Fear that he might be right.

'You're not suggesting that he was murdered? Come off it. It was his parachute. No one else would have packed it or touched it. He was fanatical about that. They all are.'

'And you can't remember the organizer?'

'The charity committee, I suppose.'

'Did you know any of them?'

She shook her head.

'No. I never got involved. I . . .'

'Yes?'

She closed her eyes and took a deep breath.

'This is getting crazy.'

'What is?'

'Montague James is chairman of the hospice committee.'

'I see.'

'This is bizarre. It is a simple coincidence. He could not

have had anything to do with it. Impossible. He wasn't even there.'

'Who was?'

Her voice was reduced to a murmur.

'I don't know. I really don't. Please, please, no more.'

Leonard would check. He did not believe in coincidence. He touched her shoulder. She stiffened. He let his hand drop. He wanted her to know that he cared. Really did.

'Harriet, I'm . . . I'm sorry about this.'

She didn't look up.

'I said I'm sorry.'

When she turned, it was as if she had seen him there for the first time. Had not heard.

'What?'

'Sorry.'

'No, you're not. You may be sorry for me. But you're not sorry. You're a policeman, James. You want a . . . a result? Is that what you call it? A result?'

'I meant what I said.'

'You think you did.'

She looked straight into his eyes. Saw nothing. Picked up the small silver frame and held it to her breast, while tears she'd thought were gone seeped from tightly shut eyes.

Fifty-One

The Filipino had left during the night. The heavy-set figure who opened the door looked like a bouncer, but was the chauffeur. Leonard had called from a box. Told Montague James he would be calling, officially. James had said it was not at all convenient. Leonard had said the alternative was sending a car for him to answer questions at the police station. James had agreed to see him and Sergeant Jack had picked up Leonard from a bench at the Gay Street end of The Circus. Before they rang the doorbell, she'd had time to tell him that

333

Samson was not talking. His sons were silent. There was no sign of Dancer. But, there had been a bit of good news on the Rainbow Wood killing. They had found the clerk who once worked at the undertaker's. An anonymous piece of information. Leonard wondered if it had come from a bright-eyed lass who rolled her own cigarettes. He touched Madeleine Jack on the arm as they waited for the door to open.

'I'll leave that one for you.'

'But it doesn't prove anything.'

He had no time to answer before the door swung open and, without a smile, a word or a gesture, they were shown into the drawing-room overlooking the city.

James was standing by the marble fireplace. He was tall enough to pose with an elbow on the mantelpiece and one hand just in the side-pocket of his silk striped jacket. Only a pair of Afghan hounds were missing from what would have been an excellent advertisement for his tailor. Montague James's mother would have approved. Leonard wondered how long he had waited. The man had not left them and was standing, hands clasped in front of him over a tall, thin Doulton coffeepot. James waved a hand towards the tray.

'Coffee?'

Leonard wanted coffee. Needed coffee.

'No thank you, sir.'

The man left. The doors closed without so much as a squeak from the hinges nor a click from the lock. Sergeant Jack felt Montague James looking at her. The top button had not been left undone deliberately. But it helped – sometimes. She was used to men looking that way. This time she knew he would not be distracted. Leonard cleared his throat with the gusto of a self-important alderman. But he said nothing. Madeleine Jack did.

For the first time, Montague James really did appear surprised. He looked straight into her eyes as she spoke.

'We've just come from Church Farm.'

Montague James looked at his most quizzical and then ignored her statement and peered at Leonard's face.

'My, we have been in the wars, Inspector. I do so hope you have had that properly treated. In these sad times, one cannot be too careful.'

And then, just as Sergeant Jack was about to relaunch her opening gambit, James turned and gave her a dazzling smile.

'Coffee? Church Farm? Indeed.'

'I should warn you, sir, that Mr Samson is helping us with our inquiries.'

'Helping you with your . . .? Really, Sergeant, one did not expect to hear that anywhere but on the wireless.'

'And I should further warn you that you have been implicated in certain activities at Church Farm, Chew Valley.'

Montague James smiled the smile of a patrician. The smile of one who listens, on great occasions, to the wireless. He offered a hand towards one of the white sofas. Sighed. Placed the ignored hand inside his jacket, the thumb resting on the lapel. He looked from Leonard to Jack and back to Leonard. Leonard blinked.

'We should like to see Mrs James, sir.'

'I'm afraid my wife is not here.'

'Out?'

'That is the implication, Inspector. Out.'

'When will she be back?'

'I'm not certain. She mentioned something about going up to town. Shopping. May I ask why you wish to see her?'

'I think you know, sir.'

'I think I do not. But doubtless you'll have your own explanation.'

Madeleine Jack had casually moved a couple of steps to her right. A small move. One from the course. It always worked. Montague James now had to look from right to left, from left to right. If he did not, he would not be able to judge how he was being observed. A man like Montague James liked to know. The instructor, Madeleine Jack remembered, had called

335

it Dislocation. She had not thought much of it until she had put it into practice. It always worked. She picked up the questioning.

'Mrs James has told us that you took part in certain activities and that you knew Richard Bolt. We believe also you knew his brother, who was murdered ten years ago.'

'I believe you must be mistaken, Sergeant.'

'Mrs James was not, sir.'

'You have a statement from my wife? A recorded and signed statement?'

He smiled into the silence. They had not. Madeleine Jack continued. Perhaps too quickly.

'One of your employees paid for a headstone.'

For the first time, Montague James showed a reaction that was not in his schedule of staged reactions. A flicker of the eyelid. A hardening of the glance. A brief moment. Not a second. Then gone. But it had been there.

'Not to my knowledge.'

Sergeant Jack looked down at her small notebook. Flipped back a couple of pages and found the entry she wanted.

'A cheque, made in favour of Messrs Goldings, Monumental Masons and Funeral Directors, was signed by your employee, or subsequent employee, Steven Reece.'

'I hardly see the connection.'

Madeleine Jack continued to look at her notebook. There was nothing in it that she didn't know by heart, but reading was a good technique. It made sure you got it right, but it also made the other person think there was maybe more and whatever there was was factual.

'We have spoken to the then office manager of Goldings, who remembered the event.'

'A very fine memory.'

'Not really, sir. It seems that Mr Golding told her not to bank the cheque.'

Madeleine Jack was back at her notebook.

'"Not the way we normally did business" is what the manager told us. That's why she remembered, plus the fact that, by coincidence, the signature on the cheque was also her maiden name.'

'Am I supposed to say bravo? And, if I should, might it be taken down and used in evidence?'

'That may very well be the case at a later date.'

'I cannot see that Steven Reece's private affairs are any of my concern.'

'He does.'

This time, James did look disturbed.

'You have spoken to Steven, Sergeant?'

'We have.'

Strictly, that was true. But it was days ago. More accurately, she had not since his disappearance from London. His office was on an answerphone. James did not follow up his own query. Which Leonard thought odd. All James had to do was to ask if Reece had said that the cheque was signed on James's instructions and Sergeant Jack's story would have folded. But he did not.

Leonard continued before James recovered.

'I should also tell you, sir, that I have written evidence, in the form of notes made by the late Giles Bowles, that you hired bodyguards through Mr Bowles and that those bodyguards murdered the man we now know to have been the elder brother of Richard Bolt.'

Montague James smiled. A thin smile, but there was little difference between that and his normal expression of joy. He walked over to the inlaid table from which an age before, just the previous evening, Leonard had poured iced water for Hilary James. He wondered where she was. He did not believe the shopping-expedition story. Her husband indicated the coffee, raised his eyebrows at their blank looks and slowly poured for himself. He took his time. He needed time. He was about to speak, when Leonard did.

'And we have evidence from a third party which ties you

in with Church Farm and both the younger and the elder Bolt.'

Montague James stirred chips of coloured sugar into the strong black liquid and looked sideways at Leonard.

'May I ask who this curious third party might be?'

Leonard said nothing. James did.

'Presumably the one person who dislikes me more than anyone I know in this city. I believe she still calls herself an artist. "A pornographer" would be a better description.'

'And then, sir, there's the video tape.'

'I beg your pardon?'

'Yes, sir. The video tape.'

Montague James laughed. It was a noisy laugh. Not a warm, developed chuckle. And Leonard felt uneasy.

'Not very amusing, sir. If I may say so.'

'Why, my dearest Inspector, you may say so indeed. But it is, it is so very amusing. A video tape. How melodramatic. And may one ask what this, ah, cinematographic curiosity is supposed to show? Or is that part of your playlet? Is this the point where you put on your trenchcoat and intone "You're probably wondering why I called you all here"? Inspector, please, do tell'

'There exists a tape, there exist a number of tapes, showing what happened at Church Farm.'

'Is that it?'

Leonard had been too confident.

'It will be presented as evidence.'

'Don't you mean, Inspector, "exhibited"? Is that not the jargon? Inspector Leonard, really! I do believe I have been very patient. If you have anything beyond circumstantial ramblings, please get on with it. I have an overwhelmingly busy day ahead of me.'

Madeleine Jack looked at Leonard. James, from where he now stood, caught her expression.

'Come on, Inspector. Why, even your delightful colleague awaits with what I am sure is bated breath.'

Leonard went in.

'Twelve years ago, the lady who is now your wife lived in New York.'

'Hardly a crime. Nor a secret.'

Leonard ignored the interruption.

'She met up with a young artist. Norma. Your wife became part of a group of people who were looking for more than kicks. She was a moderately successful model who got into soft-porn movies.'

Montague James had stopped smiling. The expression was still there, but no humour.

'The soft porn turned into hard porn. Your wife did not, as far as we know, feature in them. But she moved with the group. That group got into the business of snuff movies. Movies which culminated in the filming of the murder of young girls and boys who were heavily into drugs.'

James was fuming. He picked up the telephone.

'Inspector, I am about to call the Chief Constable. I must ask you to leave. Now.'

Leonard continued. A monotonous indictment that stopped James, who replaced the receiver.

'She returned to England and came to stay with the only friend she had. Norma. You met. You married. But – and it's here where we know of your involvement – one of the stars, if that's the term, of the hard-porn films followed Norma to England and found her here in Bath. He had an affair with your wife. She was, sir, by then, your wife. That was ten years ago. You hired two ex-soldiers through Giles Bowles to have him murdered.'

'How on earth would I have known of this man's existence? Absurd.'

Leonard was on dangerous ground. He had two hypotheses, either one of which could be right. Both could be nonsense.

'Truthfully, sir, I don't know. Even the man himself might have been daring enough to tell you, hoping to blackmail you for his silence. He was, by all accounts, in desperate straits.'

'Well, at least you have the grace, Inspector, to admit this is an entire work of fiction. Now . . .'

Leonard tapped the green diaries he'd kept beneath his arm.

'On your instructions, the man Bolt was murdered and his body dumped in Rainbow Wood.'

'This is utter nonsense.'

'That might have been that, but a local newspaper reporter, Steven Reece, got too close to the truth and so you bought his silence.'

'I've already explained, in great confidence but also, may one add, with great candour, why that was necessary.'

'Like a lot of stories, sir, almost true.'

Montague James raised himself another couple of inches and his brow went back. An almost perfect combination of haughtiness and disdain.

'I do believe you are certifiable, Inspector.'

'Bolt was dead. But, this year, Richard Bolt, who was twelve when his brother died, came to Bath from America to find out who had killed him and . . .'

'. . . and became a stinking vagrant.'

The viciousness in Montague James's tone surprised even Sergeant Jack, who had been quietly taking notes. Leonard had not finished.

'Became, through Norma, an extra in your merry'go-round. The problem was, Mr James, your wife saw Richard Bolt at one of the parties. Saw him, er, performing, if that's the right term, and, to put it crudely, wanted him.'

'Get out, Inspector.'

Leonard might not have heard him.

'You had him murdered. And such was your fury, Mr James, you had him murdered in the most grotesque manner imaginable.'

Leonard had finished. He felt sickened. He felt exhausted. Montague James went to the fireplace and pressed a button. Almost immediately, the double doors opened. The man stood waiting.

'Would you show Inspector Leonard and Sergeant Jack out.'
No one moved. James smiled.

'Before you go, Inspector, some thoughts for you. Samson
is an acquaintance. A business acquaintance. Nothing more.
I have never attended Samson, nor his home, on any occasion
other than business or to discuss charities. We sit on many of
the same committees. My wife has never met Richard Bolt,
nor his brother. The so-called artist is a drug-taker and a
celebrated, if amateur, harlot. There isn't a person who knows
her who doesn't know that. She is what I believe you would
call an unreliable witness to anything but her own compulsive
mendacity. As for a video game of so-called parties, such a
tape does not exist. If it did, you would not have said "there
exists a tape", Inspector, you would have said that you have
such a tape. Clearly you have not. If there were to be a tape,
then, I will assure you, I would not appear in it. Nor would
my wife.'

Leonard started to waver, then he remembered something
else. He felt in his pocket. It was still there. He took out the
scrap of shiny paper.

'And we have, sir, a direct connection with you and the
death of a young woman in the city.'

Montague James shook his head slowly and in mock exasperation.

'Come on, Inspector. Out with it.'

'This, sir, is a picture of your apartment. In fact, sir, it is a
photograph of this room. It was found among the effects of
the dead woman.'

'May I ask, Inspector, if you get your clues from Messrs
Waddingtons? Truthfully, you are an amusing board game in
yourself, or rather you would be if this were not such an
insulting experience.'

'The photograph is not a fake, sir.'

'I don't doubt that for one moment. But is it a picture of
my home or this apartment? We have lived here for more
than ten years. How old is the picture?'

Leonard stared at Montague James for a full thirty seconds. When he spoke, there was as much firmness in his voice as he could manage.

'I would ask you to make yourself available for interview later this morning. You may wish to consult your solicitors.'

Leonard turned and got as far as the door, when Montague James had the last word.

'Indeed, Inspector, I shall, as soon as I have spoken with the Chief Constable.'

He was dialling a number as the man showed them out.

Fifty-Two

Outside, they sat in the car. Once or twice Sergeant Jack looked to the windows but saw nothing but soft curtains and expressionless panes. The first break in the weather for weeks hovered over Bath. The cloud was low. The city clammy. The fumes from morning traffic content to lie in the natural bowl in which the spa had been built. Sergeant Jack looked across at her passenger. He was slumped in his seat, clutching the green diaries. The confidence of the hour before was gone. It had all been there. She believed Leonard. What had happened?

'Sir?'

'Mm?'

'Unless we can get hold of Steven, the headstone thing doesn't stand up. Does it, sir?'

'Maybe Reece was being clever. He seems to have lived in a world of fantasies and opportunities.'

'Or sad.'

'Why so?'

'Well, sir, maybe he knows even more than he's said. Don't forget, he was long gone before the body was released. Five years? Maybe he hadn't let go of the story as James thought he had.'

'We need to find him.'

'We've got a call in to New York. He gave me his card. The number's there. And another thing, sir, he was pretty confident about the videos. You think we've blown it?'

Leonard said nothing. Slumped even further in the seat and pointed ahead like a trail boss with a herd to get to Cheyenne. Sergeant Jack started the car and it rumbled over the crescent's cobbles and into Brock Street. They had just reached The Circus, when Leonard sat up and slammed the flat of his hand on the dashboard.

'Of course! The gallery. The Minerva. Quick.'

Three minutes later, leaving his sergeant parked outside, Leonard went into the gallery. It was a mess. Sculptures lay in pieces where only nights before Bath's finest had posed and paused for the summer exhibition. An elaborate wrought-iron angular monument to excess had been thrown across the bottom of the staircase. The surly youth was sweeping broken and chipped frames and plaster into small piles. He looked up as Leonard came in, then shrugged and brushed on with the anonymity of a pool-hall janitor. He didn't want to get involved. Leonard was halfway up the stairs when he saw *Jungle Cat*. The life-size painting had been slashed in two diagonals. Corner to corner.

The door to the studio was open. Jules Benedict was lying on the sofa. He was drinking red wine from a coffee mug.

'Well, well, well, look who it ain't. Knacker of the fuckin' yard himself.'

Leonard looked about him. The room was worse than below. Racks had been turned out. Pictures stomped.

'Where is she?'

'Fucked if I know, darling. Fucked off, if she knows what's good for her.'

'What happened?'

Benedict gave a long, exaggerated belch. Leonard could smell his breath five paces away. The artist shrugged.

'As the man said when he fell off the Empire State Building, how the fuck do I know – I just got here.'

Benedict went into convulsions of laughter. Belched again and threw up driblets of wine. He was naked from the waist up and rubbed the spittle into his matted and flabby chest.

'I need to find her.'

'Too late, me old darling. She's off-fucked. I promise you. I came in for a little something, you know, and she wasn't stopping.'

He winked and stabbed his clenched fist backwards and forwards.

'Got me, sunshine? Little something? But I promise you. She was on her bike and running.'

Leonard went past him and into the back room. The place had, as Ray Lane would have said, been trashed.

Downstairs, the youth knew nothing more. He had arrived shortly after eight-thirty to find Norma pulling a few personal things together.

'Didn't she say what happened?'

'I don't think she had to, did she?'

He looked about him. The broom did not seem adequate.

'Did she say where she was going?'

The youth shook his head.

'No way. But she won't be back.'

'She say that?'

'She gives me some money. What she owes, she says. Then says I'm on my own. Right? She then says she's had it with Bath. Then she's gone. Right?'

Leonard told the youth to stay where he was, then went out to the car. He told Sergeant Jack what had happened and to stay at the gallery until a team arrived. He wanted anything at all that would show who had done this.

'You think it was James?'

'I think I now know why he was so sure that the tape was gone.'

Sergeant Jack watched Leonard trudge away down the hill.

She liked him. Liked working with him. But she knew what Stainger meant. Routine. Routine would have had statements from Mrs James. From Norma. Might even have had the tape. If it existed.

Fifty-Three

It was five-thirty. Stainger was in his chair. Marsh was in the big armchair. Leonard was in the hard seat. Samson and his sons were in their farmhouse. Montague James was in his bath.

Stainger spun his paperknife. It didn't stop pointed towards Leonard. But it would do.

'What have we left?'

'The farmhouse is clean. Spotless.'

'So no evidence?'

Marsh's voice was cruel. The barb was meant to stay buried beneath Leonard's skin.

'Nothing the CPS will buy, no, sir.'

Stainger was ticking off the failures on his fingers.

'Video?'

'They –'

'Who are "they"?'

'OK, sir, someone ransacked the gallery. It's gone.'

Marsh shifted. Irritable Marsh. He'd known from the start how hopeless this would be.

'If there was one in the first place.'

Leonard said nothing. It wasn't worth it. He believed there had been a video. Maybe there was still. Marsh had not finished.

'And your star witness, who just happens to be a bohemian junkie and leg-over specialist of the first magnitude, has disappeared.'

'Yes, sir.'

'But not before she left her mark on you.'

'No, sir.'

'You mean "yes".'

'Yes, sir.'

Stainger ticked another finger.

'The diaries?'

'The strongest point, sir. They show what happened. The initials we're checking now. If we find them, we're still in with a chance.'

Marsh sniffed. Leonard continued as Stainger tapped his ring finger. Point four.

'Then there's Mrs James. Her evidence could be crucial.'

Marsh almost roared.

'You heard his damned mouthpiece. Thanks to your tactics and insinuations, we daren't lay a finger on her. Verge of a nervous breakdown. I can see it now. The CPS would never go in with this. Harassment? Make West Midlands look like the Samaritans.'

Leonard had had nearly enough. Time for the offensive. He turned in his seat. Rubbed at his spectacles and glared at the blurred figure of Superintendent Marsh.

'Look, sir. I know this is James. I know what Hilary James said. I know what Norma said. I know what Dancer said.'

'And he's fucked off.'

'And I know what those diaries say.'

'And let me tell you something, Leonard. I know what the papers will say if we go half-cocked. I know what the influence of someone like James can do. So shove it. Shove what you think you know. Get me something that can pin down the bastard.'

The silence was for the anger of Marsh. For the amusement of Stainger. For the surprise of Leonard.

'You believe me, then, sir?'

Marsh looked thunderous.

'Of course I believe you, man. I just won't tolerate the way you do things. But what d'you think I am? Bloody idiot? Up from the sticks on the haywain this morning? Course I believe you. But I'm telling you, nothing you've done will stick.'

More silence. Stainger swung in his seat. No need for counting. There was a tap at the door and Sergeant Jack came in with a note for Leonard. She left without looking at anyone, including Leonard. He scanned the note.

'It's a check on the two soldiers. All the Ts have been done. All legit, or so it seems, except one. Now believed to be signed up with a mercenary agency operating out of Camberley in Surrey. Last known in Bosnia. Now thought to be in Afghanistan.'

Marsh grunted.

'Bugger. And the Cs?'

'Still working on them, sir.'

Stainger broke the gloom.

'You think your sergeant would like an away-day to Kabul?'

The two senior officers laughed. Leonard was gazing out of the window.

'Then there's Dancer, sir. He can't have disappeared. He'll show somewhere. He knows what we want. He knew Bolt ten years ago. He knew Richard Bolt.'

'And he's done a runner.'

'Yes, sir.'

'Should have locked him up.'

Maybe someone has, thought Leonard.

Leonard needed a shower and then sleep. He'd left Stainger's office, but not before they'd agreed to ask for an extended monitor on the farmhouse and James's telephone. It was Marsh who asked if anyone had checked alternative listings for the apartment. They did not expect too much. Marsh believed that, if James were to crack, it would take a long time. He knew, just as his lawyer knew, that at first glance every shred of evidence condemned him. He knew also that the police had nothing that the CPS would run with.

Five years earlier and Montague James would have been in custody. Not now. A hearsay tape. A witness with a reputation that the most junior counsel would destroy in sixty seconds. A story of sex parties for which there was no evidence and certainly no chance of any party-goer coming forward. Diaries which did nothing for the case until the mysterious T and C had been found.

Outside, it was still warm. Humid. Leonard needed to walk. To think. He wandered up Broad Street, looked into the empty window of the bakers, crossed by the lights into Lansdown Road and then turned into Alfred Street. A cold glass. Selsey was sitting in the window seat, talking to Harriet Bowles. He waved a hand to Leonard. She saw him. Turned away. He did not go in. He walked in a circle. Found himself in Brock Street. Said something, probably a greeting but he wasn't listening, to the dentist hurrying to organ practice in the abbey. Eventually, and without meaning to, he was walking towards his basement flat, running a finger along the rails as he had run a wooden ruler in lonely childhood.

The door wasn't open. But he knew there was someone inside. Instinct maybe. But he knew. He thought of Josie. He thought of Bolt, the younger brother. He thought of the Minerva Gallery. Now he did not care. The key made more noise than it had ever done; the bottom of the door, freed from its winter dampness, rasped at the coir mat.

Dancer was sitting in the kitchen drinking tea.

Leonard threw his keys on the wooden dresser, flopped into the high-back chair and swung his brown leather boots onto the table. Each action was pronounced. Deliberate. Leonard did not like surprises.

'I've been looking for you.'

'Not far.'

'How d'you get in?'

Dancer leered. Nodded in the direction of the river wall, the small garden, the old French windows. No. It wasn't difficult. Not for a fire-eater. Leonard had thought about a burglar alarm. Was now glad he hadn't got one. But he would.

'You left your gear in the yard.'

'Smart, Señor Plod. *Mucho* smart.'

'Why didn't you split?'

Dancer slurped from the cup. No saucer.

'Where to? You're my best protection.'

Leonard swung his legs down and took a cold beer from the refrigerator. There had been six. There were six. He waved a can at Dancer, who shook his head. Leonard grunted to himself. Hummed. Everyone was so damn pure. He looked at the dresser corner. His wooden box was gone. Perhaps not so pure after all. Dancer wanted to know. Wanted to know he was safe.

'Well? All done?'

Leonard was looking down at his boots.

'Nope.'

'Shit.'

'That's about the size of it.'

'Why for?'

'Fallen apart. I know what happened. I think I know who made it happen. But not enough to make it stick.'

He looked up. Dancer was grinning. Not an amused grin. Just something he did. He knew Dancer had in his head what had happened. He'd known that when Dancer hadn't left the city. He needed what Dancer knew. He needed to go easy. But Dancer had come. Come to him.

'You understand?'

Dancer raised his hands. Of course he did. His whole life was understanding. That's why his whole life was as it was.

'Sure, boss.'

'OK, Dancer, tell me.'

'Tell you?'

'Who killed Bolt? When? Where?'

'The crazy son.'

'Samson's?'

'Right.'

Leonard pictured Samson's two sons. The dribbler. The hunk.

'Which one?'

'Don't know what they call him. One of the twins.'

There were no twins. Just the dribbler and the hunk.

'Describe him.'

The hunk. Leonard looked at Dancer. Disappointed. Another witness gone down. The hunk wasn't a twin.

'Why d'you say he's a twin?'

It was Dancer's turn to look disappointed.

'He is.'

Maybe Leonard was too tired. It took a long time to sink in.

'How many sons are there?'

'Three. How many d'you want?'

Leonard was sitting up. He swigged at the can. Wanted to call Stainger. But not yet. Not quite yet.

'What happened?'

'They killed him.'

'You said you knew.'

'I've just told you.'

'No. You told me it was one of the sons. Now, what happened?'

Dancer leaned back. Held up thumb and forefinger.

'You wouldn't have . . .? No. I suppose you wouldn't.'

Leonard would have. But he hadn't. The box had gone.

'Tell me what you know.'

'The Piccolo man, the Bolt man, Everyman. He gets too hot. He tells me he's in there. He tells me they kissed his brother. Right?'

Leonard nodded. Slowly. Coaxing.

'Right. Go on.'

'So he thinks he's going to destroy them. Right? I tell him, shit. I tell him to come out. Forget it. But he says I'm shit. Right?'

'What happened?'

Dancer put up his hands in mock defence.

'It's coming. It's coming. Right?'

'OK. Go.'

'Right. He tells me they have the big parties. Screwing around. Bring in the studs for the scrawny ladies. Got some scrubbing irons for the men of this fine city. Right?'

'And?'

Dancer leaned across the table. His voice had dropped to a stage whisper.

'And my Bolt man . . . and one of the ladies steps out of line. She's just there to watch. Then one night she touches the goods. Bad news. Bad, bad news.'

'Which lady?'

'He don't say.'

'He must have.'

Dancer shook his head.

'No, boss. No. Promise. He don't say. But what he does say is that this all happened in the back parlour.'

'The merry-go-round.'

Leonard remembered. Lane had said it. The revolving bed. The merry-go-round.

'And?'

'And your man's giving her something to remember him by. But this is the big one. This lady is high-class. The Bolt man is strictly trade.'

Dancer sat back. Looked from side to side as if they were in a crowded room.

'And it's on tape?'

'Right. Your man's got the picture show. He has done the amazing. The crazy. The impossible. Switched cassettes.'

'Of him and the woman? He's got the cassette of him and this woman screwing?'

'Right.'

'And she is an untouchable.'

'Right, Señor Plod. She is fat cat's chattel. And my man has her in beautiful technicolor, screaming for it.'

Leonard swigged. Nervously. Tired.

'So that was it.'

'But wait one, Boss One. Your man has a bonus. He picks

up two cassettes. Well, if he thinks he has dynamite, then he now goes megatonnage.'

Dancer paused. Excited. He took Leonard's can and sucked it dry. Leonard leaned back, opened the refrigerator and took out two more.

'Go on.'

He put an open beer in front of Dancer.

'On this little gem is what the big guys on the block call a snuff. You hear me?'

'I hear you.'

'But for now he's just interested in the rattling lady. He's got this little arrangement in this city. Right? He has a friend. So the friend sets up a little deal. And your man meets the lady regular.'

Norma. The gallery?

'And it's on film?'

'And how. But you know why? You know?'

Leonard knew. He'd already been told. He knew. He shook his head. Dancer had to say.

'Because the little lady wants it that way. She wants the action replay. She wants to see herself in action.'

Leonard got up. Ripped the ring from another can.

'What happened to the other cassette?'

Dancer didn't know.

'But I do know the management of this establishment found out.'

'How?'

'Don't know. Maybe they guessed. But the way I heard it Bolt man gave the tapes to a close and dear one for safe-keeping. Maybe the friend tried to put the arm on the gentlemen on the block.'

Leonard was leaning against the wall. Norma had tried to blackmail. Samson? James even? Was Dancer telling the truth? He thought he was. So did Dancer. For the moment, that would do.

'Ok, Dancer, what happened to the Piccolo man?'

'You asked me before.'

'Tell me right this time.'

Dancer ran his hand along the table. Picked up the beer and took a long draught. Wiped his mouth.

'I see him. He's with us. With Josie. She saying he shouldn't go no more. She didn't know where. She didn't know anything, that one. She says it's dangerous. But he says he going once more. So they pick him up and that was it.'

'Where did they pick him up?'

'Like every time. I saw them. We both did. Little Josie bird was so sad. So sad.'

'Where? The Podium. The Roller?'

Dancer brushed his hand across the table like a seamstress smoothing material. One last explanation. One last effort.

'No. One of the comfy trucks. You know? Land-Rover?'

'The son?'

'The very same.'

'What happened this time?'

Dancer's grin was gone. The sadness in his eyes was real enough. The hand caressing emptiness.

'Last trip, boss. Last time.'

'Where did you find him?'

Dancer stopped caressing. Looked frightened. For a moment wanted to go. Then saw Leonard's eyes. It would be OK.

'Where they left him. Near the Tor.'

'Where the hell's that?'

'Glastonbury.'

Leonard didn't understand. Dancer could see that.

'He got dropped, see? Just one more traveller. Right? But it didn't go down that lane, boss. No way.'

'Because you found him.'

'Right. Same night. Maybe one, maybe two, in the morning. I see the Land-Rover. It hits the lane by the well. Josie found him. All clean. All dead, boss. Badly. We knew what they were doing. Let him burn. Let him lie. Glastonbury just a pigshit house. That's what you people think. Right? You wouldn't care. Just another travelling man. You people would go through the war dance. But no war.'

'So you decided to bring him to Bath?'

'Had to. Bring him here. Put him under your noses. Make a stink. Understand? Put him on the altar.'

Leonard nodded. He understood. Put a sinner on the high altar and the police get busy with the sacraments. The Cross Bath, one of the main tourist attractions. A very high altar. Because they believed it happened in the city, that's where the police had started turning over dustbins.

'How do you know it was the son?'

'I don't. I just know he picked him up and delivered.'

'How do you know which twin it was?'

'I worked for them. Three years back. He was shit. The one with the arm. You know? The scar? Chain-saw. Pity it weren't his throat.'

Leonard remembered the son. The hunk. The bare, strong arms. No scars. The doorbell rang. Dancer looked frightened.

'Stay there.'

It was Madeleine Jack. She was holding the pup. She put him down and he scampered into the kitchen. Dancer looked frightened. Then arrogant. Then Madeleine Jack said hello to Dancer and it was all right.

'By the way, I've got something for you.'

Leonard looked surprised. He didn't get presents. She opened her shoulder-bag and gave him the wooden box.

'Here. Not the sort of thing to leave lying around when the Forensic boys turned up.'

Fifty-Four

Stainger was impressed. Marsh had gone. He was not so impressed. Stainger had knocked down the idea of another raid on the farmhouse. There was no point. Leonard said it was keeping up the pressure. Stainger said no.

Sergeant Somers-Barclay had been called off the yard watch and sent over to see the community beat officer in the valley. He had come back with the best they had got. Yes, there was a third son. The CBO had assumed they knew that. But he had not been seen in the district for a few days. But, as Somers-Barclay had pointed out, that did not mean he had been away for days. He'd called at the farm and asked where he was. Samson had said on holiday. Had been for three weeks or so. Where? Touring. Touring where? Samson didn't know. Or said he didn't. As Somers-Barclay had pointed out to Leonard, it wasn't the usual time for a farmer to go on holiday.

A telephone call had produced his passport number and Immigration was alerted for a port watch to go with the one on Norma. If he'd gone, if she'd gone, there was no chance. The Immigration Service was so overstretched that it had a hard time pinning down anyone. The best chance was given to a fresh-faced and eager constable who was told to start checking travel firms, airlines and ferry services. Most of them were closed, but there were methods.

By ten o'clock, Stainger called it a day.

'Listen, Jamés, even if we do pick him up, all we've got is this fire-eater of yours. All he's got is that he claims the son picked up Bolt.'

'It's enough to go on.'

'For us, yes. But all the bastard has to do is deny it. This Dancer laddie has even told you that when he worked there the son gave him a hard time. What d'you think they'll do to him in the box? Yet another unreliable witness. A grudge witness we don't need.'

'If he's still here.'

'He's in safe custody. We can't do any more than that.'

'And if he walks?'

'You think he will?'

Leonard shrugged. He didn't know.

He muttered good night, even to Somers-Barclay, and said no to Ray Lane's offer of a pint in the George. He'd left his bicycle in the yard, or thought he had, but was too tired to check. As he let himself out by the Lost Property door, he stopped to breathe in deeply the cooled night air. He needed the beach. The sound of unseen night waves. And then memories came with the flood tide and he shuddered and walked on.

The porch light was on. He knew it would be. Sergeant Jack had promised to wait with the pup until he returned. She couldn't keep the animal in her flat. The other natives were not friendly.

She was asleep on the sofa. She didn't stir when he came in. The pup made scampering noises, but seemed content to sniff, not to worry. Johnson had gone to the wall. Sid? My goodness, what sort of name was that?

Leonard took off his jacket, loosened his waistcoat and leaned back, eyes closed, stroking the pup's ear with one hand, holding a large glass of Islay in the other. He knew they would get there. He didn't know when. He knew the evidence would not be enough. He knew that eventually someone would have to crack. To break.

He wondered about Reece. Would they ever get him back? And, if they did, so what? He wondered about Hilary James. Possibly last night. But now? He wondered about Norma. Gone. He wondered about Jules Benedict and for a moment grinned to himself at the thought of the slobbering artist struggling to stand up straight in a witness box. Forget it. He thought about Dancer. Taken away. Reassured by Leonard that all would be right. Tucked up safely.

Then he wondered about Samson. Prove it! The son? Maybe. Maybe the best chance of all. When they found him. He wondered about Montague James. So confident. He would only ever be convicted on Samson's evidence. Each strand not strong enough to tie a prosecutor's brief. Put them together and it might just hold. The case closed. The files filed as Stainger liked. The files. What had happened to them? He remembered Hilary James asking him if he worked for her husband. Many do, she had said. He wondered how many.

At last, he wondered about Harriet Bowles. Lovely Harriet Bowles. Lovely eyes. Bright. Amusing. Then he saw her as he'd left her. Saddened. Crying. And he ached. Maybe she'd been right. Nothing to do with justice. Simply a mystery to be solved. He heard her again. Word for word.

'You're a policeman, James. You want a . . . a result? Is that what you call it? A result?'

She was right. He wished she were not.

'Penny for them.'

It was a sleepy voice. He looked over to the sofa and the movement disturbed the pup, but not for long. Leonard whispered as if he'd been nursing a child long past its bedtime.

'Just thoughts. Wondering if we're going to get . . .'

His voice trailed off.

'A result?'

He looked at her eyes. Sleepy as her voice. Soft. Soft as Stainger had thought. Didn't look like a copper, Lane had said. Maybe she understood. He hoped so. He did not want to explain.

Fifty-Five

It was late. The abbey restoration-fund recital had gone on longer than expected. A late start. Too long an interval. And then three encores. Then the auction and now the reception showed little sign of winding up.

Montague James was in good form. But not at his best. Effusiveness did not, however, require Montague James's best.

'My dear William, you must be thrilled by the results. Twenty-four thousand three hundred indeed. A gift from heaven, I'm certain of that.'

The Bishop sipped his champagne wine. Only a sip, for he was wise as well as wet-lipped and jolly.

'We give thanks for all manna of things, if I may make a pun.'

'I'm sure you may, William. I'm sure you will.'

They all laughed as leading citizens did on these occasions. The editor, who chuckled as much as the others, had a thought.

'I'm not a scholar, but wasn't manna given to the Jews? I mean, before your lot.'

'But you are, Mr Dover. A scholar indeed. I'm afraid pedantry gets in the way of too many things for me to worry about that. I'll simply give thanks from whencever the donations come.'

There was more laughter and Patsy Bush arrived to say that the auction figure had just been added up once more and another hundred pounds had been found.

'So, let me see, that's twenty-four thousand four hundred. I'd say that's pretty da . . . er, pretty close, wouldn't you?'

The Bishop took another sip. Yes, he certainly thought it pretty damn close. Montague James chose his moment well. A slight lull.

'I wonder if you would allow me, William, to make up the total to the target?'

The general murmur showed how much they admired his generosity and of course his wealth. The Chief Constable, who had had enough of James for one day, was slightly annoyed. He'd been about to make his apologies but could hardly do so without appearing to snub James. His gruffness came as approval from them all.

'I must say, James, that's really decent of you. I mean six hundred isn't chickenfeed. I'm sure the fund committee would want to thank you formally.'

Montague James allowed himself a blush. At least he sincerely hoped it would appear as one.

'Not at all. Not at all.'

Votes of thanks may be taken to embarrassment. Bishops are versed in these matters and Bishop William was quick to slip in with an inconsequential remark.

'And what a pity Mrs James wasn't able to join us tonight. I heard she was, ah, unwell. Nothing serious, I trust?'

There was a moment's silence. But only that. A slight hesitation from Montague James. But only that.

'Yes, William, she's gone away for a few days' rest.'

Patsy Bush was a pretty straightforward woman. She'd heard no tense silence.

'Hey, that's nice. Good to get out of this place when it's full of tourists and not enough air to go around. Anywhere nice?'

'Nice? Mm. One sincerely hopes so, my dear. But quiet. She's gone to stay with friends.'

'Far?'

'No, no, not really. Ireland. Just Ireland.'

Fifty-Six

The coffee was bubbling in the espresso. It was smelling better than it was ever going to taste. The orange juice was in a frosted glass from the freezer. Johnson was lying in the morning sun on her favourite part of the wall. She had one eye on Sid. Thus far, the visitor seemed well-behaved, although one could never tell how these matters would turn out. Didn't seem much pedigree in this one. Johnson thought pedigree rather important.

Leonard had showered and was barefoot in his robe and scrubbing at his curly head with a towel. The face wasn't any better, looked worse than it was, and he hadn't shaved.

The ring at the door was the postman. A padded bag too big for the letterbox.

Leonard walked back into the kitchen bouncing the fools-cap bag in his hand as if guessing its weight. The writing on the front he did not recognize. The postmark was smudged. He tugged at the brown taped top, reached in and took out a postcard. London. The Changing of The Guard. The message on the back was simple.

> *Thought you might need these.*
> *Don't try to find me. You won't.*
> *Norma*
> *X*

Leonard reread the card. Put it down. Took out two boxes from the packaging. Two video tapes.

He picked up the telephone. Dialled Sergeant Jack's home number. They had, he believed, a result.